Lesbian Romance:

4 Volume – 4 Themed Erotic Lesbian Romance Collection

Spirited Sapphire Publishing

Contents

VOLUME 1

Lesbian Vampire Romance Collection

Story #1

Bound to Budapest

A s Julie walked down the cobble stone street she turned her face upwards towards the sun and soaked in its hot rays. "Bette! Stop sulking in the shadows! Come and enjoy the Hungarian sun with me!" Erzsebet rolled her eyes at the sound of her friend's voice shouting to her, and continued to walk close to the building where she was being shielded from the devilish licking of the sun's hot tongue. Julia and Erzsebet had grown up together in Buda, Nebraska, a city with a very large population of Hungarian descended citizens. Julia and Erzsebet both came from Hungarian families and were given Hungarian names. Julia and been fortunate enough to be graced with her name, Julia, which she further Americanized into the nickname Julie. Erzsebet on the other hand, was given a much more traditional name which only shortened into Bettie or Bette, nicknames much to plain to capture all the facets of Erzsebet's dynamic personality. The two friends were currently in Hungary visiting the city of their ancestors, Budapest. Well, Erzsebet was there to visit the city of her ancestors. Julie was more interested in the Hungarian bars and all the single women. Erzsebet knew Julie wouldn't be much interested in the architecture, museums, and culture of the city but she needed a traveling partner and Julie was the most convenient person to go with her.

Julie and Erzsebet finally arrived at the home of the generous Hungarian family that had allowed the pair to stay at their home for a cheaper rate than a Budapest hotel, and a cleaner environment than the hostels in the city. As they walked through the door they were met with the smell of a traditional homemade Hungarian meal being prepared. As they joined the family to eat dinner, the two women discussed possible plans for their evening. "It's our last night here and we have got to spend it out partying!" Julie says cheerfully.

Erzsebet sighed at her friend's suggestion. "Julie I really wanted to try and find Erzsebet's grave before we leave."

Erzsebet was named after her great-great-great grandmother, who was raised and died in Budapest. The circumstance of her great-great-great grandmother's death has always been ambiguous at best through various tales her elder relatives told, and she was always suspicious and curious as to what might have really happened. Erzsebet had always felt a strong connection to her namesake, and she often wore one of her great-great-great grandmother's lockets around her neck, a pretty antique piece with an inscription on the back that read, "To my darling Erzsy, love is eternal, Calli". Calli was the shortened name for Callidora, and through some clandestine chats with various family members, Erzsebet's learned that Callidora was the great love of her great-great-great grandmother. Apparently her great-great-great grandfather was aware of this love affair between his wife and her female lover, yet in vampire families, which Erzsebet has always strongly suspected her family was a part of, this is neither forbidden nor taboo, and in fact, it has always been quite acceptable. Stories about the pair tell of how Callidora was of noble birth and fell for Erzsy the moment she saw her, but prideful Erzsy wanted nothing to do with her. She was devoted to her husband. That, however, did not deter Callidora and she relentlessly continued to woo her until one day Erzsy had no choice but to surrender her heart to the beautiful temptress. Some of the legendary tales say no two had ever been more in love than them, and those tales caused Erzsebet to often dream of finding a woman like Callidora, a strong, beautiful woman that would see her worth and work to win her over, but so far no luck in that department.

"Bette," Julie chimes, interrupting Erzsebet's reverie. "how 'bout we go to the club for a bit, and when we get bored we can try to find your granny's old bones." Julie's disrespectful attitude bothered Erzsebet. Julie knew how important this trip was to Erzsebet but she was obviously too self-centered to care.

"Whatever." Erzsebet muttered. Julie, of course, takes the guttural noise as compliance.

"Great! I'm going to start packing so I don't have to do it in the morning. Let's leave around 7pm so we can grab some dessert before the club." Julie suggested to Erzsebet.

Several hours later, Erzsebet and Julie are at the club that Julie raved so much about. Sitting on a couch, sipping a martini, Erzsebet scans the room, people watching, and is highly unimpressed with what she sees, rapidly growing bored of the ceaseless "unst, unst, unst," of the music. Julie was off with some exotic Hungarian nympho on the dance floor, grinding holes into their pants. A few brave guys attempted approaching Erzsebet but her icy stares scared each of them off as soon as they mustered up the courage to start walking towards her. Now that a few of them got shot down, none of the other curious ogling men were up to the challenge of trying to interest and seduce Erzsebet, but that did not stop them from window shopping. Erzsebet was a very attractive brunette, about 5'7" tall. Her long-sleeved, knee-length, lace dress did not show much skin but hugged seductively onto her curves, showcasing her bulging breasts and round behind. Her dark hair was styled big and bouncing, framing her most charming and captivating feature, her eyes. Erzsebet's eyes smoldered with powerful mystery, desire and thirst, and the men who were lingering around Erzsebet obviously longed to know about this mysterious beauty, but were also somehow equally afraid to find out. This saved her the need to explain to the salivating mongrels that she preferred the attention and affections of women. Erzsebet had never been the most popular, her withdrawn nature had kept most people away often leaving them wondering what was hidden behind her dark eyes. Only people like Julie, who had known Erzsebet for a long time and who were oblivious to her attempts to push people away, stuck around.

It was getting late and it was obvious that her friend Julie was too drunk, and too into the girl she was dancing with, to want to leave to go to an abandoned cemetery anytime soon. Erzsebet sighed. Julie had been her friend for a long time but that did not make her a very good one. She stood up and scanned the room one last time to find a reason to stay. "Fuck it," she thought and walked out the door and into the night.

The night air felt like home to Erzsebet, who had always preferred the dark. She caught a cab but instead of heading back to the house where her and her friend had been staying, she decided to visit her great-great-great grandmother's grave. "I can't leave without seeing her, it's why I came," she thought. After a short drive the cab pulled up to the graveyard. Erzsebet got out and paid the cabbie.

"Would you like me to wait?" the man asked.

"No, I think I'll be awhile." Erzsebet knew that she had to be up early in the morning, but she also suffered from severe insomnia and knew that the lack of sleep wouldn't bother her. The cemetery was not very big and was thankfully well lit by a full moon, making it easy to read the names on the gravestones. Many of them, however, were quite weather worn making it hard to see the names and dates of the people buried beneath them. Erzsebet spent many minutes searching throughout the graveyard trying to find her grandmother's grave, and she found herself getting discouraged and emotionally riled. She had always felt out of place and uncomfortable with herself, and she thought that maybe finding her namesake would help her gain a sense of who she was. Erzsebet was about to give up when she spied a group of weeping willow trees in the far corner of the cemetery. Something about the way their branches danced in the breeze called Erzsebet over to them. She walked over to the three sister willows and pulled aside some of their branches, which were occluding a gravestone in a seemingly protective way. Beloved Erzsebet Marie Kovak Born: February 28, 1740 Died: May 17, 1815. Erzsebet gently knelt beside the tombstone. "Finally," she breathed with relief and gratitude. She laid a hand on the gravestone and wished she could see her grandmother's face. Erzsebet Kovak was the last of Erzsebet's family to live and die in Hungary. She grimly thought about Erzsy's children, who were the first of the family to move out of Hungary. Erzsebet's children did not willingly move from Budapest, however. The grisly truth was that her four children were run out of town after being caught enjoying a cannibalistic feast. The children were 19, 17, 14 and 10 years old. They fled town, made their way across Europe, taking care of each other, and eventually ended up in America. This gruesome story was not one that Erzsebet's family was proud of. In fact, Erzsebet only heard it once when she asked her grandmother about her Hungarian ancestors. Erzsebet was unsure about her feelings towards her cannibalistic relatives. Part of her was repulsed by their actions while another part of her longed to understand them and validate that they were even true. As Erzsebet silently pondered the cascade of thoughts and emotions that flooded forth, she began to feel calmed, as if her great-great-great grandmother were there right alongside her reassuring and soothing her angst.

"You have her eyes." Erzsebet jumped to her feet at the sound of a husky female voice coming from the shadows of a nearby tree, and a woman stepped into the bright moonlit grass in front of her. "Her eyes burned just like that." She looked like a woman but had an otherworldly aura about her. She was tall, probably close to six feet and dressed in a long dark skirt with a high collared blouse and long flowing, hooded cloak. A jeweled brooch positioned at the top of her blouse collar sparkled in the reflective rays of the moon, and it looked not only incredibly expensive but also incredibly old. Her hair appeared to be as black as the night and was styled in a part updo with loose, thick tendrils framing her face. A stream of silver moonlight fell upon her face, revealing her exquisite beauty. High cheekbones, full luscious lips and the most intoxicating blue eyes she had ever seen. "Don't be afraid," the strange woman said softly to Erzsebet, whose body stood frozen. She was overwhelmed by both fear and a strong sense of curiosity about the mysterious beautiful woman standing before her, and who exactly she was comparing her too.

"Who are you?" Erzsebet managed to whisper hoarsely.

"I am a friend," the woman replied.

"I mean, what is your name?"

"My name is Callidora, Erzsebet."

Erzsebet took a startled step backwards. "How do you know my name?" she demanded.

"A lucky guess," she replied while taking a step forward. One of the woman's arms reached outward and her fingers boldly, yet gingerly, picked up the locket that rested against Erzsebet chest to inspect it. As her fingertips brushed against her skin, Erzsebet's body trembled with an unexplainable rush of excitement. Callidora flipped the locket over, her eyes looking as if she was actually expecting there to be an inscription on the backside. After studying it for the briefest of moments, she placed the locket again against her chest and took a step backwards. They stood in silence for a moment. Callidora turned towards Erzsy's grave and stood motionless while Erzsebet took the moment to observe her face. Her perfectly proportioned nose and chin gave her a look of elegant nobility and her gaze was intense, filled with what Erzsebet thought looked to be passion. The way she presented herself, made Erzsebet feel that she was a very intelligent, well-mannered lady of high ranking. Altogether, the strange woman appeared to be an ethereal creature with an allure that Erzsebet had never encountered before. Callidora continued to gaze at Erzsy's headstone with great sadness, and she seemed to miss the woman whose name was inscribed upon it. Although Erzsebet knew that it was impossible, before she let her brain know what she was doing she asked Callidora, "You knew my great-great-great grandmother?"

Callidora turned slightly and gave a small sad smile, "Yes. Yes I did."

She turned back towards the tombstone and gave a barely audible sigh and then fully turned so that she faced Erzsebet again, and offered Erzsebet her arm. Erzsebet could not help feeling incredibly flattered that such an elegant woman would make a gesture like that to her, so she immediately took it. As Callidora started guiding her out of the cemetery however, Erzsebet's senses started to set in. Who or what was this woman? Why was she trusting a complete stranger to guide her to who knows where in the middle of the night, from a cemetery, in Hungary?

Erzsebet's fears however were both mixed and stifled by her awe of this quietly enchanting, beautiful woman. Erzsebet began to feel anxious, she suddenly seemed incapable of speech and her body began to feel shaky. Callidora was something that she had never encountered before and she felt a strange and desperate need in her body to please her. They approached a row of trees and passed through a gap in between two of them, and when they emerged on the other side Erzsebet was awestruck by the site of an enormous castle towering over them, reaching high into the moonlit sky. Callidora looked over at her and smiled widely, which made Erzsebet aware of her dropped jaw. She quickly snapped her mouth closed, looked down and blushed slightly embarrassed. "At least it's dark. She probably can't tell I'm red." She thought to herself. Callidora, with her free hand, softly raised her chin and looked deeply into her eyes, as she brushed a piece of hair behind her ear.

"It's beautiful, isn't it?" She remarked.

Erzsebet gave a small nod, still too embarrassed to talk, while Callidora stroked her cheek gently with the back of her slender fingers.

"Like you," she whispered so softly that Erzsebet was fairly certain she imagined her saying it. Still her heart leaped and a spike of arousal coursed through her body. Callidora and Erzsebet turned towards the castle and resumed walking towards it, all the while Erzsebet trying to hide her grin.

Soon they were at the castle's door. Callidora opened it and let Erzsebet enter first, as she quickly slipped in behind her, and before she had the chance to observe the entry way she had a hand on her lower back ushering her down a corridor to the right. The castle was made of stone walls and seemed to be decorated very elegantly, but Erzsebet had a hard time telling exactly what it looked like because the only light to see by was the soft moonlight pouring in through the windows. Callidora was now holding her hand, guiding her down the hall, and Erzsebet was surprised by how comfortable and reassuring this felt to her.

"Callidora." Callidora looked surprised to hear her say her name, as she turned to look at her. "Please tell me where we are going," Erzsebet said firmly. Callidora stopped walking and took both of her hands in hers, smiling widely.

"I would be very honored if you were to accompany me to a masquerade this evening," Callidora said with a carefully shrouded expectancy in her voice.

"Tonight?" Erzsebet asked, puzzled. Callidora nodded and Erzsebet gave her a look of confusion, yet she offered no resistance to the invitation. Somehow, she couldn't.

"Follow me," Callidora said and then led her through another set of doors into a room that was lit by several large candelabras. It was a fairly large room with a grand red sofa and matching chairs, and something that looked like a vanity mirror with a small counter and a chair in front. There was also a very large wardrobe and dresser. Erzsebet would have guessed it was a bedroom except that there was no bed. "Please, wait here," Callidora said as she motioned for her to wait on the sofa. Erzsebet sat lightly on the sofa as Callidora exited the room through a second set of double doors. She looked around and tried to assess not only where she was, but again, who Callidora was. For the first time, she had a moment to ponder how Callidora could have possibly known

Erzsebet Kovak. She died in 1815 and that was almost 200 years ago! Yet Callidora didn't look any older than her mid-20's. Was Callidora immortal? A time traveler, maybe? Her clothes did look as though she had stepped out of the 1700's. Before Erzsebet had any more time to ponder, Callidora returned, and with her she brought a young attractive woman with dark hair and eyes that looked just like Callidora's. She was dressed in an elegant looking gown, dark maroon in color. And, similar to Callidora's attire, it too looked like it belonged in a 1700's ballroom. Erzsebet was taken aback by her beauty and the woman looked equally surprised to see Erzsebet there.

Callidora extended her hand towards Erzsebet, "Erzsebet, darling." Erzsebet took Callidora's hand and rose from the couch where she was sitting. "I would like you to meet my sister, Maria."

Maria's exquisite features were arranged in an expression of perfect shock upon hearing Erzsebet's name. She quickly recovered however, and gave a polite curtsey while offering her greeting, "So happy to meet you." Erzsebet was a bit taken back by the formality, but gave a slight bow and smile in return.

"Maria, Erzsebet will be attending the masquerade with me tonight. If you have the time, will you please find her something appropriate to wear and help her to get dressed?" Callidora asked

"Of course, dear sister," Maria responded.

"I will leave you to it then." Callidora took Erzsebet's hand once more, raised it to her ruby stained mouth and brushed the back of her hand with the softest yet most electrifying kiss Erzsebet has ever experienced. As her lips brushed her skin, it felt as though Callidora had planted a lightning bolt into her hand that shot up through her arm and straight into her heart. "I will see you soon my dear," she said, and left the two women alone to prepare for the masquerade event.

Once Callidora exited the room, Maria directed Erzsebet to the chair in front of the vanity table mirror. Maria began to pin Erzsebet's hair into a stylish updo while Erzsebet carefully studied Maria's reflection in the small mirror. "Did you know Erzsebet, too?" she inquired of Marie.

"I did." Maria said simply. She paused a moment then hesitantly asked, "Did you know her as well?"

"No, not directly, she was my great-great-great grandmother." Maria smiled sadly, but said no

more. Although neither of them said much to each other, it seemed that Maria was just as comfortable with the silence between them as Erzsebet was. Although Erzsebet had a hundred questions racing through her mind, it was so rare to find a person who didn't feel the need to chit chat about trivial things that she decided to just sit and enjoy Maria's presence.

Soon Maria was finished with Erzsebet's hair. "It's beautiful," Erzsebet breathed as she admired Maria's work in the mirror.

Maria then put her hands on Erzsebet's shoulders and leaned her face in side by side with Erzsebet's. "Only because you are beautiful," she responded. Erzsebet looked shyly down at her

feet and smiled. "Now let's get you into a gown." Maria walked over to the wardrobe and opened it. Erzsebet expected her to pull out an elaborate dress like her own, but instead she came back to Erzsebet with an armful of white linen garments. "Put these on," Maria instructed, as she handed the pile of clothes to Erzsebet and turned back towards the wardrobe. Erzsebet held the clothes out in front of her, "oh," she thought to herself, "they're undergarments." By then, Maria had returned from the wardrobe holding a mess of circular wires.

"What are those?" Erzsebet asked in dismay. Maria laughed lightly.

"They are hoops, silly girl."

Erzsebet cracked a smile and giggled a little bit herself. Once all the undergarments were on and the hoops were arranged neatly on her hips, Maria returned to the wardrobe once more. This time she returned with a gown. Maria helped Erzsebet slip the gown over her head, arrange it over the hoops, and lace it up in the back. Erzsebet was about to look at herself in the mirror when Maria stopped her and tied a mask around her dark eyes. Once the mask was secured, Erzsebet was then allowed to turn around. She hardly recognized herself. Her mask was black with gold and crème colored lace trimmings and flowing black feathers. The cascading fabric of her gown matched her elegant mask. Suddenly, another masked face appeared in the mirror behind her. She spun around to face her hostess, "Callidora!" she exclaimed.

"Erzsebet, you look exquisite!" She said, smiling. Her mask displayed a slight variation to her own, and she had changed into a gown more regal than anything Erzsebet in her wildest of dreams could have imagined. Callidora extended her hand and the pair exited through the doors they arrived by. The hall was still dimly lit, but Erzsebet could see that the great room that they first entered in was now bright and she could also hear the sound of haunting classical music being played.

They reached the entrance of the great room and Erzsebet could now see and take in the detailed gothic architecture and high vaulted ceilings, along with gold ribbons and other decorations that were placed around the walls and chandeliers. Callidora and Erzsebet turned right, and a few other masked couples and individuals were headed in the same direction, towards a set of descending stairs. Callidora and Erzsebet reached the stairs, and Erzsebet look down to see a magnificent scene. Outstretched before her was an incredibly large ball room. At least a hundred masked couples were dancing to a slow passionate song, every person taking each step with unnatural precision. A live orchestra was playing just to the right of the steps, couples resting lined the walls to the left and right, and acrobats flew and flipped between the massive chandeliers. Directly across the steps sat two individuals in extravagant throne like chairs stationed upon a raised platform, overseeing the festivities.

Callidora turned her face towards Erzsebet, trying to gauge her level of shock. She was pleasantly surprised to see that Erzsebet was obviously pleased at the extravagant scene before her. She held onto her waist as they slowly descended the stairs. "Are you thirsty, Erzsy?" Callidora asked as she guided the two towards a large table of refreshments. Erzsebet felt her heart leap up into her throat upon hearing the nickname. "So much better than Bette," she thought. Callidora picked up two wine glasses and gave one to Erzsebet. Erzsebet was puzzled by the contents of the glasses. The drink was thick and red and appeared to be the only thing being served. She lifted the glass to her mouth, Callidora watching her carefully as she did the same, the contents smelled sweet and slightly rusty. She took a sip. Her mouth was instantly filled with the sickly sweet taste of human blood. She looked up at Callidora whose glass was still lifted up to her mouth. Erzsebet could see sharp fangs showing through her parted lips. Alarmed, Erzsebet looked around at her other guests. She saw people laughing, talking, smiling and drinking, all with fangs protruding from their mouths. "Vampires!" Erzsebet thought with a gasp, "She is a vampire! They are all vampires!" The revelation made sense, how else could Callidora and Maria have known Erzsebet Kovak? Callidora saw that Erzsebet had noticed her unusually sharp incisors and quickly put a hand on her arm in an attempt to calm her. Erzsebet tried to pull away but Callidora leaned in close to her ear. "I promise, no one will hurt you darling," her husky voice whispered. "You are my guest." Despite the crisis at hand, Erzsebet could not help but feel herself moisten from the sound of Callidora's voice and the feeling of her warm breath against her ear.

For a moment, Erzsebet considered running back up the stairs and out of the castle as fast as she could, but after one look into Callidora's hypnotic eyes she was seemingly spellstruck and could not help but trust her. She again had no ability to resist the situation and Erzsebet smiled to signal to Callidora her decision to stay, and Callidora returned it with a wide, seductive grin. Erzsebet then shot her wine class a combination look of dismay and disgust. "I think you'll like it if you give it a chance," Callidora said encouragingly. Erzsebet gave her a sarcastic look but took another small sip anyway. She was surprised to find that the drink had seemed to become much sweeter than her first sip. Erzsebet took another bolder drink and firmly decided it was the best thing, food or drink that she had ever tasted, and after a few more gulps, her glass was almost empty. Erzsebet began to feel her own incisors sharpen, although it could have been her imagination. She also felt an overwhelming compulsion to drink more. She set down her glass, and began to look for a fuller cup when Callidora placed an arm around her waist and laughed. "Pace yourself Erzsy!" she said with a grin. Erzsebet gave her a slightly embarrassed smile.

Just then, a couple other guests approached Callidora and Erzsebet. The couple greeted Callidora warmly. The man gave a deep bow and drew one of Callidora's hands up to his mouth to tender it with a kiss, while the woman presented a deep curtsey. Callidora returned their gestures with small nods, and then introduced Erzsebet, who then gave her best curtsey. The couple were too enamored with Callidora, however, to notice anything amiss with Erzsebet's greeting. The couple left momentarily and Callidora spent the next several minutes pointing out the many distinguished guests in the room to Erzsebet.

"That couple over there are old family friends. That man in the blue mask is a dignitary from Africa," she explained

"Dignitary?" Erzsebet questioned.

"Yes. Our kind don't exactly have a government. It's more like representatives that maintain good relations between regions. Do you see the two over there?" Callidora motioned to the regal looking man and woman sitting on the platform, above all the rest of the guests. Erzsebet nodded. "They are essentially the rulers of this land although they don't go by any official title. They punish wrong doing and keep other regions in check." Erzsebet was watching the royal couple as

Callidora spoke and she noticed Maria approaching the woman on the throne. The queen rose and gave Maria a warm hug and seemed to be admiring Maria's beautiful gown.

"Maria seems to know her pretty well," Erzsebet commented to Callidora.

"I should think so, she is our mother," Callidora said with a smile. At first Erzsebet was a little surprised at being in the company of nobility, a princess in fact! But the shock soon dissipated as Erzsebet thought more about it. With such refined exquisite features and impeccable manners, how could she be anything but royalty? "Come," Callidora said, interrupting her thoughts, "I will teach you how to dance." Normally, Erzsebet would avoid any kind of partner dancing but her body and mind seemed to be under Callidora's spell, and either would do anything she asked of her.

Erzsebet found the steps easy and fun and she caught on quickly to the graceful dances. Callidora and Erzsebet spent the next few hours dancing, drinking, laughing, and socializing. The inhibitions that Erzsebet usually felt when in a large crowd were gone. She talked and chattered and laughed with everyone, and had a grand time doing it. She also felt herself surprisingly at ease with the group of creatures around her and marveled at how no one seemed to find anything out of the ordinary with the two women dancing and intimately socializing together. Was it because they were in fact…not really human? Perhaps vampires were indeed much more open to same sex coupling.

While standing next to Callidora, sipping more of the red lifeblood, she could not help but admire her breathtaking beauty. Callirora's dark hair was styled elegantly, her blue eyes glistened with mischief and mystery, and her smile was both confident and sensual. The sight of her fangs pointing out of her parted, ruby-stained lips made Erzsebet's neck and breasts tingle with excitement. She then turned her attention back to her swiftly emptying glass, and as she was sipping, she noticed another exquisite pair dancing. Both had magnificent blue eyes and blonde hair, their features were the male and female versions of each other and both were exceptionally attractive. They were dressed in matching costumes of royal blue with white trimmings. "Who are those two?" Erzsebet whispered to Callidora.

"That is Gaston LeBlanc and his wife, Genevieve," Callidora answered in an equally hushed tone. Erzsebet gave her a questioning look and she explained further, "They are French representatives . . . and also siblings." Erzsebet's eyes widened in shock. "When the vampire species first emerged, there were very few of us, so interbreeding was nearly impossible to avoid and it was just accepted as normal. Now it is not necessary, but it is still not taboo as it is in human society." Surprisingly, Erzsebet felt more taken aback by this news, than when she realized she was surrounded by creatures who could kill her in an instant.

Callidora and Erzsebet continued drinking and dancing, and Erzsebet could not tell if the blood was having some intoxicating effects on her or if she was just happier than she had ever been in her entire life. Soon the guests started breaking off into pairs and smaller groups to leave. The orchestra was reduced to a single pianist and the acrobats began to descend from the ceiling. "If you'd like I can escort you home now," Callidora said.

"Well, if it's alright. . . . I think I'd like to stay with you. I don't need to leave until dawn." Erzsebet said with flirting eyes. She wasn't sure, however if Callidora was too much of a lady to pick up on her hint.

"Very well," Callidora said with a knowing smile and began to guide her across the ballroom and through a set of doors. The two made their way through several long halls and a set of stairs and through another door. "This is my room," Callidora informed her, as they entered. The walls in the room were made of dark mahogany and it contained a large wardrobe and dresser, a desk, sofa, chairs, a grand fireplace, and an enormous four poster bed.

"I didn't think vampires slept on a bed," Erzsebet remarked as she took off her mask. Callidora slipped off her mask as well and then grabbed Erzsebet suddenly by the waist and pulled her towards her forcefully. Their noses almost touching, she replied, "There are other things you can do on a bed besides sleep." Callidora then began to seductively kiss Erzsebet's blood-stained lips. As she kissed her, she slowly applied pressure to Erzsebet's hips forcing her to walk backwards until the back of her knees hit the bed. She lay down onto the soft mattress as Callidora slowly lowered herself on top of her. She could feel Callidora's sharp fangs on her tongue as Erzsebet licked her lips, and Callidora playfully bit her lip in return.

Callidora then moved her attentions towards her neck and as she kissed her, Erzsebet interrupted the moment and surprised Callidora by asking, "What was Erzsy like?"

"Much like you," Callidora responded between kisses. "You remind me so much of her, even the way you kiss." Callidora suddenly pulled away from Erzsebet's neck. Erzsebet looked at her with a wide eyed, questioning expression. Callidora averted her eyes and said in a soft husky voice, "We were lovers."

"Lovers!" Erzsebet thought, her expression widening. Could this be? Could Callidora be the "Calli" that had given her great-great-great grandmother the locket she wore around her neck? Could this be the woman that she had heard stories about all her life? That she had dreamed about all her life? Erzsebet could not find the voice to say these things out loud but Callidora saw into her reeling mind, knew what she was thinking and nodded slowly and sadly. If she really had been Erzsy's lover, that also meant that Erzsebet was part vampire! It certainly would explain her insomnia, her hatred of the sun, her cannibalistic ancestors, her newly revealed pleasure in the taste of blood, and many other things that before had been unexplainable. "I'm so sorry, Erzsy, I should have told you." Callidora said gently with great sincerity. Erzsebet mind briefly flashed to the sibling spouses she had seen earlier that night.

"Callidora . . ." Erzsebet breathed softly. Callidora looked up hopefully at the sound of her name. "Kiss me," she said. Callidora eagerly pressed her lips to Erzsebet's, and as she kissed her she began to glide her hand over her hips and sides. Erzsebet could feel Callidora's chest heave against her and she nervously lifted her fingers to undo the buttons down the front of Callidora's dress coat, when Callidora stood up suddenly and stripped out of her dress coat and skirts until she was standing nude in front of Erzsebet. Erzsebet was already feeling dizzy from Callidora's passionate kissing and now the sight of her full, perfect teardrop shaped tits and luscious curvy hips made her catch her breath as she felt her inner juices flow and moistened the lips between her thighs. Callidora held out her hand and pulled Erzsebet up with her. She whipped her body around so that she faced the bed, and she was behind her pressing her hips into Erzsebet's. Her slender fingers swiftly began to unlace her tightly strung gown, and Erzsebet leaned forward so that her elbows rested on the bed and her butt was backed into Callidora's pelvis, so that she could continue to feel her nude curves press tauntingly against her. While still unlacing with one hand, Callidora reached underneath Erzsebet's skirt and began caressing Erzsebet's soft inner thighs. When her fingers brushed against the wetness of her pussy lips, Callidora abandoned unlacing the dress altogether and instead focused all her attention on Erzsebet's soft creamy thighs and teasing her soft, smooth folds with the lightest of touches that made Erzsebet's knees go weak. Erzsebet felt tingles running back and forth through her body, from her hard nipples to her wet pussy. While Callidora was busy moving her fingers between the lips of her dripping flower, Erzsebet moved her arms up and out of her loosened gown and underclothes, freeing her voluptuous breasts. Callidora leaned forward and began kissing her bare back as she moved one hand around to explore Erzsebet's exposed tits. She began squeezing her breasts and pinching her nipples while continuing to expertly tease her pussy with her fingers.

Erzsebet could feel Callidora's middle finger flicking along her soft swollen bud, while almost, but not quite entering her.

Callidora then flipped Erzsebet back over so that she faced her, tore off her remaining clothes and thrust her back onto the bed where she then began to play with her swollen stiff clit with one finger, while her mouth gently nibbled on Erzsebet's large, dark erect nipples. Erzsebet let a few moans escape her lips which served to excite Callidora even further. She moved her mouth off of her tits and placed it in-between Erzsebet's thighs so she could focus all of her attention onto her wet, throbbing pussy. Callidora licked her over and over again, in slow circular movements until Erzsebet felt she couldn't stand it anymore. Heat surged throughout her body and as she opened her eyes, Callidora had stood up between her legs spreading her thighs open even further and smiled as she licked her fingers in preparation.

Using the fingers of one hand to part her pussy lips, Callidora used the moistened fingers of her other hand to gently tease the opening of Erzsebet's wet cunt. Slowly sliding her fingers into the warm moistness, Callidora couldn't take her eyes off of the jiggling flesh of Erzsebet's huge tits. Erzsebet's cunt hungrily welcomed Callidora's fingers and she rode them rhythmically while her eyes watched Callidora's fangs protrude pronouncedly from behind her plump lips. Somehow, the sight of the incisors only served to excite her further and her hips rocked faster and harder against Callidora's fingers. Callidora suddenly withdrew her hand and raised it to her lips so that she could suckle the musky dew of Erzsebet's pleasure from her fingers. A low, husky moan escaped her mouth and Erzsebet could have sworn that she saw Callidora's eyes flash red with a look of lust-filled hunger. Callidora jammed her fingers back into Erzsebet's wet cunt and thrust them back and forth as her mouth headed for Erzsebet's creamy white neck, her fangs gently teasing at the soft flesh beneath them. Callidora grinded her own soaking wet pussy against Erzsebet's thigh while her hand was vigorously finger-fucking her cunt. She watched as Erzsebet's eyes rolled back and her head turned slightly to the side. With her own juices flowing freely by now, Callidora could feel Erzsebet's pussy begin to tighten around her fingers. Just as Erzsebet's body went stiff with orgasm, Callidora pressed her fangs into the side of Erzsebet's neck, just deep enough to retrieve a sampling of her deliciously tart blood. Callidora licked at the droplets of blood as Erzsebet cried out, her screams a mix of pleasure and pain.

Ecstasy coursed through their bodies, unifying the women in more ways than one. Once the waves of orgasm subsided from Erzsebet's body and Callidora had drunk her lover's blood to satiety, the pair collapsed side by side on the bed, panting and exhausted from their wild romp. They looked at each and Erzsebet suddenly felt inexplicably bound to the beautiful, mysterious woman lying next to her. Callidora lovingly brushed a piece of hair behind Erzsebet's ear as her lips trailed soft tender kisses along the curve of her neck. Erzsebet's pussy was still throbbing, but her body still wanted and needed more. The sensual fun began all over again and continued on throughout the remainder of the night.

When the light of dawn came, Erzsebet was reluctant to leave the castle, and Callidora, but she was leaving Hungary today and knew Julie would be anxiously waiting for her. Callidora managed to find the dress that Erzsebet arrived at the castle in last evening, and she put it back on for the journey home. Neither Erzsebet nor Callidora had much to say while walking back to where she had been staying with Julie during her time here and Erzsebet spent the time silently trying to convince herself that she couldn't stay in Hungary. "What about school?" she thought. She also had no job here, no friends or family. The only person she could technically say that she knew here was Callidora, and considering her history with romantic relationships, she probably was already over her. Plus, there was the bizarre fact that she was a relative. A very, very, very distant relative but it certainly didn't feel that way.

As they approached the house and paused a moment on the porch, Erzsebet was about to thank her for the wonderful night when Callidora interrupted her. She grabbed her hands and held them tightly, "Stay with me Erzsy, please, don't leave! You are a vampire. This is your home, and you belong here. With me! Love and blood will keep us together forever and I give you my heart!"

The two were then startled by another voice, "Bette! Where have you been?" Erzsebet heard her friend Julie say, as she came out of the front door of the house. In that moment, the sound of that ugly nickname and her friend's voice made Erzsebet despise Julie. "Who's your friend?" she then asked, looking towards Callidora.

Erzsebet did not immediately respond to her friend's inquiry, and the three of them stood for a long moment in silent anticipation of what Erzsebet would say next. "Julie, I finally found what I was looking for last night. In fact, I found a lot of things I've been looking for, for a long time." Turning to face Callidora, she wrapped her arm around her neck and looked deep into her intense eyes as she declared her intentions. "I'm staying here in Hungary. This is my home. This is where I belong, and this is the woman I belong with."

Julie's jaw dropped in silent dismay and confusion, as Callidora leaned forward to kiss Erzsebet passionately on the lips. Erzsebet's journey and quest had been fulfilled as her heart was now forever bound in Budapest.

Story #2

Lured to The Embrace:

A Lesbian's Immortal

Transformation

"Whee-whoo!" Vivie heard a man whistle at her as she exited her cab. She raised her middle finger in the general direction of the offender and turned to walk into the apartment building lobby, secretly smiling to herself. Although she thought that the catcall was rude, it also reassured her that she had chosen the right outfit for the evening. Vivie was wearing nude colored high heels and a one shoulder crimson cocktail dress that left her other shoulder naked and exposed. The dress hugged her in all the right places, showing off her robust chest and generous behind. Vivie had her brunette hair styled in big bouncing curls, her eyes were fringed with dark lashes, and her lips were painted red to match her dress. She was dressed to impress and ready for her night out.

She buzzed the apartment of her friend, Haley, and then returned to wait in the cab. Haley soon joined Vivie and the cab driver drove the pair towards their destination. Mulling in thoughts of her recent break-up, Vivie suddenly couldn't contain her emotions. "Maybe I shouldn't go. It's going to be awkward! I don't want to see her!" Vivie's tone started out calm but by the third sentence she was frantic, "She probably won't even care if I'm there! What if she already has another girl!" Vivie was now panicking. Her ex-girlfriend was rumored to be attending the festivities tonight, and the possibility of running into her was very high.

"Deep breaths, hun." Haley put her arm around her friend and patting her knee said "Repeat after me. You are smokin' hot and ready to have fun. You don't care about her. You are going to have a fucking awesome night no matter what!" Vivie chewed on her bottom lip nervously and nodded slowly. It wasn't a great pep talk but she was glad for the support. "Stop that! You'll ruin your lipstick," Haley scolded her. Vivie began to reapply and Haley watched as Vivie slowly smoothed the scarlet color over her plump lips and she felt herself get wet. Haley wasn't usually attracted to girls but Vivie was so beautiful and intriguing that everyone was attracted to her, even longtime friends like Haley.

"Here we are!" Haley chimed excitedly when the cab pulled up to an old, run-down, office building. Here we go, Vivie thought to herself. The two stepped out of the cab and headed towards a side entrance into the building that wasn't visible from the main street. They walked towards the door where a tall bulky man was guarding the entrance.

"I pray you, do not fall in love with me, for I am falser than vows made in wine." Vivie informed the bouncer, who then stepped aside after hearing the correct secret entrance phrase, and opened the door for the girls. The two were immediately met by a scene of wild debauchery. A thick wall of music permeated the air. Vivie could feel the pulsating beat deep in her chest, vibrating out through her breasts. The girls linked arms, and mouthed, Oh my god!'s to each other. They had been to this underground club a few times before, but there had never been this many people there before. The music seemed louder and the vibe was cooler than it had ever been before. The dance floor was packed, as were most of the booths and tables around it, and the bartenders' hands blurred from the speed at which they were working.

Vivie scanned the very large main area to assess who was there and who she wanted to talk to. She spotted a very hot woman and noted where she was standing so that she could talk to her later. She also noticed Stephanie at the bar, a woman who is a regular at this particular club, and Vivie gave her a smile and small wave. She continued her scan and was caught off guard at the sight of Taylor, her ex, nearby, with a gorgeous spikey-haired blonde hanging onto her arm and every word she was whispering into her ear. Vivie's heart began to race and her chest felt tight with anxiety. She turned towards Haley but she had her back to her, flirting with someone else already. Vivie frantically looked about the room for a way to escape before Taylor noticed her standing all by herself and her eyes came again to Stephanie and she started to walk in her direction.

Stephanie was tall, with long, jet black hair and piercing green eyes. Tonight, she was dressed in a strapless, black leather dress and wore a beautiful black beaded choker around her neck.

"Joining me so soon, darling?" Stephanie asked in a husky Russian accent, as Vivie sat on the barstool next to her. Stephanie was always sitting at the same place at the bar, enjoying her usual bloody mary, and she had many times generously played the part of a girlfriend when Vivie was trying to avoid another woman, or man. Usually however, she came to Stephanie when the night was almost over and she didn't want to go home with the person she had been flirting with all night. Smiling, Stephanie looked over at Vivie, but her expression soon changed when she noticed her forlorn look. "Darling," she said gently, "What's the matter?" Vivie smiled but Stephanie could see the tears beginning to well up in her eyes. She gently stroked her back, "There, there, you're alright," she said a bit uncomfortably. Stephanie was not used to dealing with others' entangled emotions.

"I'm so sorry," Vivie said, embarrassed. She tried to reign in the tears that threatened to leak from behind her eyelids. "It's just. . . Taylor. . ."

"Ah," Stephanie said understandingly. "Say no more, darling." She then motioned to the bartender who brought back a lemon drop martini, Vivie's favorite. She smiled, grateful for Stephanie's support. "Why do you let her upset you so much?" Stephanie asked gently, yet with genuine intrigue over this dance of emotions between lovers.

"Well, I thought I was prepared to see her. But then, as soon as I walked in, some pretty blonde girl was all over her! I mean, it's only been like a month!" Vivie had her elbows on the bar counter and put her face in her hands, upset.

"Which one is she, love?" Stephanie asked. Vivie looked up and around.

"Taylor's over there, with the spiky-haired blonde," she responded with a motion of her hand and then returned her attention to the drink before her.

"Well, I wouldn't be too jealous. I think the blonde woman likes the overt attention and promise of your ex-lover's financial capabilities a bit more than her." Vivie glanced back at her ex to see her buying her new playmate and her three friends a round of drinks. Vivie laughed lightly, and smiled widely at Stephanie for genuinely making her feel better. Stephanie had surprised Vivie, she usually was more reserved, not from shyness but from a general disinterest to other people's drama. In addition, usually by the time Vivie found herself sitting next to Stephanie, she was too inebriated to really pay attention to what she was saying.

Stephanie began to pick out other girls in the club who were also flirting for favors. Soon the two were leaning in close to each other, people watching and analyzing the characters they picked out from the crowd. "Look! Look at her!" Vivie pointed out a young woman who was going back and forth, flirting, between two men. The men were oblivious to each other's presence but as the woman's state of sobriety was rapidly decreasing, so were her efforts to keep the men from each other. Stephanie laughed heartily at the scene and Vivie giggled to herself, pleased she had made Stephanie laugh and pleased at the charming way she did it.

Suddenly, Stephanie stood and grabbed hold of Vivie's hand, pulling her off of her barstool. "Wha. . .?" Vivie started to ask but answered her own question once she saw Taylor noticing the pair. She looked back at Stephanie who was smiling mischievously.

"We can't let her go unpunished now can we?" She asked jokingly. "Come, let's dance, darling." Vivie allowed Stephanie to lead her onto the dance floor because she knew that it would make Taylor wildly jealous, but she also felt a twinge of confusion. Although she had always enjoyed Stephanie's company, she was always so distant that she couldn't imagine her doing anything other than sitting at the bar, especially doing something as intimate as dancing.

Once they reached the dance floor Stephanie began to sway confidently but not zealously to the beat of the song. Vivie was unsure of what to do, most of the couples dancing were vigorously grinding, but Vivie didn't think that that's what Stephanie intended when she asked her to dance. She positioned herself in front of her, about two feet apart and began to swing her hips and arms to the music. Oh goodness, she thought, now Taylor is watching me make a fool of myself. Stephanie could sense that Vivie was unsure about what she was doing, which she found very endearing. She again gripped Vivie's fingers but this time led her in a twirl. She caught her with her free hand and quickly pulled her close, looking directly into her dark eyes. Their bodies pressed close, Vivie could feel her breasts pushing into Stephanie's own ample bosom, which seemed to cause an immediate surge of heat to ripple throughout Vivie's body. She swallowed nervously as she gazed into Stephanie's hungry eyes that held an expression she had never seen in her before. Stephanie smiled, for she knew that in that moment she had unquestionable control over Vivie's body and emotions. Before she knew it, Stephanie pushed Vivie's hips away from her and guided her into another series of spins, and twists, and steps. Even though this kind of partner dancing was not typical of this club, Vivie was unable to think about that. She was too dizzy and distracted from the spins and turns and the grazing passes of Stephanie's luscious body against her. Suddenly, Stephanie ended the series of dizzying dance floor moves by once again pulling her close against her body. Vivie's tits tingled this time as Stephanie pushed them tighter against her own chest, and Vivie could feel her skin flush at the feel of Stephanie's cleavage spilling slightly out of the top of her strapless dress. Inexplicably entranced and her body filled with a lust and longing she struggled to comprehend, Vivie's body felt frozen in place as she stared into Stephanie's hypnotic green eyes.

Vivie awoke from the trance Stephanie had trapped her in to find a few fellow club go-ers around her clapping and cheering at the pair's performance. She smiled and gave a playful bow. Stephanie, still holding her hand, led them off of the dance floor and towards a big horseshoe shaped booth far away from the dance floor. They scooted towards the center of it and Stephanie motioned one of the bartenders, ordering another bloody mary for her and another martini for Vivie. Soon they were once again sipping their cocktails and laughing together, but this time Vivie suddenly felt much different about Stephanie. Now, she had to try very hard not to bat her eyelashes or playfully caress her fingers along Stephanie's silky, slender arms. Stephanie also didn't try to hide her hungry glances into Vivie's cleavage whenever she was taking sips at her martini. Vivie was now overwhelmingly drawn to Stephanie, as Stephanie was, and has been for a while, to her. It just wasn't in a way that most expressions of couplings occurred.

Suddenly Haley emerged from the crowd, "Hey, girl, there you are!" she exclaimed, and then gave Vivie a quizzical look once she noticed who her drinking companion was. Vivie only smiled widely at her friend as she approached the booth, but her smile quickly wavered when she spotted who was coming up directly behind her friend, Taylor and her new blonde playmate.

"Mind if we join you?" Taylor announced as they approached the booth. Vivie was a bit too shocked to respond, but Stephanie quickly answered her so that no one would notice Vivie's sudden muteness. As the three began to slide their way into the booth, Stephanie reached her arm around Vivie and placed it on her far hip, pulling Vivie towards her to make room for the new comers. Vivie was forced much closer to Stephanie than necessary, but she didn't mind. No, she didn't mind in the least. Stephanie felt Vivie's soft bare thigh press against her leg and began to think about what lie above her hemline. Vivie herself felt as if electricity was intermittently pulsing through her body as the bare skin of her leg pressed against Stephanie's, and her mind flashed back to when their breasts and bodies were pressed tightly against one another just minutes earlier on the dance floor.

Vivie snapped out of her reverie and found herself directly across from a woman she spent two years loving mildly and the past few weeks hating passionately. This was the first time that Taylor and Vivie had seen each other in a month and the last visit involved a lot of throwing things and name calling. Vivie was uncertain how to act around her, and Taylor's female companion only increased her nervousness. Vivie had to admit that she was very attractive, and even though she wasn't exactly her "type", she was definitely a head turner. Her spiked hair was just the right shade of blonde, accented by big gold hooped earrings, and her braless breasts poked teasingly through the thin fabric of her sleeveless blouse. No wonder Taylor picked her as a rebound lover. Why, if Vivie was looking for a rebound affair, she might have even picked this blonde, nipple showing specimen herself.

Suddenly, she felt Stephanie's firm grip around her thigh while she vaguely heard Taylor say something like, "How have you been Vivie?" Vivie's face flashed an expression of surprise for a very brief, hardly noticeable moment, which quickly then changed into a wide posed smile.

"Yeah. . . Um, yeah, I'm great," Vivie said smiling and slightly giggling, still recovering from the initial shock of Stephanie's hand on her leg. "Uh, what about you, Taylor? What have you been up to?"

"Yeah, well I've been pretty great too. Recently at work I received that promotion I had been hoping for and a big raise to go along with it. . ." Taylor began to ramble on about how great her life has been since she and Vivie went their separate ways. Vivie was smiling and nodding without actually hearing any of the bullshit that Taylor was trying to tell her about and instead her mind was focused on the feeling of Stephanie's skilled fingers sliding back and forth along her inner thigh, getting closer to the hemline of her dress with every stroke.

Vivie was still not paying any attention when she heard Haley begin to speak, "Oh wow!" she exclaimed. "That sounds amazing! I've always wanted to go there. Vivie, you've been there haven't you?" Vivie's attention was brought back into the conversation by the sound of her name, but she had no idea what place Haley was asking her about.

"Oh, um . . ." Vivie laughed, as her face flushed with embarrassment. "Where was that, Haley? What were you talking about?"

"I was mentioning how you went to that same art gallery down town a few weeks ago, didn't you?" Haley responded, with obvious irritation.

"Oh, of course, the art gallery! Yes, I thought the show was amazing. The artist used a lot of different materials to make these wonderful sculptures that, oh! Um…. the sculptures were, ah very nice, and oh! Very cool. They were very cool!" Vivie awkwardly responded, while the others began looking at her strangely. When she had began her sentence Stephanie was still caressing her thigh with short, soft strokes, but as she continued to talk Stephanie began to inch her fingers up closer to the edge of her panties until eventually she was stroking the lips of her pussy from outside of her thong. When she did that, Vivie could barely continue thinking let alone talking so she made her reply much briefer than she had originally intended. Vivie grabbed onto Stephanie's hand to stop her motions. Although she liked her caresses she simply couldn't concentrate on anything else around her while Stephanie was touching her like that.

Once she grabbed hold of her hand, Stephanie announced to the table that she and Vivie were going to dance some more and exited the booth pulling Vivie out with her. Stephanie headed towards the dance floor with Vivie in tow, but upon reaching it she started to make her way around the crowd rather than stopping to dance. Due to their hastened zig-zag pace Vivie had no chance to question her on where they were going. Stephanie quickened her pace even more, making Vivie unable to talk to her while they were walking. She maneuvered them around the crowd and off of the main floor, and then she then led Vivie to a corner of the club that Vivie had never explored before. Stephanie turned down a deserted hallway where Vivie finally had the chance to stop and speak. "Where are we going?" she asked, a little concerned.

Stephanie turned and looked intensely into Vivie's eyes. Smiling at her, she replied, "Darling, somewhere I can finger you and no one will bother us." Vivie was much too shocked to respond. She was used to girls, and even guys, hitting on her, but no one was ever quite so direct. In addition, out of everyone in the club, Stephanie was probably the one she would least suspect of wanting her as anything more than a friend. However frank she was, the thought of Stephanie's fingers sliding into her excited Vivie tremendously, and the way she said it in her Russian accent only added to her anticipation.

Stephanie led her over to an elevator, and they rode it to the top floor. Vivie took notice to how Stephanie certainly seemed to know exactly where to go. She led them past old offices and abandoned cubicles to a room at the very end of the hall. As Stephanie opened the door, Vivie was taken back by the drastic change of scenery. Where she thought would be someone's long forgotten office, there was what appeared to be a very elegant, modern studio apartment. There was a plush black sofa surrounded by a couple of chairs and a long coffee table, as well as some lounging chairs huddling around a large flat screen TV and a gargantuan sized antique looking bed. The entire western wall was no wall at all but a window that ran along the entire length of the room, overlooking the bustle and bright lights of the city.

Oh my. . . Vivie thought as she approached the expansive glass. This view of the city was more beautiful than any she had ever seen before.

"What is this place?" she whispered.

"I guess you could call it my apartment." Vivie quickly flashed a look at her, puzzled. Then Stephanie simply said, "Actually, darling, I own the entire building." Vivie stood for a moment, watching all the bustling people and speeding vehicles moving in blurs on the streets below. As she stood Stephanie approached her, her eyes flashing red with hunger, yet it went unnoticed by Vivie who seemed fascinated by the cityscape below her. Stephanie wrapped her arms around Vivie's breasts from behind and began to gently kiss her exposed shoulders. Vivie's skin tingled with goose bumps as Stephanie's soft lips traced moistly across her skin. Hypnotized, Vivie closed her eyes and leaned back against her. Stephanie felt her push her firm buttocks into her pelvis and Vivie, in turn, enjoyed once again feeling Stephanie's tits press against her, this time from behind.

Suddenly, Stephanie's gentle kisses turned into frisky bites. "Oh, ow! Careful." Vivie giggled. Stephanie turned Vivie around, and looked like she was about to say something, but no words came out of her mouth. Strangely, Vivie felt as if Stephanie was 'talking' to her, yet she too spoke no further words. Stephanie grabbed one of Vivie's hands and led them over to the expansive bed where she threw Vivie down onto it. Vivie let out a sound which was a combination laugh and moan, absolutely thrilled with Stephanie's show of dominance. In one swift move, Stephanie slipped out of her strapless dress and tore off her panties, discarding them onto the floor as she was silently sizing up how quickly to proceed. She let out a soft, abbreviated laugh as she followed Vivie's eyes scanning every curve and crevice of her body, enjoying the moment of anticipation for just a bit longer than was necessary.

Straddling Vivie's legs which were hanging off of the bed, Stephanie leaned down and began kissing her slowly…softly…passionately. As Vivie's body responded to her tender kisses, she then moved one of her hands to the front of Vivie's dress and just as quickly as she had unsheathed her own evening attire, Stephanie ripped Vivie's dress off of her luscious body in one clean jerk. Smiling to herself as she heard Vivie gasp, Stephanie swiftly repositioned herself on the floor in front of the bed directly between Vivie's thighs. Continuously alternating the speed of her movements, Stephanie slowly slid her fingers along the inside of Vivie's thighs until she reached the pretty black lace of the panties she wore, flicking her fingers teasingly across the outside of the moistened thin fabric. Vivie's hips began to rock and the rise of her scent further served to agitate the lustful need within Stephanie's body. In a flash of movement Stephanie tore off her thong, exposing her smooth wet pussy and spreading Vivie's thighs apart even further so that she could take in the full beauty of her pretty pink lips and protruding, erect clit.

Vivie's hands tugged at Stephanie's hair, pulling her mouth closer between her parted legs, as Stephanie teased her just a bit longer as she trailed her wet tongue slowly along Vivie's inner thighs before licking, sucking and teasing her pussy lips and clit with her tongue. A series of moans escaped Vivie's mouth as her body received such deliciously intense pleasure. Stephanie rose and her mouth grabbed hold of one of Vivie's tits, as one of her hands slid up squeezing and groping the other breast while her other hand slid downward back between her thighs. While still sucking eagerly on her breast, Stephanie began to softly stroke Vivie's swollen pussy lips with her fingertips. She gently probed her opening without actually entering her, getting her fingers wet with her obvious arousal. She then brushed up along her inner folds until her finger hit Vivie's engorged clit and she began to rub it in tiny quick circles. Vivie moaned even louder and arched her back upwards like a cat in heat. This excited Stephanie, who then plunged two of her fingers deep into Vivie's moistness and began gliding them back and forth as Vivie's arousal quickly soaked her hand. Vivie cried out as Stephanie so expertly finger fucked her, stopping before she could climax.

Vivie's body was teetering on the edge of ecstasy as Stephanie then lay down onto the bed next to her. She reached for one of Vivie's hands and directed it between her thighs. Vivie's fingers quickly parted Stephanie pussy lips and she again moaned loudly when she discovered how wet Stephanie's pussy was. Stephanie returned her fingers into Vivie's cunt and the two hungry lovers finger fucked one another as they kissed and groped at each other's tits and mouths.

Stephanie began again to kiss Vivie's neck and bite at it slightly. "She sure likes to bite," Vivie thought, as the biting was becoming more and more frequent and slightly more aggressive with each nibble. Vivie moved both of her hands up Stephanie's body and cupped them around her full tits. Stephanie continued to finger fuck her…harder…faster…harder still. Vivie felt her body edging towards orgasm when suddenly Stephanie bit her harder than she cared for. "Ow! Stephanie!" She cried in pain, and pushed Stephanie away from her neck. Vivie gasped in horror. Stephanie pulled away from her baring a pair of huge fangs in the space where her incisors previously inhabited. Vivie began to struggle against her, trying to get away from those sharp teeth that had appeared out of nowhere, but Stephanie was on top of her, appeared to have some type of non-human strength, and she was not about to let her go.

"I've wanted you for so long, Vivie. I throw this stupid "invite only" party every weekend, hoping that you'll come, hoping that you will talk to me." Vivie was panicking and struggling against the hold Stephanie had of her body. What was she talking about? Why won't she let me go! "I've wanted to turn you, yet I have tried to resist you for so long! I thought that having sex with you might sate my desire, but this desire, it's too strong! I can't hold back! I must have you in all ways!" Stephanie's husky Russian accent was now frightening, rather than seductive, thought Vivie. Turn me? Turn me! What does that mean? What could that?..... Vivie suddenly came to a startling revelation when she again glanced at Stephanie's menacing fangs.

"No! NOOO!!" Vivie screamed. Stephanie bent her head down once more towards Vivie's neck and sunk her fangs deep into Vivie's flesh. Vivie's vision went black for a moment, and then, as the pain exploded in her neck, she saw bursts of purple, blue, and green, like neon explosions against the backdrop of a darkened sky. The poison began to spread through her veins, bringing the feel of fire with it. She felt the fire-like pain spread up her neck and into her temples, as well as downward, into her shoulders and even causing her breasts to tingling with heat. She felt as if every blood vessel in her body were about to burst. She could only think about the pain… or was it pleasure? …and the confusing dazzling lights in front of her eyes. Vivie vaguely felt as though Stephanie was continuing to make love to her. She couldn't tell if it was her rubbing her clit vigorously or if it was the heat of the poison rushing into that area of her body. Soon her entire body was being eaten by fire. Every blood vessel tingled. Her toes curled, and she felt a deep burning sensation in her belly.

Stephanie continued to pin her down as Vivie's body tightened and struggled from the poison Stephanie had injected into her veins when she bit into her, while simultaneously suckling the blood from her body. She watched her carefully, as Vivie's face contorted to a mixture of orgasm of pain. Stephanie could then see in Vivie's eyes, her transformation happening. Her skin had turned white and stone-like, and she had never before been more beautiful than she was right now. Stephanie stroked Vivie's clit and licked at her nipples as her body continued to gently writhe from the transformation. Seeing Vivie becoming like her….she couldn't help herself.

As the fire began to subside, Vivie felt Stephanie plunge her fangs into the other side of her neck while simultaneously plunging her fingers back into her cunt. This time, her shock came not from the bite but from Stephanie's fingers sliding inside of her. Stephanie began to thrust her fingers back and forth inside of her, going faster and getting more excited as she watched the final effects of Vivie's transformation play out before her hungry, lustful eyes. Simultaneously, Vivie's body and mind were being bombarded by a mix of sensations. The fire raged through her veins while pleasure radiated out from her sweet spot. The two feelings mingled together creating the most ecstatic high that she has ever felt before. Eventually, Vivie's body almost lifted off of the bed as she orgasamed, and at that moment of pure emotion and pleasure, Vivie knew she had been "turned". There was no turning back and she would from this point forward, forever belong to Stephanie in her immortal transformation. In the following moments Vivie's mind began to fully clear. The flashing lights faded into the blackness, which, in turn, melted away as well. The fire receded, and Vivie emerged...... a vampire.

Story #3

Confessions of Counsel: "I See Vampires!"

Her office was a large room, paneled with dark mahogany and dimly lit by two small desk lamps. Dr. Grayson explained that this was to provide a calming atmosphere for her patients but Lilah saw rats and beetles darting in and out of the shadows cast by her desk, and the chairs and sofa. For her, it was not calming at all. Dr. Grayson sat with calm poise in a high-backed chair, just like one you would expect to see a psychiatrist sitting in. Lilah sat opposite of her in a similar chair and beside her was a fainting couch, slightly raised at one end with no arms or back, to lie on if she ever was feeling too emotionally distraught, which she sometimes did. All three pieces of furniture were covered in a very soft, deep red fabric. There also hung two large mirrors on two different walls of the office.

"How have you been since our last visit?" Dr. Grayson inquired. Lilah, stared at the ground and playing with a lock of hair, only shrugged in response. Lilah was of average height, with thick curly dark hair that she often swept to the side, and dark green eyes. She was a young woman, 23 years of age, and extremely skinny for her height but with perfect perky breasts and an equally perky behind. Suddenly, Lilah's eyes widened and began to dart back and forth wildly, as if watching something on the ground moving very quickly. "Lilah, master your delusions. They only have power over you if you give them that power." Lilah brought her eyes back up towards Dr. Grayson, but could still see the rats in her peripheral vision, scurrying underneath the desk. "Lilah, how do you think you have changed since our sessions began?"

"I'm functioning, I guess," she shrugged again sarcastically. When Lilah began seeing Dr. Grayson, about six months ago, she was constantly seeing rats run along the walls and beetles crawling up her arms. She would see the beetles shells shine in various hues of green and blue climb up a stranger's arm and into their mouths. She often opened closet doors and cabinets to find a swarm of bats flying out of them chaotically. There was more though. Lilah constantly saw dark figures in the corners of a room or in an alley way, and sometimes at the foot of her bed at night. Sometimes the shadows were bolder, and she would see them trying to disguise themselves as normal humans at the grocery store, at the mall, or walking down the street. These figures appeared as both men and women with pale white faces, deep purple lips and dark menacing eyes. They would watch Lilah intently as they walked past her, because they knew that only she could tell who they really were, or rather, what they really were. When their purple lips curled into an equally menacing smile, long, sharp incisors were revealed. These frightening creatures were Lilah's worst fear: vampires. Since her counseling sessions began, Lilah still saw the beetles and rats but she was better at ignoring them. The vampires however still followed her everywhere, but she had since stopped warning people of their presence.

"I've noticed that you've started dressing differently that you did before," Dr. Grayson commented. Lilah crossed her legs and leaned forward in her chair. Her button down blouse had more buttons unfastened than would normally be appropriate, and even though Dr. Grayson tried to resist looking, she couldn't help peeking just for a second, down past the jeweled necklace that hung lowly between Lilah's braless firm breasts.

"You like my new look?" Lilah said softly with a slight smile, and then gave a short sarcastic laugh while leaning back into her chair.

"You look nice. However, I can't help noticing though that you remind me of the delusions you've been describing to me." Dr. Grayson observed. Lilah was looking past her at the wall and started smiling. Although Lilah tried to respond with vague answers and act aloof, Dr. Grayson had an annoying way of figuring her out. She now felt obliged to explain her actions.

"I thought that if I dressed like them they might think I was one of them, and leave me alone." Lilah explained slowly.

"I understand." Dr. Grayson responded simply, "Well, I do like that lipstick on you," she said, smiling warmly. Lilah looked down at her hands in her lap and smiled back, genuinely flattered. Dr. Grayson was an attractive woman, older than her by about 10 years, but very fit, tall for a woman, and extraordinary graceful in her mannerisms. She had light brown hair, which she mostly wore in a professional updo of some sort, and the most captivating eyes Lilah had ever seen. While it was true, that Lilah was seeking counsel from Dr. Grayson for her own dark demons, Lilah couldn't help but wonder what dark secrets of her own did the beautiful Dr. Grayson harbor, for reasons she couldn't quite explain.

"It makes me feel more confident too," Lilah continued, feeling encouraged, "I feel as if I am one of the hunters, rather than one of the prey."

"And you like being a hunter?"

"Yes," she said shyly, "It makes me feel . . .well, powerful." She looked up at Dr. Grayson with her eyes burning brightly.

Dr. Grayson felt drawn to her client's intense stare but mentally shook off her desire and continued on to say, "Less afraid, perhaps?" Lilah nodded in response. "Do you think these delusions represent some other fear that you are too afraid to even admit you have?" Dr. Grayson questioned. Lilah's benevolent looks quickly turned sour, and any ground that Dr. Grayson had gained vanished when she suggested that the vampires Lilah saw only existed in her mind. She gave Dr. Grayson a sharp look, leaned forward, and hissed.

"They aren't delusions! I know what I see! I see them watching me! Following me!" she stood, angry fire rushing through her body. "They are there! And they know I am not a fool! They cannot trick me!" Lilah strode past Dr. Grayson's chair to stare angrily out of the window. Her arms were crossed and she focused her attention on keeping the wrath trapped inside her trembling body. She felt anger in her bones, in her toes and fingers, forearms and forehead. Every part of her ached with raw emotion. So many people talked to her as if she was a child, or mad, or stupid. She could tolerate that kind of reaction from some, but she couldn't take Dr. Grayson talking to her like that as well.

She felt a hand on her shoulder. The hand startled her as she did not hear Dr. Grayson approaching her, and she was not used to any physical contact from her either. She recovered from her surprise quickly and returned her focus on her anger. Dr. Grayson placed her free hand on her other shoulder. "Forgive me, Lilah. I didn't mean to offend you." The tender way she spoke her apology began to make her anger fade. She turned around to face Dr. Grayson. Her bright hazel eyes pierced through Lilah's resistance and the closeness of her presence seemed to fill her body and mind with a hypnotic resonance. At this very moment, she had never felt anything more intimate.

She moved one hand to the curve of Lilah's lower back and led her to the couch. Lilah couldn't help but feel a twinge of excitement from the doctor's firm, yet gentle touch. She lay on the couch on her side, facing Dr. Grayson who sat back down in her chair. "Tell me about them. Tell me what you wish you could tell everyone else." Lilah swallowed nervously and felt her throat close up, making her incapable of speech. "Don't be afraid, Lilah you are safe here."

"I'm not quite sure what I want to say," Lilah explained.

"Maybe the journal that you keep with you can refresh your memory," Dr. Grayson said plainly.

Lilah sat up, slightly shocked. Then trying to regain her composure, she slowly responded, "I don't have a journal."

"Really? I could have sworn you kept it in the inside pocket of your blazer."

"How could you know that?" Lilah asked, alarmed. She did keep a journal there, but was careful not to get it out or even touch it during her sessions with Dr. Grayson.

"I'm a psychiatrist," she explained, "It's my job to notice things in a person that others miss." After a short pause she went on to say, "Please, I'd like you to read some of it to me."

"Well it's not really a journal... it's more of a ... research log."

"Research log? Like you are studying these people's behaviors?" Dr. Grayson asked. Lilah nodded shyly while pulling the small book out of her inside jacket pocket. She hesitated a moment and then handed the book to the intrigued doctor. Dr. Grayson opened the book and slowly began turning the pages. Lilah watched her expression carefully. Suddenly terror struck her. What have I done? She thought. Dr. Grayson already knew that she was delusional and obsessive, but what if the detailed journal entries convinced her that she should be institutionalized? She leaned forward and covered her mouth with one of her hands, chewed on her bottom lip and anxiously awaited Dr. Grayson's judgment.

Dr. Grayson opened her mouth as if to make a comment but when she looked up to see that Lilah was clearly upset, she seemed to change what she was going to say. "Lilah," she said, concerned. She looked so distraught that Dr. Grayson actually moved from her own chair to sit next to her on the couch. She put her arm around her, "Lilah," she repeated, "What's troubling you?"

"I just... I ... when you saw the book... I thought maybe ..." Lilah looked up at Dr. Grayson, her big eyes magnified by the tears beginning to form. Her expression was so perfectly sad and beautiful, that Dr. Grayson couldn't help but feel an urge to protect the fragile creature sitting next to her. Before she could put her urges into check, Dr. Grayson reached out and gently brushed a lock of Lilah's curly hair behind her ear. Lilah felt another rush of excitement shiver down her body. Dr. Grayson was the first psychiatrist that she had been to, so she was a bit unfamiliar with profession boundaries. Still, she was fairly certain that these gestures might be considered borderline inappropriate.

"Lilah," she said, this time in a much more professional tone of voice while removing her arm from around her. She cleared her throat slightly and continued on to say, "You needn't fear. Everything said-and read-in this room is confidential." Dr. Grayson then opened the journal to a page with an illustration on it of a pale woman with long black hair and a high collar. She looked out from the page, proud and terrible. "Can you tell me about this woman, Lilah?" she coaxed gently.

Lilah took the book from the doctor's hands and into hers. "I don't see her as much anymore. I would see her often as I was walking to class. She would always pass me at the same time every morning. The first few days she didn't notice me, and I wasn't sure why I noticed her. After a week or so she made eye contact with me. The kind of eye contact that sends shivers down your spine. Her eyes pierced mine right down to my heart, and I felt a black fear take hold of me. Soon, I didn't see her on campus anymore. Instead, she would appear in the shadows of my house and against the walls of alleys. One night, she was standing in the corner of my bedroom. I watched her for hours, terrified and paralyzed with fear. Slowly dawn crept in through the window and she vanished at the first ray of light."

"What do all these symbols and tally marks on the page next to her mean?"

"This row stands for how many times I've seen her. And this column of symbols – each symbol stands for the places I've seen her." Lilah ran her hand over the page of strange markings and smiled wistfully, "You know, I decided to write in these symbols so that if anyone found my book they couldn't read it and mistake me for crazy." She laughed heartily, "I think I've defeated the purpose!"

Dr. Grayson gazed at the page. She couldn't deny that the whole thing looked like the markings of a lunatic, but of course she didn't say this out loud, instead she said, "It was a logical thing to do."

"I suppose," Lilah responded, not believing her at all.

"Show me which vampire frightens you the most." Dr. Grayson then said. Lilah smiled up at her. She had never heard her use the word vampire before. Dr. Grayson had always been careful to only refer to them as delusions or hallucinations. Using the term vampire thrust all of Lilah's trust into her. She flipped to the page that contained the information on the vampire that she was most afraid of. Although she was terrified of the horrible creature, she was excited to be showing someone what she had found out about her. Plus, the vampire didn't seem so frightening when talking about her during the daylight.

The illustration on this page was vague and nondescript. It was of a shadowy figure mostly hidden in the dark. The pages next to it were filled with scribbles and symbols all jumbled together, and were almost illegible. "I started seeing this woman about 5 and half months ago," Lilah began nervously. "Since then I've seen her almost every day. She follows me wherever I go. She stays hidden in the corners and shadows but I still know that she's there. She watches me while I walk to class and the grocery store. She stays outside the house window while I'm eating dinner, and she hides on the other side of the curtain while I'm taking a shower." Dr. Grayson started fidgeting a little and she appeared to be growing nervous as Lilah told her story.

"Have, uh. . . Have you ever seen this woman's face?" Dr. Grayson asked.

"No. . . It's always been hidden in the shadows." Lilah responded. A wave of relief seemed to pass over Dr. Grayson's face. "But," Lilah continued on to say, and Dr. Grayson looked at her with great anticipation, "but, I have seen a part of her arm." The relief quickly dissipated from Dr. Grayson's face as quickly as it had come. "She has a small tattoo on the inside of her wrist. It looks something like three intertwined symbols. I can't quite tell what the symbols are but it looks something like this." Lilah turned the page showing the doctor the picture she had drawn of the vampire's ominous black tattoo.

With a sudden start, Dr. Grayson stood up from the couch and silently walked to the window. Lilah sat confused. "Did I say something wrong?" She thought to herself, feeling rejected. Dr. Grayson continued to stand at the window, motionless. Lilah thought of how she was standing in front of that same window moments earlier, and how Dr. Grayson was there to comfort her. She stood, and slowly approached Dr. Grayson, the uncertainty of what was happening frightening her. She stopped just behind her. "Dr. Grayson?" she asked gently.

"You can call me Nicoletta, or just Nicki, if you'd like."

"Uh, ok. Nicki," Lilah said tenderly. Dr. Grayson turned towards her, her eyes downcast. She took Lilah's hands gingerly. She looked down at Lilah's hands in her own and felt a great sense of intimacy. One of her blouse sleeves was slightly pushed up, revealing part of her forearm. Lilah's eyes spied some black ink peeking out from Nicki's pushed up sleeve, and it looked to be in the same pattern as the vampire's. Lilah dropped Nicki's hands and gasped in horror, as she was coming to the terrible realization that the woman standing in front of her, whom she told all her deepest secrets and worries, was also the same woman who stalked her in the night. Nicki ceased standing and now had turned into a small winged creature, flying towards his desk. Bat! Lilah thought, as she watched it land out of sight behind the great mahogany desk. Lilah stood, frozen and terrified. After several moments of anticipation filled silence, Lilah tentatively began to inch her way towards the door in order to make her escape. She kept her distance from the desk, but decided to peek around it to see if the monster was still there. The bat was gone, instead there was a woman crouched down, practically underneath the piece of furniture.

This woman was surely the person she was talking to a few minutes before, but instead of the poised, intelligent Dr. Grayson, or the frightful creature that had been haunting her, this person was obviously and overwhelmingly upset. Lilah couldn't stop herself from pitying her. She slowly made her way towards the desk and stooped down. "Nicki?" She asked timidly, to the woman whose back was towards her. Lilah reached over to her and placed her hand on Dr. Grayson's shoulder. "Nicki?" She asked again a little more confidently. Dr. Grayson responded this time by placing a hand on top of Lilah's on her shoulder.

"I am so sorry, Lilah, so very sorry." She spoke in a whisper.

"Can. . . Can you tell me why?"

Dr. Grayson turned to face her, simultaneously moving Lilah's hand from her shoulder so that she could hold it in her lap. "When you started coming to see me, I was taken back by your uniqueness and beauty. Your fiery spirit and unwillingness to confide in me frustrated me and intrigued me at the same time. Then when you started telling me about seeing the vampires, I couldn't tell if they were just hallucinations and paranoia, or if you really were able to see my brethren. I began to follow you. I told myself it was only to see if the vampires you saw were real. As I was following you, I never saw another vampire but I wasn't really looking either. I loved watching you." Nicki's voice grew earnest and desperate. "You are so beautiful and interesting. I wanted to know what you were thinking, and feeling, and what you would do next. It became so that almost every day I would fight the urge to go and see you, a fight that I usually would lose." She took Lilah's face gently into her hands, "Forgive me, Lilah! I never meant to frighten you!"

Lilah pulled away from her hands, unsure what to think or feel. The woman she was currently talking to had already transformed too many times for Lilah to trust her completely. She had come to greatly admire Dr. Grayson, and she was always wise and incredibly patient and understanding during their sessions. And today, while still believing she was solely Dr. Grayson, she had come to feel a sudden sense of indescribable intimacy with her and even excitement at her tender touches. Yet, the creature who stalked her in the night terrified her. Although still frightened and unsure what exactly was to come of this extraordinary revelation, Lilah stood and offered her hand to Nicki. Despite her fear, Dr. Grayson had been a true friend to her these past six months and she would not abandon her now.

They smiled warmly at each other while Lilah attempted to help pull Nicki to her feet. While she was getting up from her position on the floor behind the desk, Lilah examined her closely. Suddenly taking notice to Dr. Grayson's seductive curves made her a little weak, which resulted in her knees buckling slightly, which in turn made Dr. Grayson lose her balance as she was getting up. She grabbed onto Lilah's waist for support and to regain her stance, and the feel of her small slim figure under her hand further stirred Dr. Grayson's desire for her. They both laughed nervously, and holding hands, moved to sit next to one another on the sofa.

As they sat, Lilah held Nicki's hand in her lap and traced the lines of her palms with her fingers. "So . . . a vampire, huh?"

"Yes," she laughed gently.

"How...I mean. . .What do you eat?"

"I try to live mostly on animal blood. If I am ever feeling particularly weak, however, I have a friend who works at a hospital and has access to blood donated by volunteers."

"Oh. . . that's a relief!" Lilah smiled.

Dr. Grayson laughed loudly. "Yes! I imagine it is!"

Lilah turned her attention away from Nicki's palms, and was now moving her fingers up along the doctor's arm and pulling back the sleeve of her blouse in order to see her tattoo. She traced the swirling pattern with her fingers as she thought about all the times she saw the tattoo flash through the shadows in her bedroom. Nicki had an idea about what she was thinking and put a hand over the one she had tracing the tattoo. "You don't need to fear me, Lilah, I promise." She said softly.

"I know," Lilah responded while leaning her head against Nicki's shoulder. Nicki wrapped one arm around her and kissed her head. Her free hand, she placed on Lilah's thigh. As they embraced, Nicki subtly stroked Nicki's leg with her index finger. Lilah felt a spike of excitement grow from the spot on her thigh that Nicki was stroking, and shoot up her leg and throughout her body. Suddenly, Nicki then let go of her and moved back over to her usual chair.

"I'm sure you have a lot of questions," Nicki said, back in therapist mode. Lilah found it highly odd that she would try to resume their session like normal, but thought that perhaps revealing her true identity to Lilah had taken an emotional toll on Nicki as well.

"What does your tattoo mean?" Lilah questioned.

"I don't quite know for sure. I got it before I was this way ...before I was a vampire, that is. I had a wife back then, or a lover, or some kind of sweetheart, I can't quite remember. But the tattoo has something to do with her, I think."

"A wife? Really?"

"A wife, or girlfriend, or lover...something like that. It was so long ago. . ."

"How long?"

"At least 700 years. . ." Nicki said with a smile.

Lilah's eyes widened in astonishment. "700 years! How. . . What. . oh my!" Lilah knew that vampires were immortal creatures, but she was still blown away by how old she was. Nicki laughed heartily at her astonishment and Lilah couldn't help but giggle a little along with her. "That's just. . .well, so much history!"

Nicki motioned with her hand towards the desk. "Middle drawer," she stated. Lilah gave her an inquisitive smile but headed toward where she indicated. She walked over to the desk and opened the middle drawer. Inside was an old photo album. She pulled it out, set it on top of the desk and began looking through it. She randomly opened to a page in the middle of the photo album and found herself gazing at a picture of Nicki. She looked the same as what she was used to except that she was posed in stiff old fashioned clothing and had no smile. The photo was black and white but with a sepia overtone. The writing next to the picture read Nicoletta Grayson 1857. She started to turn through the pages, gasping in awe as she saw snapshots of Nicki throughout the decades. There were photos of her at the construction of the Eiffel tower, in the board rooms of presidents, at Woodstock and even Olympic games. "She certainly traveled well." Lilah thought to herself. There were many pictures of her doing everyday things as well, like swimming with friends and casually lounging at parties. In each photo she was dressed in a different style and had a different hairstyle.

As she was looking through the photos, she noticed how in each one Nicki was strikingly beautiful and her eyes shone bright through the old photographs, entrancing Lilah. Nicki quietly got up and made her way over to the desk to stand next to her. Se stood behind Lilah peering over her shoulder at the photos. Every now and then Nicki would tell her a story that went along with a photo. As she spoke, she moved closer, and Lilah's skin prickled at the feeling of Nicki's close proximately. Soon, Lilah felt her lips barely brushing against her ears and Nicki's hands sliding down to her hips. In return Lilah leaned into her, her buttocks pushing into Nicki's pelvis. She turned her face to look at Nicki over her shoulder, and Nicki leaned in and began kissing her passionately. As they kissed, Nicki moved her hands up Lilah's body, sliding her hands in between the opening of her blouse so she could grope her breasts. Lilah gasped as Nicki squeezed her mounds and pinched at her already erect nipples. Lilah then felt a twinge of fear come over her when she felt Nicki's lips lower onto her neck. But the fear quickly melted into pleasure when she realized that she was only thirstily sucking at her neck.

Lilah felt one of Nicki's hands slide off of her breast and back down towards her hip, but the hand did not stop there. Nicki glided her hand across Lilah's stomach as it continued traveling south. She then slipped her fingers underneath Lilah's skirt and held onto her pussy mound with her palm pressing into her. If Lilah had any doubts about Nicki's intentions, they were gone. She turned around and continued to kiss Nicki's mouth while fumbling to unbutton her blouse. She could feel Nicki's velvety soft skin on her fingertips as she pulled back the satiny fabric. Sliding the blouse off of her shoulders and letting it fall to the floor, Lilah then unhooked the front clasp of Nicki's bra freeing her voluptuous breasts from containment. Nicki's dark, rosy nipples became erect as Lilah pinched at them with her fingers, and she took notice to how Nicki's tits, stomach and arms felt strangely cool in her hands. "Was it because she had vampire blood?" Lilah thought silently to herself. "Did she even have any blood in her? She had to, didn't she?"

Nicki unbuttoned the last few fastens of Lilah's blouse and threw it to the floor. Staring hungrily at her naked breasts, she pushed Lilah back into the edge of the desk and lifted her up slightly so that she could sit on it. Nicki put her right arm around Lilah, feeling the delicate skin of her back and pressed her body up close to her. Nicki's left hand she placed on Lilah's bare right breast, and she squeezed her firm, perky tit and pinched and played with her nipple as her mouth was exploring around the other one. Lilah moaned as she felt Nicki's tongue roll over the sensitive skin of her nipple. She sucked and licked ferociously, and hungrily, and every now and then she gave Lilah a playful, frisky bite.

Nicki then took her arm back from around Lilah's back and held on tight to the breast she had just been sucking on. She pushed Lilah's titties tightly together and put both nipples into her mouth as she began flicking her tongue back and forth between the two of them. As Nicki was sucking her breasts, Lilah could feel her pussy throbbing for attention, and she was getting wetter every second. She reached one of her hands underneath the skirt that had slid up to her hips, moved aside her lacey thong and began furiously stroking herself. Her fingers slid across her soft pussy, every stroke bringing her more pleasure than the last.

Suddenly, Nicki stopped her sucking, reached down, pulled off Lilah's skirt and panties, and grabbed hold of the underside of Lilah's knees and spun her around so that her legs were now on top of the desk and Lilah's back was to her. A lamp was knocked to the floor and papers were flown through the air from the maneuver, but Nicki had other things in mind than the state of her desk. She forced Lilah onto her back so that her head was at the edge of the desk and she was now looking at an upside down version of Nicki. Nicki moved closer to her so that the only thing in Lilah's field of vision was Nicki's pelvis. She watched as Nicki slowly and deliberately unzipped the back of her skirt and slid it down off of her hips. Lilah guessed by the sliver of wetness that she saw on Nicki's panties, causing the fabric to stick to the folds of her pussy lips that she just might be as turned on as she was. Abruptly, Nicki ripped off her panties, grabbed Lilah's jaw and forced open her mouth. She then kneeled on the edge of the desk, her knees straddling Lilah's head, pressed her wet pussy against her mouth and began rocking her hips back and forth. The taste and feel of Nicki's wet, smooth pussy rubbing back and forth across her mouth turned Lilah on, and she licked and sucked excitedly at Nicki's lips and clit every time they glided across her tongue.

As Nicki was thrusting her pussy back and forth across her mouth, Lilah's vantage point allowed her the view of watching her gorgeous firm ass rock back and forth above her head. While Lilah was enjoying the taste and the view, Nicki had snuck a finger down between her thighs and Lilah was startled by the sudden feeling of a finger entering into her, but the surprise quickly melted into pleasure as Nicki expertly moved her finger in and out of her warm, wet pussy. As Nicki finger-fucked Lilah, she also joined her down there, and once again Lilah began stroking at her clit as Nicki's fingers played with her. Nicki loved seeing Lilah's pert tits jiggle and the glistening of her fingers as she played with Lilah's moist, swelling cunt.

Soon, the site and feeling overwhelmed Nicki, and she abruptly pulled her pussy off of Lilah's mouth and her finger away from her pussy. She then pushed Lilah first back up into a sitting position, and then over onto her hands and knees. Lilah scooted forward and gripped the edge of the desk, bracing herself for what she thought was about to come, but it wouldn't exactly be what she thought. Nicki's excitement further surged at the sight of Lilah's pink, wet pussy waiting eagerly for her touch. Nicki pulled open the bottom drawer of her desk and pulled out a strap-on dildo. She pulled on the faux cock in lightening speed and tightened the thigh straps, just as Lilah flipped her head upwards and asked what she was doing. Nicki quickly "ssh'd" her and positioned herself onto the desk just behind Lilah, also on her knees. Her hands however, she placed on either side of Lilah's delicious ass.

Lilah looked around her and took notice of the two large mirrors hung in Nicki's office. One was directly in front of her and another was to the right. Lilah turned her head to look into the one on the right, and as she looked into the mirror her eyes widened when she saw Nicki wearing a massive dildo. Before Lilah could say anything, Nicki thrust the rubber cock deep into her throbbing, wet cunt. She felt it slide fully into her, filling her up. She gasped a little at the size of it, for nothing that big had ever been inside her before. Nicki began fucking her hard, thrusting into her roughly as Lilah watched her in the mirror. Nicki in turn, was watching them in the mirror that was positioned in front of them, and her hips banged into Lilah faster and faster at the sight of

Lilah's tits bouncing from the force of the dildo slamming in and out of her. Nicki reached over Lilah's hips and tried playing with her clit but she was now too caught up in her own pleasure and excitement to continue that for long. Once Nicki stopped, Lilah almost went crazy. She was almost to the point of orgasm and didn't want the pleasure to stop. Once again she reached down to her clit and furiously began rubbing at the swollen nub, when she again looked back at the mirror and was shocked to see Nicki doing the same to herself. Her hand had reached underneath the hanging rubber cock and Lilah could see Nicki's fingers flashing in and out of her pussy with a hungry, lustful fury. Lilah's body responded to both the sight of Nicki pleasuring herself, as well as to her own finger diddling of her clit. Her body suddenly became flush with heat, and just as she started to climax, Nicki cried out in ecstasy as her own orgasm rocked her body and she shivered and shook against the back of Lilah's ass. While Lilah's body was still enjoying the ripples of climax, Nicki flipped Lilah back over onto her back and shoved her mouth between her legs. She gently sucked Lilah's clit into her mouth as she shoved a couple fingers deep inside Lilah's drenched pussy, enjoying the sight of Lilah's body as it bucked and squirmed on the desk.

When it was over, Nicki helped Lilah down from the desk and they both gathered their clothes and dressed. Lilah glanced up at the clock. They had taken more than twice the time as usual. Nicki walked over to Lilah and embraced her warmly, again surprising Lilah with the brief display of tenderness. "I suppose you have to go now," Nicki said.

"Yes," Lilah sighed, "I am having dinner with my mother this evening."

Nicki walked her to the office door holding her hand. Lilah opened the door and was about to walk through it, when she hesitated and turned back to face Nicki. Sensing her thoughts, Nicki replied to her silent question. "Yes, I'll see you next week," she said, and then kissed her softly on the cheek. Lilah exited the office and walked through the building and out into the dusk-colored late afternoon, suddenly unafraid of what, or who, might be hidden within its shadows.

Story #4

When Teacher Bites: Professor's Lesbian Slut

"Page 17, everyone," Professor Lessing instructed her students. She then began to read a loud, "She was not herself when she spoke, but driven to distraction by her illness and the crying of the hungry children, and it was said more to wound her than anything else. For that's Katerina Ivanovna's character, and when children cry, even from hunger, she falls to beating them at once." The professor read a few more lines out of Dostoevsky's Crime and Punishment, and then began discussing the final essay that was due on Monday over the book.

"I'd like to write about Katerina from a feminist perspective in my paper. Is that topic alright?" A fellow student asked.

"Well, I'd prefer to see a more serious issue be covered, but if that's what you feel best equipped to write about go ahead, I suppose." The professor responded. I saw the girl who asked the question turn her face down towards her open notebook and blush deeply, embarrassed by the professor's response. What a bitch, I thought to myself, as I witnessed the exchange.

"I wonder if Dostoevsky also thought his character wasn't serious," I whispered to my friend, and roommate, Lilly.

"I don't care how much of a bitch she is, I'd get with her in a minute," was Lilly's response. There was no denying Professor Lessing was smoking hot. She was tall, with shoulder length black hair that perfectly framed her face and highlighted her piercing hazel colored eyes that had the uncanny ability to look deep into a person's soul. Although she usually wore stylish blouses with either a skirt or slacks most of the time, it was easy to see by the way her clothes fit her frame that she had a nice plump ass and equally plump breasts. Although I genuinely enjoy reading and studying classic literature, I admit that the main reason I enrolled in this class was because I had heard that the professor was the sexiest thing alive. Although the rumor about her good looks did turn out to be true, the gossip had failed to inform me that she was also a highly opinionated bitch who never seemed to be satisfied with any of her students, often demeaning them publicly. She dismissed the female characters of the stories we read in class as unimportant and trivial, and whenever a female would work up the courage to comment on something during class, Professor Lessing would respond by calling her ideas quaint, or cute, or charming, deliberately trying to make her feel inferior. It didn't make sense. Her behavior was akin to male chauvinism, and certainly unexpected from a modern day woman. When class first started, I didn't pay much attention to her offensive comments and instead concentrated on her seductive face and curvaceous figure. But after a couple weeks of hearing her ridiculous opinions, I had a hard time even showing up to class, and even just looking at her was becoming unbearable. I tuned back in to hear what the professor is saying.

" '. . . He was so immersed in himself and had isolated himself so much from everyone that he was afraid not only of meeting his landlady, but of meeting anyone at all. He was crushed by poverty, but even his strained circumstances had lately ceased to burden him.' " Here, Professor Lessing paused from quoting the book to say, " Is Dostoevsky trying to convey what happens to a guilty soul, or is he giving us an idea of what having a mental illness was like in Russia at the time? I hope this gives you some ideas. Your papers are due next class."

Students began filing out of the classroom. Other like-minded students, unsurprisingly mostly male, gave Professor Lessing a smile, or wave, or other greeting as they exited. At present, two girls were talking to the professor, asking her questions and overtly posturing in a flirtatious manner. It was obvious what they wanted and it looked like Professor Lessing was certainly enjoying the attention. Some of the more enlightened females shot the professor dirty looks as they walked out. I was one such female, but when I looked up to give the professor my customary sarcastic smile she motioned for me to join her. Surprised and curious, I told Lilly that I'd see her later and made my way towards the professor.

As I walked over to her, the professor told the girls that were talking to her that she'd see them next class. The girls each gave me a dirty look as they passed by, jealous of me being by myself with the professor. I rolled my eyes at them and stopped in front of the professor. I disliked her so much I could not even bring myself to say hello or ask what it was she needed. "You haven't turned in your past two essays, Karrie," Professor Lessing informed me. I just shrugged my shoulders in response but when she said nothing more, I could see that she wanted a verbal response.

"I still have a B," I say grudgingly.

"I know," she responded. "But if you keep it up you won't even have that. These assignments are important to your education. They aren't just busy work." The professor pauses here to obviously assess my attitude. When she saw that I was trying my best to spite her, her tone of voice changed to become more demanding. "You know what? I can see that this isn't getting through to you, so I am going to need you to get those two assignments to me by tonight." She spouted angrily.

"What! Tonight? How am I supposed to get both the papers done by tonight? And the final essay is due on Monday! How am I supposed to have time to do all three?" I asked indignantly.

"I'm sure you'll find a way. If you don't, you'll fail this class. I'll be in my office until about 11pm tonight. You have until then to turn it in." At this point she gathered up her papers and exited the classroom, leaving me feeling bewildered and angry. I stormed out the door behind the professor, despising her now more than I did before.

"Professor! I really don't think this is fair, if I don't do the assignments, I'll still have a passing grade!" I said, hurrying after her. The professor's pace was brisk, and as I'm on the shorter side, I was having trouble keeping up with her.

"You won't have a passing grade if I give you an F." She responded while glancing back to give me a hateful smile. At that moment, it took all of my will power not to push her down onto the floor and walk across the top of her body.

"Could you at least give me the weekend to get all of the assignments done?!" I ask, growing desperate.

"Students are turning in their Dostoevsky paper on Monday so I will have that to grade."

"Tomorrow, then!?" I pleaded.

"I'm afraid I'm going out of town tomorrow afternoon. And now, as you've chased me all the way to my office, I know that you know where it is so you won't have any trouble finding it tonight." The professor shut her office door suddenly and a bit obnoxiously immediately after she finished speaking.

I turned and marched down the hallway. My temper was on fire. I had never felt so embarrassed or humiliated before. I was also certain that Professor Lessing did not care at all about the two essays. The dominating, opinionated bitch obviously only wanted to pull a power trip on me and see me suffer. I walked back home slowly, sad and defeated. Although I was disappointed in myself for letting Professor Lessing walk all over me, there was one positive to it. Tonight I had plans with my friend Lilly to dress up and hit up every club in town, and I had been looking for an excuse to get out of going. These essays were now that perfect excuse. My girlfriend and I had broken up about a month earlier, and Lilly had recently found herself single again as well. She had planned this recently single's night out in order to celebrate our new relationship statuses but instead, fortunately for me, I would now be spending the night studying and writing.

When I got to our shared apartment, I told Lilly that I wouldn't be able to make it that night. "What? Why?" She sputtered, obviously upset by my announcement.

"Professor Lessing told me that if I didn't turn in the two essay assignment that I didn't do, she would fail me!" I explained.

"When do you have to give her the essays by?" she asked.

"Eleven o'clock tonight. I'm supposed to deliver them to her in her office by then." I answered.

"Eleven! Karrie! Then you have plenty of time to go out after you drop them off!" Lilly concluded. Inwardly, I cringed. Usually I am a much better liar, but my encounter with Professor Lessing had left me so bewildered I didn't think to keep the eleven o'clock due date to myself. I had no choice but to agree to this new plan. With 7 hours to go until my deadline, I immediately got to work on the assignments.

After working on the essays for about six and half hours, I had completed one and was about halfway through the second. My brain was practically mush and I knew that the essays were complete bullshit, not even worth turning in. I stopped here. Knowing that my brain couldn't take anymore, I decided to bring what I had to Professor Lessing and see if I could plead with her to accept the work that I had done so far, and let me turn in the rest of the second essay at a different time. I printed out the pages I had, and began to get ready to meet Lilly at the night club. We had decided, that I would meet her there right after dropping off the papers to Professor bitch asshole.

I looked through my closet and picked out an outfit. I put on a tight, short black skirt and a black tank top. I didn't wear a bra because the shirt's neck line plunged all the way down to just above my belly button. It was a little cold out so I also decided to wear a pair of tights. The tights were black and similar to fishnets but were in a zigzag pattern. I then slipped on a cute pair of black ankle high boots with spikey silver studs on them. I took one last look in the mirror and headed towards the door. As I was walked down the hall, I stopped at the closet. Because it was chilly out, and because I was uncomfortable with Professor Lessing seeing me so scantily clad, I grabbed a long jacket that buttoned down and tied in the front, and put it on as I went out the door. I crossed the street, onto campus and began walking towards the professor's office.

I don't get scared easily, but I was filled with relief when the building containing Professor Lessing's office came into view. During the day the campus bustled with people, but at 10:45 at night, it was deserted and dark, and I was frightened of all the imaginary things that might be hidden within the shadows. I quickly ran into the building only to find it almost as dimly lit as outside. Only about every sixth or seventh light was turned on, creating a very eerie atmosphere. I hurried down the hall and finally came upon Professor Lessings's office. I hesitated a moment, trying to decide if I was more frightened of the dark night or of Professor Lessing. I eventually gathered up the courage, took a deep breath, and knocked on the door.

"Come in," I heard her call. I opened the door and saw her smile widely. "Ah! Karrie!" Professor Lessing exclaimed, "I was beginning to give up hope that you would come."

The professor's office was lit only by her desk lamp, but felt warm and cozy in contrast to the dark halls. The wall to my left and the wall behind her desk directly in front of me were lined completely from the floor to the ceiling with bookshelves. The book shelves were mostly filled with just what a person would expect – books, with a few trinkets mixed in, and against the wall to my left was a large brown leather sofa. Professor Lessing was sitting at her desk, grading papers. This time, no long-sleeved blouse or loose fitting slacks covered up her curves. I noticed the blouse that she had been wearing in class was now hung up on a hook on the wall next to one of the expansive bookcases, along with her beige colored tweed slacks. Professor Lessing sat with only a tight fitting lavender t-shirt on, coupled with a pair of equally tight fitting jeans. At the sight of her braless tits pushing through the t-shirt fabric, I felt my pussy quiver and start to moisten, which surprised me because of my deep dislike for the woman. The room was suffocatingly warm, so as I stepped inside the office I untied and took off my jacket. While I removed it I saw Professor Lessing's eyebrows rise up slightly and I remembered why I had put it on in the first place. I felt myself blush deeply because of my skimpy outfit. Professor Lessing laughed lightly and stood while she said, "Don't be embarrassed. It's Friday night. I'm sure you're going out after this?" I nodded shyly. I had never heard her use such a gentle tone of voice before. I stepped forward to hand her the essays.

"Here…" I began, but never finished, because as I began speaking my fingers let go of the papers before Professor Lessing's fingers had actually gotten a hold of them. The papers dashed around the room and eventually floated to the ground. Professor Lessing stooped to pick up the ones nearest to her, while I turned around and bent over to pick up the loose papers that had landed near me. After I had gathered up a couple pages I came to a horrific realization. I was bending over like a person wearing pants would, not like a girl wearing a mini skirt should. If Professor Lessing was looking in my direction, there would be no way she missed my fish-netted ass cheeks peeking out from underneath my hemline. I quickly shot upright and turned around, my eyes wide with fear. Professor Lessing's eyes were carefully trained on the ground. She finished picking up the couple of pages left around my feet and then stood straight. I couldn't tell if she'd seen anything or not, but I decided she didn't, mostly because it would be unbearable to think the opposite. Professor Lessing went to stand at her desk and organize the papers.

"Sorry, I don't have a stapler," I said nervously and apologetically.

"That's quite alright," she said, turning to smile kindly at me. I felt a little baffled at her unusual demeanor. Rather than the harsh and criticizing professor I was used to, the woman standing before me was kind and understanding. I stood still and studied her closely as she organized the papers back into their proper order. The Professor's face was incredibly radiant, and her eyes and skin had an unusual luminesce glow to them. The tight fitting t-shirt she was wearing let me see for the first time the perfect tear dropped shape of her breasts, and I could faintly see the outline of color of her nipples underneath the tight fabric. The sound of Professor Lessing's voice pulled me from my observation.

"Have you begun your paper for Monday?" She asked while stapling the essays together.

"I've started putting together an outline," I responded.

"Good! What topic have you chosen?" She questioned further. I hesitated to answer, but encouraged by the professor's new manners I told her.

"I'm writing about Sonia's development as a character," I said this slowly, afraid of what reaction would come from the professor.

"Excellent. Sonia's character has a lot of depth to it, and she is much more important to the plot line of the story that most people think." She replied. Although pleasantly surprised, I was confused by her sudden change of attitude towards the female characters in our reading, as well as...towards me. Professor Lessing then moved over to the brown leather couch and sat. While flipping through my papers she said, "Karrie, you seem to be missing some parts here."

"Oh! Yeah," I said while sitting down beside her on the couch, a couple of feet away. "I meant to ask you at the beginning...I can't...well...there is just no way that I am going to be able to complete both of the essays tonight, so I wanted to ask if it would maybe be ok if I turned in the rest of the second essay to you on Monday." I asked this not holding on to much hope, but to my great surprise she immediately responded by saying,

"Well, the other essay I assigned today is due on Monday. How about you turn this one in to me on Wednesday? That should give you plenty of time to finish."

I looked at her smiling, yet confused. I shook my head a little, and she smiled at me and cocked her head to the side as little as if to say, what? She had never been so adorable. "You're just. . . You're not what I expected." I told her.

"Oh? And what did you expect?" She asked with a grin.

"Well, there are a lot of rumors." I responded nervously and squirming a bit against the back of the couch.

"Like?" The Professor inquired.

"Like. . . that you are incredibly beautiful, but also.....well, also a bitch from hell." I told her boldly.

"Really? And is the rumor true?"

". . .uh…Well, you do make some comments in class sometimes."

"I do act that way in class, but I promise, it is only to illicit a reaction. By acting indignant or overly opinionated, I inspire my students to write passionate essays and papers trying to convince me I'm wrong." She said, her smile fading a little. It touched my heart to see her beautiful face looking troubled, so next I said much more light-heartedly.

"People also told me that you were super sexy."

"And? Were they right?"

"Very," I said while giving the professor a seductive look up and down. She laughed charmingly.

"Continue. I'm curious. What else have these rumor-spreading people told you about me?"

"They say you'll give an A to the first person who finishes their test. And, they also told me that sometimes you work as a stripper on the weekends."

Professor Lessing laughed openly at my last comment. "Anything else?"

"Well...." I began, while playfully scanning the room with my eyes, checking for imaginary eavesdroppers. I scooted over closer to Professor Lessing and whispered in her ear, "Some even say that they think you're a vampire."

"I guess sometimes those rumors turn out to be true." She said while bringing her mouth close my neck, and placing a hand on my thigh. My pussy began tingling wildly and I felt dizzy with raw primal attraction. An hour ago, I could have spent hours ranting about how much I hated this woman, and now my breasts ached for her touch. The professor's lips brushed against my neck, and I waited in anticipation for a playful love bite. It came, but a little harsher than I expected.

"Oh, ouch," I said with a giggle. She pulled away from me and grinned, revealing large sharp teeth were her incisors had been. My body stood frozen for several seconds with fear, before I jumped up and tried to make my move towards the door. But before I could get there, Professor Lessing had blocked my way with inhuman speed. She pushed me up against a bookshelf, and grabbed the tops of my arms, effectively pinning my body against the tightly packed rows of books.

"Don't be afraid," she whispered in a low, husky voice. Professor Lessing moved my arms so that now she could restrain me using only one hand. Her free hand she placed on my waist. Once more she moved her mouth in the direction of my neck. I closed my eyes, bracing myself for a fatal bite. Rather than sharp pain however, I felt a few frisky bites, right in a row. Then she began to suck and kiss the tender, sensitive skin of my throat. My fear quickly melted into pleasure. Soon, little moans of joy were escaping past my lips, out of my control.

Professor Lessing's hand slid down my body, spreading chills and goose bumps as she boldly explored my curves. Eventually, she slid her hand underneath my skirt and began rubbing my inner thigh over my tights. I couldn't believe what was happening. I was terrified, I was wildly excited, and I didn't want her to ever stop touching me. Did I really see those fangs or was it only my imagination? They couldn't have been real. As if she had heard what I was thinking, Professor Lessing pulled away from my neck smiling at me, baring her impressively sharp looking fangs. My eyes grew wide with fear, which seemed to greatly delight her. The professor's smile grew bigger and she kept steady eye contact with me, as she slid her hand even higher up my thigh until she reached the waistband of my tights. She then grabbed the tights and my panties, and with one violent motion ripped them both completely off my body with a strength and speed that both scared and titillated me, leaving my pussy bare and exposed underneath my skirt. Professor Lessing moistened a finger with the juices flowing from my pussy and began slowly and deliberately stroking my clit.

"I love virgins, you get wet so easily."

I opened my mouth in protest, but before I could say anything Professor Lessing shushed me and said, "Don't try to deny it. I could smell it on you the first day you walked into my classroom." I looked down, slightly embarrassed. What she had said was true, and was also part of why my last girlfriend and I had broken up. The professor said to me, "Don't be ashamed, dear. More women should be like you. Anyways, you're not going to be a virgin much longer." She released my hands and roughly pulled aside the plunging sides of my top to expose my breasts. Professor Lessing grabbed them both hungrily and squeezed them in her hands. She then began sucking on one tit while pinching and playing with my other nipple. My eyes watched as her tongue flicked and teased my erect nipple, and my pussy throbbed for the same attention. I could feel her pelvis pushing into mine with force, and I longed to see, smell and touch what lay underneath her tight fitting jeans. Oh how my body was suddenly silently screaming to feel her fingers touch me, and to be deep inside me.

With a sudden jerk, Professor Lessing had pulled me off of the wall and pushed me forcefully onto the ground. "Luckily for you," she said, "since I'm a different kind of creature, my cunt is warmer and sweeter tasting than any other pussy you'll taste after me. I've also lived hundreds of years, which means my mouth and fingers have had plenty of experience and are incredibly adept at pleasing. She said this while pulling the lavender t-shirt over her head and throwing it to the floor. A heat surged through my belly at the sight of her perfect tits and dark nipples staring back at me. Professor Lessing then peeled the fabric of her jeans down and off her legs, and not wearing any panties, there also was her perfect smooth pussy mound and slit taunting me of what was to come. "Take the rest of those fucking clothes off," she commanded me. Loving her dominance, I removed my skirt and top, and bashfully crossed my arms and legs. This was the first time I was ever completely naked in front of a woman, and I felt a level of vulnerability I had not yet experienced. I was eye level to her pussy, and Professor Lessing was right…her pussy must be sweet tasting because I could already catch a hint of sweet aroma from my vantage point.

"Crawl over to me," the professor commanded next. I obeyed, which forced me to expose my own tits and pussy in the process. I could feel her hungry eyes upon me as I positioned myself within an inch of her pussy. "Now, using just your tongue I want you to slide it between my pussy lips and lick me nice and slow until I tell you to stop."

Trembling with fear and excitement, I obeyed. I was about to get my first taste of pussy and I could feel my own juices flow in anticipation. My nipples hardened and I was experiencing a pulsating rush deep within me that I had never, ever felt before. I stuck out my tongue and nervously touched it against the professor's smooth lips. I wasn't sure what to do next, but it kind of just happened naturally. My tongue slipped between Professor's Lessing's pussy lips and touched against a small hard bud. "Oh my god!" I thought. I just touched her clit!

"Lick me!" the professor commanded in reminder.

I moved my tongue slowly up and down between Professor's Lessing's pussy lips and I swear it tasted like sweet musky honey. She was right. Her pussy tasted amazing. Still unsure, I licked at her a little faster and then moved my tongue up towards her erect bud.

"Stop!" She commanded, and then forced me onto my hands and knees and positioned herself behind me. "I want to pop your virgin cherry first, so then I can clean it up and get on to other things."

My hands gripped onto the throw rug on the floor. My mind wanted this, yet I was afraid. My body yearned for it, but it trembled in anticipation. I felt the tip of Professor Lessing's fingers press into the opening of my pussy and stay there on the cusp for a few minutes, slowly moving it all around the folds of my smooth lips. I then felt her enter me slowly and gently, guiding her fingers in just a little farther into me, a little at a time. As my pussy lips opened and wrapped around her fingers, I could feel yet another finger enter me, and without warning the professor then gave a sudden thrust forward. Pain and pleasure shot through my virgin cunt, filling my body with heat and vibrations, while my mind was filled with visions of color and the sensation of out-of-body travel. She gave a few more quick thrusts and once she was sure that she had broken the membrane, Professor Lessing pulled out her fingers, and I could feel the warm blood flow from my pussy. She flipped me over and began lapping up the red liquid coming out of me. My body tingled with pleasure as her tongue glided over my vulva and clit. "Virgin blood is exquisite. It tastes so divine and it gives me energy for months," Professor Lessing explained between licks.

Although it seemed she had gotten what she really wanted, my untainted virgin blood, Professor Lessing apparently wasn't satisfied with simply popping my cherry. After she was done lapping up my virgin blood, she made me return to my hand and knees and resume my attention to her own cunt. I shyly licked at her lips, which now glistened with a dewy moistness, and Professor Lessing used her fingers to spread open her pussy lips so that I could lick deeper between them. Using her free hand, the professor pulled a chair up behind her and sat down on the edge. She propped both of her feet up against one of the bookshelves and shoved her cunt against my mouth. "Take my clit into your mouth Karrie and suckle on it gently," the professor instructed. Like a good virgin slave I obeyed, not needed much coaxing, only some direction. As I suckled on her clit, I could taste the professor's sweet juices that escaped from her. I again could feel the electric pulses within my belly and sensory overload threatened to overwhelm me. Was this the beginning of what an orgasm felt like? As I sucked at her clit just a little harder, Professor Lessing grabbed for one of my hands. "Slide a couple of your fingers into my cunt while you suck on me. Glide them back and forth and don't stop until I tell you to."

Doing as instructed, Professor Lessing's body was now pushed back against the chair and her hips bobbed up and down against my mouth. Since she didn't say anything, I figured I was still correctly doing what I was supposed to do. The professor then suddenly grabbed at my hair and shouted "faster". Not sure what I was supposed to do faster, I hesitated. Professor Lessing became frustrated and yanked at my hair. "Fuck me faster with your fingers!" she commanded. "Now!" I began sliding my fingers faster and faster into her cunt. My fingers were so wet and the escaping juices had moistened the chair that Professor Lessing was sitting on. Her fingers were still entangled in my hair, and I felt her tug harder and harder, my head now being intimately smashed into her spread pussy. Suddenly, Professor Lessing bayed out loud and a spurt of wetness shot out against my face. Imprisoned in my position, I bear intimate witness to the Professor Lessing's orgasm while also having the experience of having her squirt her warm, sweet juices onto my face. My body now ached like never before, and I so desperately wanted to feel what she just felt.

Sensing my thoughts, Professor Lessing spoke not a word yet she rose out of the chair and kicked it aside with her foot. Her foot then pressed up against one of my tits and pushed until my body fell back onto the floor. She then kicked open my legs and positioned herself on her stomach between them. The first strike of Professor Lessing's tongue as it slid up in between my pussy lips sent me reeling. Pinching and pulling at the sides of my pussy lips with her fingers while her mouth and tongue explored my folds and clit was enough to make my entire body tremble….but, there was so much more pleasure to be felt. Darting her tongue in and out of my hole Professor Lessing gently pinch at my clit with her fingers causing it to swell even more. I didn't understand why she would do this until she guided her mouth upwards and sucked onto my swollen bud. My clit was so fucking sensitive and the slightest of her licks and touches now sent shiver after shiver to ripple throughout my body. Gauging my readiness, the professor slid a finger into my wet pussy. This time, there was no pain, only pleasure. I felt my pussy lips grab around her finger, as she then inserted another and thrust them together in rhythm in and out of my wet cunt. I felt Professor Lessing's tits press against my thigh and longed to caress the fleshy mounds with my mouth and hands. While still finger fucking me Professor Lessing licked fast and gently at my clit, causing another new wave of sensations to flood my body. My eyes rolled back into my head and waves of colored flashed behind my eyelids. I could only feel heat, pleasurable ripples of heat, and pulsating sensations in my belly and cunt. I couldn't think, I couldn't move, and then as my body suddenly went stiff and shook with climactic pleasure, Professor Lessing held my body tightly as she continued to lick me until my shivers subsided and my body went limp.

After a brief pause to refresh ourselves with water, the professor and I spent the next several hours exploring ecstasy as she taught and showed me so many Sapphic delights. I was powerless, and I was inexperienced, yet she brought me to orgasm each time we tried something new. She frequently told me, that she loved how sensitive virgins were. It was true, my pussy throbbed and ached so much that a few strokes sent me into ecstatic climax. Because Professor Lessing was not human, she enjoyed a stamina that no mortal could understand and she was able to please me over and over again. I also grew ecstatic knowing that the professor used me for her own pleasure, and I inexplicably wanted to be the professor's little lesbian slut. I wanted Professor Lessing to be my mistress and I was already hungry to please her in every way.

After my virgin body was thoroughly and delightfully ravaged and I experienced orgasm after orgasm throughout the evening, the first rays of daybreak peaked through the curtains of the professor's office. Professor Lessing gently helped me to redress and we parted ways. It was early morning by now, so I headed back to the apartment. When I got there, Lilly was asleep on the couch. I woke her trying to walk by.

"Karrie, you never showed up to the club. Where have you been all night?" she asked sleepily.

"I've been with a girl," I answered vaguely. Lilly was too tired to question anything, and quickly returned to her slumber. From then on, I was Professor Lessing's little slut. I would stay behind after class and she would fuck me on the floor before her next class came in. We would meet in an empty room by the cafeteria during her lunch break, and she would finger fuck me from behind. I loved sneaking into her office between classes, and if Professor Lessing was there, she would fuck me. I loved taking it any way she would give it to me, and if she wasn't there, I would get upset. I was her slut and needed to be used. I would think about her experienced fingers penetrating me and furiously masturbate, angry at her for not showing up. My life revolved around how many times a day I could get her fingers into me and her mouth and tongue on my pussy. Every few weeks she would ask me to cut myself and she would carefully tend to my wound, eagerly lapping up the thick ruby drops of blood that dripped across my skin. I was fascinated by this beautiful creature, and I was equally as fascinated with the creature that had been awakened within me.

Eventually, the semester ended and summer came. I saw Professor Lessing less and less and began to see other girls. None of them ever gave me the same kind of thrill or pleasure as the professor had though, nor did they have the stamina or the primal sensual nature that she possessed, so I still spent a lot of time masturbating. The professor taught me so many things that semester and gave me a lot of lessons, both in the classroom as well as outside the classroom. I had to work very hard to keep up with it all, but in the end, it was worth it. Professor Lessing gave me an A in her class, and she instilled in me a thirst. A thirst for something I knew that forever forward I was always going to seek to be quenched.

VOLUME 2

Lesbian Cowgirl Romance

Collection

Story #5

Cowgirl Chivalry:

Erotic Mountainside Adventure

Abby's knuckles were white from her intense grip on the steering wheel, as she maneuvered her car up and down and around all the hairpin turns on the roads that snaked through the Colorado Mountains. Oh, the scenery was majestic, for sure, but she wasn't really able to enjoy it like she would have liked to. Instead, her eyes were constantly focusing on the dangerously close mountain sides, loose fallen boulders and short guardrails, or more often than she cared for, lack thereof. She also couldn't understand why people were just speeding past her, unless they were locals and they had more faith in their trucks than she did in her 12 year old car. Her car obviously wasn't made for mountain driving, and she was starting to worry if she'd even be able to make it out of the mountain passes.

When the mountains seemed to subside and she thought the worst was over, there were the foothills and the Eastern Colorado plains. Abby was able to relax a bit now and allow her eyes to take in the scenery, only what she saw now didn't look very healthy. The drought was certainly taking a toll on the residents of Colorado, and especially the ones who still maintained active ranches and grew things in order to make money to feed their families. And, though there were few and far between, Abby also noticed that there were some pretty expansive and elaborate looking ranches out in this area. She couldn't decide if being semi-isolated was a good thing, or a bad thing. All it would take is one blizzard and the roads around them would be closed. But, folks who lived in the country, especially cowboy country, certainly were well versed in self-sufficient living.

Abby wasn't so sure she'd be as self-sufficient. Just last night, Abby had encountered a nasty fog that slowed driving to 10 miles an hour, and that was enough to almost give her a full-blown panic attack. It also didn't help, that her car was old and becoming unreliable. But, at least Abby had some form of entertainment while she was driving. There was no cassette or disc player in her car, but the radio in her old Hyundai still worked even if other things had been slowly breaking down on her. What did she expect? The car, a gift from her father twelve years ago, was practically an antique now and really had too many miles on it for her to be traversing through the mountainsides in it. She often joked with her friends that she needed to get a specialized license plate for it listing it as an 'antique' when she renewed her tags every year.

A blink of light caught her eye, and a quick glance at her dashboard revealed that the car's warning lights were illuminated. Abby rolled her eyes. They always were lit up. She could refill her windshield wiper fluid and the low fluid light would turn off for five minutes, and then come back on. Every time she stopped to get gas, the check engine light would come on right after restarting the car. Abby's mechanic told her it was just dirty fuel injectors, and he told her to buy a cheap bottle of fuel injector cleaner and add it to her gas tank before she filled up with gas the next time. She did, and sure enough that particular warning light flickered off. There was always some selection of warning lights lit on her dashboard, and some of them remained on even if the problem was fixed. Hell, even the emergency brake light flashed at her to warn her that she was driving with her emergency brake on, the same emergency brake that was currently in its proper resting position. Abby was chalking it up to faulty sensors, and that nothing was seriously wrong with her car. It was just old, getting senile, and losing its mind. Maybe her car was a hypochondriac. It always thought something was wrong with it. Still, it got great mileage and for its age, it had taken Abby to a lot of different places. She wasn't quite sure how she was going to give it up, even when she could afford to upgrade to a newer more reliable vehicle, but right now all she really wanted was for her car to get her through this trip and returned safely back home.

"Piece of shit lights," Abby mumbled at the illuminated dashboard, looking like it was all lit up for a fourth of July party. So used to seeing all the glowing red warning lights being on, Abby's eyes failed to spot something that was genuinely amiss, and that was the elevated temperature gauge on the far right side of the dashboard. That was something her father and every mechanic she had ever talked to, told her to absolutely not ignore. It meant that the car's radiator was empty or leaking, and either situation was bad. The sudden smell of something burning caught Abby's attention. Rolling down her window, the smell became even more obvious, and smoke started to escape from the edges of the car hood. Abby then noticed the elevated temperature gauge and hoped that maybe the temperature gauge was just going up because it was hot outside. Without even thinking about it, she cranked up her air conditioning and rolled down all her windows. Maybe that would help cool the car down.

Abby fought the urge to panic. Out in the middle of nowhere, the only assistance she could think of calling, was her insurance company. She reached a hand into her purse that was laying on the passenger's seat, to search for her cell phone. When her fingers finally grasped onto her phone she hit the main menu button only to be met with another warning message, and that was a no cell phone service signal. "Dammit!" Abby exclaimed, as she tossed the cell phone in frustration onto the passenger seat next to her. She anxiously watched as the gauge reported the temperature as getting higher and higher, and the needle was now flickering into the highest red zone it would monitor. Less than a minute later, her vision was completely obscured when the entire car hood erupted like a volcano with billowing plumes of smoke. Abby had no choice now but to pull over to the side of the road, muttering a long string of unladylike curse words.

Abby maneuvered her car to a stop into the grass and gravel that lined the sides of the roadway. Thank goodness she was at least on flat terrain, and not on one of the dangerous switchbacks of the mountains. Jumping quickly out of her car, she ran around to the back of it and popped open the trunk. She did keep a small selection of emergency car supplies in a crate, and she knew she had a jug of antifreeze-coolant in there. Pulling the crate to the trunk's edge she reached in to get the jug of coolant, but she could already tell by its smashed appearance that the coolant jug, like her radiator, was also empty. Growling in frustration, Abby slammed her trunk shut and went back to the front of the car. She grabbed her keys, her purse, her currently useless cell phone, and a couple bottles of water that she had in the back seat. Her only option now, was to seek out some help from the closest living local, so she started walking back in the direction of one of the expansive ranches she had driven past a short while ago.

It was hot outside, with zero cloud cover and a blazing sun positioned over her head. Abby's hair was already sticking to her neck and the sides of her face from sweat, and she was wearing a sundress with sandals, which was not exactly the best of walking attire. She hoped that she could cover some ground quickly and reach the ranch for some help. She also hoped like hell, that someone would actually be home and willing to help her. As Abby walked along the side of the road, she at least had some comfort in knowing that she wasn't going to have to worry too much about getting run over by speeding traffic. In fact, it was just the opposite. She was worried about there not being enough traffic. Expecting a tumble weed to roll past her like an old Western movie was something that would've made her laugh, but her current situation had sapped her of any possible humor. So, Abby took her frustration and anxiety out by walking faster and faster towards the still distant ranch, but her fast paced footsteps could not outrun the harsh heat of the midday sun. She was almost out of water already, her toes were starting to bleed from rubbing up against the sandal straps, and her mood was turning more sour by the minute. She now desperately hoped that the ranch she saw earlier when driving past wasn't just a mirage, a false image of hope sprung from her dehydrated brain.

Over an hour had past, before Abby heard the sound of a vehicle coming up behind her. She edged even further away from the side of the road, but the vehicle wasn't passing her. It was slowing down to drive beside her. Abby suddenly felt vulnerable and tried not to look at the slowing driver, but her peripheral vision caught a glimpse of an old pick-up. "Oh god, I'm going to die at the hands of some back roads serial killer!" Abby thought to herself, her dehydrated state was creating delusional thoughts of her impending dramatic demise, and so she just stared straight ahead, trying to avoid a confrontation with a madman.

"Need a ride Miss?" a pleasant sounding female voice inquired.

"No thank you," Abby said, looking straight ahead, although she was surprised to hear a female's voice and not some husky male one.

"So, you are just out for a nice walk along this incredibly long highway in this heat?" the female voice joked back at her. Abby didn't find it humorous at all. What was happening? She was in search of a human out here in the middle of nowhere to assist her with her predicament, and now that one has appeared, she was too frightened to explain her circumstance.

"I need to get to a ranch I saw awhile back," Abby finally replied, still walking and the truck still keeping pace with her. A small voice inside of her was warning her about giving away too much information.

"Well, most people use vehicles around here," the female voice joked again, speaking over some country music that was playing on the truck's radio.

Abby turned to face the truck and its driver, as it halted to a stop, with her hands on her hips. Did she really have to put up with this right now? She arched an eyebrow at the truck's driver and pursed her lips together. The driver looked to be several years older than her, probably in her mid thirties, but still quite youthful looking and much more beautiful than she imagined a serial killer would be. Abby noticed some loose strands of long brown hair peeking out from under a worn cowboy hat, and the woman's smile and demeanor certainly didn't suggest….. "I'm looking for someone to kill today."

Abby's defensiveness subsided a bit, as she figured it was probably ok to explain her situation to the beautiful cowgirl in the pickup truck who was offering her a ride. What other choice did she have? She was sunburned, dehydrated, her feet were bleeding, her phone had no signal to call for help, and she felt her composure start to weaken as she thought of her current predicament. Trying to fight back tears, Abby started to explain her circumstance. "My car is back there," she said pointing over her shoulder, her voice rising suddenly. "Stupid piece of crap overheated, and now I am out here walking my ass off to some ranch I thought I saw, because I can't get a phone signal to call my insurance company for roadside assistance, and no one in their right mind out here probably even owns a cell phone, given that there's no cell phone service out here in farmville!"

Abby was surprised how much came out of her mouth in one breath, and she immediately regretted it once it left her lips. She had finally found someone who could help her and here she was being rude, and insulting the woman and the place where she probably lived. She wouldn't be surprised at all if the woman just drove off. All of it made her want to cry, and Abby bit her lip in an effort to prevent that from happening.

"Yeah, here in farmville cell phone service is spotty at best," the woman said with a smile, which both surprised Abby and put her at ease. "And, I happen to know for a fact that the ranch you're headed to has a working landline phone," the woman continued with a compassionate smile, as she reached over to open the passenger side door of her truck for Abby. "Come on let me give you a ride to that ranch. I know the guy that owns it, and he's a good honest cowboy, just like most folks are here in Colorado. You can get freshened up, have a decent meal and then we'll see to fixin' your vehicle for you and gettin' you back on the road."

Abby knew she'd be a fool to resist the woman's offer. She certainly seemed genuine and polite, and of course, the fact that she was sexy as hell in a rugged cowgirl kind of way certainly helped. Walking towards the truck, Abby was suddenly feeling very aware of her appearance. She nervously ran a hand through her wind blown hair and held the bottom of her sundress down as she hoisted herself up into the cab. The fabric of her sundress was not exactly the stretchy kind, so when she lifted her leg to get in, she was sure she flashed her beautiful rescuer a peak underneath. The woman noticed Abby self-consciously tugging her dress down as she took a seat in her truck, and she politely looked away hoping that that would make her nervous passenger feel better. She wasn't some weird sex starved dyke, after all. She just saw a tiny peek of what appeared to be black lacey panties. No harm in that.

"My name is Laura," the woman said, as she took off her cowboy hat and put it on the bench seat between them. Her long brown hair fell in messy waves around her shoulders, and Abby tried not to stare, yet a stirring in her belly indicated her obvious attraction to her rescuer. "You are in luck," Laura continued. "I actually know quite a bit about vehicles, kind of a necessity out here. We'll still need to go to the ranch first, and get you some food and water and let you freshen up. Plus, I'll need to bring some tools and other supplies with us when we go back to get your car fixed and running again for you."

Abby looked at Laura on the verge of tears. Could someone really be this nice and generous to a complete stranger, especially, in today's world? She had a hard time believing that this is what happened to normal people when their cars died out in the middle of nowhere, but maybe it did in some parts of the world. Wasn't she supposed to just call some tow truck that promised to arrive in ten minutes, only to show up an hour or two later? She was beginning to feel incredibly relieved, and incredibly lucky.

"Thank you so much Laura. I'm Abby and I'm sorry for all the farmville comments," Abby admitted, as she looked down at her hands in her lap. "I didn't mean to offend you. I guess I was just scared. Plus, I'm a city girl, which you can probably tell, and I'm not used to genuine hospitality from strangers, so I wasn't sure how to take your offer of assistance at first. I can tell you now though, that I really can't tell you enough how much I appreciate you're helping me.

"No offense taken Abby and it's my pleasure to be able to help you." Laura replied, as she put the truck into drive and headed down the road towards the ranch. "The terrain really messes with communication signals around here, and we really could use some more cell towers throughout the state. You should get your city friends to come build us some. We might pay you a lot of money to do it," Laura said as she took a right onto the long dirt road that led to the ranch, "or we may pay you in cattle and horses." She couldn't resist a small chuckle, and to her surprise, Abby chuckled back, obviously more relaxed than a few minutes ago.

As they drove along the bumpy dirt road, Abby stared out the window at the beautiful landscape that surrounded them. Colorado really was a majestic state of natural beauty. Abby knew she should be polite and at least make small talk with Laura, but she didn't quite know what to say. Laura didn't seem to mind the lack of conversation, and she began singing in a seductive soft voice to the country songs that came on the radio. There was something about her easy going manner and seductive voice that caused Abby's body to once again tingle in response. She even fiddled with the few buttons at the top of her sundress, to modestly allow air to travel down between her breasts. If Laura noticed Abby's busy fingers she didn't say anything, but that didn't stop Laura from getting a big ol' grin on her face just the same as they approached the ranch.

The look on Abby's face revealed her awe. The ranch looked impressive from the distant view of the roadway, but up close, it looked like it should be on the show "Lifestyles of the Rich and Famous". It was absolutely enormous, and breathtakingly beautiful. She spotted what appeared to be several horse barns set back from the main structure, and various smaller buildings were peppered all along the expansive acreage. She noticed large fields of crops that weren't noticeable from the roadway, a large chicken coop and an impressive greenhouse that even made Abby want to try her hand at gardening. "What do ya think city girl, not bad for back country living, huh?" Laura said with a playful smile, as she swung her old Ford pickup alongside a couple of other trucks that were parked in front of the main ranch house, and shifted the truck into park.

Abby took closer notice of Laura's attire as she opened her door and leaned out before hopping down onto the dust and graveled covered ground that served as parking for vehicles. Laura had a simple white t-shirt on, and since her truck lacked air conditioning, her sweat dampened shirt clung nicely to her chest giving Abby a clear view of her dark nipples which showed clearly through the thin wet fabric of both her bra and shirt. Abby loved how the wind blew Laura's long brown hair haphazardly around her face, and her tight fitting faded jeans well complimented her other natural attributes. The way the denim fabric molded around her firm ass would've made any supermodel at an underwear photo shoot jealous. Abby found herself wishing that Laura would get back in and out of the truck again, just so she could watch her behind flash before her again.

Instead, Laura walked around the truck over to Abby's side and opened the door. "Wow," thought Abby, "how chivalrous!" Laura offered up a hand for Abby to hold and steady herself as she exited the truck, and when she took a step down, Laura could feel her body react to the beauty of her damsel in distress. Abby's wind strewn auburn hair perfectly complimented her light green eyes, and her smooth milky white skin looked luminesce against the lavender color of her sundress. The sundress clung seductively to her sweat moistened body, and the fabric around her breasts where she had unfastened several of the top buttons obviously revealed that she wasn't wearing a bra. Laura had to bite gently on her tongue to prevent a moan escaping her lips when her eyes locked onto Abby's erect nipples that were pressing against the thin, sweat-moistened fabric. The bottom of her sundress pushed upwards on her thighs as Abby leaned into Laura's hands and hopped out onto the ground, and she caught glimpses of Abby's well toned inner thighs leading to something much more appealing that she wouldn't mind seeing at all.

"Let's get you inside so you can freshen up and we can get something to eat and drink," Laura said, trying to push out the other more intimate thoughts she was suddenly having about the sexy city girl. "It'll help clear your head and I work much better on a full stomach."

As they walked to the front door, Laura rang the doorbell and within a minute they were greeted by Laura's friend Owen, who was the ranch owner. "Laura! What a nice surprise," Owen said, as he pushed open the screen door.

"How ya doing Owen?" replied Laura. "This here is Abby," Laura continued, turning her head in Abby's direction. "Her vehicle broke down about ten miles back and I picked her up walking this direction. She spotted your ranch while driving by and she was headed back this way for some help. You ok if we grab something to eat and drink and let Abby freshen up a bit?"

"You know that's not a problem," Owen answered. "There's always food cooking for our friends and passerby's, and you are more than welcome to freshen up and use whatever you need to get this pretty little lady's vehicle running." Abby was more than relieved to hear that, and she continued to be blown away by the generosity and hospitality being shown to her by complete strangers. Maybe there was something to this rural, country living. "Now, I've actually got to tend to some business out in the fields, but you know where everything is at Miss Laura, so make yourself at home and you and Abby help yourself to anything you need.

As Owen walked out to his truck and drove it out into the fields in the direction of one of the horse barns, Laura and Abby entered the ranch and headed towards the kitchen. The smell of something delicious permeated Abby's nose and she realized now just how hungry she was…and how incredibly thirsty she was. As if reading her mind, Laura had already pulled out a couple bottles of water from the fridge and handed one to Abby. Unscrewing the cap and drinking the entire contents of the water bottle in just a couple swallows, Abby could finally feel herself relax with a confidence that she was in good hands, hands that she certainly wouldn't mind feeling touch her body, but those thoughts she'd have to keep to herself.

"See, I told you everything was going to be ok. We look out for each other out here in the country. Oh, the guest bathroom is right around the corner," Laura pointed out. "There's a pot of chili going, so I'll get everything ready to dish us up a couple bowls while you go and freshen up." Laura looked like she wanted to come over and give her a hug, or maybe that was just Abby's mind running wild. Goodness. How did thoughts of fixing her vehicle become secondary to thoughts of being intimate with this incredibly pleasant and incredibly beautiful cowgirl?

"That sounds great. I would love to wash this sweat and dirt off my face and body. Thanks Laura," Abby replied, searching Laura's eyes to gauge if there might be any mutual attraction on Laura's part. "I'll try to be quick." Abby stated as she then went to freshen up in the guest bathroom, which was incredibly, about half as big as the kitchen. She started to run some water into the deep sink so that she could wash off the dirt and sweat from her body, but once she spied the beautiful stone walled shower behind her, she decided that perhaps a quick jump in the shower might be easier and quicker. Plus, she had never showered in anything that looked like it came straight out of a high-end spa catalog. Stripping out of her sundress, panties and sandals, Abby located a large, fluffy towel and some shampoo and liquid soap. Once the water temperature was to her liking, she opened the glass shower door and stepped inside. The warm water cascading over her body felt like heaven. After first washing her hair, she soaped up her body, and imagined it was Laura's hands running across her pert breasts, stomach and ass.

In the kitchen, Laura had pulled out two bowls, silverware and prepared some fixin's to put on top of the chili. She also uncorked a bottle of red wine that she found in the wine cabinet in the next room. After pouring two glasses of the merlot, Laura set everything out on the kitchen table and sipped from her wine glass as she waited for Abby to return from freshening up. Laura was glad to have the distraction of fetching them something to eat and drink, because she was having a hard time focusing on anything but being intimate with the auburn haired beauty in the next room. Abby's first display of city rudeness when Laura offered her help was slightly off-putting, but she quickly realized it was just Abby's self defense responses and not her true personality. She was actually quite pleasant and she was definitely gorgeous. She also seemed to be surprisingly pleased with the offerings of country living, which was another turn on for Laura. She would love to show her more of her way of life, and Laura was willing to bet Abby would be quite surprised at how much she enjoyed it.

Looking up at the clock, Laura realized that Abby had been gone for over 20 minutes. Laura didn't mind eating cold chili, but she was wondering what was taking so long. Grabbing both wine glasses, Laura walked out of the kitchen towards the guest bathroom. As she stood in front of the closed door, she could hear Abby humming, and it sounded like the shower was on. The mere thought of her naked body standing just to the other side of the door made Laura's pulse race. She wanted to go in and see if Abby needed any help, which would be silly, but fun nonetheless. She also wanted to mind her manners, which true cowgirls do, so Laura wrestled her primal urges to the side and just knocked on the bathroom door instead. "Are you alright Abby," Laura called through the closed door, knowing it was probably a rhetorical question, but she could think of nothing else to say. The answer she received both surprised and excited her.

Abby was taking a much longer shower than she had anticipated. The water felt heavenly, she felt safe, she knew her car would be fixed, and she was distracted by the fact that she was admittedly very attracted to the pretty country girl who had come to her rescue. Perhaps she was just trying to prolong the moment as long as she could. While Abby was lost in thought and humming to herself underneath the showerhead, she heard a knock on the door. She jumped slightly, but then when she heard Laura's voice on the other side of the door, a moment of possible opportunity flashed through her mind. Laura had inquired if she was alright, which was sweet. Could Laura possibly be interested in more than just seeing if she was alright and assisting her with her vehicle? Did Laura feel an unexplainable pull of attraction between them, like she did? Gathering up her courage, Abby decided that there was one way to find out the answer to those questions. And, if Laura didn't respond the way Abby hoped she would, there would be no embarrassment. She could just finish up her shower, get dressed, eat and help Laura fix her car.

"Yes, I'm alright. The door's open. You can come on in, if you want to," replied Abby, feeling a knot of anticipation swell up in her chest.

There was a moment of silence, and then she heard the door squeak open. Now, her chest was absolutely pounding, and she wasn't so sure her implied invitation was such a great idea. She faced her body towards the back shower wall and continued to rinse her body, waiting to hear what Laura would say next.

Pausing after hearing Abby's reply through the door, every ounce of primal instinct that Laura had been trying to resist came bubbling to the surface. Was Abby really inviting her into the bathroom with her? Possibly, even into the shower with her? After a brief tug-of-war in her mind over what to do next, Laura's hand opened the bathroom door. The large bathroom was filled with steam, and she could see the flesh colored silhouette of Abby's body in the shower. Laura downed the last of the wine in her glass and then set both of the wine glasses on the sink's vanity top. "It's been a while, so I was checking to see if you were alright," said Laura, while facing the steam covered sink mirror. "I brought you a glass of wine, for when you're done with your shower."

"Thank you Laura, wine sounds delicious. But, I'm actually not quite done with my shower yet," replied Abby as she swung open the glass shower door, her wet naked body exposed for Laura's viewing pleasure. "I think I'm going to need you to help me wash my back," Abby continued with a wink.

Water sprayed out onto the floor rug as Abby boldly stood there awaiting Laura's response. Abby felt a tinge of relief that she wasn't being turned down when she saw Laura start to strip out of her clothes, all the while never taking her eyes off of Abby's naked body. Abby had already anticipated what may lie beneath Laura's dusty clothes, but when Laura stripped off the last of her clothing and was too standing naked, Abby gulped at the perfection in Laura's form. Her legs and arms were lean and toned like a trained athlete. Her stomach was washboard flat and her tits were....well, fucking amazing! Full, perky and with small dark nipples that were now standing erect. "The country lifestyle sure does keep a woman's body in sexy fit condition," Abby thought to herself, as she could feel herself moisten.

Laura grabbed Abby and kissed her hungrily as she entered the shower and closed the glass door behind them. Laura gently pushed Abby back up against the shower wall and allowed her hands to explore Abby's soapy wet curves. Her just-the-right-size pert tits felt incredible in Laura's hands, and the curve of her slender hips were perfect for pulling the pretty little city girl's body up against her own. As the warm shower water flowed over their sexually charged bodies, Laura turned Abby around to face the shower wall and guided open Abby's legs so that she could explore the treasure that lie between her thighs. Laura slid a hand around Abby's thigh and gently parted Abby's smooth pussy lips with her fingertips as her other hand reached around to squeeze and massage her tits. Feeling Laura's fingertips flick at her clit made Abby push her ass upwards, like a cat in heat, while her hands grasped at the slippery wall for support as her knees began to weaken. A moan escaped Abby's mouth, her body yearning for more, as she leaned her head back against Laura. Laura leaned in to kiss the slender outline of her neck, and as Abby turned her head over her shoulder, their lips met and their tongues danced with urgent passion.

As Laura's hands continued to explore Abby's body, waves of pleasure rippled throughout her from head to toe. While there certainly was an urgency to their intimacy there was definitely no roughness, and Abby marveled at how soft and tender Laura's lips and kisses were, and how sensual and gentle her hands were. And, when Abby finally felt Laura's fingers delicately tease at her moist opening, her knees buckled and her body fell against Laura's. Laura quickly guided Abby onto a shower bench inside the huge shower stall, and as she sat down on it, Laura knelt down in front of her and gently parted Abby's thighs. Laura's hands caressed the insides of Abby's thighs as her lips trailed kisses further and further upward until she reached those sweet pretty lips. Abby let out another moan of pleasure as she felt Laura's tongue gently part the folds of her pussy, and softly flick across her throbbing clit. Abby's hands grabbed gently at Laura's shoulders, pulling her body in even further between her legs and pressing her face against her mound. Abby's hands were able to reach Laura's plump tits, and she squeezed at those delicious mounds of flesh and pinch at her nipples as Laura continued to expertly worked her mouth and tongue on Abby's pussy lips and clit. Abby felt dizzy and surges of heat coursed through her like bolts of lightening. Just then, Abby felt Laura slide a couple of fingers inside of her, while never letting her mouth leave her swollen bud. First slow, and then faster, Laura glided her fingers in and out of Abby's warm moistness, still sucking and licking her clit. "Oh Laura!" breathed Abby. Waves of pleasure rocked her body and she climaxed against Laura's hand and mouth.

"My god, you taste so sweet," Laura said, leaning up to kiss Abby on her mouth.

"Your turn, cowgirl. Come sit on this magical shower bench. It must have some kind of built-in vibrating device," Abby said with a smile.

Laura switched places with her, and this time it was Abby who was positioned on her knees in between Laura's legs. Abby looked up at her, as she teased the innermost top of Laura's thighs with her tongue. Laura's eyes about rolled up in her head, but she didn't want to pass up the amazing visual pleasure that went along with the physical pleasure. Laura's hands played with Abby's wet hair as her eyes took in the view of Abby's gorgeous round ass, shapely toned back, and her firm pert tits. Abby then surprised Laura by jamming her tongue in and out of her hole as her fingers stroked small circles around Laura's clit. Laura's body started to quiver and she pushed Abby's head away from her. Not because it didn't feel good, but because she didn't want to cum just yet. Laura had been aroused ever since she helped Abby out of her truck and never expecting this intimate interlude between the two of them to happen, Laura wanted to prolong it just a moment longer.

"Stand up in front of me," Laura said, pulling Abby's body up from between her legs.

Abby stood up and then straddled Laura's thighs like she herself was a cowgirl getting ready to ride her horse. She rested on her knees against the bench, her tits conveniently positioned in front of Laura's mouth. Laura pulled Abby closer as her mouth quickly found one of her stiff nipples and sucked and tucked at it gently. Laura could feel Abby's spread pussy lips teasingly brush against her thigh, and she slowly slid a hand down Abby's side and around the curve of her ass until her fingers made contact with those smooth parted lips. Laura teased her fingers at Abby's opening, moistening them with the dew of Abby's arousal, and then sucked Abby's tit into her mouth as she pushed a couple fingers deep inside her cunt. Abby moaned as she threw her head back and pushed herself down a bit against Laura's hand. Laura began to finger fuck Abby, while eagerly sucking on her tits and biting at her nipples. Abby once again began to feel an incredible surge of heat pulse through her body and she pushed aside one of Laura's thighs so that she too could work some finger magic. While riding Laura's hand, Abby slid a couple fingers into Laura's pussy and began finger fucking her in rhythm with Laura's movements. Faster and faster both of their hands rammed into each other's pussy, until Laura could feel Abby's pussy begin to tighten and pulse around her fingers. Wanting to give her pretty city girl another beautiful climax, Laura didn't stop and continued to thrust her fingers in and out of Abby's cunt even as she started to feel her own body inch towards the edge of her own orgasm. Abby's body stiffened as she let out a loud moan and shook against Laura's hand, her fingers slipping out of Laura's pussy. Laura wasn't expecting anything more, but once Abby's body relaxed she kneeled back down on the shower floor in between Laura's legs and shoved her mouth against her pussy. Abby's tongue flicked rapidly across Laura's clit as she slipped her two fingers back inside her pussy and resumed finger fucking her. Laura grasped at Abby's hair as her legs squeezed against Abby's shoulders and her body stiffened against the shower bench, twitching in ecstasy.

It took a few minutes before either one of them noticed that the shower water was no longer warm. Laura quickly got up to turn off the cold spray and opened the shower door to grab some towels. They both dried off, while exchanging kisses and caresses. "Wow! Talk about cowgirl chivalry. This is some one of a kind roadside assistance!" Abby exclaimed with a laugh.

"My pleasure pretty city girl," Laura replied with a wink, as she pulled on her clothes. "And, speaking of roadside assistance, we'd better eat quick so I can head back out and take care of that broken down vehicle of yours."

"Sounds like a plan. Besides, if we don't leave this bathroom, I may just need to take another shower!" Abby responded playfully.

Laura smiled and surprised Abby as she quickly got undressed again. "Well pretty city girl, I'm happy to oblige you!"

Story #6

Cowgirl Bridesmaid:

Intimate Reception Rendezvous

Tara rolled over in bed to answer her cell phone's pleading beeps and tones. It was a string of text messages from her best friend, Renee. Renee was slightly losing her cool, in these final hours before her wedding. She wasn't second guessing her decision to marry Matthew, a man she had met while out of town in Colorado, she was just letting all the hyperactivity of the occasion get to her. This kind of pre-wedding stress happens to brides all the time. But then, there was also the tremendous amount of stress Tara had put on herself, by volunteering to coordinate her best friend's out of state wedding.

Rising from her comfortable hotel room bed, Tara lengthened her body like a cat and let out a nice long stretch. She ran a hand through her long, black hair and walked over to the window to open the room's curtains. It was late summer in Denver Colorado, and the view from her hotel window was nothing short of magnificent. The sun was already peeking out from behind the Rocky Mountains, and the brilliant hues of red and orange leaves on the trees gave the landscape a beautiful luminescent glow. Tara greatly appreciated the majestic beauty of the mountains, but being a lover of the water, the lack of ocean was making her miss her home in San Jose, California. Even with the amount of fascinating traveling she had to do for her job, Tara knew that no other place would be home to her like California would.

When Tara and Renee first met in San Jose California, they had just been two young college girls who went out on the town several nights a week, and as many college girls do, they shared many intimate conversations with one another about their lives. Renee knew that Tara was a lesbian, and Renee herself was bisexual. Tara was always the "chick magnet", always having some hot sappho to hang with, while Renee enjoyed her time dating both men and women. Both of them had demanding school and work schedules so neither Tara or Renee had ever desired to be tied down in a serious relationship. Then, after graduating college, both women landed demanding jobs that required lots of travel and long hours. Tara was enjoying a successful career while still enjoying "playing the field" with the ladies, but when Renee met Matthew after one particular business trip to Colorado, Tara knew their relationship was the real deal for her best friend. After all, Renee and Matthew had been together an entire year, and it wasn't an easy year since they were dating long distance. Tara was seeing less and less of her best friend, but she was genuinely happy for her. Still, when Renee finally decided to give up her San Jose apartment to move to Denver and be with Matthew, it devastated Tara.

Many of Tara's friends were one-by-one deciding to settle down into serious relationships, and it made her a little sad to watch all her girlfriends branch out to start new lives with their partners on their own. Truthfully, it also made her a little envious. She knew it was just a part of life and growing up. The problem was she wasn't sure if she herself was ready to contemplate settling down just yet. She was still having far too much fun traveling and earning money so she can buy her dream home by the ocean.

Despite her personal reservations about settling down just yet, if there was one thing Tara was good at it, it was event planning, and that included wedding planning. It had taken the past three months to coordinate this fairy tale Colorado ski resort wedding, and she owed it to her best friend to make sure everything went as smoothly as possible. That of course, included calming the bride down whenever she needed it. Tara headed into the bathroom to get showered and dressed for breakfast. She wondered what list of great disasters her friend would have for her this time. Flowers? In-laws? Ice sculptures?

Tara put some finishing touches to her minimal makeup and then met Renee down in the hotel lobby for breakfast. They both looked like they could use more sleep, indicating that neither of them had a restful nights sleep. Tara glanced around the large dining room and identified various friends and family members who were also there to enjoy some breakfast. The groom, ironically enough, was nowhere to be seen. Tara silently wondered if Matthew had some last minute fitting or something else he needed to attend to.

"Good morning to the beautiful bride," Tara said, as she pulled her friend Renee into a hug. Instead of smiling, the poor bride looked to be on the verge of tears. Tara stroked her back to reassure her that everything would be okay. "What is it, Renee? What's wrong?"

"My mother is trying to change the music," Renee whispered so her mother wouldn't hear her across the room. "If I don't walk down the aisle to the song that was playing when Matthew and I first danced, it will be the absolute worst wedding in the history of weddings."

Tara couldn't help but chuckle at Renee's overreaction, and she gently hushed Renee having heard enough. Tara was both the maid of honor and wedding coordinator, and these things could be easily handled. "I will take care of it. You will get the song you want," Tara said, as she rubbed Renee's shoulders in reassurance. "Now, you need to go and get your hair and makeup done as soon as possible. Did you eat anything?" Renee nodded. Apparently, people had been trying to feed her all morning. Tara honestly thought that her friend looked like she was going to throw up, so maybe food wasn't the best idea right now.

"Okay, off you go. I will meet you in the bridesmaid's dressing room soon. It won't take any time at all for me to get ready, and I'm looking forward to seeing how gorgeous you will look in your dress." Tara said, pleased to see a small smile appear on Renee's face. Renee headed back towards the elevators, and she was quickly followed by half a dozen other women that were Renee's other bridesmaids, some by choice, and some not by choice.

Tara poured herself some orange juice with champagne. It was never too early to start drinking at a wedding, especially if you were in the wedding party. She almost regretted not demanding Renee have a drink with her, but then again she didn't want the bride puking everywhere. Looking across the room, Tara cleared her throat, and strode over to take care of the music situation that had Renee in a tizzy. A short conversation with the wedding DJ would easily put things back on track for what Renee wanted on her wedding day. After the music snafu was handled, Tara went around doing last minute checks to ensure everything was in place, caterers, flowers, seating, etc. And now, there were only a couple things left to do before the grand event happened. Tara met the other bridesmaids upstairs in their dressing area, and got her hair done by one of the hairstylists. After then putting on her bridesmaid's dress and matching cowboy boots, she had to go check on Renee and make sure that all was well with the bride-to-be.

"You look beautiful!" Tara beamed to her friend. "I am going to go tell everyone to get the hell out of the way, so we can sneak you downstairs." Renee looked grateful. She also looked a lot better than when Tara first checked in on her at breakfast. Maybe it was because her mother wasn't in the room with her at that moment. Tara knew what was expected of her. She was the loving friend, supporter and organizer. She would stand by her friend's side during the ceremony and after the crying and saying "I do's", Tara would help start off the reception by giving her toast to the new couple and drink absolutely more alcohol than she planned to in order to get through the reception. It was a party after all. Plus she knew how to handle her liquor, and there were lots of lovely ladies in attendance that she was eager to mingle with. In fact, there was one lovely lady in particular, and Tara suddenly found both her heart and body responding to the very thought of wining and dining with her. But, time was zipping by and she did not have the luxury to daydream about hopeful possibilities.

In the small side room adjacent to a much larger room where all the wedding guests were filing in, the bridesmaids were congregated in a parade of purple flowered dresses with simple straw cowboy hats and pretty white and purple flower bouquets. Of course Renee stood out in a remarkable custom made white wedding dress with a brilliant bouquet of purple. There was the typical buzz of anticipation in the air. The older people were walking around correcting the ring boy and flower girls on the small things, like how and where to walk. The bridesmaids were all gossiping and laughing nervously. Only the groomsmen seemed to be unabashedly joking and having a good time before they had to pair up with their respective bridesmaid for the iconic walk down the aisle.

Tara glanced over at the bridesmaids, and one particular beautiful specimen stood out. Her name was Tess, and Tara had the pleasure of meeting her several times during the past year. She had shoulder length sandy brown hair, was incredibly fit from riding horses, was funny and smart, and she always seemed to be surrounded by people who she loved to charm and make laugh. Today was no exception. Tara had noticed how both men and women were inexplicably drawn to the charismatic and beautiful bridesmaid, and Tara watched them blush and giggle at Tess's jokes and tales, like bees lapping up honey.

Tara always wondered if Tess's male or female admirers realized that their flirtatious efforts hadn't won over the vivacious cowgirl. Like Tara, Tess was also a free spirit enjoying her time and freedom, and one of the reasons Tara and Tess may have gotten along so well from the start, is because they both didn't want to seem like the desperate single friend to their married and partnered couples friends. So, they both enjoyed all the wedding preparations and activities without feeling the need to troll for a future life mate, and just enjoyed each other's company and interactions.

Tara walked over to a table against the wall to grab a bottle of water and survey the happenings, to make sure everything and everyone was in the right place and doing what they were supposed to be doing. "Hey good looking," Tara heard a soft female's voice purr in her ear. She turned around to see none other than Tess, one of Renee's other bridesmaids standing in front of her. Tess was not only part of the bridesmaid party, but she also helped Tara to organize some of the wedding particulars. Since Tess both lived in Colorado and worked at the resort, she was able to book the reception hall at the ski resort for the wedding, due to her connections. Tara certainly didn't mind all the long distance phone calls to this gorgeous cowgirl, and she also didn't mind the attention Tess paid her whenever they had the opportunity to be together.

The two had chatted frequently ever since Tara had arrived in Colorado four days ago, mostly about the wedding plans and trivial matters. However, the rehearsal dinner last evening had them sitting right next to each other, and the pair enjoyed a spirited conversation filled with lots of flirtatious gestures and innuendos. Tara had teased Tess for being a Colorado cowgirl and Tess had teased her for being a California beach bum. Tess worked the summers on a busy working ranch, and spent the winters working at the ski resort. Her line of work was quite physical and her stellar physique would make any professional athlete envious. Tess was also quite an eclectic woman with diverse interests and Tara really enjoyed her company a lot.

"Ready for the big event?" Tess asked, as she not so subtly gently stroked her fingers along Tara's arm. Tara smiled as she remembered a certain promise they both had made to each other during the course of their long distance wedding planning for their friends. They promised that they would enjoy each other's company as a couple during and after the wedding, and that included some intimate pleasure just as soon as they could manage it.

"Ready as I'll ever be," Tara replied. "Don't you ever have a bad hair day?" Tara joked at Tess, noting that while she was perfectly well groomed, she always seemed to have that just perfect sexy tousled hair look. Coupled with the light tan colored cowboy hat that all of the bridesmaids were wearing that made Tess look like she was about to do a rustic pinup girl photo shoot, Tara's body definitely responded to this woman's incredible sex appeal with some internal tingling that she hoped didn't distract her during the wedding ceremony.

"This messy mane?" Tess said, while touching her hair and faking an innocent smile that only made her look even more sexy. "Are you saying you want to mess up my hair?" Tess toyingly ran a hand through her wavy tresses and her infamous mischievous grin made Tara want to rip Tess's clothes off and have sex with her right then and there. But, there was a wedding ceremony to be had first, so she tried to divert her sexual hunger by continuing to banter with her.

"Ahhh," Tara half moaned. "Stop teasing me cowgirl, otherwise I just may have to carry you off to one of these rooms and delay the start of the wedding." She gave Tess a playful bump with her hip since their arms were still closely interwoven. Tess looked down and couldn't help but admire how nicely Tara's dress hugged the curve of her hips, noting that she had always found Tara extremely sexy and desirable.

Tess opened her mouth to say more, something clever that would make Tara show off her amazing smile, but their moment was interrupted when they heard the bridal party music begin to play.

"Oh Tess!" the mother of the bride shouted in their direction at the last minute. "Hurry up and take your spot in the lineup." Suddenly Tess was ripped from the snug hold she had on Tara's arm, and Tara stood with her mouth open about ready to cuss someone out when she suddenly found herself being taken by the arm by the best man, ready to escort them both down the aisle. As the doors opened, flashing a sparkling smile when all eyes turned to look at her and the best man as they walked down the aisle, Tara's mind flip flopped between thoughts of the wedding and thoughts of the reception afterwards and to her hopeful rendezvous with Tess.

During the ceremony, Renee appeared to have lost her jitters and she looked absolutely radiant. However, Tara couldn't help but be slightly distracted with thoughts of Tess, and she kept glancing over at her during the ceremony. Tess looked beautiful as ever, and she stood perfectly poised and attentive during the vows. Tara thought that was possible only because she wasn't in high heels, since all of the wedding party was wearing cowboy boots, but still, Tess's graceful posture and her manner were quite poised for a free spirited cowgirl.

Although Tara didn't notice, Tess too had been stealing some glances her direction during the ceremony. Her long black hair at every other event so far had been hanging down her back, where it rested against her California tanned skin. Today, for the wedding, a portion of it was twisted and curled and placed on top of her head. The style, combined with the tiny flowers that were sprinkled in it, made Tess think that Tara looked like a beautiful earthy goddess.

The bridesmaid standing directly behind Tara started sobbing, and any bridesmaid wedding veteran knew enough to tuck at least one tissue in your bra for just such an occasion. The bridesmaid behind her however, did not foresee this need. Tara reached into her bra as slowly and as discreetly as possible to retrieve a tissue for her, while attempting to hide her hand from the view of the audience by moving her bouquet upwards in front of her. This did nothing to block Tess's view however, and she suggestively raised her eyebrows to Tara. Tara caught Tess's look while handing the tissue over to the sobbing bridesmaid, and motioned with her eyes that she should pay her attention forward to the bride and groom. Still, that didn't stop Tara from noticing that Tess's hands were crossed in front of her and hung down past her waist. Tess's eyes locked with Tara's as her fingers were ideally stroking at the soft fabric of her dress, conveniently at crotch level. Tara wondered what Tess was getting at. Even if she wasn't getting at anything at all, it did not stop Tara from turning her attention and thoughts to what might be occurring between Tess's legs.

As the couple finished up the ceremony, and were pronounced husband and wife the people in attendance stood and clapped while the newlyweds, followed by the bridal party, filed out of the room. Renee and Matthew looked happy, the members of the bridal party looked happy, and the people in attendance looked happy. And now that the serious part of the festivities was over, everyone was looking forward to the reception for some wining, dining and dancing. But before Tara could enjoy some one-on-one time with Tess, they had to first undergo the mandatory post wedding ceremony picture taking.

All the traditional picture poses were captured. The groom and groomsmen were all together in one shot. The bridesmaids were in another shot surrounding the bride, Renee. The parents stood proudly by their kids in a group shot, and then each set with their respective son or daughter. Renee also made sure she got a group picture of her and her maid of honor Tara, alongside Matthews and his best man. While picture after picture was being flashed, Tara looked over at Tess to give her a playful, suggestive wink. Everyone was relieved when the photographer said that he was done taking photos for the time being, and the wedding party was allowed to go on to the reception hall, where the guests were already congregating. Tara and Tess linked arms as they headed out to the reception area, and Tara quickly noticed that some of the other bridesmaids and guests were staring at them and whispering behind their bouquets or drinks, but she didn't care.

As the food was been served, Tara looked across the room at all of the wedding guests from her place at the bridal party table. It was definitely one of the biggest weddings she had ever been to, and once everyone finished their meals and started dancing and milling around, nobody would even notice her absence when she snuck off for an intimate rendezvous with Tess. However, she couldn't quite sneak off yet. As the maid of honor, she had a toast to make to the bride and groom. So, for the moment, she just enjoyed the lingering scent of Tess's perfume that clung to her dress from when they were pressed side by side during the picture taking. Longing to also smell the scent of her naked skin and the feel of her tits pressed against her, Tara's pussy started to throb with anticipation on their interlude.

While eating, the photographer worked his way around the reception hall taking more pictures, and as Tara ate her prime rib meal her eyes perused the other side of the bridal table with all the groomsmen. They were laughing and swigging beer right from a tower of bottles that was forming on their end of the table. Tara always wondered why men were almost expected to act wild and uninhibited at weddings, but the women were expected to act prim and proper? Tara was all too ready to get a little wild and uninhibited herself, and she wanted to do it with the sexy cowgirl who sat seated just a few seats down from her. While Tess looked sexy as ever in her bridesmaid attire, Tara couldn't wait to free her body from it and enjoy her taut, voluptuous, and very naked body.

Tara was startled out of her sexy daydream when she heard the clinking of glasses and someone announcing that it was time to give the speeches. The best man rose and in gentleman-like fashion offered the microphone to Tara first, who politely refused. She motioned for the best man to go first so she could take a moment to collect her thoughts. Tess noticed the exchange and winked seductively at Tara, which certainly didn't help Tara reel in the fantasy her mind was enjoying. The room fell silent and almost hypnotized by the best man's surprisingly eloquent words, and the cool manner in which he spoke. He was a natural speaker, and Tara suddenly wished she wouldn't have to follow such a commanding performance. He had the crowd laughing, and even Renee's mom, who was typically an uptight stick in the mud, was laughing and responding to best man's storytelling. As soon as the best man made sure that all of the guests had heard a few select embarrassing things about he and Matthew's shenanigans, he brought the speech back to a serious sentimental note that made everyone all teary eyed.

"And it is with a happy heart that I congratulate my best friend,

Matthew, and his lovely bride Renee, on finding and embracing a union of unbridled love, joy and passion. May you always respect, support and treat each other right, and have a lifetime of happiness with one another. Let's hear it for the happy couple!" the best man ended. The crowd applauded and Matthew stood up to give his best friend a great big hug.

The best man offered his most charming of smiles to the crowd and then walked over to Tara to give her the microphone. After handing off the microphone to Tara and walking back to go sit back down with the rest of the groomsmen, Tara was startled when Tess stood up and came over to stand right behind her with what appeared to be no intentions of moving while she gave her speech. Tara rose from her chair and stood next to Tess, who to the crowd looked unassuming as she stood silently behind Tara while holding onto her glass of champagne. Tara felt Tess's eyes watching her, and she herself was all too aware of her body just mere inches her own. What was Tess looking at? Her hat? Her ass? A small part of her wondered if Tess was getting a decent shot of her breasts if she was looking down her dress, and Tara felt her knees slightly weaken at the flash thought of Tess's hands freeing her tits from the constraints of her bridesmaid's dress.

Trying to focus on the task at hand, Tara raised both her champagne glass and the microphone so she could deliver her maid of honor speech to the newlyweds. Tara thankfully had a natural knack for giving spontaneous, heartwarming speeches at weddings, and as she crafted her kind words for Renee and how much she respected and honored Matthew for being so good to her, Tara's body was given a little jolt of surprise when she felt Tess's fingers start to suggestively draw shapes on the back of her shoulder's before trailing down her back and around her ass. She did not let it distract her as she congratulated the couple and even brought the whole speech in for a perfect ending.

"Renee, you know I've known you a long time and I cannot think of another person who deserves the happiness you have found with

Matthew. I know you guys will love each other with all your hearts and set an example for all of us here today on what the power of true love can stir in all our hearts. Congratulations, girl! I love you and I am so happy for you"

Renee wiped away a few tears and Tara knew that that meant she gave a good speech.

"That was lovely," Tess whispered into Tara's ear. Her breath felt hot and suggestive on her neck and she couldn't help but shiver a bit. She grabbed onto Tess's hand to pause her actions as a wave of relatives began to swarm Renee and Matthew again at the bridal table.

"You think so?" Tara commented. "I have been told I do write lovely speeches. Your show of support during my speech was quite moving too. It touched me, right in here," Tara replied suggestively, bringing her hands to her breasts. Tess's eyes followed her hands and she bit her bottom lip hungrily.

"I think this would be a perfect time to escape. Let's go find someplace a bit more private for us. They won't even notice that we're gone for awhile," Tess whispered back to Tara. "My hotel room?" Tess suggested, her anticipation only growing as she felt Tara trace her fingers around the curve of her hips. Tara's anticipation was growing too and she knew that at this moment, when their friend Renee had just committed to having sex with only one person for the rest of her life, Tara didn't mind adding another girl to her list of experiences, and Tess was the one. She was like minded on this matter, and the two had agreed to have some unbridled fun and enjoy each other while Tara was in Colorado.

"Not enough time," Tara whispered to her. "They will be cutting the cake soon and we need to be back here for that, otherwise our lack of presence will be obvious." So, Tara held onto Tess's hand and led her out of the reception hall and down a couple adjacent corridors, looking for a place where they could have some private intimate fun. She spotted the designated coat check room for the wedding, and it was obviously not presently being attended to. Tara pulled Tess into the room, deliberately not turning on the light so as not to draw any attention, and she walked them to the far back wall of room.

"Perfect," Tess whispered in the dark. Tess had to move jackets and coats away from her, but her hands were perfectly aware of where everything else was, and she pressed Tara's body up against the wall directly behind the rack of coats. Tara mildly noticed that some of the coat hangers were swinging delicately on either side of her head, but her attention was much more focused on Tess's hands that were gently running up the inner sides of her legs. The light fabric of her dress easily bunched up around her hips, and to Tess's surprise when her fingers reached the innermost top area between her thighs, Tara wasn't wearing any panties. Had she planned this? It certainly would seem so, and Tess delighted in the fact that Tara was such a free spirited vixen. A groan escaped Tess's lips as her hands brashly pulled down the front of Tara's dress, freeing her tits for Tess's viewing, feeling and tasting pleasure. Tara whispered words of profanity as Tess's mouth found her erect nipples and she suckled on them like a hungry newborn.

Tess's intimate attention to her tits was making Tara extremely wet, and as her mind wandered to thoughts of touching and tasting Tess's pussy, she felt the thrust of Tess's fingers deep inside her cunt. Tara's hips bucked against Tess's hand, as her own hands grasped at the dangling coats on the coat rack, pulling several of them from their hangers. "Oh my....fuck....don't stop," Tara hoarsely whispered, as Tess finger fucked her to the edge of orgasm.

Tess stopped suddenly before Tara could climax, and she stood so she could be face to face with her. Tess's lustful eyes penetrated Tara as she swiftly pulled her own bridesmaid dress over her head and let it fall to the floor. While Tara had deliberately took off her panties before the ceremony, she gasped when she saw that Tess wasn't wearing panties or a bra, and her shadowy nude form stood tauntingly before her, making Tara want to just forget about ever returning to the reception and just spending the next 24 hours exploring, and re-exploring every inch and curve of Tess's delicious naked body. Tara leaned forward and kissed Tess with a hungry desire that her body could no longer contain.

Tara's hand grabbed at Tess's voluptuous tits while their tongues and mouth passionately explored one another. The mixed scent of Tess's perfume and natural body scent drove Tara absolutely wild and she had to mindfully try to keep her moans and verbal expressions muted so as not to alert any passerby's. While Tess stood with her hands holding onto one of the coat racks, Tara kneeled down on the floor and spread apart her legs with one hand while squeezing and caressing Tess's ass with the other. The silky, smooth feel of Tess's skin, her intoxicating aroma, Tara was all about to burst if she didn't get a taste of this enticing cowgirl from Colorado. Without the luxury of time to fully take her time in exploring all of Tess's attributes slowly, Tara pulled Tess's hips towards her face and buried her mouth in her mound. Her tongue quickly parted the soft folds of Tess's pussy and Tara wasted no time in running her mouth softly up and down the slit of her lips. Using her fingers to spread open Tess's pussy lips, Tara's tongue expertly darted back and forth across Tess's clit, eliciting soft moans and twitching in return. Just as Tara had imagined, Tess tasted like fucking sweet honey and she couldn't get enough of lapping at her soft, moist lips. Tess began to rock her hips against Tara's mouth, and Tara slipped in one finger, and then two, into Tess's moistness.

Coats and hangers began to swing on the coat rack as Tara finger fucked Tess. Sucking Tess's clit gently into her mouth, Tara's fingers thrust alternately between slow and fast into Tess's cunt. Tess's pussy juices had soaked Tara's hand and just as Tara was going to change positions, she felt Tess's body tense and quiver in climax against her mouth and fingers. "Holy fuck!" Tess exclaimed in a loud whisper.

Before Tara could reply, Tess had whipped Tara's body around on the floor so that she was on her hands and knees and Tess knelt down on the floor behind her. Pressing her hips against Tara's ass, Tess reached between her thighs and slipped her fingers easily into Tara's already wet pussy while reaching around to grab at one of her tits. As if riding one of her horses, Tess grabbed a handful of Tara's long black hair, effectively messing up her styled do, while finger fucking her with fast hard thrusts. The sound of distant voices passing by the entrance of the coat check room indicated that the women needed to hurry up and return to the reception, yet Tess wanted to make sure that Tara was satisfied, at least once, before they paused their intimate enjoyment of one another until after the reception. "Don't stop," whispered Tara, and Tess wasn't about to. Tugging harder on her hair, Tess slammed her fingers deep inside Tara's cunt and thrust them in and out until Tara's body reached that glorious moment of ecstasy and bucked upward like an unbridled mare.

Collapsing from pleasure, Tara's body fell forward onto the carpeted floor and Tess straddled her while trailing kisses upward along Tara's back and along the side of her neck. The musky smell of their sex permeated the air around them, and while Tess was definitely ready for more, she knew that the two of them really needed to get back to the reception before their absence was noticed. They exchanged deep, passionate kisses without saying a single word for several minutes before Tess broke the hypnotic sensual spell they were both under. "I guess we should probably make ourselves look presentable again and get back to the reception."

"Yeah, you're right," replied Tara.

Tess located her dress and slipped it back on before running her hands through her wavy hair to make herself presentable and re-donning her cowboy hat. Tara reassembled herself as well, and tried to feel with her hands if her hair was messed up, which it was, so she quickly removed the hair pins that had been holding a portion of her hair up and just let her hair fall naturally down her shoulders and back. She knew people would notice, but it would be better than returning to the reception with "I just got fucked hair"! Now that their eyes had adjusted to the darkness in the coat check room, Tara noticed a slew of coats lying on the floor around them, obviously stripped off their hangers by the couple's recent activity. Tara carefully replaced the coats back onto the hangers while Tess helped her, hungrily looking at her like she was ready go at it again. "Ready to get back to the party, sexy lady," asked Tess with a devilish grin.

"Yes, I'm ready. You think they'll notice my hair?" Tara asked.

Tess laughed and nodded. "Yes, but nobody will dare say anything." Tess thought it looked beautiful, and was almost aroused to the point of keeping Tara in the coat check room for another round of sensual fun. "Besides, if anyone asks, just tell them you got sick of it being up," Tess said.

As the pair made their way out of the coat check room successfully unnoticed and then back down the corridors to the reception hall, they were just in time to hear someone announcing on the microphone that it was time for the cake cutting. "Whew, just in time," Tara said with a satisfied grin.

Tess leaned in and gave Tara a soft kiss on her cheek just before they re-entered the busy room as if nothing out of the ordinary happened at all, and Tara and Tess walked over to the wedding cake table where Renee and Matthew were waiting for them. As the couple cut the cake, and more pictures were flashed, Tess flashed her devilishly sensual smile at Tara, and whispered in her ear that there was more intimate pleasure to be enjoyed after the reception concluded. Tara purred softly in response, anxious to resume their intimate reception rendezvous.

Story #7

Cowgirl Rides:

Erotic Wild West Vacation

Sitting on a plane on the way to New Mexico, Kelly wondered how in the world she had ever let her friends talk her into this. The girls had insisted that she needed to get out of her office and stop being the "secretary slave" to her boss. They also had insisted that alongside of her break from work she needed some quality female attention that wasn't from a coffee shop girl or restaurant waitress.

It wasn't as if Kelly was against the outdoors. She loved growing up in the city where you were smarter to walk everywhere and there were parks wherever they could be squeezed in, if you felt like exercising. It was just that city exercise, and out-in-the-middle-of-nowhere exercise, were two entirely different worlds and she wasn't so sure she'd be able to keep up. The girls had said that they wanted to go to New Mexico to get a taste of Wild West country. They wanted camp fires, horses and lots of sexy cowboys and cowgirls. Kelly's friend Julia was a lesbian, like she was, and their friend Trish was straight and loved "bad boys". The camp fires and cowgirls part sounded perfect, it was the horse part that had Kelly worried. The only horses Kelly had ever interacted with, were the ones hooked up to a carriage and had a driver in a top hot looking to make a few bucks around Central Park by offering ride to tourists. Her friends also promised that a dude ranch vacation would offer lots of "adventure." Kelly was all up for the adventure part, she was just hoping that that adventure didn't involve being chased by a steer, a run in with poisonous snakes or flash floods. She knew she was being a bit overdramatic, but she was a city girl after all and she knew she was going to feel like a fish out of water in the middle of the desert.

When they arrived in New Mexico, one of the first things Kelly noticed was the stifling heat. She had heard that New Mexico wasn't as hot as most parts of Arizona, Nevada or California, so she was hopeful that it wouldn't be too bad. But, New York doesn't typically see 100 degree days as an average, so even though the humidity was much lower, the heat was definitely intense. She could definitely understand why desert wildlife comes alive during the evening hours when it's cooler. Well, it was probably better than vacationing somewhere where the temperatures were constantly below freezing.

After retrieving their luggage at the airport carousel, a special shuttle bus from the ranch picked-up Kelly and her friends, along with a few other passengers who were also headed to the same location, and drove them on a scenic drive out to the dude ranch. Kelly was surprised by the amount of green trees and grass she saw during their drive to the ranch, as she was expecting a much more arid, tumbleweed filled desert environment. She was beginning to see why people would want to vacation and even live out here. The driver was a New Mexico native, and he offered a lot of fascinating tales along the way. Kelly's anxiety filled perception over vacationing at a dude ranch quickly changed from feeling like a fish out of water, to one of excited anticipation and discovery.

When they arrived at the dude ranch, it couldn't have looked more inviting. There were several large main buildings and the driver, who also turned out to be one of the main ranch hands, explained to the arriving guests that one was the dining facilities building, another was the activities and entertainment building, and the third was the main ranch office and living quarters of the family that owned and operated the ranch. There were several dirt roads that directed people and horse traffic throughout the expansive acreage of the ranch, and the guests quarters consisted of 50 separate small cabins which were set back from the three main buildings and situated on either side of the dirt roads. There were also several large horse barns and designated outdoor areas where guests could learn horse back riding, roping and other ranch related activities. The ranch hand continued on to explain that some of the other daytime activities included gardening and canning, outdoor trekking and ranch survival skills. Some of the nighttime activities included evening bonfires, cowboy and ghost tales, and square dancing and line dancing lessons.

As the group of newly arriving guests was being led along one of the dirt roads getting their cabin assignments, Kelly felt a sharp nudge in her side. "Hot cowgirl candy, straight ahead," her friend Julia whispered in a not-so quiet way. Kelly looked up, putting a hand on her forehead to shade her eyes from the sun. A group of three horse riders were heading down the dirt road in their direction, two of them were men and one was a naturally beautiful woman. They all wore dusty cowboy hats, long sleeved shirts, despite the heat, and were all tanned enough to confirm that they all most likely worked here at the ranch. The horses were as good looking as their riders, and they walked obediently next to one another side-by-side down the dirt road. As the trio passed the group, Kelly took sharp notice to the rider closest to her, which was the only female rider. As she tipped her hat to the group, Kelly noticed that she had dirty blonde hair and the most beautiful green eyes a woman could ever have. By the length of her legs, she appeared to be quite tall and the fabric of her snug denim jeans and tight plaid shirt couldn't disguise the fact that this woman's body was obviously in magnificent shape. The cowgirl wore a bandana tied around her neck and the way she sat so confidently and in-charge in the horse's saddle caused a little stir in-between Kelly's legs. The cowgirl winked at Kelly as they trotted by, and Kelly was surprised by the lurching feeling she experienced in her chest.

Noticing Kelly's reaction, Julia had to poke a little fun at her friend. "I see that a certain cowgirl has already gotten your attention." Kelly scoffed and waved a hand at Julia, motioning her to be quiet.

"Shhh," Kelly said in return, feeling a flush come to her cheeks. "I am on vacation and I am just enjoying the sights." Kelly laughed lightly, watching the backside view of the horses and the cowgirl rider as they continued down the dirt road, heading towards one of the horse barns.

Kelly thought she heard the ranch hand who was guiding them mention that one of the horse rider's names was Samantha. Given that she was the only female rider, it had to be her. "What a perfect name for a cowgirl," Kelly thought to herself, as she was given her cabin assignment.

Listening to the exchange between her friends made Trish kind of envious. She was the only one in the group who wasn't lesbian, or single, and somehow she knew that being surrounded by drop dead gorgeous cowboys, in a setting one has to experience to appreciate for the next week, was really going to put her relationship with her fiancé to the test. She would just have to live out that fantasy vicariously through Kelly, and hopefully, it would indeed result in one juicy fantasy.

It was already mid-afternoon, so the three women decided to get settled into their cabins and they would meet up again at the dining hall later for supper. Their guide explained that the dinner chow bell rang promptly at 5 pm each day, and dinner was served for only 1 hour. Every evening there was a large campfire that started at roughly 8pm, and guest could roast marshmallows, drink beer and whiskey from camp mugs and listen to the ranch hands play music and tell tales of cowboy ghosts and Wild West history. It all sounded like so much fun, and Kelly and her friends couldn't wait to start enjoying all that the ranch had to offer. In fact, Kelly was already starting to enjoy what the ranch had to offer. While she hadn't even planned on having any kind of vacation romance, the sight of that blonde-haired, green-eyed cowgirl quickly changed her mind and she hoped that she'd run into cowgirl again sooner vs. later.

Unfortunately, Kelly did not run into her blonde haired cowgirl at supper that evening, but she did cross paths with her fairly often while coming and going to the many ranch activities she participated in over the next several days. Kelly figured out that one of her blonde haired cowgirl's main duties was to tend to the horses, because every time she passed by the horse barn closest to her cabin Kelly saw her there. She was either grooming or training the horses, or saddling them up for the guests to take on one of the ranches daily horseback riding sessions. Kelly always walked slower by the horse barn whenever she spotted her, and she wondered if the pretty cowgirl caught on to the fact that she was attracted to her. While Kelly always saw her and all the other cowboy ranch hands wearing long sleeve shirts while out riding the horses, Kelly noticed the cowgirl was often only wearing a tight fitting t-shirt when grooming and training them in the stable areas. Her arms were both incredibly tanned and toned, her stomach was flat, and her breasts jiggled as she stepped up and down on the step ladder when washing and grooming the horses. And, as Kelly suspected, she was tall. The cowgirl's long, lean legs suggested that she was probably between 5' 10" and 6' tall. She always wore the same tan colored cowboy hat that matched the color of her hair, and her smooth sun kissed face bore a natural beauty that Kelly was so attracted to.

Today, Kelly was headed to meet a group of ranch guests that were going on a guided day hike in the mountains. Julia and Trish were meeting her there at the meet-up point, so at the moment Kelly was walking alone. Maybe it was because of this fact, that when the blonde haired cowgirl caught sight of her strolling by the horse barn unattended by her friends, the cowgirl waved and called her over. Kelly stopped and walked over to the fence that encircled the stable area. Kelly's heart started pounding in her chest as she watched the beautiful ranch hand walk over to her, her body already reacting to the sight of the cowgirl's tits bouncing against the fabric of her shirt. "Be cool Kelly, be cool," she breathed to herself.

"Well hello there pretty thing," she greeted Kelly with a tip of her hat. "I notice that you are a new guest here on the ranch. How are you enjoying your stay so far?"

"Uh, it's been great so far, thank you," Kelly replied, her body feeling the aura of natural magnetism the woman exuded, as she stood with her arms on her slender hips just several feet away from Kelly on the other side of the fence.

"I haven't seen you on any of the daily trail rides. Most guests can't wait to saddle up a horse and take a ride through the beautiful countryside. By the way, my name's Samantha, but most folks just call me Sam."

"Nice to meet you Sam, I'm Kelly. A ride in the countryside sounds wonderful actually, but I confess that I've never even been on a horse before. If you put me on a horse by myself, I'm pretty sure my nerves would spook the poor beast." Kelly was thankful that she was wearing sunglasses, because her eyes couldn't help but enjoy the magnificent sight of Sam's gorgeous physique, and steal glances at her nipples which were suddenly hard and poking through her shirt. Goodness, maybe Kelly should let herself be thrown from a horse just so she could feel the cowgirl could put her arms around her and help her up off the ground.

"Well, that's exactly why I'm here. I've got plenty of seasoned horses for all levels of rider experience, including first timers. I'd be happy to personally give you riding lessons and a personal trail ride if you'd like. In fact, I might even let you wear one of my lucky hats," she said with a wink.

"Yeah, you ranch types sure don't like taking off your cowboy hats do you?"

"Well, we don't too often. A real cowboy or cowgirl keeps their hat on almost all the time. Typically, we take our hat off when we eat, when we enter someone's house, and when we are in bed, sleeping or otherwise," Sam explained.

"So, does that mean that real cowgirls don't wear their hat when they're having sex?" Kelly was surprised by her boldness, but hey, she was on vacation and the environment and scenery were definitely having an effect on her.

Sam flashed Kelly a great big smile, as she answered. "Well, you let me know if you'd like to research that inquiry."

"Are you flirting with me cowgirl?"

"Why yes I am. Are you flirting with me pretty thing?"

"Why yes I am," Kelly responded with a laugh. "But, I've actually got to get going right now. I'm headed over to meet my friends at the meet-up point for today's day hike in the mountains. But, I'd like to take you up on your offer for a personal riding lesson and trail ride. I'm free tomorrow, if you are."

"I'm most definitely looking forward to it. I'll have one of my best horses ready for you tomorrow. Just meet me here around 10am. Enjoy the view on your hike," Sam said, tipping her hat and turning to walk back towards the horse barn.

"Oh, I'm already enjoying the view!" Kelly whispered out loud, and with that, Kelly strode off to meet her friends, with visions of a naked cowgirl wearing nothing but her cowboy hat dancing in her head. "Damn, this dude ranch vacation thing is turning out to be one hell of a great idea!" Kelly thought to herself, also knowing that her friends were going to tease the hell out of her when they found out about her intended plans with Samantha. Kelly hoped that tomorrow she'd be experiencing all of the "horses, cowgirls and adventure" that her friends had promised her, and all in one shot!

Kelly arose the next morning as the sun was rising over the mountain tops. Anxiously looking forward to her 10am riding lesson with Samantha, she tried to keep herself busy to make the next 4-1/2 hours go by faster vs. slower. After having breakfast with Julia and Trish in the dining hall, Kelly went over to the ranch's gift shop in the main building and purchased a pair of cowboy boots. They were cute, plus she figured she might need them for her riding lessons. Kelly then returned to her cabin to freshen up before heading over to meet Samantha. After smoothing lotion all over her skin, Kelly brushed out her long blonde hair and applied just a touch of makeup. She then pulled on a cute little sundress that matched nicely with her new cowboy boots, along with a pair of large silver hopped earrings. Lastly, she spritzed on a bit of light perfume and headed out the door to meet Samantha over at the horse barn.

As she locked up her cabin door she noticed that the skies had turned overcast, which Kelly appreciated, welcoming any small relief from the heat. Her heart pulsing in her chest, Kelly hoped that she wouldn't look overly anxious when first seeing Sam. Kelly was of course looking forward to her personal horse riding lesson from her, but she was also secretly hoping that there might be a different type of personalized lesson from Sam as well. Turning at the end of the dirt road, she caught sight of the horse barn, but she didn't see Sam or any horses out front. As she approached the side entry to the horse barn, she guessed that Sam was probably inside getting her horse ready for their lesson. Walking inside, Kelly noticed that almost all of the horse stables were empty except for a few horses occupying the stables at the far end of the row. "Hello? Samantha? Sam?" she called out. Getting no answer in return, Kelly wondered if Sam had forgotten about her promise to Kelly for a personal riding lesson. Feeling a tinge of disappointment, Kelly started walking along the hay strewn barn floor towards the horses at the end.

Kelly had never been inside a horse barn before, and she was surprised by how clean it was. As she got closer, Kelly noticed the few horses watching her curiously, while chewing on whatever it was that horses chewed on. They were admittedly quite beautiful creatures, and Sam obviously took extremely good care of them. Their coats and manes were very well kept and shiny, and she also noticed that they appeared to be quite content and happy. The only thing that bothered Kelly was the fact that these beautiful creatures were so much larger up close than she anticipated. Trying to overcome her anxiety about the horse's size, Kelly slowly reached out a hand to pet the side of its head. "Hello there, my name is Kelly", she whispered as her hand glided along its silky soft coat.

"I see you've met Stella."

Startled, Kelly swung around to see Samantha standing there with a big grin on her face and holding a saddle in her hands. Did this mean she didn't forget about their riding lesson? "Sam, you scared me. I was just making my acquaintance with the horses."

"Well, the horse you were making your acquaintance with is Stella, and she is who you'll be riding today. She is very patient and is excellent with first time riders," explained Sam as she set down the saddle. "She's a beauty isn't she?"

Kelly nodded in agreement, also thinking just how naturally beautiful and mesmerizing the woman standing next to her was. Sam was wearing a long sleeved brown and white plaid shirt with jeans that conformed perfectly to her amazing ass and legs without being too tight. She of course had on cowboy boots along with her worn tan cowboy hat. Kelly hoped Sam wasn't reading her thoughts, which involved stripping Sam out of her clothes and rolling around naked in the hay. While Kelly was deep in thought, Stella had stuck her head over the edge of the stall and was sniffing her hair. Sam smiled as she watched her favorite horse bonding with Kelly.

"Well, I need to get this saddle on Stella before we start that riding lesson," Sam stated as she reached out and pulled a piece of alfalfa from Kelly's hair, which Stella had left behind during her exploration of Kelly's own pretty mane. As Sam gently tugged the twig from Kelly's hair, she allowed her fingers to softly trace down the side of Kelly's cheek. "I think Stella is going to enjoy having you on her today."

Surveying Kelly's appearance, Sam certainly wasn't complaining about how sexy she looked. Only problem was, Kelly wasn't exactly wearing proper riding attire. She was wearing the proper footwear of course, but the sundress might pose a modesty problem. The hemline fell to just above her knees, and Sam could already tell by glancing at her creamy legs that the dress was going to rise quite a bit when she got on the horse. Sam could feel a stirring in her belly as she thought about it, and she wondered if she should suggest to Kelly that she change her clothes. Not wanting to risk her getting embarrassed and calling off her riding lesson Sam decided to speak up about it.

"While I personally think you look incredibly pretty and sexy in that sundress, it may not be the best thing to wear while riding a horse. If you wanted to change into something else, I can wait," Sam suggested, while moving her eyes along Kelly's legs so she would get her meaning.

"Oh," Kelly said almost embarrassed. She had dressed with the intention of wearing something sexy for Samantha, not even thinking about the sensibility of proper riding gear. Kelly was worried about being embarrassed by getting kicked or thrown off her horse, not if she was showing too much leg…or more. "Well, I think it should be okay, unless you think I need to change."

"Well, I'm certainly not going to complain if I happen to catch sight of your pretty legs," Samantha laughed. "I just want you to feel comfortable." Kelly couldn't help but smile back at her, while thinking how sexy Sam's laugh was.

"Alright then, that's settled. Now, let me get this saddle on Stella and we can start your riding lesson." As Sam opened the stable door Stella's tale started twitching, yet she remained very still as Sam mounted and secured the saddle on her. Stella was staring at Kelly, and there was something in Stella's eyes that made her feel calmer. It was as if she was conveying a message that she wouldn't let her fall, and this was going to be a gentle pleasant experience.

"Stella and I have been friends a long time, and we have a very personal connection," Sam said as she reached up to fit a bridle around her face. Stella didn't resist her at all. "I helped birth her into this world almost seven years ago now, and she's the only horse that I've personally raised, and trained since birth."

"Really?" Kelly said with a surprised tone. "That's pretty incredible. Sounds like you're a true born and bred cowgirl."

"Yes and no," Samantha replied as she maneuvered around the horse securing all the straps and buckles. Kelly could not help but notice how Sam's perfect form moved underneath her clothes. She looked so physically fit compared to Kelly's thin build. There is a big difference between toned and thin, and Samantha's body was toned to perfection, obviously the result of all the physical requirements of ranch life.

"My parent's owned a ranch when I was a kid," Samantha continued, as she put the finishing touches on securing Stella's saddle and bridle. Her continued talking allowed Kelly to relax a bit and she liked listening to Sam, as her voice was soft and calming. No wonder Stella was letting Sam do whatever she wanted to her without even so much as a curious glance. There was a complete trust that Kelly admired, and she wanted to feel and enjoy the calm sure touch of Samantha's hands, the way she was sure Stella enjoyed every time she was with her. "I knew I had a knack for animals, particularly horses, and so I left to study veterinary science at Colorado State University. I missed the ranch life tremendously while in school, and once I graduated, I knew I didn't just want to open an ordinary vet practice. I wanted to raise and care for horses on a ranch. And, so here I am. Living my dream life and loving what I do." Kelly was highly impressed with that little story snippet, and she suddenly realized that Samantha wasn't just some wannabe dyke ranch hand. She possessed a depth of admirable qualities that far extended her being a good looking cowgirl that knew how to handle horses.

"Alright, I think we are ready to go. Let's walk Stella out into the corral and I will get you two better acquainted. Here, take these sugar cubes and keep them in your hands. If Stella comes your way, just hold one out for her in your open palm. "

"Okay, I'm ready...I think," Kelly replied with a sudden nervously she hadn't expected.

Sam clicked her tongue and Stella obediently followed her out of the barn. The sheer size of her moving towards her made Kelly step back, but Sam moved her eyebrows towards the treat in Kelly's hand.

"Oh right," Kelly said, finding some confidence. She held out her hand, and it was almost as if Stella's eyes lit up. She moved her head quickly, but not too quickly, towards Kelly's open hand. A long tongue shot out and over Kelly's palm to sweep up the sugar cube. Kelly couldn't help but notice how flat her teeth were. "Wow," she muttered.

"Good girl, Stella," Samantha whispered to her horse, as she stroked her head. "See, horses are gentle giants. You treat them with trust and respect and they trust you back. If you approach them nervous and scared, they get spooked because they don't know what your intentions are. Stella here," Sam stopped to pet the horse's muscular side a bit, "she's more trusting than other horses because she's been around this ranch her whole life. Stella is used to different people riding her, and she trusts me. She knows I won't let someone who is too panicked or too aggressive ride her."

Kelly smiled and held out a hand. She looked to Sam. "May I?" she asked, and Sam nodded. Kelly ran her hand down the horses' long nose. Stella closed her eyes and Kelly could almost feel her smiling. She stood perfectly still too. That seemed like a lot of trust to Kelly. "I can see why she is so special to you."

"Yes, she is," Sam commented looking only at Kelly. When Kelly noticed that Sam was looking at her, not Stella, she blushed.

"Now, are you ready to get up on her?" Sam asked. Kelly looked up at the horse, and upon looking at Stella's calm gaze, something told her that it was okay to venture outside her comfort zone. She nodded her readiness to Sam.

"Ok, getting on a horse is like getting on a bike or motorcycle, you gotta know where to put things," Sam commented as she began pointing out certain pieces of the saddle, the reins, and where Kelly was going to put her feet. Her phrasing of "you gotta know where to put things" was a phrase that sounded a lot like what you had to do when making love, but maybe that thought connection just popped into her head because she was so incredibly turned on and attracted to Samantha, especially as she was finding out more about this beautiful cowgirl.

"So, put your foot here," Sam said pointing to the stirrup and snapping Kelly out of whatever thought she was having that involved Sam with no clothing on.

"All the way up there?" Kelly looked at Sam, uncertain if she wanted to ride all the sudden.

"It's okay, I am going to help you." Sam offered her a hand while Kelly positioned one of her feet into the center of the stirrup. "Great. Now reach up and grab onto the saddle horn if you can. That will help support you as I help you up into the saddle. Now, nice and steady, give yourself a little bounce and then pull yourself up into the saddle. I will support you to make sure you don't fall, so don't worry about that." Sam stepped closer to Kelly, finding any excuse to touch her arms as she walked around her student and the horse. Kelly welcomed each intentional or unintentional touch, and she hoped that Sam would touch her even more as she continued to instruct her.

Kelly took a couple of deep breaths and then gave herself a little bounce as Sam instructed. As she held onto the saddle horn trying to pull herself up, she felt Sam slide a hand along the side of her body and down to her thigh in a way that made Kelly blush. It was of course to support her so that she wouldn't fall, but the only thing Kelly could think about was the fact that Sam just got a clear view of the full length of her legs and most likely her panties too. Sam had warned Kelly about her attire already, so she was thankful that Sam didn't repeat herself. Instead, Sam just tried to keep her grinning to a minimum.

"Keep going… swing your other leg over…and there you go!" Sam congratulated Kelly as she successfully made it up into Stella's saddle. Samantha kept her hand on Kelly's thigh, but she did lower it back down to just above Kelly's knee. When she realized that maybe she was being a little intrusive, Sam quickly removed her hand.

"It's okay," Kelly said smiling down at her. She wanted Samantha to touch her. Sam smiled back at Kelly, her embarrassment draining out of her face. Sam felt comforted that the flirting was mutual.

"Ok, now you want to rest your calves here," Sam instructed as she walked around Kelly, stopping to stroke her calves, her ankles, and at one point Kelly thought she felt lips on her right leg. Sam said she was just leaning in to check something.

"Now as you ride, you move your legs like this," Sam said showing Kelly first what to do when Stella was standing still, "Ready for her to move?" Kelly nodded and Sam made the sound for Stella to move forward.

"I can't believe it! I'm riding!" Kelly said excitedly, and Sam smiled as she moved to stop Stella again. "Let me show you how to keep your hips and back," Sam said as she stood on top of a stool to be at Kelly's level. Stella had been moving just fine and Kelly was riding just fine, but Sam wanted an excuse to be close to Kelly and put her hands on her. Kelly almost wished Samantha would just climb onto Stella and ride with her so she could feel her chest pressed against her back, her breath on her neck and her toned arms wrapped around her. Between Samantha's touches and her own racing thoughts, Kelly couldn't hold back the intense arousal she felt between her legs.

"Okay, just like that. You look beautiful," Sam whispered loud enough for Kelly to hear. When she looked at Sam she revised her speech, but Sam couldn't revise the look of wanting on her face, "I mean, your stance, the horse, you both look great!"

Sam hopped off of the stool and began to lead Stella out of the corral area with Kelly on top, all the while keeping her body extremely close to Kelly's. "I have the perfect trail in mind," Sam said as she began walking Stella down one of the dirt roads and towards a slightly wooded area that didn't appear to have any other horse or people traffic.

"Aren't you going to ride with me?" asked Kelly.

"Not today hun. My attention is focused solely on you and making sure you have a comfortable and pleasant first time riding experience. Plus, I'm enjoying every minute of it," Samantha said with a wink.

As they walked along the trail, Kelly was surprised by how confident she felt riding Stella. She was certain it had everything to do with the way Sam expertly and lovingly handle Stella and also by the way she patiently instructed her. Kelly couldn't help but notice she didn't see any of the trail marker signs that she saw when she was hiking the previous day with the other ranch guests. "This isn't part of the main trail, is it?" she asked Sam curiously.

"Nope, this is a special trail," Sam replied giving her a suggestive smile. Kelly wondered what she might be implying, but she already trusted Sam. Sam hadn't let her fall off of Stella and she certainly seemed to know what to do to keep the massive beast she was riding on sure-footed, calm and happy.

"I think I hear water," Kelly commented. Sam directed Stella down an even more secluded path, and just around a bend a beautiful brook emerged. Kelly almost didn't see it due to the trees and high grass that were growing near that water. Stella eagerly trotted towards it for a drink without Kelly expecting it. "Woah," she called out nervously. Sam stopped Stella and lifted her arms up to help Kelly down. She laughed and welcomed Samantha's steady arms around her waist as she guided Kelly slowly down to the ground.

As they stood face-to-face with just inches between them, it took every ounce of restraint for Kelly to not throw herself at Sam. Searching deeply into her eyes, Kelly silently recounted all of Sam's amazing qualities. She was incredibly pleasant, she had a depth about her that many women don't, she was self sufficient, she obviously cared for animals, and she smelled and looked so damn good! "Guess she was thirsty," Kelly commented trying to make conversation. Sam quickly silenced Kelly with a kiss, her lips brushing softly against hers as if it were a test, to see if she would get slapped or not. "Wow," Kelly whispered as Sam pulled away. Sam's eyes searched Kelly's reaction to see what she might do or say next. Kelly answered her silent query by placing her arms around Sam to pull her into a deeper kiss, displaying that Kelly wanted her just as much as Samantha wanted her.

"I don't want you to think that I do this all the time" Samantha whispered, hoping she wasn't about to do something to make her lose her job.

"I know you don't," Kelly whispered back to her, as her fingers silently began unfastening the buttons of Sam's shirt. By the quickening of Sam's breath, Kelly could already tell that she was aroused, just as she was. In fact, Kelly had been aroused for awhile now, ever since Sam started making all those gentle grazes against her while helping her with Stella and speaking instructions with hidden innuendo.

Samantha put her hands on top of Kelly's, signaling her to pause. "Wait, just a minute," Sam smiled as she took Stella's reins and tied them securely around a tree. Stella immediately went about grazing on some grass, too busy to notice too much what was happening. After Stella had been taken care of, Sam resumed her position beside Kelly. Her hands were back on Sam's shirt now and Sam thought that for someone who was hesitant of horses, Kelly certainly didn't seem hesitant to initiate some afternoon delight in the woods. After unfastening the last of the buttons, Kelly glided the shirt off of Samantha's body and tossed it to the ground. She then worked her fingers inside the waistband of Sam's jeans, unzipping and pulling them down her legs as Samantha then stepped out of them and stood before Kelly now wearing only a pair of panties and her cowboy boots. Kelly stood silently for a moment, her eyes openly admiring Samantha's perfect form. The smooth skin of Sam's large breasts were lighter than the tanned skinned on her arms, neck and face, and even though it was hot outside, Sam's rose colored nipples became hard and looked to be begging for some intimate attention. Samantha kept her eyes on Kelly as she slowly slid off her panties, revealing a smooth shaved pussy that Kelly was now dying to get a touch and taste of.

"Too bad we don't have a blanket," Kelly said, staring hungrily at Samantha's nudeness.

Samantha smiled and retrieved her shirt from the ground. She spread it on the ground and then motioned for Kelly to lay down on it. Samantha's desire for Kelly grew with intensity as she watched Kelly position herself suggestively on her shirt. Lying on her back with her knees bent up and resting on her elbows, Kelly's sundress rode up to the tops of her thighs and Samantha had a clear view of her pink lace panties. Never taking her eyes off of Kelly, Sam's hands reached down to finish what Kelly had started and tugged off her cowboy boots and socks, leaving her wearing nothing but her cowboy hat, and looking even more beautiful than Kelly had imagined she'd be.

"Take you sundress off for me," Samantha gently commanded, still standing above Kelly. Kelly sat up and pulled her sundress over her head in one quick movement. She then reached behind her back to unfasten her bra, sliding it off to expose her perky breasts. Her fingers then reached under the waistband of her panties, and leaning back she pulled them off her hips and up the length of her legs before tossing them off to the side. As she reached towards her boots, Samantha stopped her. "Keep your cowboy boots on," she said, as Samantha laid her naked body next to hers.

Kelly lay on her back as Samantha softly outlined the contours of her face and neck with her fingers. Sam was propped up on one arm, so her face was above Kelly's. "You are so beautiful," Samantha whispered as she leaned down to kiss her, thinking how her lips felt as soft as flower petals and she smelled as good as flowers too. Their kisses started off tender and sweet, before transitioning into a deeply passionate dance of lips and tongues. Kelly could feel every inch of her body respond to Samantha's touch and scent, as her fingers pulled her face even tighter into hers, knocking her hat to the ground. Kelly's body was already electrified by Samantha's kisses, and when she felt her pussy lips being gently parted by her fingers, an involuntary moan escaped from Kelly's mouth. Sam's fingers slowly glided along the soft delicate folds of her pussy until she reached her clit. When Sam's finger started tracing circles around her erect bud, Kelly's breath quickened as she arched her back and leaned her full body weight into the side of Sam's body. Sam slid a finger into her moistness as her thumb continued massaging. Kelly had one hand caressing Samantha's hips and ass, while she placed her other hand on top of Sam's, pressing her fingers in even deeper inside her. Feeling lightening bolts of heat surge through her belly and her pussy start to pulse around Samantha's finger, Kelly knew that it wouldn't take much for her to cum, yet she didn't want to cum just yet.

When Kelly could not stand it anymore, she broke away from Sam's kisses to allow another string of moans to escape her. Samantha glanced over at Stella who didn't seem to be bothered by the sounds of their intimate liaison. Kelly fell backwards, her body already reveling in the waves of pleasure Sam had instigated in her. Samantha was only beginning. Sam rose from the ground and positioned herself between Kelly's legs. Parting her thighs open further, Sam leaned in and gently slid her tongue between the parted folds of Kelly's wet pussy. Sam's tongue slowly lapped at her wetness, and she reinserted a finger inside of Kelly's cunt and began thrusting it slowly, and then faster, in and out, and in and out. Kelly bucked her hips in rhythm with Samantha's finger, raising her ass off of the ground and her hands clutching at the loose grass on either side of Samantha's now rumpled shirt that she was laying on. Samantha slowed her movements as she felt Kelly's body inch closer and closer to climax, and she crawled up Kelly's body to suck on her hard, erect nipples. Kelly grasped at Sam's ass as Sam sucked and nibbled on her tits while rubbing her hips back and forth against Kelly's mound. Samantha grabbed onto one of Kelly's breasts with one hand while reaching down with the other, to this time insert two fingers into Kelly's very wet pussy while simultaneously rubbing her clit with her thumb. Moving her mouth up to Kelly's, Samantha kissed her deep and hungrily as she finger fucked her in a steady fast rhythm. More moans managed to escape Kelly's mouth as her orgasm slammed into her without warning, and Kelly's body trembled against Samantha's mouth and hand and waves of ecstasy rippled throughout her body.

Beads of sweat covered Kelly's perfect perky tits, and her erect nipples taunted and begged for more attention. Just as Sam was leaning down, Kelly stopped her with her hand. "Sam, I want to return the pleasure. Kneel over my mouth."

Samantha's pussy was already throbbing for attention, and now this pretty little ranch guest was offering to give her some. Samantha positioned her knees on either side of Kelly's head and lowered her pussy lips just over Kelly's mouth. Samantha's body shook when she first felt Kelly's fingers tickle and stroke at her pussy lips. "Oh, she is a tease," Samantha thought to herself. Kelly's hands caressed and squeezed at Samantha's firm ass as her lips slowly licked around and just between the slit of Sam's pussy. Sam's knees started to tremble at the expert way Kelly was teasing her and she couldn't imagine what it would be like if the two of them were able to spend an entire day and night together. Sam's eyes rolled shut as Kelly's tongue now found her clit and flicked at it softly back and forth. Her fingers spread open Sam's pussy lips and while still licking at her bud, Kelly inserted her thumb into Sam's cunt while one of her fingers flicked at the tight opening of her ass. "Holy shit!" exclaimed Sam, as colors flashed behind her closed eyelids. Samantha wasn't sure what exactly Kelly was doing with her thumb, but her pussy was throbbing and pulsing louder and faster than her heart was. Rocking her pussy against Kelly's mouth and hands, Samantha put her hands on the front of her thighs to keep her balance, as she felt her body begin to contract and tremble. Sam thought she felt Kelly's finger slide in her ass as she climaxed, and Samantha bayed out in pleasure to the wilderness.

As the waves of pleasure subsided, Samantha laid back down next to Kelly, her fingers gently tracing patterns along Kelly's stomach and breasts. She nestled up to Sam, resting her head on her shoulder and Sam leaned in to sniff the flowery aroma of Kelly's soft hair. They enjoyed the after glow in silence, until a soft whinny from Stella broke the hypnotic spell in the air. "I think that might be our cue," Samantha whispered in Kelly's ear. "I would really like to see you again while you're here at the ranch, and if you like, even after you leave the ranch to return home."

Kelly turned her head to look up at Samantha and knew by the look in her eye that she was being sincere. "Well, I certainly like that thought. I think I would very much enjoy getting to better know cowgirl Samantha from New Mexico," she replied with smile.

"And, don't forget Stella."

"And, of course I wouldn't forget Stella," she replied laughing.

"Alright my pretty thing, I think we better get dressed and let Stella get some more exercise." After they both dressed and brushed all the loose grass and twigs from their clothing and hair, Samantha helped Kelly back up into Stella's saddle. After untying her reins from the tree where she was secured, Samantha handed her cowboy hat up to Kelly.

"Here, I would like for you to wear this."

"Wow, you're really going to let me wear your hat?" Kelly asked as she positioned Sam's hat on her head.

"Well, when a cowboy or cowgirl puts their hat on a lady it means that they like her and are interested in her."

"I'm flattered! And, by the way Sam, I happen to like you and am interested in you as well."

Samantha guided Stella and Kelly back down the trail towards the horse barn, the three of them enjoying the moment in silence, while Kelly was secretly marveling at how amazing and promising her erotic Wild West vacation was turning out to be.

Story #8

Cowgirl Winter: One Snowy Romance

Erin stared out of the large western facing window in her cabin, as the sun was settling behind the mountains that graced her ten acres of land in White Fish, Montana. She was trying to perfectly match her paint colors to the shades of orange and red of the setting sun, and their unique winter hues as the colors reflected off of the cold, frosty air. Dabbing her paintbrush onto her palate, she resisted the urge to mix more white into the rustic color she had already created. Erin always took great care in the planning and execution of her paintings, and she was a perfectionist when it came to all the smaller details of her paintings. She believed it was all those perfected smaller details that made her paintings "pop" and come to life with realism.

"I am not letting you get away," she said out loud to herself, as she maintained her feverish pace of painting at her easel.

Since leaving Chicago, Erin's primary objects of artistic creation were the beautiful landscapes of the mountains, foothills and plains of Montana that now surrounded the land around her. In Chicago she had primarily painted people or strangers in the city's north side area where she lived, and her paintings were wildly popular. She enjoyed capturing the emotion and details of a moment in a person's life, and most people were surprised by how well that was conveyed in her paintings. A woman embarking on a new phase in her life in her early thirties with no husband and kids, Erin suddenly found herself getting restless in the city and desiring to move to someplace much more rural and live a rustic country lifestyle. She also felt herself being pulled to paint life from a different perspective, and what better contrast to city living, than country living.

Erin had been in Montana for about six months now and things seemed to be falling into place. The cash she had earned from selling her prime location condo in Chicago was proving to be enough for her to live on, so that she could continue her vocation as an artist and work from home. The environment was exactly what Erin needed to let her creativity flow, and several art studios in the southwestern state region had already contacted her with interest in having her paintings put on display in their various locations across the states. The ten acre parcel that came with her cabin was definitely rustic, and she had a whole lot more living chores to contend with than she ever had while living in Chicago. There was a lot of physical labor involved, and between that and her painting, Erin was certainly never bored, was in the best shape of her life, and she found that to be true of her mind as well as her body. And, the more acclimated Erin got to all the aspects of living the country life, the less she struggled. That was... until the storm hit.

Erin knew that winter storms were common in Montana and her realtor had warned her about preparedness and self-sufficiency. As desolate as rural country living can be during the best of weather, it was twice as bad when the weather acted up. This storm was far beyond anything she had ever experienced in the city, where disruption in road travel, heat or electricity was always kept to a minimal, even in Chicago where winters can be rough. The snow hasn't let up for the past two days now, and sometime during the afternoon of the first day of blinding snow, her electricity, which was also her main source of heat, was knocked out. When she purchased the house, the realtor had also pointed out that there wasn't much cut wood on the property, which was for using in either the fireplace or the wood burning stove that she had in the cabin. Her property had an ample amount of trees, but they needed to be cut and the wood allowed to season for 6 months before it would be ready for use. Her realtor advised her when she moved in to immediately go out and start cutting some wood to stock, or to go out and buy some wood. Maybe it was because Erin was so used to her city life, where heat was available with just a turn of a thermostat dial, but she never got around to it and now she has been without electricity or heat for two days and no wood to remedy her circumstance. The winter storm was showing no signs of letting up and Erin was now deeply regretting that she overlooked that critical piece of helpful advice. And, there is only so much cold food a person can eat before everything is just horribly unappetizing and the only thing your body can feel is the constant intense chill that has permeated you, right down to your bones.

"You're not going to help me much without any wood, are you?" Erin said to the wood burning stove in her kitchen, watching her breath frost and hang suspended in the air in front of her. Deciding that she wasn't going to freeze to death, Erin decided to take action, which meant that she was going to have to face the even cooler air and more hostile conditions outside. She went to her bedroom to dress in as many layers as she could wrestle onto her body, and then tugged on her boots, hat, scarf and gloves. Erin did remember one stroke of good luck, the property had left her with a snowmobile and she was hoping that it had some gas in it so she could seek out some wood or help from a neighbor in the area. She hadn't officially introduced herself to any of her nearby neighbors since moving in six months ago, probably because of the distance situation. She approximated that the nearest neighbor was about two to three miles away. Attempting to travel that distance in the current extreme conditions wouldn't be the wisest of things to do, but traveling that distance by snowmobile would be quite doable…as long as the snowmobile worked.

After a few unsuccessful minutes of trying to start the snowmobile, the machine's motor finally turned over. Grateful beyond belief, Erin settled herself onto the seat and drove the machine around in a few circles before she finally got the hang of it. She then aimed the machine towards the direction of what she knew to be her nearest neighbor and hoped with all her might that someone would be there when she arrived. The snowmobile didn't have a windshield, so the prickly blowing snow against her face only served to further induce her body into a freezing state, but her determination to find someone to help her was enough to ignore the feeling of not being able to feel anything. The harshly blowing snow also made it hard to see, but Erin had a general idea of where she was going. Thankfully it was daylight hours otherwise she was sure she would get lost due to still being so unfamiliar with the surrounding area and trying to travel in these conditions. After maneuvering the snowmobile through the deep snow, she finally caught sight of her nearest neighbor. She didn't see any lights on, but she hadn't expected to. "Please be home, please be home, please be home," she kept saying to herself. She got within about half of a mile from the house, when the snowmobile died and she couldn't get it restarted. She figured it was most likely because it ran out of gas, so she rewrapped her scarf tightly around her face and started to walk the remaining distance to the house. By the time she reached the door she was sure she had frostbite on her face.

Erin knocked on the door with frozen knuckles, attempting to stomp down the snow as best as she could. Her heart leaped with relief when she heard the door being opened, which was then immediately followed by pleasant surprise at the sight of a very attractive female standing in the open doorway. She looked to be around her age, and she greeted Erin with a look of confusion mixed with genuine concern.

"Hello there. My goodness, what are you doing out in this storm?" the woman asked as she eyeballed the gorgeous frozen woman who has seemed to stumble upon her door step out of nowhere. The woman was briefly tempted to follow-up her inquiry with a flirtatious response and ask this Sandra Bullock look a-like if she was late for her movie star job when the woman began to speak, but given the circumstance she thought better of it. In fact, she somehow already knew that the half frozen woman on her doorstep was in some sort of predicament, because nobody in their right mind would attempt to travel out in these conditions unless it was absolutely necessary.

"Hello. You don't know me, but I just moved to the area six months ago and I live a little more than two miles from here," Erin started to explain. "My electricity went out two days ago, and I foolishly didn't stock up on any wood, so I have no way to heat my house. I was starting to worry that I might freeze to death, so I decided to seek out some help and that's why I'm here. I…I can pay you…for any extra wood that you might be able to offer, and…and, I promise that…that as soon as the storm is over I…I will get out and stock up on wood for my place." Erin started fumbling over her words a bit as she was talking, and she wasn't sure if it was because her body was so cold or if she was distracted by the incredibly beautiful presence standing in front of her. Pert braless breasts were clearly visible, even in the woman's tightly buttoned flannel shirt, and just the right tightness jeans hugged her ass and legs in all the right places. And peeking out from her tresses of brown hair, which were being wildly whipped around her face by the wind, were the deepest most mesmerizing brown eyes Erin had ever seen.

The woman raised her eyebrows at Erin, "How did you get here?" she interrupted, her eyes scanning past her, mostly likely looking for a vehicle or some other clue as to how she landed on her doorstep. Erin was grateful for the verbal intervention. She had suddenly lost track of everything she was going to say, after having laid eyes on the intoxicatingly beautiful woman that she realized was her neighbor.

"I…I took a snowmobile for most of the way, but it died out on me about half a mile back. I walked the rest of the way."

"You must be frozen to the core!" the woman said, "My name is Casey, and first things first. Come inside and let's get you warmed up," Casey said opening the door all the way for her to come inside. Erin walked through the doorway, and the instant feeling of warmth almost made her crumble with relief. But, what was odd, was the fact that she was almost manic just minutes before, in search of heat or a heating solution, and now this woman's presence has distracted her discomfort to such a point that she was immediately looking for signs of a spouse or partner in her home. Erin wasn't seeing any, and the fact that the woman was not wearing a wedding ring or commitment type looking ring, did not go unnoticed.

"I am so sorry to intrude, but I was getting desperate and didn't know what else to do." Erin started explaining again. "I'm a city girl from Chicago, so I guess I underestimated the self-sufficiency needed for country life."

"It's quite alright, and you are not intruding," Casey said, "I know how intense Montana storms can be, and if this is your first winter here, it's probably going to seem a little overwhelming for a city girl like yourself. You are always welcome to come by if you need anything, but I am surprised that your husband didn't think to keep some wood around," Casey said as she extended an arm to welcome Erin into her expansive living room. Her last remark was also a little bit of a fishing expedition, to see if the pretty snow covered lady in her house was married or attached in any way.

"Thank you for being so understanding, and to answer your question, "no", no husband, no boyfriend, no girlfriend. It's just me."

"Gotcha. Sorry if I was being presumptuous or rude." Erin's last remark definitely caught Casey's attention, when she included not having a girlfriend in her response.

"No, you're not being rude it's an obvious general question. Actually, I'm long since divorced. I was married briefly after college, but quickly realized that I prefer being with women so my marriage ended hastily without any children." Erin explained turning to directly face Casey, and drink in those deep brown eyes that so quickly held her fancy. Erin's artistic mind instantly wanted to capture the woman's gorgeous face and mesmerizing eyes with her skilled hand and a paint brush, and then hang that picture somewhere in her house where she could look at it everyday.

"How about some nice hot coffee….um,…?" Casey started as she began to walk past the beautiful woman who sat shivering in her living room. "I'm sorry I didn't catch your name."

"I'm sorry. I'm Erin," she replied, in a melodic voice that Casey was finding quite irresistible.

"Erin." Casey repeated slowly out loud. "That is a lovely name." Walking over to her own wood burning stove, she started gathering the supplies to brew a pot of coffee. "Erin, why don't you get comfortable near the fireplace, it will help warm you up faster until I can get this hot coffee made for you."

Sitting down on the floor in front of the fireplace, Erin had to admit how welcoming the heat radiating off of the burning logs felt. After a of couple minutes, she was actually warm enough to remove her hat, scarf, gloves and coat. Her multiple under-layers of clothing were still damp however, so she moved a little closer to the fire so that they might dry as well. "So, what makes a city girl from Chicago decide she wants to move out to a rural area like Montana?" Casey asked, as she handed Erin a steaming hot cup of fresh coffee.

"Aahh, that was just what I needed," Erin moaned as she took a couple sips of the warm java. "Well, I found myself suddenly needing to be away from the bustle of city life, and I wanted to connect with nature and the more simple aspects of country living. So, I bought the ten acres with the cabin on it that's just north of here. I knew it was going to be quite different from city living, but I guess I underestimated by just how much. I'm embarrassed to say that I didn't prepare myself well, and that I don't even have any cut wood for heat." Casey nodded empathetically as she listened to Erin, and Erin couldn't help but notice how absolutely hypnotizing Casey's eye contact was. She couldn't explain it. Erin had literally just met her, but Casey's attentiveness and concern was so comforting, that Erin literally felt like she could talk to her all day and about anything at all.

"Well, with ten acres to be responsible for, you'll be able to get the hang of things pretty quickly. As long as you aren't opposed to some physical labor, which you don't look like you are," Casey said smiling appreciating that Erin had removed some of her outerwear clothing. "I run my main ranch here, as well as manage a handful of others that I have spread across over one hundred acres. That's of course far too much to handle alone, so I have lots of ranch hands that are permanent residents in all of my ranch houses, except this on. I'd also be more than happy to help show you some of the best and most efficient ways to manage your home, especially when it comes to sticking it out through the harsher weather months."

"Wow, one hundred acres!" Erin exclaimed as she took another sip of her coffee. It was the first hot thing she had consumed in days and it tasted like heaven on her tongue. Looking at Casey, her mind was filling with some other things she wanted to taste, to see if they were also just as heavenly. It had been too long since she had been intimate with someone. Erin knew there was no shame in desiring this woman, but she needed to scout the situation first. "Your husband and kids don't mind all the work involved in keeping up with one hundred acres?" Erin inquired, purposely probing the idea of marriage and family to size up the situation of her new wonder woman hero in flannel.

"It's just me," Casey said quickly, almost too quickly. She didn't want to come across like some horny teenager, but her beautiful new neighbor was appearing to be everything that Casey was looking for. She couldn't help but think this circumstance was not just luck, maybe it was fate too, "I am split from my ex as well, and my kids both live out of state with their mother," she admitted freely to Erin as she went to grab the coffee pot and refill their mugs. "My partner and I adopted two children, but she didn't much care for the country way of life, and she and the kids moved back to Phoenix where she has family. The kids come out to stay with me during the summers."

"She?" confirmed Erin. "So, you also prefer women?"

"Yes, new neighbor, I also prefer women. I hope that does not bother you," replied Casey, silently hoping that the vibes that she had been picking up from Erin weren't just her imagination.

"Of course it does not bother me. I'm just pleasantly surprised to know that there are women like me... like us... out here in Montana."

"Yes, women like us are out here, we just can't live as openly as you can in the bigger cities. So, don't go wearing any rainbow colored bandanas or shirts when you go into town." Casey replied with a laugh.

"Duly noted."

"Sugar?" Casey asked, as she offered a small porcelain bowl to Erin.

"I would love some...hun," Erin replied with a jester's smile, holding out her mug. Casey smiled back with a laugh. Erin's play on words, suggesting that Casey had called her 'sugar' when offering her sweetener for her coffee, was cute and clever. This woman was turning out to be too good to be true. She was drop dead beautiful, smart and witty. Casey's concern for helping Erin out in a time of need was absolutely genuine, yet instead of helping her and then getting her out of her house right away, Casey found herself thoroughly enjoying Erin's company and she was hoping that she could find a way to extend Erin's stay as long as possible. Admittedly, it could get lonely, even for someone who was used to living out in the country, but Casey's interest in Erin was proving to be more than just neighborly.

Casey added a couple sugar cubes to her own coffee and then resumed her spot next to Erin in front of the fireplace. "Well Erin, you are certainly more than welcome to stay as long as you want until the storm passes over and the electricity gets restored so that you have heat at your place. I have plenty of room, food and wood. It's just..." Casey hesitated, her mind filling with what she needed to say before she spit it out. Erin was going to need clean, dry clothes to wear and visions of Erin wandering around the house out of her frozen clothes, naked, made Casey's cheeks flush and burn with both embarrassment and lust.

"It's just what?" Erin inquired, urging Casey to continue. She was hoping Casey's next words were not the words that threw her back out into the storm. Erin had done a spouse check. She had made sure to ask about kids. What could possibly be said to suggest that she should go back to her own cold and lonely house?

"Well," Casey said with a small suggestive smile, allowing her eyes to look Erin up and down unabashedly before she bluntly stated, "if you decide you would like to stay, you should really get out of those wet clothes. You can wear whatever is around here that'll fit you."

Casey' eyes boldly lingering across her body caused an instant internal reaction. Erin could now feel a surge of heat, which happened to be located in the uppermost region between her legs, when Casey boldly stated that she should get out of her clothes. In her mind she saw flashes of Casey's bare skin against hers, and her lips exploring areas that had long since gone numb.

"Yes, yes I would like to stay," Erin said rising from her place in front of the fireplace, wondering if Casey could read her thoughts. "I don't mind wearing whatever you have that is clean and dry, and it would be most appreciated," she replied, her hands peeling away another layer of clothing. Casey's eyes were so focused on Erin's fingers unfastening the buttons on yet another layer of her snow soaked clothing that she nearly missed the coffee table when she went to put down her empty coffee mug.

"Well, you just, uh," Casey was suddenly finding it hard to speak. Erin's hands kept moving and it was making her lose focus on everything else. The strong cowgirl in Casey wanted to just take over and do it for her. Casey wanted Erin to let her manage things so that she could do it the best way she saw fit. "Come on, follow me," Casey finally spit out. "Let me show you around so you can pick a room to stay in. I promise you, they are all very clean and comfortable. Cowgirls take pride in our horses, land and property, and we always keep them in tip-top condition."

"That sounds lovely. Is it ok if I first take off a few more layers of these wet clothes and leave them here by the fire to dry? I think keeping them on is what's preventing me from getting thoroughly warm." Erin peeled off another layer of wet clothing articles, while silently desiring to take all her clothes off and simply stand before Casey naked. Erin wondered if she would be prepared for that. Would she be prepared for Erin's brown hair falling down around her shoulders in wet, tight, curls? Would she be prepared for her erect nipples, assaulted from the icy weather and now awaiting to be assaulted by her tongue? Would she be prepared to entwine her own nakedness around Erin's in a way that would make them both completely occupied with each other for days of raw love making? Perhaps she was thinking too boldly, but she noticed the way Casey was now looking at her.

"Of course it's okay," Casey answered, trying not to let her voice give away her immense desire to just strip Erin naked herself and make love to her right in front of the fireplace. Casey's eyes watched intently as Erin peeled off almost all of her remaining layers. The poor thing had tried to dress for the trip, but a Montana snow storm knows no boundaries. She was wet right down to her last sweater, which also had been completely soaked through, and Casey couldn't help but notice the outline of a black bra underneath the wet, thin fabric. It was the style of a bra with the lovely U-shapes that curved and dipped so beautifully on the skin of a woman's breast. Trying not to stare too much, Casey extended a hand out to Erin. It was a gentle gesture, and perhaps it would help peel her eyes off of Erin's perfectly studded nipples that were prominently protruding from that luscious bra.

Erin took Casey's hand and let her lead her through the expansive house to where the bedrooms were. Erin knew that her sweater was soaked through, and by the way Casey was staring at her tits, it was obvious that her erect nipples were poking through the fabric. But it's not like she could take it off right then and there. Casey was going to show her the living arrangements first. Plus, Erin needed to wait for the right opportunity to see if things between them might get a little more heated that what the fireplace and coffee could offer.

"This room has only a twin bed," Casey said as she gestured inside one of the bedrooms. The room was fairly dark and cold, but Erin noticed that it had its own small fireplace situated across from the bed. "This room has a full bed instead, and a small fireplace of its own as well," Casey pointed out as they entered the third bedroom, and Erin couldn't help but notice that the rooms were indeed well kept and clean just like Casey said. They also looked like they had already had another woman's touch. It was something that Erin would've been suspicious of had she not already known that Casey was split from her ex.

"And, this room has a nice big adjacent bathroom for you to freshen up in," Casey said, as she pushed open another door. "In fact, you should really take a nice hot bath to warm up. I put in a brand new Jacuzzi style bathtub this past summer, and I have to say, it's pretty darn comfortable." Erin followed behind Casey into the room. It looked like it had been the room Casey was occupying before Erin had knocked on her door. There were candles everywhere and an overturned book was lying on the bed with a page bent back keeping Casey's place. "Go ahead, take a peek into the master bath," Casey motioned to the adjoining door.

"Wow! That is hardly a bathtub Casey. It's a small pool!"

"Well, it's definitely a luxury I enjoy after a hard day's work on the ranch," Casey replied laughing. "Seriously, why don't you take a bath? I would be happy to bring up some boiling water. Probably can't fill it too much, but it'll be enough to get you warmed up."

Erin hesitated slightly. Did she really want this poor woman carrying boiling water all the way to this room just for her? "Oh Casey, it seems like such an inconvenience. Maybe I just need to borrow a robe or a shirt, I…" she started before Casey interrupted her.

"Nonsense! Consider it done. I'll start boiling some water now. Besides, I can see that you're shivering again," Casey said while shuffling around her so that she could make her way to the kitchen. As Casey passed by, her fingers brushed against Erin ever so slightly, and she felt her body shiver. "See?" Casey whispered. "You're shivering again." Erin silently yearned for Casey to locate the cause of those particular shivers, and she felt a little weak in the knees. All of the sudden a hot bath, even if it was only a partial bath, sounded like a good idea.

"Ok, if you're absolutely certain it is no trouble," Erin responded softly. And honestly, she didn't want to resist anything Casey had to offer. Watching Casey bring the boiling water to the bathtub took longer than Erin thought it would, but then again, of course it would take time to boil large amounts of water. Erin sat down on the side of the tub and enjoyed the view being offered each time Casey reentered the bathroom to splash more hot water into the tub. "I really appreciate you doing this for me."

"Don't mention it," Casey said as she poured in another bucket of steaming water. The steam was making sweat pour down her face, and Casey stopped to unfasten a handful of buttons on her flannel shirt. Erin tried not to gasp, as she caught glimpse of Casey's firm pert tits peaking out from behind the parted shirt fabric, and she could feel herself moisten at the sight of Casey's small pink nipples becoming erect as the cool room air brushed across them.

"I just don't know how I can make it up to you," Erin said twirling her hair around her fingers suggestively. It was a cheap line, yes, but by the way Casey looked away from her, and then back suddenly, it was quite clear that Casey was on to her train of thought. She put the empty bucket down on the floor and stared boldly into Erin's eyes, before allowing her own to trail down Erin's neck, chest and legs, and then back up to her beautiful mouth. Erin noticed Casey's chest start to heave as her breath quickened, and she knew Casey was contemplating the moment.

In two long strides, Casey stood in front of Erin and pulled her up off the edge of the bathtub. Looking intensely into her eyes, Casey saw the look that she was searching for, the look that said…"take me". Casey's body was screaming inside, but she pushed those primal urges aside for a moment to show some cowgirl chivalry as well as to make sure that she was actually being invited to partake in the carnal pleasures she was pretty sure were suggestively being offered.

Casey glanced towards the tub and then back into Erin's pretty blue eyes. "Are you suggesting I take a bath with you?"

"I hope I'm not being too forward, but yes, that is what I'm suggesting," Erin whispered in reply. "I think the tub is full enough," she added. "If you'd like to join me, why don't you help me off with the rest of my wet clothes?"

Casey gave Erin her answer by leaning in and kissing her mouth with soft, passionate kisses, as her hands slowly pulled Erin's wet sweater off and tossing it to the floor. As her fingers fumbled with the clasp of Erin's bra, Casey couldn't help but notice how cold Erin's skin was, and she wanted desperately to warm Erin's beautiful body in every way that she knew how. Once she released the bra and slid it down and off Erin's arms, Casey's hands slowly traced up along Erin's slender sides until they reached her full round breasts, and she gently massaged the cold mounds in her hands while letting her lips and tongue explore Erin's mouth. Casey then moved her hands down to unzip Erin's wet pants and after some tugging, because they were sticking to her skin, she managed to slide them off her legs. What a beautiful sight she was.

"Here, let me help you into the hot water," Casey said holding out a hand for her. Erin took her hand and stepped into the large tub, never taking her eyes off of Casey as she slid her body down into the water.

The tub was only half-filled with water, which conveniently stopped just below her full tits, and Casey just stood there for a moment enjoying the incredible view.

"Join me?" Erin invited Casey, eager for her to be naked just as she was. She didn't have to ask twice. Casey first tugged off her cowboy boots and dropped them near the bathroom door, before kicking shut the door with her foot to try and contain what little heat the hot water was giving off in the bathroom. Casey's fingers then quickly unbuttoned her denim jeans before sliding them down her legs, along with a pair of red panties that she had been wearing, revealing gymnastic like toned legs that made Erin squirm in the water. With only a few remaining buttons to unfasten on her shirt, in seconds Casey had tugged off her flannel cover fully revealing those pretty pert tits that Erin had gotten a peak of earlier. Erin's hands gripped at the side of the bathtub, enjoying the view and eager to feel Casey's naked body pressed up against her.

Casey stepped into the half filled tub of water and as they both lay back in the tub, Erin appreciated how large the bathtub was. They had more than enough room for both of their bodies, and on either side of them were small pockets of space that allowed both of them to intertwine their legs around one another. Casey leaned Erin against the side of the tub first, her toned, lean legs straddling her hips while she kissed her deeply. The warm water swirling around them was warm and sensuous and Erin couldn't tell where her aching lubrication stopped and the warm water started. Casey's hand cupped her tits, no longer cold but warm from the water, and she gently pinched and tugged at her nipples until they sprung erect in her fingers. Erin leaned back against the tub and Casey leaned down to suck and lick at her beautiful breasts. Erin's fingers played with Casey's thick brown hair, and as her hips lifted upwards she could feel Casey's spread pussy lips press down against her thigh. Casey's hands took over where her mouth left off, and as she squeezed and massaged Erin's plump tits, her lips came up to taste some more of those sensual kisses on Erin's soft lips.

As their kisses deepened, Erin gently pushed against Casey, guiding her body towards the opposite side of the tub and positioning her ass onto one of the top steps, while small gentle waves splashed around their bodies as they moved. With Casey's body now out of the water, Erin guided apart her legs and lowered herself into the water in between Casey's smooth thighs. Casey pressed her hands against the edge of the tub to steady herself, while watching as Erin's tongue licked and kissed up and down her thighs. Her mouth felt so soft against her skin and when Erin's tongue made its first electrifying pass across Casey's pussy lips, Casey's hips almost lurched upward in response. Slowly Erin traced her tongue in between Casey's smooth folds as her hands reached up to pinch at Casey's nipples. Casey's mind was silently racing, while her body was outwardly responding. Ripples of sensation and heat were coursing through her belly, and again Casey's hips almost lurched upward when she felt a couple fingers slide into her wet cunt. Erin used her free hand to spread a part Casey's pussy lips and locate her erect clit. While sliding her fingers slowly in and out, Erin alternated between using her mouth and fingers to tease at Casey's bud. Casey's pussy was tight and gripped intimately at Erin's fingers, coating them with her sweet fragrant juices. Erin stood up in the tub so that she could kiss Casey, never removing her fingers from the gorgeous cowgirl's moistness. Casey kissed Erin feverishly as she took a hand to pull Erin's body closer against her so that she could feel her tits press against her. Erin increased the speed of her thrusting, finger fucking Casey at a steady hungry pace. This time, Casey's hips did come up off of the tub step and she bucked her hips in rhythm against Erin's hand. Their bodies moved like an erotic tango, until Casey's body slipped past the point of no return and she tensed and twitched as her orgasm rippled through her body. When Casey's body relaxed, they both slipped back into the cooling water, their mouths still hungrily seeking out each other's lips.

Casey's hands were particularly commanding as she stood and pulled

Erin up out of the water with her. Casey spread a huge towel onto the floor next to the tub and motioned for Erin to come lay on it. Parting Erin's thighs with her hands, Casey was eager to return the favor and she did not waste any time in locating Erin's clit. Gently parting her soft pussy lips with her fingers, Casey nibbled and sucked on the tiny bud until it became engorged and plump. Casey then inserted a couple of fingers into Erin's pussy and glided them back and forth at the same speed at which she was also now licking across her clit. Erin's tits jiggled as her body was being rocked by Casey's finger thrusts, faster….and faster….and faster. Coming up for air, Casey pulled out her fingers and licked Erin's sweet juices from them. Surprising Erin, Casey flipped her body around into a "69" position and Erin moaned in appreciation as Casey lowered her pussy above Erin's mouth. Using her fingers to spread a part Casey's lips, Erin lapped at her pussy, teasing her hole with her tongue and using a finger to make teasing slow circles around her clit. Casey could hardly concentrate as she buried her face into Erin's mound. Her smell was intoxicating and she tasted like sweet musky honey. There was no need for communication as they both silently knew that this was the next step in their quest for ultimate ecstasy. Casey's tongue flicked softly and rapidly across Erin's clit while her fingers tickled and tugged at her pussy lips. Erin pinched at Casey's swollen bud as she darted her tongue in and out of her hole, causing Casey's ass to quiver over her head. When Casey slipped a finger inside of Erin's pussy, she knew that she was close to cumming by the way Erin's pussy latched onto it. Gliding her finger in and out as she continued to lick at Erin's clit, Erin was no longer able to contain what was about to happen. Ramming a couple of her fingers into Casey's cunt, she started finger fucking her while her own body started to lose control. Casey held onto one of Erin's thighs as she never let up, and she continued to lick and finger fucked her until Erin's body twitched uncontrollably in ecstatic climax. As Casey felt Erin's legs go limp, she was surprised when she felt a couple fingers being reinserted into her pussy and then being thrust rapidly in and out, and in and out while Erin's tongue sucked at her clit. It took mere seconds for Casey's second orgasm to take her body over the edge, and her hands pushed against the floor as she tried not to let her body fall on top of Erin.

Finally rolling over onto the towel next to Erin, Casey grabbed at a second towel to throw over the top of them and then pulled Erin's body up tight up against her. Erin turned to face her, and kissed Casey with all the gentle passion her mind and body were feeling in that moment. Erin wasn't quite sure what was happening, but she sure liked it, reveling in the complex feeling of sensual contentment, security and romantic optimism.

"As long as you are here in Montana," Casey started, as she propped herself up on one elbow and looked intently into Erin's eyes, "you'll never have to be alone and unprepared again. I would like to take care of you and show you how to survive in this part of the country."

"Truly?" Erin replied, wide eyed.

"Truly." Casey returned. "I don't know what just happened, but it happened. You reawakened something in me I wasn't sure I'd ever feel again, and I don't know how to explain it, other than I would like to share my life with you and make you happy.

Erin replied to Casey's sentiment by snuggling into her shoulder and wrapping a leg and arm across her body. Erin knew in that moment that her move from Chicago to Montana was definitely the right choice. She had a beautiful home, a million landscapes to paint, and now Casey, an authentic and beautiful cowgirl who just declared that she would do anything for her. Earlier that day Erin had set out to find help from a blinding snowstorm. Who'd of thought that what she'd really find, was to be blindsided by one snowy romance. Life sure couldn't get much better than this.

VOLUME 3

Lesbian Women in Uniform Collection

Story #9

First Alarm Love

"**S**omething sure smells good. Hope we get time to eat whatever is cooking," Cheryl stated to one of her coworkers.

"You and me both," replied a guy named Ted. "It's Tony and Mike's turn to cook and they're making a big pot of chili.

Cheryl was a firefighter, and she was already pretty exhausted not even midway into her shift as her engine company has been responding to back-to-back emergency calls all morning. While many people think that firefighters just sit around in the fire station, just basically waiting around for an emergency, it's really an almost non-stop working job. In addition to responding to calls, you had to keep equipment and supplies constantly stocked, there is the transporting of patients to the emergency rooms, and then there was also the constant meetings and training in-between all of that. Being a firefighter is a very mentally and physically demanding vocation, and more often than not, your shifts were in constant work mode with very little time to relax. Therefore, you ate when you were able to, and grabbed a quick shower whenever you were able to during a shift. Additionally, every crew had station duties, including rotating kitchen duty. Today it apparently was Tony and Mike's turn on kitchen duty, and both were quite skilled in culinary creation.

Cheryl was glad that there was a pause in the constant stream of emergency calls, and while her stomach grumbled with intense hunger, her body itched for a quick hot shower to wash away the several layers of soot and sweat from the mornings calls. Cheryl grabbed her bag and headed toward the women's locker room for a shower. On her way, she passed through the kitchen area where Tony gave her a brotherly slap on the shoulder. "Hey, you're not boycotting my famous chili are you?" he said laughing.

Cheryl lightly punched Tony in the arm, "Hell no. Can't wait to dig in. Just need a quick shower before chow."

As Cheryl showered, she thought back on how far she has come with her relationship with her coworkers. She has been with the New York Fire Department for ten years now, and the first few years were admittedly rough. Cheryl has a beautiful tomboy look about her, naturally blond hair, and a tight, toned body. The guys in the firehouse initially would give her a hard time, as well as hit on her, every single shift when she just started working. This was partly because they were testing her, just like they would any other new rookie on the department, and partly because they were.....well, guys. Cheryl was extremely nervous about how much to reveal about her life at first, because you can't be part of a firehouse crew and be elusive. A firehouse crew is your family. Cheryl spent the first couple years proving her capabilities as a firefighter, and talked about her family just as any other guy would. However, she masterfully managed to skirt around the dating and relationship questions by answering them ambiguously, while at the same time finally making it clear that she wasn't about to date one of her fellow male firefighters. It was during her third year that she finally felt comfortable enough to disclose to her shift coworkers that she was a lesbian, and when she did, it went much smoother than she could have hoped for. They kidded her, of course, but nobody stopped respecting her, nor did anybody start harassing her. In fact, Cheryl's relationship with the guys has progressed so well over the years that they treat her like a sister, and they even try to set her up with other women. A gesture Cheryl finds endearing. They are all very much a family, close knit and happy together. No-one ever gets left behind, and work doesn't always feel like work when you work with people who you cared about and they cared in return.

Cheryl managed to get in her shower, and the crew even found time to sit down to Tony's famous chili. They were eating and chatting when a call came in for an apartment fire. They all jumped into work mode as silverware was dropped and gear was quickly being put on, and the crew was pulling out of the station just a couple minutes later driving towards the address of the call. The sirens squealed as their trucks skillfully snaked their way through the busy streets of New York. They arrived to find utter chaos at the location, and police crews closing off streets and trying to manage crowd control for the fire trucks to make access to the fire hydrants and the apartment building. Cheryl and her crew immediately went to work to put out the fire, as well as search and evacuate any tenants that may be in the building. Thankfully the fire was contained to just one apartment, thanks to the crew's quick and skillful actions, yet there was still a significant amount of work to be done after the fire was extinguished to remove the heavy smoke that snaked its way through the apartment building hallways, as well as do a secondary search to make sure there were no physical injuries sustained by anybody. Cheryl remembered seeing a small dog in one of the apartments during her initial search, but when she tried to rescue it the dog kept running away from her. She went back up to search for it and Cheryl found the little dog cowering under a bed in one of the apartments that was still pretty heavily filled with smoke. He wasn't hurt, but probably did have some smoke inhalation. And, he was definitely scared, which was evident by his poor little body shaking against her arms. She took him out and down to the fire truck and gave him oxygen and some water to drink. As Cheryl was tending to the dog, a woman who appeared to be its owner came running up to her.

"Oh my God! Max! Is he okay?" she knelt down beside Cheryl, inspecting her dog.

"He's fine, just a little scared. There was a fire in one of your neighboring apartments, but your dog wasn't injured. I just gave him some water and oxygen, because of the smoke inhalation." Cheryl informed her.

After ensuring that her dog was ok, she introduced herself to Cheryl as

Max's mom, Tina. Tina was grateful that somebody cared so much for a little dog that they would go back up into a smoke filled building to rescue it. She found herself instantly attracted to Cheryl, whose soot stained face and thick protective gear around her body couldn't hide the fact that she was beautiful. She was the sexiest firefighter Tina had ever seen. Genuinely grateful, she thanked Cheryl profusely for going back up for her dog. She then retrieved Max from Cheryl's arms, letting them linger for just a moment, along with what she had hoped was telling eye contact, and then she left leaving Cheryl to finish up on the scene with her crew.

Though Cheryl was on duty, she couldn't help but acknowledge the stirring in her loins because of her encounter with the dog's owner. Not only was she gorgeous, but she was obviously compassionate towards animals, and very nice and engaging. Cheryl tore her mind away from Tina and returned to help her team with their clean-up activities. That night, after her shift was over, Cheryl headed home to her own apartment with thoughts of Tina filling her mind all through the night. She found herself inexplicably intrigued by her, and she just had to see her again. Fate always has a way of creating circumstance for paths to cross. Was today's moment at the apartment fire fate's way of ensuring that their paths crossed? Cheryl wasn't sure. She wasn't even sure if Tina was a lesbian. But, she was determined to find out.

A few days later, on her day off, Cheryl decided to head out to a small café for lunch. The café was conveniently located right across the street from the apartment building fire from a few days earlier, the same apartment building that Tina just so happened to live in. Cheryl desperately wanted to cross paths with Tina again, but she wasn't sure how to contact her. She was hoping that by having lunch across from Tina's building, she might be lucky enough to catch her coming or going while she was there, even though it was the middle of the day and Cheryl had no clue what Tina did for a living or what kind of work hours she had. She was obviously hoping to get lucky, and luck didn't happen unless you co-participate.

After finishing lunch and her third cup of coffee, Cheryl was feeling a bit deflated over any possibility of running into Tina. She motioned for her check and was pulling out her money to pay her bill when she caught glimpse of Tina coming out of the building with her dog Max on his leash. Cheryl quickly paid the bill, leaving a generous tip, and quickly made her way across the busy street to where Cheryl was minding Max as he went about his doggie business.

"I see Max is doing well," Cheryl called out as she made her way down the sidewalk.

Tina looked up, hesitated for a moment, and then smiled in recognition as Cheryl approached them.

Hello again. I'm Cheryl. I was one of the firefighters that responded to your apartment building fire a few days ago and brought Max down for some water and oxygen. How are the two of you doing?"

"We're both good, thanks to you and your fire crew," Tina responded with a smile that Cheryl was silently trying to interpret. "Well, you're obviously not working now since you're in civilian clothes. Do you live nearby?"

Feeling a flush rise to her cheeks, Cheryl was suddenly not too sure as to how much she wanted to share with Tina. She wanted to let her know she was interested in getting to know her, but she certainly didn't want to appear to be a stalker. Bending down to pet Max gave her a minute to organize her thoughts before speaking.

"I don't live too far. I was actually having lunch across the street just now when I saw you and Max coming out of the apartment. I figured I'd come see if little Max was doing ok, as well as him mom. In fact, I wouldn't mind knowing if you're doing ok over dinner or drinks, if you feel comfortable with that."

Tina paused for a moment, not sure how to respond, but feeling every part of her body scream "yes!" as she fidgeted with Max's leash.

Did Cheryl actually read her mind when she took Max from her after getting his dose of oxygen? Did Cheryl actually know that she was attracted to her, or was she just being friendly? Shit, why was it sometimes so hard for lesbians to be forthright? Finally, after a long pause, Tina responded. "Sure, dinner sounds great. Should I consider this to be a date?" throwing the ball of clarification back into Cheryl's court.

Cheryl smiled with relief, for Tina's hesitation in answering caused her a moment of anxiety. "I would like for it to be a date, but I will leave that up to you. I'm not sure if you are a lesbian, but I am. I picked up on a vibe when our paths crossed the other day, and I admittedly would very much like to get to know you, if you are interested."

"Yes, I'm definitely interested," laughed Tina. "I confess that I too picked up a vibe with you the other day, and I look forward to our future dinner date. Say, I'm sort of on my lunch break myself, and was about to take Max for a walk. Would you like to join us?"

"Sure, that'd be great."

Cheryl couldn't believe her luck. Not only did she actually cross paths again with Tina, but she agreed to have dinner with her, a dinner date to be specific, and she was taking a walk with her now. On their walk, they told each other a little bit about themselves. Tina was a freelance writer, which provided her with an extremely flexible schedule. She grew up in Westchester County; her family was middle class. She had a pretty stable childhood, with one brother. Her parents were still married and still living in the home she grew up in. Tina told her that after working a regular nine-five job and seeing no growth, she decided to quit and work for herself. It was the best thing she ever did, even if it meant less money. "Less stress, a schedule on my terms, and a lot more free time are priceless," Tina told her.

"Ok, enough about me. Tell me more about you. How can a firefighter be so caring, strong and sexy?" Tina said with a wink. "In fact, what made you decide to become a firefighter?" Tina queried.

"Well, it was actually a fire I was involved in when I was only five years old. My mom had left me with a neighbor so that she could go to the grocery store, and there was a lit candle that caught a curtain on fire. I was trapped in the room and was saved by a firefighter. I was truly grateful, and obviously so was my family. As soon as I fully understood what happened, I vowed to help other people the same way that the firefighter helped me. Now here I am." Cheryl found her conversation with Tina to flow smooth and effortlessly, the way it does when two people have known each other for years.....or, when two people instantly connect with one another.

The two women talked some more as they finished walking Tina's dog, exchanging numbers and making arrangements for their dinner date later in the week when Cheryl would have another day off of work. Tina needed to return to her apartment do work on a writing project, so the women parted with a hug in front of Tina's apartment building. Cheryl felt giddy with possibility and went home with a huge smile on her face. It gave her an amazing feeling to know that she would be going on a date with such an incredibly wonderful woman. There are many women who are beautiful on the outside, but to find one who was just as beautiful on the inside was a treasure. She didn't get that fake vibe from Tina that she often got from other women. She seemed genuinely nice, intelligent and sincerely interested in Cheryl. Cheryl found herself admittedly quite anxious for Friday evening to arrive.

The next several days passed with text messages and a couple short phone calls between the pair, and Tina agreed to meet Cheryl at the fire station where she worked after her shift ended on Friday. Cheryl brought along a nice outfit to change into, and was thankful there wasn't a last minute call that the crew needed to respond to, so she was able to take a quick shower, change and freshen up for her dinner with Tina. Tina arrived at 7:30 pm, and Cheryl introduced her to a few of her ever curious station crew members. After the brief introductions, they hopped in a cab and went to a really nice Hibachi restaurant where Cheryl had made reservations. Dinner went even better than Cheryl could have hoped for, and she just couldn't help but feel that the woman sitting across from her had the potential to be "the one". No, Cheryl was not one of those "U-haul lesbians", in fact, she was just the opposite. Fiercely independent and preferring a partner who was also independent, she somehow could envision the two of them melding their lives together in harmony without either one of them losing their identity. Their first official date ended with them sipping glasses of wine in the restaurants sushi lounge, and Cheryl getting the nod that the bar was about to close and it was time for the ladies to leave.

"Wow, I can't believe its 2 am already," exclaimed Cheryl. "I really like you. I hope you've enjoyed our time together as much as I have."

Tina responded by placing a hand on Cheryl's leg and leaned in to give her a soft kiss on the mouth before finishing her last swallow of wine. She knew it was not the wine that was making her insides tingle and her heart leap in her chest. No, it was the amazing vibes emanating from Cheryl that were making her feel like a school girl looking into the eyes of potential love. The pair donned their jackets and headed outside to hail a cab. They sat quietly in the back seat with Tina resting her head against Cheryl's shoulder on the ride back to the station house, where both Tina and Cheryl had their cars parked. The women concluded their first date with a long hug and soft passionate kiss. The kind that left both of them secretly yearning for more as they both made their way home.

Cheryl and Tina began communicating via text and phone regularly after that night, and on Cheryl's days off of work they would go out for dinner, shoot some pool, or take in one of the many neighborhood cultural events that were always going on. About three weeks after their first date, Tina invited Cheryl over to her apartment for dinner. Cheryl had been to Tina's apartment twice before, but the visits were always fleeting. This time Tina was preparing a romantic meal for the two of them, followed by movie-in night and some wine. Cheryl hoped that it was a sign that they were about to take the next step in their relationship. Cheryl was a little nervous when she arrived at Tina's apartment that night with flowers and wearing a spritz of new cologne, which she didn't usually use. Sex, or potential sex, with a new partner was always nerve wracking, no matter how much you have fantasized about it. Tina buzzed Cheryl into the apartment building and seemed calm and happy to see her when she opened the door, easing much of Cheryl's anxiety over her anticipation of the evening's events. The food was perfect and so was their evening. They ate alfresco style on the balcony, with a small gas heater keeping them warm while they wined and dined to a panoramic view of the city and Max sleeping contently beside them.

After cleaning up from their meal, they sat down on the couch to watch a movie. The ambiance was perfect, Cheryl was thinking as she wrapped an arm around Tina's slender shoulder. She then leaned in and gently kissed the side of Tina's neck. Tina loved it and snuggled closer, leaning her head to the opposite side so Cheryl had more room. Their cuddling soon led to kissing as Tina turned to face Cheryl opening her lips to her probing tongue. And, this time, their kisses displayed an urgency about them that bridged them into the next moment, the moment that they both acknowledged and surrendered to their feelings for one another. Yes, it happened, love and passion took over.

Deepening their kiss, Cheryl began removing her clothes. Piece after piece, she threw them onto the floor next to the couch. Finally, she was naked, and Tina was feasting her eyes on her new lover's perfect body. She was perfectly proportioned; narrow waist, broad hips, with average sized breasts. Tina cupped her breasts and kissed them, before getting up to remove her clothes.

They were a perfectly matched couple, both beautiful and passionate women. Cheryl pulled Tina into her arms, molding their bodies together. She felt the rise and fall of her chest press against her as she breathed. Her breasts were deliciously full and firm. Cheryl positioned Tina on the center of the couch and gently guided her body back up against the thick cushions as her free hand slowly parted her legs.

"Are you ready for pleasure baby?" she asked.

Tina responded by opening her legs even wider and moaning in anticipation as she glided her fingers through Cheryl's hair. Silky soft hair that caressed the skin of her thighs as Cheryl's mouth headed straight for Tina's pleasure zone. Cheryl gently sucked Tina's clit into her mouth as her body responded with moans and the arching of her back in ecstasy. Cheryl's hair knotted in Tina's grip as she continued to gently and steadily suck and lick her, giving her immense pleasure. She then slowly inserted two fingers inside of her wet furnace and massaged her from the inside. The licking and stroking filled Tina with pleasure; her moans echoing throughout the room. Cheryl pressed on her G-spot as she stroked her, and she immediately felt Tina's walls tightening around her fingers, pulsing and squeezing. Her moans grew louder and louder and finally, she bellowed out her delight as her orgasm overtook her. It took Tina a few minutes to regain her composure, after which she led Cheryl into her bedroom where their lovemaking lasted all throughout the rest of the night. Both sated with pleasure, they slept in each other's arms until ribbons of sunlight tickled their eyes awake the next morning.

Tina made them breakfast and Cheryl was thankful that she had brought her work bag with her, so she could just head off to the station after breakfast for her shift. Their relationship blossomed over the next few months, both of them becoming very important parts of each other's life. Neither lost their individual identities, yet they intertwined like fine woven tapestry, improving their joy and satiety of life to a degree that neither had enjoyed when they were single. They met their respective parents and things were about as perfect as either could have hoped for in a relationship. Both expressed that they had found their perfect match of a partner, and those who knew them found them to be incredibly compatible.

Cheryl had just started an evening shift at the station about six months into their relationship, when a call came in for them to go to respond to a multiple vehicle accident scene with serious injuries. Cheryl and her crew quickly made their way to the accident scene, which was only several miles away from the station, but as they approached, Cheryl's heart stopped when she recognized one of the vehicles. It was Tina's. Cheryl couldn't stop the scream that escaped her mouth as she pictured Tina being badly injured......or worse. Tina's car was wrapped around a traffic light pole, and Cheryl has responded to enough accident scenes to recognize the severity of what her eyes were witnessing.

Things seemed to move in slow motion as Cheryl grabbed her gear and jumped out of the truck as soon as it stopped, but her fire captain grabbed her before she could rush over to Tina's car and told her to tend the other car and accident victim. "No! I have to go to Tina!" she shouted.

"I can't let you do that, and that's an order," he told her, turning her in the direction of the other car on the opposite side of the intersection.

Mario, one of her crew members, grabbed Cheryl and pulled her over towards the other vehicle with him. "Tina's in capable hands Cheryl, you know that. I need you to think straight right now and help me. Can you do that?"

Cheryl stood momentarily paralyzed and Mario yelled at her to bring her back into reality....back into the moment.....at least for now. "Cheryl! Let's go!"

The sounds of police sirens now approaching the scene snapped

Cheryl out of her fog, and she went about assisting Mario who was securing the other driver so that they could safely remove him from his badly damaged vehicle. As they worked on the male victim, Cheryl overheard some of the witnesses telling the police what happened. Cheryl looked at the driver sternly, trying to avoid a public capturing of her pure rage against the man who lay unconscious and covered in blood on a flat board. The accident appeared to be the man's fault. She wanted to let him die for hurting Tina. What if she never saw her again? What if she was already dead? Though her mind was running a mile a minute, oscillating with pain and anger, she knew she couldn't let the man die. It would go against everything that she had ever believed in. She knew Tina was in good hands with her captain and the rest of the crew, and she just had to put her faith in that. Cheryl and Mario had just finished loading up the male victim into the back of the ambulance, and as she was shutting the back of the ambulance door when she looked over towards Tina's car to see her bloody, glass-shattered and lifeless body being transferred to the ambulance on a stretcher. Cheryl screamed and ran over to her. She was supposed to be in the ambulance with Mario transporting him the nearest trauma center, but emotion took over. Cheryl's captain quickly instructed another one of the crew members who was also a paramedic to jump onto the ambulance with Mario and the male victim, as he knew that Cheryl was too distraught to function in a professional capacity at this point. Not knowing whether she was dead or alive was utterly unbearable and Cheryl begged someone to tell her how bad Tina's condition was.

"Let's go Cheryl," her captain said. "Get in the truck. We're heading to the hospital where they are taking Tina." Cheryl jumped in the truck, as everything around her seemed to move like a surreal slow-motion movie.

Her nausea came in waves as they arrived at the trauma center just a few minutes later. A trauma team was ready when they got there, and Cheryl was promptly surrounded by her fellow crew members for support as the medical team immediately went to work. Tina was alive....but barely. She was rushed into emergency surgery for severe head trauma and abdominal bleeding. Cheryl couldn't catch her breath as she heaved with tears of grief, and she now had the daunting task of calling Tina's parents and informing them of the tragedy. Tina's parents arrived in less than an hour, and while Cheryl and Tina's parents waited for an update on her condition, they were informed by one of the responding police officers of how the accident happened. Witnesses collaborated that the other driver ran the red light at a pretty high rate of speed and slammed into Tina's car. The impact sent Tina's vehicle sailing across the intersection and straight into the traffic light pole. Hearing this only made their pain worse. To know what Tina had just experienced and now she was literally fighting for her life, was almost too much to bear. Cheryl prayed that Tina would live, and she also prayed that Tina would have no memory of what had happened. Cheryl's parents also came as soon as they heard and Cheryl was thankful for all the loving support from her co-workers and family.

Cheryl ran out of tears and just sat staring into space. She became numb. Tina had texted her a few hours prior telling her that she was going to the grocery store this evening. The groceries scattered around her car meant that that was where she was coming from. How could a grocery store run end up in this terrible accident? The hours dragged on, it felt like forever before they got any news on Tina's condition. The lead surgeon came out and asked for her parents.

"Mr. and Mrs. Henry, your daughter was very seriously injured. She made it through surgery and is being transferred to ICU right now, but we're definitely not out of the woods yet. The first twenty-four hours are the most critical. If she makes it through that, then we take one day at a time."

Tina's parents thanked the doctors and Cheryl could feel her knees threaten to give out as she listened to the doctor's update. It was a huge relief that Tina was alive and made it through surgery, but not knowing whether she'd still be alive in another twenty-four hours took away the relief and they were left with just worry. They were allowed to see Tina one-at-a-time about six hours after she came out of surgery and was settled into ICU, unconscious and hooked up to more machinery than one could imagine. Cheryl's heart felt like it was being pummeled as she viewed her lover's lifeless body still covered with dried blood, bandages, traction devices and tubes all over her body. Her eyes were completely swollen shut and in addition to the head trauma, she suffered multiple broken ribs and a broken arm, and her liver was perforated, which was what caused all the internal bleeding. Looking at her, Tina was barely recognizable, and for the first time in her firefighting career, Cheryl truly understood the emotional trauma of family members following the physical trauma their loved ones might have received during a car accident, fire, or other major incident.

Tina's parents and Cheryl helped support each other during those first few very rough days. Cheryl's captain let her take a leave of absence, allowing her to stay by Tina's side which she was grateful for. The bandages came off of her eyes on day three, but she was still unconscious. She was in a medically induced coma, which the doctors said was necessary while there was still swelling in her brain. This allowed her body's energies to focus on healing vs. daily bodily functions. Then, during her second week in ICU, Tina opened her eyes. She was groggy and couldn't move, but she recognized Cheryl and understood what had happened to her. Unfortunately, the doctors had to heavily sedate her again to ease her crushing pain. Cheryl only every briefly left Tina's side, which was typically to check on both of their apartments, shower and change into clean clothes, and take Max for a walk.

Around week number three, Tina was able to remain fully conscious and not be maddened by the pain. It was bearable by then, with enough medication. She truly appreciated the outpouring of love and support she was receiving from her family and friends, especially when she heard that Cheryl hadn't been going to work and that she had taken unpaid leave to be by her side. Cheryl's coworkers had also been to the hospital to see Tina, since she was now part of their close knit family. Throughout this terrible tragedy, not once has Cheryl's love or commitment to Tina wavered. In fact, it only strengthened her resolve to build a happy forever life with the love of her life. And, almost having death destroy their happiness brought them to the realization that life is short and time shouldn't be wasted waiting on the right moment for anything.

After some initial hardcore physical therapy, Tina was finally released from the hospital two months later and Cheryl moved in temporarily to take care of her. Helping her with her readjustment was just as hard on Cheryl as it was on Tina. She hated to see the defeated look on her face when her injuries prevented her from doing something. Tina cried one day when Max was stuck under the table and she couldn't bend down to pick him up, she felt useless to everybody. Cheryl hated to see her sad and she did everything she could to cheer her up. Eventually, it worked and she came out of her dark hole. As Tina continued to heal, the smile slowly reappeared on her face. She started making jokes again and staying in the kitchen with Cheryl while she cooked, and the feeling of joy was back in the apartment. They watched movies together, took Max out for short walks and Tina even started doing some part-time work again, taking on small writing projects.

Their intimacy slowly returned as well. All throughout Tina's healing process, Cheryl was afraid to touch her intimately, out of fear that she would hurt her. Tina recognized this and realized that Cheryl would never be the one to make the first move, out of fear of hurting her. So, one day while Cheryl was preoccupied with cooking dinner for the two of them, Tina snuck up behind her and gave her a gentle kiss on the shoulder. Cheryl turned and kissed her back, but she didn't press her body against Tina as she always did. Tina used her good hand and pulled her into her. She felt a little tinge of pain still in her ribs, but the pleasure of feeling Cheryl's lips on hers and her body pressed up tight against her after all this time was definitely worth it.

As Tina continued to heal and Cheryl had gone back to work at the fire station, life slowly resumed a normal rhythm. Cheryl had continued to stay at Tina's apartment, both of them under one roof, each of them working again, resuming their social life and sharing the events of their day with one another over dinner all just felt so perfect. Cheryl was desperately in love with Tina and she put a lot of thought into spending the rest of her life with her. Living without her was not an option and she didn't even entertain the thought. Her only fear was that Tina wouldn't be ready to make such a commitment. Being in a relationship was one thing, shacking up another, and getting married was....well, a huge step. Tina had never expressed an interest in marriage and Cheryl was convinced she herself would never be interested in marriage, but Tina had changed all that.

After several weeks of serious contemplation, Cheryl decided that she was going to do it. She was going to propose to Tina. Nothing felt wrong about it. In fact, the only thing that felt wrong would be in not asking Tina to marry her. While out and about on one of her days off of work, Cheryl perused the many jewelry stores in their area before picking out an engagement ring that she thought would look perfect on Tina's long, slender fingers. She loved the ring and she loved Tina.

Later that same evening, a slightly nervous Cheryl was busy preparing one of Tina's favorite meals for dinner, clams in red sauce over linguini along with a bottle of her favorite merlot.

Cheryl was unusually quiet as she cooked and Tina knew that something was going on when Cheryl told her to stay out of the kitchen; she didn't need her help. Was Cheryl mad at her? She couldn't imagine why, but she had no idea why Cheryl was so adamant that she leave her alone. Maybe something was going on at work that she didn't want to talk about. The spring weather was quite balmy, so Tina stayed out on the balcony with Max until Cheryl told her to come inside for dinner. The dining table was breathtakingly beautiful and there were flowers and scented candles all over the room.

"What's going on?" Tina asked a little suspiciously, as she sat down at the table.

Smiling, Cheryl said, "Just a romantic dinner for my special lady."

"Oh, baby, you're amazing. This is beautiful!" replied Tina, as she took her place at the table.

The food was delicious, the setting was perfect, yet Tina noticed that Cheryl was a bit on the fidgety side. Maybe something really serious was going on at work, yet she didn't want to spoil their beautiful dinner by asking. Cheryl hardly uttered a word all throughout the meal and Tina was now becoming concerned. She didn't know what was going on and wondered why Cheryl was acting so weird. Did she lose her job?

Cheryl sensed Tina's growing concern and knew that she had to act fast before the atmosphere became awkward. She could see that her nervousness was rubbing off onto Tina, who kept glancing at her with a mixed look of suspicion and concern.

Taking a sip a wine and clearing her throat, Cheryl finally decided now was the time. "Tina, do you ever think of the future? Of our future, that is?"

Suddenly scared that Cheryl might be breaking up with her, she hesitantly answered, "Yes….uh, I do, as a matter of fact."

"Could you see yourself spending the rest of your life with me?"

Tina looked startled as realization hit her…the careful preparation of her favorite meal, candles and flowers. Was Cheryl about to propose? "Oh my God," she thought to herself, trying her hardest not to scream. She was so excited and happy, but she didn't want to ruin the moment.

She wanted to give Cheryl the chance to ask her, so she stifled her scream and tried to keep a neutral look on her face.

Tina nodded again, in response to the last question.

Cheryl then came around the table and got down on one knee.

Holding out her hand with the ring, she said. "Tina Marie Henry, I have loved you from the first time I laid eyes on you. I almost died inside when I thought you were dead. I do not want to live without you. Please do me the honor of spending the rest of your life with me. Will you marry me?"

Tina was shaking with excitement and when Cheryl finally asked the question, she screamed "Yes, yes, yes!" Her ribs protested, but all she could think of was the future, their future, the future that she would spend with the woman that she loved. Cheryl presented the ring to Tina and slid it slowly onto her finger as she embraced her as gently as she could, her heart bursting with happiness.

The pair celebrated the occasion and their future by going into the bedroom where they made passionate love to each other. Cheryl disrobed Tina and gently guided her naked body onto her stomach on the bed. She got the massage oil from the side table and drizzled it onto her back and gave her a slow and sensual massage. Her hands moved lower and lower with each move, until her hands crested the mounds of Tina's ass cheeks and she gently guided her fingers around and down until they parted the soft petals of her pussy lips finding the bud of her clit. She used one hand to slowly massage her clit, and the other she used to insert two fingers into her warm, wet pussy. Being stimulated inside and out was heaven for Tina and she lay writhing and moaning, her body displaying her pleasure. She exploded on Cheryl's fingers over and over again until she felt like she couldn't take any more.

Tina changed positions with Cheryl and gave Cheryl her massage while she lay on her back. Tina used her good hand to stroke her G-spot while using her tongue to lick Cheryl senseless. Cheryl's hands stroked Tina's hair as her hips gently bucked back and forth beneath her. She felt Tina's fingers working magic at her core. She enjoyed every stroke, every push and release of pressure, and she was so wet that Tina's fingers were covered and dripping with her juices. Each moan brought her closer and closer to the end. Tina teased her, until finally, she sent her over the cliff. The waves washed over her and she slowly floated down, her body and mind lost in the sensation of ecstasy.

They spent the rest of the evening planning for their future, outlining the anticipation of all the joyful experiences that they would share throughout the years. They were on a high, drunk in the liquor that was their love.

Story #10

To Serve and Protect

"Oh, God, what a day this has been." Thirty-six year old grade school teacher Lexie Larsen huffed, as she unpacked her last box for the day. It had been a busy week, and all of it was spent arranging furniture and unpacking all of her belongings into her new rental home.

For years now Lexie was wanting to move back to her home state of Texas, yet her current job as a teacher prevented her from doing so. The economy was horrible, people in every vocation were getting laid off monthly, and she couldn't gamble on haphazardly quitting her job in California in hopes that she'd just land a new job once she arrived back in Texas. Instead, she had to wait for a job opportunity to present itself in Texas before she could relocate, and her opportunity came when her sister informed her of an opening at the school they had both attended as children. Lexie waited with bated breath for over two weeks after she had flown out for the interview, and quite literally jumped for joy when she got the call that she was hoping for….the call offering her the job. Her family, who were scattered in cities across Texas, shared her joy, and they were just as excited as Lexie for her return. California had been her home for many years, but her family and heart were in Texas.

Lexie moved during the first week of summer break from school to give herself the entire summer to adjust to her new home and surroundings. Gardening and cooking were her favorite things to do, and she planned to do as much of them as possible. Her new home was an older, but nice looking place, but the asset that made her fall in love with it was the huge backyard. Lexie was anxious to get all of her unpacking and arranging done inside the house as quickly as possible, so she could quickly get about to tending to her new garden for the summer. Her tools had already been unpacked and were sitting in the shed in the back yard.

After emptying and breaking down her last box of household items from their moving box, Lexie stripped out of her clothes and headed off to take a long, hot shower. Tired, and not in the mood to cook, she decided to take a drive over to a nearby Chinese restaurant for some take-out. She felt nostalgic as she drove through the town. Memories of her childhood and moments spent with her family, friends and a couple early lovers came flooding back. As Lexie parked her car and walked across the parking lot, the scent of the food hit her as she approached the restaurant, and suddenly she became extremely hungry. Lexie ordered her food and left less than 10 minutes later when it was ready.

Lexie drove back home, and as she grabbed her take out bags of dinner and headed towards the front door, her heart took a serious leap in her chest and her feet stopped dead cold in their tracks. Her front door was swinging open. It appeared to have been kicked open because there was a huge hole in the lower center of the door. Lexie backed away from the door, ran back to lock herself in her car and fumbled for her cell phone to call 911.

"911, what is your emergency?" a voice answered.

"Hurry, please, I just got home and my front door was kicked open. I think someone broke into my home," she told the operator, feeling her body get shaky as the reality of situation started to sink in

"Ma'am, give me your address, I will send a couple units to you immediately."

Lexie gave her the address and the operator instructed her to remain in her vehicle.

Lexie realized she was scared shitless as she waited for the police to arrive. She never expected a break-in to be the first thing that happened to her after she moved to her new neighborhood. "What if the robbers are still inside? What if they came back out and spotted her?" She thought to herself. Her mind was going a mile a minute, and she was elated when the two squad cars drove up. She was impressed by how quickly they arrived, though she never imagined that three short minutes could feel like a lifetime.

The officers motioned for her to remain in the car and they went inside guns drawn to scope the house. A female officer came out to her car a few minutes later and told her that the house was clear and that she could come inside so that they could take her statement. As Lexie stepped through the door, her heart broke at the sight of her home. Everything that she had just recently unpacked and put away was scattered all about the living room. Her eyes panning the debris strewn room, Lexie noticed that her TV was gone, her laptop, her only piece of artwork that she won at an auction in Los Angeles, and pretty much every piece of expensive item was gone and most likely on its way to a pawn shop to be quickly exchanged for cash. Lexie had worked hard for years to purchase everything she owned, and to know that someone just took her possessions as if they belonged to them, made her very mad. But, more than just feeling mad, she felt violated, knowing that somebody was in her personal space, in the home that should have been hers alone. The police instructed her not to touch anything yet, because they would be dusting for fingerprints. They asked her if she had a home security system and she informed them that it was scheduled to be installed the following weak. She really didn't see the point of that now though, as the damage had already been done. Hadn't they already taken everything that was of worth?

After the police finished processing the house, the assisting officers left, leaving only one female officer behind. She was a beautiful Mexican Latina, and as Lexie walked around the house with her, she couldn't help but notice her voluptuous figure. Her uniform did nothing to hide her beauty. She had broad hips and a small waste, her jet black hair was in a bun under her hat and she wore little make-up. Lexie was very much attracted to her big, brown eyes and her olive skin tone that looked so sexy against the dark blue color of her uniform. As the officer, whose name was Mary Padilla, took a very detailed report from Lexie, she could see the look of concern and fear on her face and she wished she had the courage to tell her that being curled up in her arms would have been all the comfort she needed. Officer Padilla was genuinely concerned for Lexie, but she tried to lighten the atmosphere with her pleasant smile. At the conclusion of her report, she gave Lexie her personal business card and told her she could call whenever she needed any kind of assistance.

"I work the night shift and I will do some drive-bys throughout the night whenever I'm on duty to make sure that you are safe," Officer Padilla told her.

Lexie was grateful for the help and felt a sense of security, knowing that somebody would be looking out for her. The slightly ambiguous language and tone used by the Officer to offer the 'assistance' made Lexie wonder if the 'assistance' was an open-ended one. After the Officer left, she decided that she was just being melodramatic, the offer of assistance was probably nothing more than just that, with no meaning behind it. Her loneliness had finally sunk in; she mistook every act of kindness for flirting. She distracted her rambling thoughts by calling her family over to help her clean up the mess in her house; plus their company would help to put her at ease.

As Mary drove away from the house and put herself back in available to respond mode with dispatch, she couldn't take her mind off Lexie. It had been a rough past hour, trying to remain professional while on the job. Never before had Mary been so tempted while working, but she was glad that she had remained professional. She found Lexie to be very beautiful and articulate, and was very much attracted to her. Lexie was very confident, but not in an 'oh, I'm hot' way. She was an educated, down-to-earth kind of woman and Mary felt herself drawn to her in a very profound way, which felt strange to her, considering the short amount of time that they were in each other's company. As she drove,

Mary found herself pondering Lexie's gender of preference for her romantic partners. She knew she shouldn't put much effort into finding that out though as she had to be careful to not give the impression that she was using her position of authority to proposition citizens. That didn't mean that she stopped thinking about Lexie. Quite the contrary, in fact, as thoughts of Lexie were at the forefront of her mind for days.

Mary followed through as promised and drove by Lexie's house one to two times every night that she was on duty, looking out for any suspicious behavior. Her duty to serve and protect wasn't the only thing that led her to be so diligent in her promise though. It was coupled with her attraction to Lexie, and her hope that Lexie would come out to thank her for her vigilance one night. She knew that was a rather far-fetched fantasy, but one she held onto nonetheless, for it was the only possibility of an "accidental" run-in with her potential love interest that she could think of without jeopardizing her career.

Fate happened to be on Mary's side one day when her co-workers took her to an upscale sports bar to celebrate her birthday, and she spotted Lexie there playing darts with a man and a woman. Looking ravishing in blue jeans and a sleeveless purple blouse, Lexie's infectious laughter could be heard each time she missed the bull's eye. All during Mary's birthday gathering, she kept looking over at Lexie and trying to think of a way to accidentally 'bump' into her. Her distraction was evident to her friends, who kept asking her if she was okay.

"Sure, I'm fine. I just need to use the bathroom. Will you excuse me for a second?" She got up from the table and walked the long way around the bar area to the bathroom so she could 'bump' into Lexie. Her heart raced as she approached her, she could actually feel the blood pumping in her head. Seeing that she was deep in conversation with her companions, Mary knew that Lexie would never notice her, so she took the lead.

"Hi, it's Lexie right? What a surprise running into you. How is everything at home?" she asked nervously. She couldn't remember the last person that made her nervous, but she certainly did remember the woman's name even though she tried to passively play it off like she wasn't sure.

Smiling in recognition, Lexie replied. "Oh, hi, Officer Padilla. Things are thankfully pretty quiet. Thanks for asking. How are you? Enjoying a day off of work?"

"Actually, I am. And, please, call me Mary," she replied.

"Okay, Mary." She turned to her companions, she said. "This is the very kind officer that was so helpful to me on the night of the robbery." She returned her attention to Mary. "Mary, this is my brother Martin and my sister Ellen. They dragged me out of the house because they think that I am isolating myself too much after what happened."

"Sounds like good therapy and you seem to be having fun. I am actually here with my co-workers for a casual birthday celebration," Mary replied.

"Oh, well happy birthday!" Lexie exclaimed, and being a little tipsy from one too many drinks, she proceeded to give Mary a long birthday hug. "Listen, I love to cook. Why don't you come by one day before work or on a day off and let me whip you up a real home cooked meal. I'm sure the food here at the bar certainly can't be considered birthday worthy."

Surprised and elated beyond words, Mary quickly accepted the invitation before she thought better of it and changed her mind. They arranged the dinner for the following Wednesday on Mary's day off and exchanged contact numbers.

On the days leading up to the dinner, to say Mary was nervous was an understatement. She was anxious for the day to arrive, yet at the same time, she was worried about how things would turn out. Was Lexie's invitation strictly platonic? Lexie had no idea that she was a lesbian, and she wasn't sure if she would have gotten the invitation, had Lexie known her sexual orientation. She was also unaware of Lexie's own sexual preference but she certainly hoped that the evening would play out in her favor.

Wednesday evening came and Mary arrived trying not to look too eager, but she did come bearing a bouquet of mixed flowers and bottle of wine. Lexie opened the door looking absolutely amazing wearing a simple white sundress and Mary tried hard to not let her extreme attraction to her be obvious. Lexie took the flowers and wine as she invited Mary inside. "That was so thoughtful of you to bring these, thank you."

"Well, your place definitely looks much better without broken glass and things strewn all over the place," Mary joked.

Lexie laughed. "I agree. Please, make yourself comfortable, I need to check on dinner real quick. I'll only be a minute."

She went into the kitchen to check on her chicken in the oven, leaving Mary in the living room. Mary walked around the room, looking at pictures on display and she took notice to a large group photo on one of the end tables that included a woman bearing no resemblance to Lexie's family. A strong physical family trait seemed to be dark hair and brown eyes, yet the woman in the group photo was a blonde with light eyes and very fair skin. When Lexie returned Mary inquired about the family photo.

"Wow, you seem to have quite a large family."

"Yes, it extends pretty far. This photo was taken at my grandmother's 80th birthday party celebration. Those are my parents, my brother, my two sisters, a handful of nieces and nephews, and my ex-girlfriend," she said casually, as she pointed to all the people in the photo.

Mary smiled and she sent up a silent prayer of thanks at the revelation.

"Oh, so you do prefer women," she said open-endedly.

"Like you didn't know," Lexie smiled coyly. "Come on let's go into the dining room, dinner's ready."

The confirmation from Lexie that she was a lesbian gave Mary the courage she needed to flirt. She had been anxious for days over the matter. She figured that the worst thing that would happen would be that she would make a new friend. Admittedly she was much happier at the possibility of more than just a new friendship. After the question of "is she" or "isn't she" was put to rest, Lexie couldn't ignore the passionate tension that suddenly filled the air. She dished out their meal while Mary poured the wine and complimented her before she had even tasted anything. She said the divine aroma was enough to tell her that it was going to be absolutely delicious.

As they sat down to eat, there was a moment of pause as their eyes locked and silent back-and-forth transmissions of each of their hopeful desires scurried between them. Mary broke the pleasant tension by gazing down at her plate and pulling her chair in closer to the table. "Oh my goodness, this is amazing," she offered, after taking a bite of her food and washing it down with a sip of wine. "You weren't kidding, you certainly can cook!"

"Thank you. I'm so glad you like it. So, Mary, tell me a bit about yourself," Lexie nudged with genuine curiosity.

"Well I grew up in a pretty normal home. My parents have been married for almost forty years, and I have one sister. I knew I wanted to join the police force when I was still in high school. I've just always had this strong desire to protect others, and I do have compassion for the public. Going into nursing didn't seem to fit my personality and after one of those career days at school when my friend Mike's dad came in to talk about his job as a police officer, well I knew right then and there what I wanted to do."

"Sounds interesting. Have you ever been married?" Lexie asked.

"Actually, no, I haven't. I guess I just haven't met the right woman yet," Mary replied as she stared into Lexie's eyes and reached for her hand. "I like you Lexie. I find you interesting, intelligent, creative……and, well, beautiful." She wasn't sure if Lexie would be okay with her openness, but she knew without a doubt that they were both attracted to each other. She ran her hand through her hair and visibly relaxed when Lexie smiled and snuggled up to her hand.

They talked all about their lives, discussed what they liked to do and places that they loved to go. After dinner they finished off the wine as they both did the dishes, talking and laughing. When they were done, it was obvious that they both felt comfortable and relaxed in each other's company. It was also clear that their strong attraction to each other was mutual. As Mary was leaving, she made her boldest move yet and pulled Lexie into her arms for an intense and passionate kiss. Lexie melted; she molded her body into Mary's. She felt light-headed as they kissed, their tongues meeting in a highly erotic way. Mary's mind was in a delicious fog that night as she drove home. She had gone into that dinner hoping to find out if Lexie was interested in women, but she came out with so much more. After Mary had left, Lexie lay in bed unable to fall asleep because she couldn't take her mind off of the beautiful police officer who made her heart race. Once she arrived back at home, Mary sent Lexie a text message thanking her for the wonderful evening and her amazing company. She also complimented her on her humor, grace and beauty. Lexie felt giddy as she read Mary's text for she was very much attracted to her, and she quickly shot off a text message reply.

"I enjoyed your company too. Hope we can do it again sometime!" She hit the send button and hoped that waited anxiously for a response.

Mary responded immediately. "I couldn't agree more. Tell me the date and time."

Lexie's heart skipped as she replied to Mary, telling her to let her know when her next day off would be so they could make plans to get together. She fell asleep with happy thoughts that night. Her move to Dallas was finally going the way she hoped it would go. She had recovered from the robbery, and was spending a lot of time doing her gardening and cooking. She still had the rest of summer to enjoy before school started again in the fall and now....well, now there was a love interest in her life.

Throughout the following weeks, Mary and Lexie would call and text message each other whenever they were each able. Mary would often drop by Lexie's house to have dinner before she started her shift at work and they were enjoying each other's company so much that pretty soon, they no longer felt like strangers trying to get to know one another. Lexie felt like a really important part of Mary's life, and that was what Mary had become to her. She was no longer just the cop that helped her out when her home was broken into. She was somebody that Lexie was slowly falling in love with. Lexie was very selective when it came on to her partners. She was getting older and she didn't want to be playing around and just 'dating'. Mary matched up to all her requirements and expectations in a partner; Lexie was very hopeful about the future of their relationship.

They had a picnic in the park one day, and when they finished eating, they lay down in each other's arms on the blanket and nothing had ever felt so right. Lexie took a snapshot of the moment in her mind. The warm breeze caressing their skin, the distant sounds of birds, and the big puffy clouds that glided along in the sun-filled sky. Then there was the scent of Mary's hair, the smoothness of her arm wrapped around her shoulder and the flutter of her beautiful, long eyelashes when she blinked.

"Are you happy?" Lexie asked.

"I am. Thanks to you, I have been a happy woman for a while." She leaned in to kiss Lexie tenderly her on the lips and smiled.

"I'm happy too. In fact, I would like to introduce you to my family." Mary looked a little panicked at the suggestion, but after some discussion about family openness and acceptance levels of various family members, Mary agreed.

That evening, Lexie took Mary to her parent's house for dinner. Mary was nervous, but Lexie convinced her that there was nothing to worry about. Her family was very welcoming and they all made her feel at ease. She eventually relaxed, and was able to enjoy their company and Lexie was happy that her family liked and accepted Mary. In fact, a couple of her nieces were enthralled at the fact that Mary was a police officer and wouldn't leave her side. Her relaxed attitude with the kids made everyone fall in love with her. She was totally at ease with them and did her best to entertain them. After dinner, Mary dropped Lexie off at her house before heading to her own to get to bed. A mandatory early morning meeting at the police station called for an early night and was going to make for an extra long day since she had to work the night shift later.

At the meeting the following morning, Mary's captain informed all of the officers and a couple of lieutenants that the break-ins had started up again, at a rate of one to two a day. The main neighborhood being targeted was Lexie's neighborhood and the thieves had a pattern, they robbed persons that recently moved in or were in the process of moving out. Summer was always a busy time for people moving, and it appeared the thieves were attempting to take full advantage of this fact. The thieves were becoming more brazen, the level of danger was significant and rising, and orders had come down from the Mayor's office to increase their efforts into catching the criminals. Patrol presence was increased in the area as well as dialogue with many of the residents. The robberies were very traumatizing for them, and they would often call 911 when they heard the smallest sound.

One night while on duty, as Mary was driving her squad car around the neighborhood, she and her partner received a call to report to a house close to where Lexie lived. Mary was nervous as she drove to the address. She didn't like the fact that danger was so close to Lexie. When they arrived, they found the owner and her children crying by the door. They were extremely frightened and it took Mary and her partner a very long time to console them. There was glass and their belongings scattered all over the house. This time, the robbers not only stole many of their valuables, but they appeared intent on destroying everything that was left. Were they getting arrogant? This was a dangerous sign that the thieves would not hesitate to inflict physical harm to anyone who might stand in their way.

"Were you in the house when all of this happened?" Mary asked the woman. She was a single mother, who lived alone with her three kids.

"Yes, we were all in the house when it happened. My kids were scared to sleep alone because it is a new house, and I allowed them to sleep in my room. When I heard the commotion, I locked the door and called the police. We hid in the closet until I was sure that they had gone."

It was evident to Mary and her partner that the woman and her children were highly traumatized.

Mary felt for the woman and promised to do everything she could to keep her safe. She realized that the drive-bys in the neighborhood needed to happen more often, and promised to get another unit to patrol with her. The other unit left the scene and Mary and her partner took a full report from the woman while a forensic team dusted for fingerprints and took pictures. Mary also requested that at least one unit be in the neighborhood at all times since things appeared to have taken a dangerous turn.

Over the next few days, break-ins were being reported every single day within one of the two adjoining neighborhoods. The entire department was in an uproar over what was happening, as they had never before seen such a brazen string of robbery activity in the entire history of the city. Resources were being pulled from wherever they could to address and rectify the growingly dangerous situation. Mary had even more reason for concern, since Lexie lived in the main neighborhood that was being targeted by these criminals. To see the fear and devastation on the faces of the residents was taking its toll on her. And, to know that Lexie was living smack in the middle of all that was happening only gave Mary more resolve to assist in catching the unconscientious criminals.

The following day Lexie called Mary in a panic. "Baby, I'm scared. When will this end? Are the police getting close in catching these guys? This isn't how I remember Dallas to be."

"Don't worry, it will all end soon. We are in the process of trying to figure it out. In fact, I'm headed into a meeting about it now, so I'll call you later baby." Mary hoped her words brought some comfort to the woman she loved, yet she herself was greatly concerned over the way things has escalated over the past couple of weeks, and the biggest fear was that the thieves recent brazenness would potentially lead to someone getting hurt, or worse.

At the meeting, various tactical team leaders offered their suggestions on how to stop the robberies in the meeting, and one in particular stood out. Lieutenant Daley suggested that since the robbers seemed to prey on people just moving in or about to move out, that they go undercover as moving company employees. It would make for a perfect undercover operation, and they'd have the added benefit of using a couple large moving trucks to transport personnel and keep surveillance equipment inside. It would also afford them the ability to remain in a location for an extended amount of time without raising suspicion. If the robbers took notice to one of their undercover moving trucks, they most likely wouldn't make anything out of it.

The undercover operation was approved, and things quickly went into motion to acquire the moving trucks and uniforms for the officers that would be working undercover. Their undercover operation was planned out with a 7 day anticipated time frame, with various teams set to begin immediately. Mary was chosen for the night shift undercover operation, and she was actually relieved that she'd be able to be close in proximity to Lexie, even if it was while on duty. Mary wanted to tell Lexie about the undercover operation to catch the robbery team to help put her mind at ease that they were getting close to catching the thieves, but disclosure was strictly prohibited by the department. Any leaks at all could mean a heads up to the thieves, which would only compromise the operation and potentially the safety of all the officers involved, not to mention the citizens of the neighborhood. Additionally, with all officers required to pull 12 hour shifts daily even on their scheduled off days from work until the thieves were caught, Mary could only comfort Lexie via brief phone calls and text messages.

Two nights later, Mary's team was on duty when they spotted some men who fit the description of the robbers. They made their intentions obvious to the undercover cops when a stack of boxes that they were rolling out on a dolly fell over and they were empty. They were obviously "dummy boxes" made to look like they were moving something. The pair disappeared between two houses, yet the cops could still see the tops of their heads over a row of bushes as they made their way towards the backside of a row of houses. Were they checking to see which homes were occupied? Were they seeing if any windows or doors might be unlocked at those houses? A few minutes later they made their way back to their parked moving truck, which was only about 100 yards away from the one Mary and her team were taking cover in. They watched as the men opened up the back of the moving truck and one of the men pulled out what looked to be like some tools from a zippered duffel bag. Break-in tools, perhaps? The men appeared to be talking to each other, and Mary's captain noticed the two men putting on gloves and shoving something into the side pockets of their overalls. Were they packing guns?

"Ok, here we go. Everybody on the ready and wait for my signal," Mary's captain announced quietly to the team inside the undercover moving truck.

The men appeared to have a plan and they set in motion towards what appeared to be their target house....Lexie's house!

"Oh shit!" Mary hissed under her breath, as her heart thumped wildly in her chest. "Not again!" Knowing that she had just seconds before her captain would order them into action, Mary hastily sent Lexie a text, telling her to lock all the doors and windows and not to open them no matter what. Knowing that the woman she loved was in the direct path of danger gripped at her chest and the full realization of just how much she loved that woman hit her in that moment. She would be damned if those lowlife thugs were going to take away the chance for her to tell Lexie how she felt.

"We're a go! Move!" shouted Mary's captain, and the team sprung out from the back of the moving truck.

As Mary's team sprung into action, she didn't get to see the reply text that Lexie had sent her. They pulled out a couple of moving dollies from the empty moving truck, and all of their weapons and communication devices were strategically hidden in their mock moving uniforms. Mary's heart was beating harder than it has it a long time, mostly because she had a personal interest at stake, but she took comfort knowing that Lexie's house was currently being surrounded by police officers. The officers pretended not to see the thieves as they headed towards the back of Lexie's house. The thieves were oblivious to the presence of the officers who were quickly positioning themselves at various points around the perimeter of Lexie's house, and as one of the men jumped effortlessly over the fence into Lexie's backyard the other appeared to be fiddling with the lock at the door. And that was when the cops made their move.

The officers that were still near the truck sprinted towards Lexie's yard to apprehend the man trying to pick the door lock while Mary and the other officers jumped the backyard fence to apprehend the second individual. Just as the thief broke the glass to Lexie's back patio door, the officers tackled and handcuffed him all in a matter of seconds. Radio traffic indicated that the other officers had successful apprehended the man by the front door, and with both of the thieves now in custody, a wave of relief flooded through Mary's body. Within minutes, squad cars lined the streets, and there was police everywhere securing the moving truck that the men used, which was apparently stolen, along with all of the stolen belongings inside. Another group of officers raced into Lexie's house to check that no other thieves were inside as well as ensure that nobody was hurt.

Once both of the men were placed into separate squad cars for their ride down to the police station for processing, and the other officers cleared the house, Mary ran into the house to ensure that Lexie was safe. Though the thieves were in the hands of the cops, she had to see with her eyes to be certain. The thief had already broken the back patio door open, so Mary didn't need to wait on Lexie to let her in. She ran through the house, calling out Lexie's name. Lexie came running down the steps and straight into her arms.

"Oh my God baby, I was so scared." Lexie clung onto Mary tightly, not wanting to let go.

"I am moving in with you. I'm not even asking you, I'm telling you. I love you Lexie, and if anything would have happened to you tonight....well, I just wouldn't have been able to handle that." Mary said between the kisses she placed on Lexie's forehead, cheeks and mouth.

"You love me?" Lexie responded with questioning eyes.

"Are you kidding? More than anything, and I want to protect you in every way that I can. Which means for starters I'm going to drop you off at my apartment before I go and finish out my shift for tonight, and we can discuss our moving in together details tomorrow." Lexie didn't object, but for the moment their exchange had to be abbreviated since Mary had to return to work. Her captain ok'd her driving Lexie to her apartment before heading back to the station, and knowing that her lover would be safe there meant everything.

After Mary dropped Lexie off at her apartment, Lexie was left alone with her thoughts. The incident had brought the issue of safety to the forefront of her mind. What if those robbers had been armed? Maybe they were and she just didn't know it. What if Mary had gotten hurt? Would she always worry whenever Mary went to work? Lexie was second guessing being involved with a police officer and the collision of all her thoughts were driving her crazy. Danger would always be present every time Mary went to work, yet how could Lexie ask the woman that she loved to not do the work that she loved. As much as she tried, she didn't get a minute of sleep that night. She got out of bed early in the morning to make breakfast, so that she and Mary could eat together when she got home and breakfast was hot and waiting on the table for her when she walked through the door.

"Morning baby, did you get any sleep?" Mary asked as she pulled Lexie into her arms.

"No, actually I didn't sleep a wink. I do feel a whole lot better though now that you are here. I made us some breakfast. I figured you'd probably be starving after the long night you had."

"Baby, can the food wait a bit? I missed you," Mary replied.

Smiling, Lexie covered the food and Mary led the way into the bedroom. Mary helped Lexie out of her clothes and gently laid her naked body back onto the bed. Mary then started to remove her uniform, and as Lexie watched her undress, feelings of intense desire tingled in the innermost region between her thighs. She was nervous as she lay naked on the bed, yet she couldn't take her eyes off of Mary's amazing body as piece after piece of clothing came off revealing full, curvy hips and a plump ass. Mary's dark brown nipples became erect as her tits sprung free from her bra, and her voluptuous tits swung in front of Lexie like a sweet treat. It would be their first time making love together and Mary could see that Lexie was excited....and nervous.

"Relax baby, we can't both be nervous," Mary said with a grin.

Mary slowly crawled on top of Lexie's body and leaned down to softly kiss her lips. As their tongues danced and played in each other's mouth, their bodies melted together smashing their tits against the others, while they kissed and caressed each other, proclaiming their love with their actions.

"I love you," Mary whispered in Lexie's ear as she kissed her way down her silky body, suckling at her tits and licking her stomach until she reached that delicious point between her thighs. Gently parting the smooth lips of her pussy, Mary gently sucked her clit into her mouth while her fingers teased at her opening.

"Ahh....oh, shit," Lexie moaned, as her hips rocked up against Mary's mouth. She ran her hands through Mary's hair which hung free from the tight bun she usually wore it in while working and the velvety feel of her long, black hair brushing against her skin drove Lexie wild. The sensations were maddening, and when she felt Mary slide a couple fingers into her cunt while sucking rhythmically on her erect clit, she knew it wouldn't be long until she was pushed over that delightful edge. Lexie felt her orgasm coming on as her breath quickened and her body stiffened and up and over she went, moaning in ecstasy as her climax rocked her body.

Mary smiled, as she licked Lexie's sweet juices from her fingers. Not expecting anything in return, Mary was surprised when Lexie suddenly flipped her over onto her back. "Now it's your turn baby."

Lexie licked her in one, long stroke down her body and then lustfully, and skillfully, she licked her way back up and sucked one of her nipples deep into her mouth. While using her finger to play with Mary's clit,

Lexie kissed and bit Mary's mouth with such a hungry passion that had they been standing, Mary was sure that her knees would have buckled. Lexie glided her finger up and down the length of Mary's pussy lips, and feeling her moisture, she slowly inserted two fingers. Mary's moans filled the room as Lexie's finger expertly caressed her from the inside. Lexie massaged Mary's walls, forming a rhythm with her fingers and tongue. She would stroke, massage and then kiss her lips. Her maneuvering was too much for Mary to take, and she was soon moaning and writhing on the bed as her climax rippled through her body.

They lay sated in each other's arms on the bed, before Lexie heard Mary's stomach grumble. "Let's go eat," she said as she pulled her up off the bed.

Mary pulled on a robe while Lexie just put on a pair of panties, and they went into the kitchen to nosh on the lukewarm breakfast that Lexie had prepared.

Silence was the farthest thing from the table as Lexie needed her concerns to be addressed. "Mary, I'm worried about the dangers associated with your job. I know I'm going to worry every time you go to work."

"Lexie do you know that you could be teaching at school and a tornado comes and the building down around you? Do you know that you could be a bus driver and your bus crashes? Or that you could be a dog walker and one of the dogs attacks and mauls you? There are dangers in every job."

"I know baby, I really do. And, I would never ask you to stop doing what you love. I guess I just need to express my feelings, maybe as much to myself as to you. It's because I love you, I really, really love you."

"And I love you too, which is why I want us to move in together. I want to protect you and be there for you all the time. I want to enjoy you every moment I can. I want to share my life with you. Say 'yes' Lexie, say 'yes'."

"Yes!" replied Lexie, as she came around the kitchen table to embrace Mary. Mary hugged her tightly and started laughing. "What's so funny?" Lexie inquired.

"What's funny is, as hungry as I am I can't focus on eating breakfast with your beautiful tits pressed against my face!"

Lexie pulled off the only thing she had on, her panties, and led Mary into the living room where she wasted no time in satiating Mary's hunger. Yes, life back in Texas was going to be amazing!

Story #11

Mission Complete

Michelle Murphy plopped down on her cot in the tent she calls home. Listening to shots being fired all day had taken a toll on her. She knew she would never get used to hearing them and seeing dead bodies around her every day. What made today different from every other day was the fact that a member of her squad was shot, right before her very eyes.

To say she was fed up with military life was an understatement. Michelle was tired of the death and desolation that permeated their base. Tired of the sadness she saw on the faces of her squad mates and her sergeant. She was praying for the day to come when she would be allowed to go home.

Michelle reached for the stack of letters underneath her pillow; initiating her daily escape. Her long term partner Kelly lived in an apartment they shared back home in Seattle. They communicated as much as they could via Skype, emails and letters. The internet connection at the base was very inconsistent; one day they would have connection and then another, they wouldn't. They tried as much as they could to keep the communication going and the only way for them to do that was to write letters to each other on a daily basis. The letters were oftentimes delayed, so they wrote one every day, just in case they received it a week or sometimes even a month later.

She ripped open the envelope of the top letter and lie back to read it.

Hey baby,

I miss you so much. I spoke to your mother last night and it seems like she is the only person that misses you as much as I do. The restaurant was jam packed last night and I felt like I was going to pass out. I was so tired. I was surprised that after getting home and reading your letter, I no longer wanted to sleep.

I really do miss you, your soft, sweet smile; your gentle hands caressing my body. I had an absolutely intense orgasm thinking about the passion we share. The thought of feeling your mouth suck on my tits and clit, made me so horny and wet. When are you coming home? I really need you.

Write back as soon as you can.

Xoxo Kelly.

Feeling the usual frustration and nostalgia she felt whenever Kelly sent her such letters, Michelle reminded herself to find out if her application for leave had been approved.

Kelly's letter had really turned her on; she fanned herself with the envelope as she looked around the tent. Looking to sneak in a quick masturbating session in the middle of a military base could be quite challenging, especially for female. But, it was a risk that she was ready to take, and things around her appeared to be quite for the moment. She was really missing her woman and was in dire need of a release.

Kelly's words invaded her mind and after ensuring that there were no eyes on her, she covered herself with the sheet and slid a hand underneath the elastic of her boy shorts. She stared at the ceiling and slowly moved her hand in a circular motion. She needed this, she had to do this. She rubbed her clit while thinking of making love to Kelly. She imagined it was Kelly's fussy fingers, struggling not to moan as she massaged her pleasure knob. She saw a movement at the other end of the tent and stilled; waited to see if she had been discovered. A few minutes passed and no one indicated that they saw her and she got back to business. Her mind was going a mile a minute, lost in the sensations of her body. Pressure on her clit proved to not be enough and she slid two fingers into her now wet and dripping hole. She bit her teeth to keep her moans in. Oh what a sensation it was; absolutely amazing. She felt her fingers pressing against her g-spot and imagined it being Kelly's tongue. In and out she stroked, feeling the pressure building and sniffling every moan. Her orgasm came just as her sergeant walked into the tent. She closed her eyes, pretending to sleep and blocked him out. She was close, the pressure building; she was no longer in Afghanistan, she was back home with Kelly, being stroked by her expert fingers and tongue. She bit her lip as her orgasm took her body over the edge, letting go and forcing herself to not make a sound. She somehow managed to remain still until the waves of pleasurable sensations subsided.

I need to go home, she thought once more. Opening her eyes, she saw that her sergeant was sitting at the door to the tent, his mind seemed preoccupied. She knew she had to formally request leave, but they had discussed it informally before and she decided to go ahead and approach him. Unaware of her flushed cheeks, she tried her best to appear as normal as possible.

"Sergeant Grey, may I have a minute?" She asked.

He looked up at her. "Sure private Murphy, what is it?"

"I had spoken to you previously about my application for leave. Will it be granted?"

"Oh, yes. I remember that conversation. I had planned to let you go in a month's time, is that good enough?"

Now utterly ecstatic, Michelle replied, "Yes, sir. That is great. Thank you!"

She returned to straighten her cot in glee. After one long and tedious year, she would finally be able to see Kelly. She enjoyed serving her country, but she missed her family and friends. She penned a letter to Kelly immediately, to tell her the good news.

That night, she was awoken by loud chatter. A few members of her squad had been ambushed during a convoy mission. They planned an attack for the next morning. While Kelly loved to serve her country, she was tired of always fighting and risking her life. What if she died in this attack? What if she never got to see Kelly again and instead returned home in a casket? This thought scared her and she firmly decided then and there not to re-enlist. This continuous cycle of war after war no longer made sense to her, and too many lives were being sacrificed, not to mention the collateral damage to spouses and families when their loved one returned from their tour of duty. All this took a serious toll on Michelle and she got very little sleep that night.

Their mission the next day went as smoothly as one could hope for, with only one of Michelle's fellow soldiers being wounded during the attack. Kelly submitted her application for leave and informed her sergeant of her decision to not re-enlist. Having been in the army for many years, he completely understood why she wanted to get out. Kelly had no idea that Michelle's tour would be coming to an end in a month. Michelle didn't mention it because of her previous plan to re-enlist.

The mood at lunch was very somber. Her squad consisted of nine soldiers. There were a number of squads scattered about the country, but she was extremely close to the members of hers. She was closest to David, he was a member of the team she trained with and they had become really good friends. Though they were friends, David, like all the other soldiers, was unaware of Michelle's sexuality. She was constantly afraid that she would be threatened, blackmailed, hazed, or even risk receiving a dishonorable discharge, if she opened up about it.

To lighten the mood in the group, a private named Mark showed them pictures of his children that his wife had recently sent him. They were beautiful kids, with blonde hair like their dad. That made the team homesick; each sharing what they missed the most about their family. David spoke of his mother and siblings. He was twenty-three years old and was not married. He told them that the reason he enlisted was because his father was a very evil person and he wanted to bring some honor to the family. Having come from a small town, everyone knew you and your mistakes never go away. The men shared their stories one by one. Michelle had hoped that they would just skip her if she didn't volunteer to tell them, but she had no such luck.

David slapped her on her shoulders. "Michelle what about your man? Who will you be going home to?"

Michelle, being the only female member of the squad, was always treated like one of the guys. She had previously thought the guys were now seeing her as a woman, but the slap on the shoulder proved to her that they didn't.

Leaning back in her chair, she recited the lies she had practiced so many times. "Well, I do have a man back home waiting for me, his name is Ken. He is the love of my life, and his letters are what gets me through these tours. Man, I will be so happy when I am back in his arms."

"Where did you guys meet?" David asked.

"He is the manager for a high end restaurant in Seattle. I took my mom there for her birthday three years ago and that's how we met. It was love at first sight, we moved in pretty soon after and he basically holds the fort down. I didn't want to get in a relationship because I had already enlisted in the military, but he didn't care. It turned out to be the best decision I ever made, I have never been more in love." Michelle got a mushy, 'in love' feeling whenever she thought about her relationship with Kelly, whom she referred to as 'Ken' when speaking to her military comrades. Some people endure horrible relationships, others have an 'ok' relationship; but her relationship with Kelly was perfect. She couldn't have asked for a better partner.

The only issue they faced was discrimination. Though society thinks that it no longer exists, they are mistaken. That is the main reason

Michelle keeps her sexual orientation hidden from her comrades in the military.

David interrupted her thoughts. "Well Murphy, Ken seems like he is definitely worthy of you. Tell him he better not ever hurt you, or he'll have us to reckon with," he finished with a smile.

"I will." She replied. "Okay guys, that's enough from me."

The conversation slowly dwindled as the squad dispersed; going for a midday rest in various areas of the site. Michelle went to read another of Kelly's letters, needing it to take her mind off the sad events she sees daily.

Hey baby,

It's me again. You would never believe what happened today. I got into an accident and my car was badly damaged. Now I have to be using a rental that is costing me a lot of money. I mentioned this to my mom and she told me to stop complaining and just be grateful that I have my life. That was true and it made me feel bad that I am here complaining about my damaged car when you are there risking your life for your country every day.

I miss you and can't wait until you get home. I am anxious and excited. The dogs are excited too, Sally has gotten so big. She looks completely different; you might not recognize her when you get back. So much has changed since you left, but one thing remains the same – I am still madly in love with you. Have you realized that we have been apart for most of our relationship? Yet our love is the strongest I have ever known. My love for you knows no bounds. I am so anxious for you to get home so that we can enjoy our love in the way so many others do, with you being out of danger, and me in your arms.

I wonder where my life would be had I not met you that night at my restaurant. I don't think that I would have been this happy with anyone else. You alone have my heart, my mind, my body and my soul. I know that we will be one of those fairy tale couples who defy all odds and live a long and happy life together. We are going to have the most beautiful children (with some help of course) and have a wonderful life together. Growing old and watching our grandkids playing in our yard will bring us such joy. I know I am rambling now, but this is what I imagine our life to be.

I hope this letter finds you safe and doing okay. I so love and miss you.

Xoxo Kelly.

Kelly's letters always made Michelle happy and sad at the same time. It was a really hard situation to be in; not having your loved ones with you, knowing you could be killed at any moment. The feeling of loneliness filled her days, and the fact that she had to hide the fact that she is a lesbian and wasn't able to openly discuss her relationship with Kelly had her on edge at all times. Her guard had to be up, she had to ensure that she never let it slip because she had no idea how the members of her squad would react to finding out. Kelly's mind had never been at ease since she got deployed. She hoped for the day that tolerance was really shown to members of the gay community. Her secret was like a heavy burden on her shoulders and she longed to be free.

She penned a response to Kelly.

My love,

I know you miss me and I miss you terribly also. Life is such a priceless and precious thing. Being here has made me more appreciative and I know that we will have a happy and fulfilling life together. Knowing that I will be coming home to you pulls me through each day. You are my inspiration, my love, my life, my world. The future looks so bright with you standing by my side.

I often wonder how our children will look. I know you will be the one to carry them, and you will make an amazing mother. I hope our daughter has your long hair, slender, feminine body and looks just like you. Do you think you are ready for this journey with me? I am twenty-eight years old and you are twenty-six years old. We aren't old, but we are also not particularly young either. Having children is a big step, but it is one I am ready to take with you. After all this time of being away from you, I am just ready to begin the rest of our lives.

I will be home soon, my love. Keep holding on.

Michelle

Michelle spent the rest of the afternoon doing some exercises with her squad. She was comfortable around them to an extent, having been with this team for over a year. The anxiety came when the topic of family and lovers came up; the shield around her would go up in an instant.

After training, she decided that she would reach out to one of her friends back in Seattle to help her plan her very own surprise party for her return. She would have her friend arrange a 'retirement party' at Kelly's restaurant, and Kelly would be none the wiser that the party would actually be for Michelle's coming home. Nor would she know that the 'retirement party' was in celebration of Michelle's official leaving of the Army. As Michelle scribbled down notes regarding the arrangements of the party, she tried to image the look on Kelly's face when she walked through the door, giving Kelly the surprise of a lifetime. Kelly knew that Michelle was trying to get leave to come home for at least a visit, but that is all she knew. She didn't know when, or even if it was going to happen.

Michelle's next issue was to figure out how she would pull this whole surprise thing off, since she was all the way in Afghanistan, without Kelly finding out. Her mother would spill; she couldn't keep a secret. Her sisters couldn't keep a secret either, so they would definitely let it slip somehow. The only person she could think of was their mutual friend, Ana. Michelle knew that Ana would be able to do a good job and no one would suspect a thing. As Michelle was writing a letter to send out to Ana, Sergeant Grey informed her that she would be able to go home two weeks earlier than was originally expected.

Michelle was so happy, she jumped up and danced in front of all her comrades; something she never did because they always teased her that she looked like she was doing a touchdown dance. She was beautiful, but she was also buff and athletic and quite striking at five feet, eight inches tall. She didn't mind the teasing really it was just a part of military life, and all in good nature.

She scrapped the letter she was writing. There was no way it would reach the states in time for her to get a response from Ana. Since Michelle had a couple of hours before their next convoy mission, she headed over to the makeshift internet café on base to try and reach Ana and discuss her plans for her early return home, and of course, her surprise party at Kelly's restaurant. Ana was happy to help as Michelle told her exactly what to do. She was to plan a retirement party at Michelle's restaurant and invite all of their friends and family. Nobody was to have any idea that Michelle would be coming home early, especially Kelly, or that the party was in her honor. She fully trusted Ana's capabilities to pull this off and to not be found out.

As Michelle returned back to her tent barracks to ready herself for their next convoy mission her mind wandered to being reunited with Kelly. She and Kelly have been together for a little more than three years, and Michelle has been away on military tour for a full two of those three years. That kind of patience and tenacity displayed a level of testament and commitment to their relationship that touched Michelle at the very center of her heart, and her eyes began to tear as she thought of how lucky she was to have Kelly in her life.

Two weeks later, as her tour and term of military service was coming to an end, Michelle was pre-occupied with all of her out-processing and was unable to contact Kelly. She missed her daily letters with Kelly, but she was just so busy and overwhelmed that she barely had time to sleep. She was okay with it though, because she knew that it was just for a few more days and then she'd be heading back in the states, back in Seattle, and most importantly, back into the arms of her love.

Back in Seattle, Ana was busily planning the 'retirement party. Making the reservation and inviting the guests was a breeze. She went over the details with Kelly, being very careful with everything she said, so as not to give away who the 'retirement party' was actually for. Kelly sounded tired and exhausted on the phone and looked even more worried when they met to view the private room for the party.

"Kelly, are you okay? You don't look so well," Ana asked.

Looking extremely worried, Kelly sat in a nearby chair. "Ana, I am really worried. I haven't heard from Michelle and I'm afraid something might have happened to her. We communicate regularly, even if it is just a brief letter, but I haven't heard anything from her in almost two weeks and I am so scared."

Ana felt a strong tinge of guilt. Kelly was obviously in serious distress over Michelle's wellbeing, but she gave Michelle her word that she would keep her early return a secret, no matter what, so she kept her mouth shut. Ana knew that Michelle was safe and well, and Kelly's worrying and agony would be over very soon. "Oh, Kelly, I am sure that there must be a reason why she hasn't contacted you. Surely everything is okay." She replied, wrapping her arms around her worry-stricken friend.

"Ana, you don't understand. I would die if something happened to her. Why hasn't she written in over two weeks, or emailed, or anything?" Kelly was now sobbing and Ana felt really bad for her.

Deciding on a tactic to take her mind off of Michelle, Ana turned the conversation to business and the 'retirement party' she had booked at

Kelly's restaurant; explaining to her how everything should be and asking her to take notes. That did the trick, for Kelly was always able to use her work as a distraction from her problems. Within a matter of minutes she was able to concentrate solely on planning the party and not on her missing lover.

Distracting herself was a lot harder when she got home that night, however. There were pictures of Michelle all over their Seattle apartment and Kelly curled up with one of her dogs and sobbed. Her sobbing ended after she ran out of tears and she re-read a letter that she had received from Michelle a few months back. In a part of the letter Michelle had written that should anything happen to her, Kelly would be able to know. She explained that the bond they shared connected them in some way and that if either one was ever hurt, the other would be able to know. Kelly was beside herself with worry, but she did not 'feel' in her heart that Michelle was hurt. Communications from Afghanistan to the United States was always sketchy, and if there was a security issue, then that only complicated things further. Those thoughts comforted her in some way and she somehow managed to sleep that night.

Over the next couple of days, Kelly devoted all of her time and energy into work. It was thankfully really busy and she barely had time to think about anything other than work related matters, especially since she was preparing for Ana's retirement party for her friend. Two days later, Kelly was overseeing the hectic happenings at work, with her time being split between overseeing Ana's party and running the rest of the restaurant. Ana arrived at six p.m. to greet her guests, many of whom Kelly was also acquainted with, but by that time everything had already been set up and Kelly was no longer needed in the private room. Therefore, Ana didn't have the uncomfortable situation of explaining just who exactly this 'retirement party' was for. After all, Kelly would find out for herself soon enough.

A few minutes before seven o'clock, Kelly was busy in the main restaurant area when Ana came to ask for her assistance. She asked Kelly to follow her back to the private room where the party was being held, which Kelly nervously did. Worried that her staff may have done something wrong, Kelly looked cautiously around the room as she entered. Amy asked her to have a seat and Kelly felt her whole body tense up in anticipation of what disaster might have just occurred.

Ana seemed to be stalling and something just felt weird about the whole situation to Kelly. Just as Kelly was about to ask what was going, she heard a small commotion near the room door entrance and all eyes in the room turned in that direction. At first thinking her eyes were deceiving her, Kelly watched as the crowd parted and Michelle walked into the room, her eyes obviously scanning for her love. Kelly's heart leaped out of her chest as she jumped out of the chair and ran straight across the room and straight into Michelle's open arms.

"Michelle….," her words and emotions caught in her throat, as she made across the floor. "Is it really…."

"You're home! You're home!" She said through heaving tears after a long moment of embracing. Kelly was surprise she was actually able to speak. Her knees were weak and if Michelle had not been holding her tightly in her arms, she was sure she would have collapsed to the floor.

"I was so worried. I thought something happened to you when I hadn't heard from you in over two weeks." Tears streamed down Kelly's cheeks and Michelle gladly kissed them dry. "Are you ok?"

"Yes, baby, I'm ok," replied Michelle.

"I've been trying to keep my mind off of negative thoughts with work and organizing Ana's party, and …..hey, wait a minute." Kelly's gaze alternated back and forth between Ana and Michelle. "Ana, who is this friend of yours who is retiring?"

Ana just smiled, but didn't respond. She let Michelle unveil the surprise.

"It's me baby, I'm the one retiring," Michelle said looking intently into Kelly's eyes. "I not only got my leave request granted early, I also decided to not re-enlist. As of this morning, I am officially retired from the Army and all yours."

"You mean…no more leaving?"

"No more leaving."

Kelly jumped into Michelle's arms and the flash of camera phones lit up the room as their friends commemorated their heartfelt reunion.

Still hugging Michelle tightly, Kelly asked, "So Ana knew all along that you were ok, and you two planned this party as a surprise?" She looked over at Ana for an explanation, who nodded in acknowledgement.

Hugs, kisses and congratulations were going all around as friends came up to congratulate Michelle on her retirement. Of course, nobody was more excited than Kelly who had to hold herself back a bit to allow Michelle's friends time to express their support. She would have her to herself soon enough….well, not soon enough, but later that evening. After two four-year enlistments and three tours overseas, Michelle was finally done with her military service. It was finally over. Kelly was again speechless and all she could do was cry tears of joy. She was so happy that this was finally over and that they would be able to begin a new chapter in their lives.

The party was a success, and Kelly was able to get her manager counterpart to come and close the restaurant that night so she could go home early with Michelle. All they wanted to do at this point was to go home and spend the rest of the evening together, alone. They said their goodbyes at around eleven o'clock and drove the short distance home to their apartment.

The dogs barked excitedly and jumped up onto Michelle as soon as she walked through the door, and they licked her face eagerly letting her know that they missed her just as much as Kelly had. Words could not describe how happy Michelle was to finally be home, and this time, for good. She missed its scent, security and most importantly, its occupants. Michelle sat down on the couch and Kelly sat down beside her, placing her head on Michelle's shoulder. No words were said, nothing needed to be said. They both knew how much they meant to each other and how much of a happy moment this was. Having spent most of their relationship apart due to Michelle's military tours, this was the ultimate moment for them, the moment they had waited their entire relationship for…..the beginning of forever.

Michelle kissed Kelly softly on the lips before heading off to take a hot shower. "Let me freshen up for you lover, and I'll be right back to show you how much I love you."

It had been an exhausting day, but Kelly was no longer tired. Her whole body tingled in anticipation of her lover's touch once again. She ran around straightening up their bedroom, for she hadn't been anticipating Michelle's return. She lit some candles and put on one of their favorite soft jazz stations on the radio. Then she changed out of her clothes, freshened up her hair and spritzed on some sexy musk perfume. Not sure which piece of lingerie to put on for Michelle, she just decided to go sans any. Kelly lay naked on the bed in their candlelit bedroom, allowing Michelle to take in the beautiful view as she emerged from the shower.

"You are absolutely stunning, Kelly." Michelle said, breathing heavily. She wanted to just ravage every inch of Kelly's beautiful body, but restrained herself from moving too fast.

Michelle let her bath towel fall to the floor as she walked over to the bed and straddled herself on top of Kelly's curvaceous hips.

"I missed you so much, but now, here you are, back in my arms. You are finally where you belong," Kelly said. Michelle leaned down and kissed Kelly softly on her lips, increasing the intensity as the seconds went by. Kelly moaned into her mouth, feeling connected to her in every way that mattered.

After a long, passion-filled kiss, Kelly pushed Michelle's body upright and took control. "Sit there for me baby." Kelly said, pointing to a chair in the corner of the room. Michelle eagerly obeyed and Kelly positioned herself at the edge of the bed with her legs open. She knew Michelle loved watching her masturbate and it had been a long time, it was time to give her a treat.

She ran one hand slowly along her inner thigh and used the other one to caress her pert breasts. She could see Michelle's nipples stiffen and knew that she was as turned on as she was. She ran her fingers along her smooth pussy lips and then made slow circles around her swelling clit, as a soft moan escaped her mouth. She rubbed her clit in a figure eight motion, being careful to not apply enough pressure to cause an orgasm, only enough to make her writhe on the bed. Her moans now filled the room and her juices glistened at her entrance. Michelle licked her lips and Kelly knew the temptation was maddening.

Unable to stay in the chair for one more second, Michelle dove right in for the prize, licking Kelly's juices from her entrance, all the way up to her clit, causing her to let out a long and loud moan. She sucked Kelly's pussy into her mouth, relishing the delicious taste that she had been deprived of for over a year. She licked every crevice of her, reaching a hand up to hold and massage her beautiful tits with her hands. Kelly was in pleasure land, moaning and writhing beneath her lover. Michelle inserted one finger, then another into Kelly's dripping wet furnace. Kelly moaned even louder, placing her hands on Michelle's head.

Wanting to return some of the pleasure she was feeling, Kelly motioned for Michelle to go above her into the '69' position. Michelle happily obliged. Their love-making was to continue all through the night, making up for time lost. Kelly licked at Michelle's pussy like it was a melting ice-cream cone, while her hands reacquainting themselves with Michelle's taut, lean body.

Michelle fetched Kelly's favorite vibrator from the bedside table. Kelly was so wet that she needed no artificial lubrication and the vibrator slipped in easily. Kelly's moans could surely be heard next door, but she didn't care. She was lost in ecstasy, existing to feel only pleasure. Stroke after stroke brought her closer and closer to yet another orgasm. She was weak and trembling as the sensations took over her body. She felt the pressure building, the intensity rising. Up, up, she went riding on the waves of pleasure, her orgasm seemingly lasting forever. Then finally, she crashed. Wave after wave, and down she came, until her breathing returned to normal after a few minutes. Kelly was eager to return the pleasures bestowed upon her, and she caressed and kissed, licked and sucked until Michelle was having an explosive orgasm of her own.

They lay sated in each other's arms after a repeat of climactic pleasures, neither of them wanting the moment, or day, to end.

"That was just as beautiful as you are Kelly." Michelle kissed her lover tenderly on the forehead and hugged her tightly against her body.

Kelly nestled her head in the crook of Michelle's arm, feeling safe and at home. "Are you ready for tomorrow, and the next day, and the next?" She asked.

"With you by my side, I am ready for anything." Michelle answered. "I love you Kelly."

"I love you Michelle."

They fell asleep in each other's arms, content and happy as visions of lifelong happiness filled both of their dream state bliss.

Story #12

Anatomy of Love

D r. Vickie Morris grabbed her purse and work bag as she exited her car in the doctors parking area of Cook County Hospital in Chicago, Illinois and headed towards one of the employees only entrances into the hospital to start her 12 hour night shift. Life at the hospital was anything but boring, yet it was exactly this fast-paced, hectic and unpredictable environment that her personality was best suited for. As she walked towards the room at the end of the hall that was designated for the residents, she saw a male nurse eyeing her and she pretended to not see. She knew that some of the hospital staff had suspicions over her sexual orientation, but no one had ever been bold enough to ask, at least not outright. Used to getting attention from both sexes, Vickie knew how to easily brush off unwanted interest and advances. Standing at six feet tall, she was a strikingly beautiful mulatto woman with short, curly hair. She often heard that men were intimidated by taller women, but never in her thirty-four years had she ever felt that that had been the case for her. Men seemed to flock to her like moths to a flame, and the only thing about her that she thought intimidated men was her intelligence. It had nothing to do with her height. Well, then there was the fact that she preferred the fairer sex, but she was highly guarded as to whom she let that artifact be known to.

Ready to get to work, Vickie exited the resident's room and headed towards the main nursing station in the emergency room. Walking towards her, she spotted the sexy nursing student that she had been secretly lusting after for the past couple of weeks, whose name was Blanca. As they walked past one another, she opened the door and nodded. Blanca was a refreshing addition to the hospital staff. She had a very pleasant personality and was obviously very eager to learn about patient care, although truth-be-told, Vickie wasn't so sure the E.R.

would be the best location choice for Blanca once she received her nursing license. While Blanca proved to be more than capable with many of the emergency room patients, in the more traumatic cases of gunshot and stabbing victims, industrial accidents and extreme domestic abuse, Blanca's reactions outwardly told of her ability to handle the more extreme trauma cases that often come through a level 1 emergency room. Nonetheless, Vickie thought Blanca was professionally capable as well as sexy as hell and desirable. However, Vickie has always been nothing but professional and has never thought of any of her fellow staff members in a sexual manner, that is, until Blanca. Though she was very much attracted to Blanca's long, black hair, dark brown eyes and signature Mexican figure, she knew that she had to keep things professional. Crossing that line could mean risking both of their professional careers.

She was doing her residency in emergency medicine, under the guidance of the chief trauma surgeon at the hospital. Vickie was updated on the evening's happenings and was preparing when the next trauma case came in. She hadn't been sitting down for three minutes when she heard the call for the trauma team and they all sprung into action. The paramedics that brought in the bloodied patient were shouting out what details they knew including the fact that the victim had multiple gunshot wounds and a team comprised of Vickie, some other residents, nurses and the chief trauma surgeon worked feverishly to assess and stabilize the young man. Vickie realized that Blanca was part of the responding team, and because Blanca was a nursing student, she had to work by the instructions of the charge nurse and her main job was to primarily observe, stay out of the way, and to only do what she was told by her. Vickie just gave her a passing glance, as she had to focus because of the urgency of the situation.

The life threatening situations in the emergency room meant that they all had to be keen alert, and move very fast and accurately without deviation. All trauma cases were handled by a trauma team, and every player performed their particular duties with precious precision. Like a fine-tuned orchestra, they each had a role to play that contributed to the overall outcome, and just like a conductor, the lead trauma surgeon directed and instructed everyone accordingly, ensuring the expediency of which medical care was doled out to the victim. Everyone stood in their usual places around the patient, and having worked together for a while, they were able to move swiftly around each other with a fluidity that was typically incomprehensible to most, yet most appreciated by patients as well as their anxious loved ones.

The E.R. was a drastically different experience from the other clinical rotations Blanca had to do for her required nursing credits, and light years away from her exposure at her previous job. She had been working as a Certified Nursing Assistant (CNA) in a nursing home for six years, and although she enjoyed her job, she needed a change. She wanted to expand her education and career options, and since she really enjoyed the aspects of healthcare and helping people, she enrolled in nursing school. Currently in her final block of schooling, Blanca could now see herself approaching the coveted finish line. All of her class blocks exposed her to a well-rounded array of health specialties and the ability to hone her craft within each niche, but never before had she been exposed to so much, in such short time, as she had now during her final clinical rotation in the E.R.. The only thing that was bothersome to her was the gruesome cases they saw come in, and on such a regular basis. There were gunshot victims, stabbing victims, drug overdoses and domestic violence cases. These types of violent, trauma cases often left Blanca feeling shell shocked by the end of her shift. She was both surprised and saddened at the level of neglect, indifference and violence that humans were capable of inflicting onto one another. The fact that little thought, if any, was given as to the consequences another person would suffer as a result of the persons inflicting the pain onto another was hard for her to come to terms with. Her experience in the emergency room didn't change her mind from completing nursing school. She certainly didn't plan to give up after investing so much time and effort into a field she genuinely enjoyed. However, working in the E.R. only made her positive that that was not the area in which she ultimately wanted to work, and Blanca had nothing but the utmost respect for all the medical personnel that worked constantly under those circumstances. The physical and emotional part of the job was very demanding and one had to be strong on both accounts to be able to do it.

The lead trauma surgeon quickly spat out orders for CAT scans, X-rays and blood work on the gunshot victim and Blanca watched in awe as all of that was done within about five minutes right there in the room. The trauma team concluded that he had suffered a perforated liver and lung from a couple of the bullets, and the patient was packaged and rushed upstairs for emergency surgery to remove the bullets from his body, stop the internal bleeding and repair what they could to his damaged internal organs. Blanca watched the pretty doctor working hand in hand with the lead trauma surgeon and realized that it was none other than Dr. Morris, the most captivating woman she had ever seen, and one she had hoped to interact with from the first day that her clinical rotations started at the hospital. But, who was she kidding. That captivating beauty was a doctor, and doctors don't pay attention to nursing students.

After the patient was sent into surgery, Dr. Morris and the rest of the team had left the room. Blanca was instructed by the charge nurse to clean and restock the trauma room immediately so that it would be ready for the next incoming trauma patient. As Blanca cleaned the room, she couldn't help but still admire the speed at which everything happened. The victim was in and out of the trauma room in no time, and afterwards the team immediately went there separate ways tending to the other emergency room patients in their unique roles, always ready to assemble for the next incoming trauma. The hands-on experience was priceless and there wasn't enough classroom experience in the world to prepare you for life in an E.R.. The other thing suddenly on Blanca's mind was Dr. Morris. Yes, the captivating, beautiful, intelligent and skilled Dr. Morris. She had taken notice to her and had been admiring her, albeit from a distance, from the first time she laid eyes on her. Dr. Morris had that complete put-together attractiveness that was rare. She was confident and proficient in her job; very engaging and attentive; she moved with grace; spoke with grace; and had this mysterious allure to her that Blanca was drawn to in a very powerful way. However, Blanca often did catch Dr. Morris looking at her strangely. Was she scrutinizing her job performance, her work appearance; her professional demeanor? If she was in any other environment, she might even entertain the thought that the lovely doctor might actually be attracted to her. The very thought of that possibility sent a ripple of arousal to stir inside Blanca. There was just something about being in her presence that made Blanca's nerves stand on end, but in a good way…a very good way… a very sexual way! Blanca reigned in her stray thoughts, determined to focus on nothing but her work for the remainder of her busy shift. Besides, deep down, she knew that the possibility of her dating Dr. Morris was probably next to impossible.

At about 12:30 am, Blanca was assisting one of the E.R. nurses to check on the many currently roomed patients. The patients were lesser emergency cases, some of whom were waiting on diagnostic testing, some who needed to have their broken limbs put in a cast, and others were waiting to be discharged. Blanca and the nurse exited a room to enter another, when she spotted Dr. Morris returning from the operating room. She had a patient's chart in her hand and she looked up from the chart and smiled at Blanca as she walked past them. Blanca felt a tingle ripple through her body. That smile almost made her melt, and she was sure that Dr. Morris smiled at 'her' and not 'them'.

They walked into the room of an elderly man who was just admitted and complaining of chest pains. He was presenting in very poor condition and they quickly set about asking the man questions, taking his vitals and hooking him up to an EKG monitor. Just as the E.R. nurse finished hooking up the leads to the heart monitor, the man went into cardiac arrest. The nurse sounded the 'code-blue' alert and a team of doctors and nurses immediately rushed into the room with a crash cart. Blanca watched as the team worked swiftly and with coordinated effort to save the man's life. Blanca noticed that one of the doctors on that team, and the first to arrive in the room was Dr. Morris. She quickly shouted instructions to the rest of the staff, and just like in the trauma room with the gunshot victim, everyone knew their precise role and not a seconds worth of time was wasted with any confusion. They administered injections and several rounds of shocks, which resulted in the man regaining a heart rhythm. Blanca was once again amazed at the efficiency of the doctors and nurses. A cardiac team was dispatched to the man's room, where they ordered an operating room be immediately readied for the patient. With no down time to be had, everyone again resumed their duties with the other awaiting patients.

Blanca stared out of the hospital window, enjoying the first rays of morning sun as she put on her coat. It had been a long night, the busiest yet in fact, since starting her clinical rotations at the hospital, and her body desperately needed some long hours of sleep to recoup from her adrenaline-filled shift. She walked over to the elevator that would take her to employee parking, and as she stood waiting for it to open, Dr. Morris walked up. It appeared by the fact that she too was wearing a coat, that she was also leaving.

"Hello Blanca. Busy shift it's been, huh?" Dr. Morris greeted.

Smiling, Blanca replied. "Hello Dr. Morris. Yes, incredibly busy. The busiest I've seen it since starting my rotation."

"Please, you can call me Vickie when we're off duty." The door slid open and they stepped into the elevator. "So, how are your studies coming along? Are you close to completing school?" she asked.

"They're going well, and yes, I'm almost finished with my schooling. This is my last clinical rotation, and then it's just a matter of studying for my license testing next month. Apart from being tired and a bit traumatized from some of the emergency cases that I've seen, things are going great," Blanca replied, catching a whiff of Vickie's scent in the close quarters of the elevator. It was intoxicating. But then again, everything about her was intoxicating. And, she knew it was her natural scent because nobody was allowed to wear perfume while working.

"So, you are almost done, that is great news. Myself, I'm doing my residency in emergency medicine. Its hard work and those of us who get into medicine know the toll it can take. But, if it's your calling, it will all be worth it my dear."

Being referred to as 'my dear', made Blanca think that there might really be a 'vibe' between the two of them, and Vickie's smile did have a flirty tone to it. Was it just wishful thinking or was it sleep deprivation? Blanca wasn't sure, but there was some kind of subtle vibe going on, she just couldn't put her finger on. "I guess it will be," she responded, and she was astonished by the words she heard Vickie say next.

"Well, please let me know if you need any help or guidance while you're here. I know the road is rough, but with help, it can be easier." Vickie smiled that flirty smile again when Blanca thanked her for her offer. Before she could say anything more, the elevator door opened and they each went their separate ways to their vehicles.

Blanca's thoughts raced as she made her way to her car. A doctor offering their assistance to a nursing student was unheard of, maybe to a medical student, but a nursing student? Blanca was literally floored by the offer. Was it just a kind gesture? Did she possibly see Blanca as more than just another potential fellow hospital employee? Was that even possible? She thought not of her traumatic night as she drove home to her apartment, she thought only of Vickie. In fact, try as she might, she couldn't get her off of her mind.

Over the next three weeks, Blanca and Vickie's paths crossed quite often in the emergency room. They worked alongside each other in the trauma room on many occasions, and on the few occasions that the emergency room was quiet, they would sit and drink coffee while Vickie gave Blanca advice on her career. Blanca looked forward to their talks over coffee. She valued the advice she received from Vickie, but her company is what she looked forward to the most. She eagerly looked forward to every shift just so she could be in close proximity with this amazing woman.

Blanca found herself constantly wondering if she was setting herself up for disappointment. Whenever she and Vickie had a moment alone together, the atmosphere was always slightly tense, but it was a good tense. It was a sexual tension that subtly, but noticeably, increased each time they saw each other. Blanca found herself looking at Vickie seductively on several occasions and she had to quickly control her outward demeanor, not to mention her growing feelings, before Vickie realized. The catch however, was that Blanca actually did want Vickie to realize. She often caught Vickie looking at her strangely, but she knew it must be her imagination coupled with wishful thinking. Sure, Vickie had been true to her word and helped guide and advice Blanca on her professional endeavors, but nothing more than that has ever been spoken or implied. Yet Blanca yearned for Vickie. She dreamt of holding her in her arms, of putting aside the pretenses and expressing her feelings.

Blanca's rotation at the hospital came to an end the following week and her emotions were torn. At one end she was ecstatic to have finished school and all of her clinical rotations, and at the other end she was disappointed, and even sad, that she would no longer be seeing Vickie. They were by no means close friends, but with the cover of 'getting professional guidance and advice' she was able to spend one-on-one time with her during her shifts. And now, even that small gift of close proximity and personal attention from the woman she has secretly yearned for during these past weeks, has reached its conclusion. Was the window of romantic opportunity now closed? Was it really ever open to begin with?

It was a Friday evening, and Blanca's friends were taking her out to a local bar that they often hung out at to celebrate her completing nursing school. Her mixed emotions had her dragging her feet as she got herself ready to join them. The combination of live music, cocktails and friends that would have once had her running to be the first one there at the local bar where they were meeting up, she now had little interest in. However, with the help of her friends, her evening panned out to be better than she had expected. They played pool, shot darts and bantered over barbeque chicken wings and other bad bar food. Her friend's companionship and lively conversation were refreshing, and just what she needed, thought Blanca. With her grueling school and work schedule, it had been a long time since she was able to just hang out with her friends and have fun. It also helped take her mind off of Vickie.

"So, what's next for you, Blanca?" her friend Eric asked her.

Blanca took a sip of her bottled root beer before answering her friend. "Well, I still have to take my state exam next month, so I'm not out of the woods just yet. It will be lots and lots of studying these next few weeks."

Eric patted her on the shoulder. "You're a brainiac, and I have no doubt whatsoever that you'll ace your exam."

Raising her glass in the air, she said, "Let's drink to that!" The group raised their glasses and drank to her success.

Blanca was physically and emotionally much more relaxed than she had been when first arriving at the bar, and they were all having so much fun that they lost track of time. Around midnight, they settled up the bar bill and were slowly getting ready to leave, when the very last person in the world Blanca had expected to see, walked into the bar. It was none other than Vickie, and she was accompanied by one of the male nurses that Blanca recognized from the hospital. Questions flooded through her mind, one after another. Had she been wrong all along in her assumptions? She was under the impression that Vickie was gay, or probably gay, or at the very least bisexual. If she was, then why was she here with that man? Of course lesbians can have male friends, she in fact had many. She was being ridiculous, of course, but it was her unspoken feelings about Vickie that were suddenly hijacking her thoughts. Was the sexual tension between them imagined? Or, was it all one-sided? She was fairly certain that it wasn't and she was trying to understand what was going on. Had she been mesmerized by a straight woman? Vickie spotted Blanca at the table with her friends and immediately walked over to say hello.

"Well, hello there Blanca, looks like you're celebrating," she greeted.

"Hi Vickie. Hi Byron," she replied a bit nervously. "Yes, we are. My wonderful friends have taken me out to celebrate my finishing nursing school and to relax and let me hair down for an evening." Blanca then introduced her friends to Vickie and Byron. Byron then excused himself and headed towards the bar to order them some drinks. Vickie invited Blanca to join them for a celebratory drink but Blanca felt funny about doing so because she didn't want to abandoned her friends. Eric either read her mind, or sensed her hesitancy and interrupted at just the right moment.

"Blanca, go ahead and enjoy a drink with your work friends. We're all getting ready to leave anyway."

"Ok then. Thanks for a wonderful party tonight Eric," she said, giving him a hug and a kiss on the cheek goodbye. "I'll give you a call tomorrow."

As Eric and the rest of her friends exited the bar, Blanca turned back towards Vickie. "Are you sure that Byron won't mind me joining you?" She almost regretted asking the question as soon as the words escaped her lips, but everything happens for a reason.

Shaking her head, Vickie's face was a bit quizzical.

"I don't see why he would be. We both just pulled a 12 hour day shift and then got held over due to a multi-vehicle accident at shift change that brought in eight patients and three of them were traumas. It's been an ultra-long and ultra-hectic shift and we're just grabbing a cocktail to relax before heading home. Besides, Bryon is married, if that's what you're hinting to." Blanca sent up a silent prayer of thanks. There was still hope that she was indeed gay.

"So, are you enjoying your freedom, now that you've finished school?" Vickie asked as they sat down at one of the pub tables.

"Well, I am not exactly free just yet. I still have to take my state exam next month, so I have some pretty intense studying to do."

"Ah, yes, your exam. You'll do great, I know it, and it'll all be over before you know it. Have you put any thought into what area of healthcare you'd like to be in?"

"Not sure yet, just trying to focus on my studying until I get past the state exam. Probably not the E.R. though," Blanca replied with a laugh. "I'll leave all that trauma and drama to those better suited for that. I think I'm better aligned for the slower-paced, nurturing opportunities."

"Slow-paced and nurturing huh? I wouldn't mind experiencing some of that," replied Vickie, hoping Blanca would catch her between-the-lines intention. Blanca's eyes widened and her pretty lips formed a sexy smile of acknowledgment. Yes, it appears that she did catch Vickie's intention.

"Was that a….um, are you asking…." Blanca's stuttering reply was interrupted by Byron returning with their drinks. He sat them down on the table, sat down on one of the bar stools and then raised his glass to toast Blanca on her accomplishment of finishing nursing school. The three of them clinked their glasses and then chatted for a while about work. After Byron finished the last of his drink, he got up to leave.

"Time for me to head home ladies. A shower, bed and wife await me. Hey, good luck on your exam Blanca, hope to see you around sometime," Byron finished, as he gave Blanca a hug and then headed out the door.

"Looks like it's just the two of us," Vickie said coyly, as she stared deep into Blanca's eyes.

"Yeah just the two of us," Blanca responded. A rush of new questions flooded her brain, and suddenly feeling courageous after having a cocktail, she decided to finally address those questions that have been tormenting her for weeks, or at least the main one.

"Vickie, are you flirting with me?"

"I suppose I am."

"You suppose? Ok, I'm feeling brave so I'm….."

"Bar's closed ladies. Time to leave," called out the bartender. Again, Blanca was cut-off mid-sentence and mid-thought, this time by the bartender.

"Looks like we'll have to finish this conversation another time," Vickie said with a smile. "Listen, I'd be happy to help you to study for your exam over the weekend, if you'd like, that is. I'm actually off from work and I have nothing planned." Vickie offered as Blanca was sitting there still trying to figure out what was happening between them.

Vickie stood, put on her coat and threw down a cash tip on the table. Still not sure what to think, Blanca quickly accepted Vickie's offer. "That would be great. Who better to help me than an actual emergency room doctor, right? What time should I get there?"

"You can come by at around five p.m.." Vickie took out a business card and handed it to Blanca. "Call me for the address and directions."

"Ladies, time to go. I got cabs outside ready to take you home," called out the bartender as he switched off most of the lights in the bar.

"Great. I'll see you tomorrow," said Blanca as she headed towards one of the waiting cabs. On the ride home, she reviewed the events of the evening as well as the past couple of months. She was sure that there was something between her and Vickie, but when Vickie didn't show anything more than subtle signs of interest, she wasn't so sure. Then, of course, her clinical rotations came to an end, as well as her crossing paths with Vickie. Her low expectations for a night out with friends this evening surprised her, and she had a really good time enjoying their company. And then, there was the surprise run-in with Vickie at the bar, and her flirtatious demeanor and remarks, this time a bit more overtly. Once again hopeful, but still confused, Blanca reached into her purse for some cash to pay the cab driver, ever curious as to what might transpire during her visit tomorrow. Even if it was only to study, it could open up the opportunity for something more. After all, she was actually being invited to Vickie's personal home. Blanca went to bed happy and contented.

Blanca woke up at 8 o'clock the next morning. Though she was tired from staying out late, she had to get up, shower and start studying. As she started a pot of coffee, instead of focusing on her future and her exam, her mind was filled with thoughts of Vickie, and last night. Their flirting at the bar was unexpected, and she wondered if she had been drunk and was just imagining that it happened. Could it be that Vickie really liked her? If she did, was there any chance of a relationship for them considering their positions? Blanca spent the day unable to concentrate on her studies, as thoughts of the sexy doctor kept invading her mind. She called Vickie just after noon to get directions to her apartment, and afterwards her eyes were constantly checking the clock, counting down the hours and minutes until it was time to leave.

Vickie had dinner ready and waiting by four-forty five, as she placed a bottle of white wine in a bucket of ice on the kitchen counter. She wasn't nervous to see Blanca, she was more anxious. She had waited for the moment to tell her how she has felt ever since she started giving her one-on-one guidance at the hospital. Now that Blanca's rotations had ended, she had nothing stopping her anymore. Having told Blanca last night that they would be studying, she knew that she had to do what she had promised, but that could be done after they got to know each other better. At least that was the way she had hoped the evening would play out, and dinner and wine was the perfect way to start the evening.

She got up when she heard the doorbell ring at three minutes to five. She opened the door to find Blanca smiling at her, coat and book bag in hand, and her shapely figure nicely filling out a white sweater and black skirt. The skirt stopped just above her knees, showing a tease of skin above her knee-high boots.

"Come on in." Vickie stepped aside to let her pass. "You look beautiful this evening Blanca." Her eyes took in the panoramic view of Blanca's figure as she walked past her and her nose inhaled the heavenly scent of her perfume, while her mind tried to temper its excitement of finally having an opportunity to cross that line between professional and personal relationship.

"You have a really nice place," Blanca said as she walked in, her eyes scanning the furniture and décor of Vickie's luxury high rise apartment.

"Thank you. Let me take your coat and bag," replied Vickie, hanging the items on the coat rack next to the door. "Make yourself at home. I made us dinner, I hope you don't mind. The kitchen is this way, if you're ready."

"That is very kind of you, I wasn't expecting dinner."

"Going straight to intense study seemed so informal, and I want you to feel comfortable around me."

As they turned the corner at the end of the hall, it opened up into a lovely dining space with the kitchen being separated by a half wall with large potted ferns sitting on top. The table was already set and Blanca noticed that whatever was cooking smelled absolutely amazing. "Wow, this looks great, and something does sure smell amazing."

"I hope you'll like it. Just sit down and relax, and let me grab some wine glasses."

"Ok, this is definitely not just a study session," thought Blanca to herself, as she sat in one of the expensive chairs at the dining table. Dinner and wine? The ambiance screamed….."date!" And the way Vickie said 'comfortable' made Blanca hopeful once more of a relationship between them. There was no way she was just being polite, that was definitely flirting and an invitation for more. Vickie returned with the wine glasses and a bottle of wine. She poured them each a glass and then went back into the kitchen to bring out dinner. She served them each a plate of eggplant parmesan with pasta, before sitting down to join Blanca at the table.

"Mmmm, oh my goodness, this is delicious," said Blanca after enjoying her first bite. "I never knew that the lovely doctor was also an expert cook. What other secrets are you keeping from me?" she continued on, only half-jokingly.

Vickie looked directly at her. "I guess I would like to have the opportunity to share some of those secrets with you."

Suddenly feeling nervous, Blanca reached for her wine glass, and as she took a sip she noticed that Vickie's eyes never left her. In fact, her stare only intensified.

"Your lips are so soft and inviting. They look like they taste nice." Vickie said unexpectedly.

Blanca felt moisture between her legs as the remainder of dinner was filled with back and forth innuendos and snippets of conversation that hinted to one another's feelings towards each other. Vickie noticed Blanca's confusion now and then and smiled inwardly. She knew how Blanca felt, because she once felt that way. Her desire to be with Blanca took back seat to her position and professional status at the hospital. Now that Blanca was no longer working there and Vickie was no longer her indirect supervisor, those shackles of constraint were removed and she was free to do as she pleased. And, in short order, she would reveal all of this to Blanca.

After their meal, Vickie led the way back to the living room for them to begin studying. Blanca took out her books and told her the topics that she needed help with. They had been studying for a couple of hours when Vickie decided to have a little fun with Blanca. "Did you know that the nerves in the nipple are so sensitive that a woman can have an orgasm from just being stimulated there?" she asked.

Blanca shifted in her seat, suddenly visibly stirred by Vickie's comment. "Um...yes, I....um, I think I do know that."

"And did you also know that the nerves in the lips of your mouth are very sensitive too? They are another excellent source of pleasure." Blanca was shifting back and forth in her seat as Vickie went a step further in her teasing. "And the clitoris is the only body part that was intended strictly for pleasure. The concentration of nerve endings there gives a woman unspeakable pleasure when stimulated, even if the contact is not sexual." Vickie smiled slyly, enjoying her guest's reaction immensely.

Blanca blushed. "Are you trying to tell me something?" she asked.

Shaking her head, Vickie replied, "Nope, nothing at all. Would you like some water?"

"Yes, please."

Vickie came back with a couple bottles of Pelligrino water and handed one to Blanca. Blanca took a sip and then idly ran her finger across her lip.

"What are you doing?" Vickie asked.

"I am feeling the nerves in my lips."

"I know a better way for you to feel them." Vickie stared into her eyes as she leaned into her and placed her lips on hers. Blanca felt her heart racing as she finally felt the lips she had been lusting after rest on hers. She parted her lips and felt Vickie's arms pull her closer as her tongue slid into her mouth. Her body felt as if it was melting. Was she dreaming? Was this true? She fully immersed herself in the sensations she was experiencing in her beautiful dream. She felt every nerve in her tongue and lips come alive as their lips danced and massaged each other. Her breasts rubbed against Vickie's as they pressed their bodies close together to feel the utmost pleasure.

Vickie was the first to break the kiss. She moved back slightly as her fingers moved towards the zipper on the back of Blanca's skirt to help her undress. "Are you ready for this? Are you sure you want to do this?" She asked Blanca.

Blanca nodded her answer and pulled Vickie down on top of her on the couch.

"I was hoping you'd say that," Vickie whispered as her hands quickly glided the fabric off of Blanca's curvaceous body, exposing her olive toned nakedness. "I'm going to show you just how sensitive and responsive your body can be."

Vickie sucked one nipple in her mouth and ran the other one between her thumb and forefinger. Blanca released a soft purr that excited Vickie even more. "Do you see what that little movement can do? I have more in store for you my beautiful anatomy student."

She kissed her way down Blanca's body, still keeping her nipple between her fingers. Blanca raised her hips when she felt Vickie's breath on her clit. She moaned out loud at the first feel of nerves on nerves. Vickie ran her tongue ever so slowly along the inside of Blanca's labia, causing her let out a long "Aaaaagh." The nerves in that area were indeed sensitive and the moisture between her legs was evidence of her pleasure. Vickie gently sucked her clit into her mouth. She circled it with her tongue, driving Blanca wild with pleasure. Blanca moaned loudly and arched her back. Placing her hand on Vickie's head, she released a loud groan. Blanca pushed Vickie away and maneuvered her body to lie back on the couch. She lay down beside her, but with her head at the opposite end of the seat. That was her favorite position because it allowed both lovers to be stimulated at the same time, giving them the chance to orgasm together.

Vickie's scent had been driving her crazy all evening. She knew she was aroused and now she had proof. She licked the entrance to Vickie's pussy and felt a shiver run through her body as Vickie did the same thing to her. Blanca flicked at Vickie's clit with her tongue and Vickie started doing the same. She realized that Vickie was mimicking her movements, causing them both to feel the same sensations. Their moans were lost in each other as they licked and sucked each other's most sensitive areas. Blanca inserted two fingers inside Vickie's wet pussy, and began sliding them in and out in a slow, steady rhythm. Blanca was barely able to hear Vickie's passion-filled moan above the blood rushing in her ears. Her moan was similar when Vickie slid her fingers deep inside of her.

Their bodies were on fire and totally in-sync. Nothing had ever felt so good, so perfect, and so right. Everything fell into place when Blanca felt her body tensing. She quickened her movements on Vickie as her breath came faster. She felt Vickie tightening and knew that they would get the chance to share the moment together. As climactic waves crashed over their bodies, they pressed themselves together, wanting to share every inch of the experience. Blanca was the first to reemerge back from her orgasmic abyss. She kissed Vickie as her orgasm subsided, content in the moment, and happy. Yes, she felt very, very happy.

"Was it just me, or was that incredible?" asked Vickie.

"It WAS YOU! It IS YOU! And yes, it was incredible!" Blanca replied.

"I've been fantasizing about being with you for a while," Vickie responded back, as she repositioned herself on the couch so that she could look at Blanca's face as they talked.

With raised brows, Blanca responded, "Really? Then I wasn't just imagining it. You really do like me. You know what I mean, are interested in me."

"Yes, I do and I am." Vickie leaned in and placed a deep, tender kiss on her lips.

"So what happens now?" Blanca asked.

"Well, what happens now is that I would love for us to get to know each other better, and for this to be more than just sex. I think you are a beautiful and intelligent woman and I would like to get to know all about you and hopefully intertwine our lives together." She looked at Blanca hopefully.

"You mean a relationship? What about our jobs?" Blanca asked.

"That will not be an issue as long as you do not accept a job at my hospital in the E.R.. Go somewhere else, or at least seek a different department to work in. Do it for the sake of us." She laughed, and pulled Blanca's smooth, delicious body up tightly against her.

"Deal! The only part of that emergency room that I'm interested in, is laying right here next to me."

The women made love to each other once more, this time even more slowly and deriving even more pleasure, now that they have committed themselves to the anatomy of their love.

VOLUME 4

Lesbian Paranormal Romance Collection

Story #13

Witch's Mirror

T aylor felt a cold chill run up her spine, for the day was unusually cold and breezy for October, especially in Los Angeles. Taylor Bradbury was a natural beauty with smooth, light colored skin, dark brown eyes, long dark blonde hair, and a smile that could light up a thousand rooms. Residing in Los Angeles, California, she works as an assistant director for a major television production company. Taylor quite literally couldn't remember the last time she had taken a vacation because she was always too busy with work, and she always kept promising herself that she would take one after wrapping up the latest movie project, or after the completion of whatever new TV show pilot just happened to be in the works. After too many years of promising herself a much needed vacation she finally got the opportunity, a month long break between movie projects, so she jumped on it. She wanted to get as far away from Los Angeles as possible, and she has always wanted to visit the New England states area. And, since it was October, she thought a great location to enjoy her vacation in would be Salem, Massachusetts. The entire town celebrated Halloween and the history of witches, making it a coveted tourist attraction this time of the year. Once her extended work day that Friday ended, Taylor went home to over-water her plants and immediately pack her bags before anything came up to prevent her from leaving. After gobbling down a late night dinner of take-out Chinese, she loaded up her car and hit the road, hoping to make it out of California before sunrise, thereby avoiding having to contend with the insane traffic of southern California.

Instead of traveling by plane, Taylor decided to add the adventure of a road trip to her vacation plans. Yes, it would be a very long drive, probably 4-5 days each way, but the long drive would give her mind plenty of time to relax and reflect. Plus, driving always afforded you traveling views and venues that you would never even be aware of via plane travel. She was also going on vacation alone, so there was no added pressure of needing to appease anyone else's itinerary demands. The second Taylor's car pulled out of her assigned parking spot at her apartment complex, she could already feel her body and mind start to relax. She popped in a relaxing Jazz CD to listen to, and took a sip from her travel mug filled with hot apple cider. "Salem, Massachusetts, here I come!"

Each day, Taylor stopped on average every 3-4 hours to stretch her legs, fill her car up with fuel and grab a drink and sometimes something to snack on. The diverse scenery that she was witness to as she drove through the various states gave her creative mind lots of location considerations for some upcoming movie projects for once she got back to work, although she really wasn't dwelling on work. However, she was surprised by how many inventive ideas effortlessly flowed into her mind during her many hours of driving each day. At the end of her fourth day of travel, Taylor entered the state of Massachusetts, and she became even more excited about being here during such a festive time. Halloween was just around the corner, and Salem is well known for all its tours and reenactments centered around the infamous Salem Witch Trials. Taylor couldn't wait to experience all of the activities, and her mind was already making a checklist of all the things she wanted to do.

Exhausted from her road travels, Taylor anxiously checked into one of the historical bed and breakfasts she had reserved a room for over the next couple weeks, and after completing her check-in, she took a long hot shower and fell asleep the moment her head hit the pillow. The following morning, without any hard set itinerary, she spent her first day in Salem visiting a museum and watching a mock witch hunt. People in period costumes were pulling people from the crowd and putting them in the stocks. While Taylor wasn't presently wearing any period attire, her looks were not only alluring and captivating, but they also resembled that of a beautiful witch. Perhaps that is why Taylor noticed a number of people staring at her in a quizzical way. Was it her long, naturally wavy hair and tall statuesque? Was it her milky white skin and mysterious eyes? She wasn't sure, but she decided to have fun with it, and she allowed herself to be put in one of the stocks. Taylor was then further surprised when complete strangers started taking pictures of her. One of the other tourists even asked her if she had any family lineage to Salem, and several just boldly asked if she was a witch!

On her way back to the bed and breakfast that she was staying at, a lady in a bed and breakfast across the street was sweeping her porch and took notice to Taylor. She waved "hello", and looked at Taylor as if she could tell instantly that she was not from this area. Or, was she too questioning if the beautiful outsider's family roots were from Salem? After waving back to the woman, Taylor entered the downstairs area of the bed and breakfast she was staying at. The owner and manager of the establishment was in the foyer area arranging some Halloween decorations on the handful of small, round dining tables that were for her guests, and she eagerly introduced herself. Her name was Sylvia, an attractive older woman with long silver hair, laugh lines around her smiling eyes, and a short plump physique. She seemed like a very nice old lady who loved to chat up her guests, sharing with them the rich history and superstitions of Salem. Taylor was all too happy to listen to her, and her interest really peaked when the woman went on to explain an artifact about Taylor's last name.

"I took notice to your last name when you checked-in last evening, and you share the same last name with a young woman who pled guilty of witchcraft during the witch trials, and was later one of the few who escaped death and was pardoned. Her name was Mary Bradbury. Do you happen to know your family history, dear?" Sylvia asked. Taylor shook her head, for she was unsure of any particulars in her family history, and had no idea just how far back her surname could actually be traced.

"Well, if you're interested, I have a guest room that I normally keep off limits to guests, but if you'd like to stay in it during your two week visit, I can help you move your things," Sylvia continued. "It's a room that Mary Bradbury was said to have lived in at one time, but I have not been able to confirm that. Either way, I thought it might lend a little bit more mystery to your visit."

Taylor thought it would indeed add a bit of mystery to her stay, and she excitedly accepted Sylvia's offer. Sylvia followed Taylor to her room, and after gathering up Taylor's things, she led them down the upstairs hallway and around a very short bend that ended with a single door. Taylor immediately took notice to the barely visible number "13" that was painted on the door, but tried not to attach any superstitious thoughts to that artifact. When Sylvia unlocked the door, Taylor's nose was assaulted by the smell of a room that obviously had not been opened or aired out in quite some time. Tiny dust particles hung suspended in the motionless air and the only light came from a small, narrow window on the opposite wall. Sylvia went over to force open the window and let some fresh air in, while Taylor put down her things and took a quick survey of the room.

"Well, what do you think? Is the room suitable enough for your stay?" Sylvia asked.

"Yes, I think it will be. Once the fresh air freshens up the room, and I wipe the furniture down, I think it will be just fine.

"Marvelous! Since you are so kind as to give the room a wipe down, I'll bring up some dust rags and a few other cleaning supplies, and for your efforts, I'll take off today's room charge from your bill."

Sylvia left, and after switching on the single artificial light source from a small nightstand lamp, Taylor decided to give room number 13 a closer inspection. One of the first things that caught her attention was what appeared to be a long oval shaped mirror that was positioned on the wall directly facing across the small twin sized bed in the room, and it was shrouded in a dust covered sheet. Looking around the sparsely furnished room, she noticed that none of the other furniture pieces were covered with sheets. Intrigued, Taylor went over to give the mirror a closer look. She had heard that in many cultures a mirror can offer a reflection of a person's soul. And, many people also believed that the mirrored reflections were a view of an alternate reality. She took the sheet off and gasped when she saw the intricacy of the handcraftsmanship. The mirror looked incredibly old and like it came from somewhere important. It had tiny etchings of suns and moons and it had an engraving of the year 1692, in roman numerals. Taylor was just awestruck by this and wondered if the mirror she was touching was actually more than 300 years old, or if it was just a reproduction. This mirror looked authentic in Taylor's mind, and she was suddenly anxious to find out more about it.

When she looked into the mirror at her reflection, Taylor could have sworn that she looked younger. Maybe it was because the mirror hadn't been cleaned in who knows how long, and she noticed that the mirror was smudged with quite a few finger prints. Sylvia had already deposited a bucket full of cleaning supplies at her door, so she grabbed one of the wash cloths, wet it, and gently began cleaning away the film of dirt and oil from the mirror. However, something peculiar happened. As soon as she touched the mirror, it sparked. Taylor removed her hand, and stared at it. She went to touch it again, and this time, as she rubbed the cloth across the surface, the mirror gave off a faint glow and it looked like something was swirling just underneath the surface. She knew she wasn't intoxicated, for she had not consumed one drop of alcohol since leaving Los Angeles, yet she was definitely seeing something in the mirror move. Perplexed and curious, Taylor slowly placed her hand up against the mirror and jumped when she saw the face of a beautiful woman looking back at her. As she jumped back and her hand left the mirror, the woman's image disappeared. Gathering up her courage, Taylor put her hand back up to the mirror, and the image of the woman returned. She seemed to be looking directly at her, and the woman raised one of her hands to touch the mirror directly over where Taylor's hand was. The woman was dressed in old fashioned clothes that looked like they were from a theatre presentation or a renaissance fair. Taylor removed her hand from the mirror, and again, the woman's image disappeared. Was Sylvia pulling her leg? Is this why she offered this particular room to her? Did Sylvia have this room, or even maybe the entire building, all set up with special affects to appease the tourists looking to have a paranormal experience? If so, this was one hell of a special effect, and Taylor knew that she had to get to the bottom off this.

While most people would have run out of the room screaming, that was not Taylor's style. There was no need to be afraid because everything has a logical explanation, or it should. As she stared intently at the mirror she couldn't help but wonder and a flood of questions came to her mind. Why was the mirror the only piece of furniture in this room that was covered with a sheet? Was it because perhaps a spirit was trapped in the mirror? Was this mirror a portal to another time? "That would be impossible though," Taylor thought out loud. "Or, is it?" She was starting to stress a bit by what had just happened, and now was perhaps a good time to go get a drink. She was now getting a weird feeling about the mirror, and Taylor wondered if there were more antique mirrors covered with sheets within the rooms of the bed and breakfast. Could the bed and breakfast be haunted by the spirits of the Salem Witch Trials? Hell, anything is possible, right? She wasn't sure if what she saw was her imagination, or if it was real, but right now she was going to find the closest bar and get a nice strong cocktail.

When Taylor returned a few hours later, she decided it would be a good idea to talk to the bed and breakfast owner about what had happened up in her room. "Sylvia, may I please talk to you about my room," Taylor asked the bed and breakfast owner, who was rushing about the front area.

"I'm a bit busy right now dear, but I'm listening, room 13, right? How is it so far?" Sylvia asked eagerly, almost too eagerly.

"It's nice, I really like the room. But, I want to ask you about something in the room. When I uncovered the mirror on the wall that was covered with a sheet, I noticed that there's something….well, strange about the mirror. Is there something I should know about it?" Taylor asked.

"Oh… well…" Sylvia hesitated for a moment before replying. "Well dear, all mirrors have powerful potential energies, some more than others. And, if you don't respect their energies and use them wisely they can sometimes be bad news. I personally prefer not to use them at all except to do my hair and for driving, that's it. Covering a mirror with a sheet, or reversing it so that it faces the wall, will help to contain any unstable energies."

Suspicious by Sylvia's answer and now even more curious, Taylor imagined that there had to be a more specific reason as to why Sylvia has an aversion to mirrors, and she was determined to extract more details from her. "Have you ever noticed anything strange about that mirror, Sylvia? Or, any mirror? Do they give off any weird vibes to you?" Taylor questioned.

"Dear, I am, shall we say a bit overly cautious about mirrors and the one that you ask about does indeed have a mysterious history. In fact, I have several mirrors like the one in the room you are now staying in. They came off of a European ship coming to Salem. The ship was a known slave ship that later became cursed by a very powerful local witch. Everything on it was said to be cursed as well. One morning the ship headed out in search of spices, raw materials, and slaves, but no one returned. The only thing that returned months later was an empty ship. The mirrors were given to people around the town of Salem and I acquired a few of them. Many people say that these ship mirrors are portals, and some of my past guests have shared stories with me, that if true, would support that theory," Sylvia claimed. "All I can say is that I urge you to be cautious."

Later that evening, Taylor was sitting on the bed in her room browsing through the handful of tourist brochures she had picked up earlier in the day, and she kept getting distracted by what she thought were noises coming from somewhere in her room. At first she thought it might be coming from one of the neighboring guest rooms, but then she remembered that her room was isolated from the rest of the other guest rooms. She happened to look up at the mirror and thought she saw a dim bluish-green glow swirling from just underneath the surface. Her heart started racing, and she stood up off of the bed and walked over to it. She hesitantly placed her hand on the mirror, the way she had done before, and the blue-green glow slowly grew brighter and brighter and swirled faster and faster. Taylor felt dizzy but kept her hand placed against the mirror. Her knees started to tremble, and just when she thought she was going to faint, the image of the same woman that she had seen earlier in the day reflected back at her and this time, the reflection of the woman looked like she was trying to grab her hand.

"Come," she thought she heard the woman say. "Come back to me." Was the woman inviting Taylor to follow her through the mirror to where she was? At first Taylor thought that she was going crazy because people don't just hop through mirrors, but her mind entertained the notion, and that was all it took. Without really knowing what was happening, or how it was happening, Taylor slowly walked through the mirror and got sucked through some kind of vortex. She had never experienced such a thing before, and if this was heaven, she wanted to experience this every day.

Things seemed quite different on the other side of the mirror. In fact, they were extremely different. Things smelled different, things looked completely different, and Taylor felt very, very different.

"What shall ye name be now fair maiden?" asked the mysterious woman.

"Um...my name is Taylor. What is your name?" Taylor was still trying to ascertain whether or not she was dreaming or if she was really standing someplace far, far away from where she was only just moments ago.

"My name is Ann, and I truly have been admiring you from afar in the mirror, the mirror that connects us."

"Well, Ann may I ask where exactly am I and what year it is?"

"You are in Salem and the year is 1692 of course. Are you daft woman?"

"Ann, you somehow pulled me through a mirror that is in a guest room I am staying in. I am not sure what is happening, but I live in the current year of 2014."

"Sshh, don't talk like that woman! If anyone hears you speak this way they'll imprison you and you what will happen then. They'll accuse you of being a witch and you'll either be burned alive or hanged!" Ann exclaimed.

Ann seemed very adamant about the witch talk and Taylor's mind was starting to grasp the possibility that maybe she did just time travel through a portal in the mirror. In which case, Sylvia would have been right about the curse, the portal, and the energies. Taylor did ignore her warnings about the mirror and now look where she was, standing in front of a woman from ye Old Salem. A very naturally beautiful woman, actually, now that Taylor took note of it. Ann was on the tall side, maybe a couple inches taller than Taylor, and was obviously very slim and shapely, despite her layers of peasant-like clothing. She had black hair, and big brown eyes, and lips that Taylor sure wouldn't mind kissing. Taylor realized that she had only just met Ann, yet her attraction to her was quite intense. Taylor had always wanted to go to olden day Salem and now here she was, or was she? She still wasn't sure. Taylor loved Ann's unique accent and there was an air of familiarity about her, although that would be impossible. In fact, Taylor still wasn't sure how any of this was possible.

"My fair maiden, am I still only able to see you through that mirror?" Ann asked as she pointed towards an old full standing mirror a few feet away from where they were. "Much time and many events have passed, yet this seems our only connection."

Taylor's eyes followed Ann's hand, and she gasped when she saw how similar the mirror she was now looking at, matched the mirror in her room. "Well...I..." Taylor once again felt overwhelmed by what was happening. "What events? Ann I do not know. I too saw you through that mirror, well my mirror, really. But, you somehow managed to pull me through it, and now here I am. I don't know what to make of it."

"My maiden, the fact that you even saw me in the mirror means that you are open to the energies. The fact that you are standing here with me now means that you are able to align with the energies. You are most powerful fair maiden!" Ann responded excitedly. "But, you must heed caution. If others find out, it could mean your head."

The very thought of that possibility put Taylor on edge, and she felt a strong desire to return to her present reality, in the year 2014. "Ann, I need to return to my room, in my present time. I need to know that I can do that. Is it possible?"

"Of course it is fair maiden. I will assist you. But, before you take leave, may I ask you to join me for a dinner feast tomorrow evening?"

As she stared into Ann's intoxicating eyes, Taylor was overcome with the intense need to discover more about her. "I accept your gracious invitation Ann."

Ann's grin told her pleasure, as she hesitantly took hold of Taylor's hands and pulled them up to her breast. "I am pleased. Wear your finest threads and I shall yearn until I see you again. I shall have our feast ready at the sundown hour. And, take this fair maiden, for protection." Ann untied an amulet from her neck and secured it around Taylor's.

Taylor was rendered speechless as Ann then politely held her hand and walked her over to stand in front of the mirror. Ann instructed Taylor to place her right hand against the mirror, and she in turn placed her left hand against the mirror. Ann murmured some words that Taylor didn't understand, though she thought it sounded like a spell of some kind, and before she knew what was happening, she once again felt herself being sucked into a vortex of swirling energies and then through the mirror.

Taylor woke up a few hours later and wondered if what had happened was all just a dream. Her fingers fumbled at the amulet dangling around her neck, and that's when she realized, "no", it couldn't have been just a dream, it was real. It certainly felt real. Her mind replayed some of the things Ann said to her, or at least what she thought she said to her. Like "Come back to me," and "Much time and many events have passed." which confused Taylor. It was as if they had a history together, which was impossible. Taylor was still extremely exhausted after coming back through the portal, and after taking a shower and enjoying a hot cup of tea she returned to bed and slept until dawn the following day.

When she woke, her thoughts immediately went to Ann and she remembered that Ann would be expecting her for dinner, at the "sundown hour" to precise. After a quick breakfast of hot scones and coffee, Taylor went out shopping in search of something just right for her return visit. She wanted to choose something that was reminiscent of old Salem, and she didn't have too much trouble finding just the right dress. She was in Salem after all, and it just so happened to be Halloween time, so a good number of shops were stocked with time period attire for men and women, along with the appropriate hats, shawls and footwear. As she shopped, Taylor kept having flashbacks of her time jump through the mirror and her brief time spent with Ann. In addition to her incredibly attractive looks, Ann seemed gentle, kind and generous. She also seemed to be well versed in things of the magical and unexplainable nature. Taylor fantasized about what it might feel like to have her body pressed up against hers and Ann's hands playing with her hair. Trying to keep her mind on the task at hand, Taylor settled on a dressy vintage, mixed hue green dress that fell to mid-calf length. It had off the shoulder sleeves with lace trim and sewn in bodice ties. Along with a pair of black ankle boots with lace ties, elbow length black gloves and a black shawl, Taylor thought her attire would be considered highly date worthy for Old Salem. She also wanted to blend in better when she traveled through the mirror's portal again, although she wasn't sure if she was going to be in anyone's presence other than Ann's.

Checking the time on her cell phone, Taylor saw that it was already 3 p.m. She wasn't exactly sure what time sundown was going to be, but she knew that dusk started to fall around 5 p.m., so she wrapped up her shopping and started walking back to the bed and breakfast where she was staying. Sylvia gave Taylor a look as she breezed by her with her handful of garment bags, a look that implied that she was curious as to what was going on. Taylor didn't have time to talk though because she really had to get ready, so she would just fill Sylvia in on all the details later. And, hopefully by then there would be lots more details to tell. It was now almost 4 p.m., and Taylor took the stairs two at a time as she hurried up to her room. She stripped out of her clothes, and laid out the ones she had just purchased. She quickly pinned up the front part of her hair and adorned it with a little green hair clip that matched her dress, and decided on applying only very light touches of makeup along with some clear lip gloss. After dressing, Taylor lightly spritzed on her favorite perfume, one that smelled of cherry and vanilla, and lastly she donned her new lace tie ankle boots. Excited but more than a little nervous, Taylor gave the room one last look as if she might never see it again.

Taking a deep breath, Taylor walked over to sit at the small table in front of the mirror, and stared into it. There presently weren't any glowing colors to discern but she was sure that she was feeling some of those "energies" that both Sylvia and Ann had both referred to, emanating from the mirror. Slowly, Taylor pressed her hand onto the mirror, and this time it felt like her hand was being held against the surface by a powerful, invisible magnet. Her eyes fluttered shut and within moments she found herself sucked back into that vortex of swirling energies and colors, before somehow effortlessly walking out the mirror on the another side of time. Ann was there waiting for her, with a smile so captivating it took Ann's heart.

She walked over to Taylor and wrapped her arms around her. "Fair maiden, it does my heart good to see that you've returned." Ann kissed her tenderly on the cheek before backing away and offering out her hand for Taylor to take hold.

Taylor was again taken by Ann's tenderness and manners, and as she took hold of Ann's extended hand, she couldn't help but again feel that all of this was somehow familiar. She also noticed that the mirror was currently in what she presumed to be Ann's bedroom, where upon her brief visit yesterday she didn't recall it being in here. Ann guided her out of the room and into a slighter larger room where there was a fire roaring in the hearth. It appeared to be a multi-purpose room, obviously used for cooking and gathering, and the aromas of whatever Ann was preparing for their meal smelled heavenly. Ann walked her over to a wooden chair, one of only two that was placed next to a small round wooden table with a frayed braided rug underneath it. She appeared to be very excited to see Taylor, and Taylor enjoyed watching her proudly finish and serve their meal while stirs of arousal rose within her belly as she watched Ann move to and fro against the backlight of the fire. Ann had prepared them homemade bread and stew, with nothing more than a few cast iron pots over a roaring fire, something that Taylor doubted anyone did in her present time of 2014.

As they ate, Ann smiled continuously at her from across the table while Taylor wondered what exactly it was that she was thinking. Taylor smiled back and she couldn't help but notice the growing feeling of arousal that was consuming her body. However, she was still trying to evaluate the totality of the situation, starting with how exactly she traveled through a mirror into a different period of time, and continuing on to where exactly was this intimate dinner with a beautiful woman from over 300 years ago leading to. And, so far, the two of them had not discussed either. Yet, when Ann was helping her to understand her time travel through the mirror yesterday she spoke rather nonchalantly about it, as if it was common knowledge…at least for some.

As they finished their meal, Ann smiled at Taylor and inched her chair over next to hers. She took the spoon from Taylor's hand, which she had been fiddling with ever since she finished her meal, and placed it on the table. Ann gently brushed aside Taylor's hair, and tenderly started kissing her cheeks, her neck, and then her mouth. Her kisses became quite passionate and Taylor eagerly returned them, showing that she was inviting of Ann's advances. As lovely as their intimate exchange was however, Taylor was questioning the suddenness of what was happening and she pulled back from Ann.

"Ann, as delicious as your kisses are, I'm afraid I'm a bit confused as to the haste of which they are happening."

Ann looked at her lovingly and held her hands in her own while she explained. "Fair maiden, tis that 'memory be'gone' potion I warned you to take caution in, before consuming. You insisted on swallowing half a bottle of that potion after they put your mother to her death. You wanted desperately to forget the traumatic memories around the event, but the potion has no discernment, and all meaningful memories with others were also erased. Only the new memories you have acquired since drinking the potion remain."

"Does that mean we are….."

"Yes, fair maiden, we are lovers. And, I promise to remind you every time you forget."

Taylor's mind was reeling, yet she suppressed the urge to search for any of those erased memories when she felt Ann's lips once again brush against her mouth. As they kissed, their lips and tongues exploring each other's mouth, and Ann stood up from her chair while gently pulling Taylor up to her feet with her. "Come, let us become more comfortable in my bed. I've already lit the fire in there, so it shall be warm for our love making."

"Love making?" Taylor thought to herself as she followed Ann into the other room. This was really happening. This was better than any dream she could have imagined, yet this was no dream. She was lovers with the most gorgeous woman she'd ever seen, and she was about to make love to her. As they entered the bedroom, Taylor's skin did indeed notice the warmth in the room from the fire. The bed was small, but looked comfortable, and her nose detected the aroma of pine in the room. Ann came up from behind her and snuggled her mouth against Taylor's neck as her hands started working to untie the corset bodice of her dress. Taylor's nose caught the faint smell of lavender on Ann's skin as her lips brushed across her neck, and a soft moan formed at the back of her throat. Ann's fingers loosened the last of the laces on her corset and she gently pulled the dress over Taylor's head, leaving her standing there naked except for her lace tie ankle boots. She was pretty sure that undergarments such as bras and panties didn't exist in the 1600's, so she had decided to forgo them when she dressed for her evening with Ann.

Ann's mouth parted with obvious hunger as she stared at Taylor's nudeness. "Your beauty takes my breath away every time we are together."

Taylor could see that Ann's corset was tied in the front, so she stepped closer and allowed her fingers to shakily untie the ribbon, all the while Ann's hands slowly caressed their way down Taylor's back and along the curve of her hips. Once Taylor had freed Ann's corset from her frame, her hands quickly found their way onto Ann's perky breasts before moving lower to unlace her skirt and watch it fall to the floor. Their bodies both stood naked in front of the dancing flames of the fire, as Ann gently lay Taylor down onto the bed. Her soft lips started at Taylor's ankles, as she slowly kissed and licked her way up each of her shapely legs. Ann's fingertips traced like a soft feather along the sides of Taylor's legs and hips and sides, while her kisses continued their journey across Taylor's stomach until her mouth reached the flesh of Taylor's plump tits and Ann gently tugged at her dark nipples with her lips and teeth, causing Taylor's body to squirm underneath her. Ann continued sucking at her tits, while she glided a hand down to guide open Taylor's thighs, seeking the sweetness of her pussy. Her fingers felt Taylor's moistness as Ann delicately parted her lips with her fingers. Taylor's body began to squirm and her breasts jiggled as her breathing became more rapid as Ann slowly traced her fingers along the inside of her pussy lips and around her hole, before focusing on her erect clit with small circular movements. Ann then slid her body down between her legs and Taylor gently wrapped her legs around Ann's back. The mere touch of Ann's soft fingers on her smooth pussy lips was already making Taylor's juice flow, but when she felt the first gentle brushes of Ann's tongue lap across her clit, her hips began to buck against Ann's mouth and her hands grasped at the bedding as she quickly felt herself getting closer and closer to climax. Ann then slightly repositioned herself, and she ever-so-gently began sucking on Taylor's clit as she slid a couple of fingers deep inside her wet pussy. Ann glided her moistened fingers in and out of Taylor's hole, slowly, and then faster, before slowing down again to prolong Taylor's pleasure as long as possible. Ann's fingers then tickled at the inner walls of Taylor's pussy while his mouth never left her clit, and Taylor's body writhed and writhed until she could no longer contain her ecstasy and she bucked up hard against Ann's mouth as her body trembled with orgasm.

When Taylor's body came down from her sensual high, she stood up from the bed and pulled Ann up off of the bed with her. She turned Ann to face the bed and guided her down to her knees before gently pushing her upper body against the bed. Taylor moaned as her eyes took in the lovely sight of Ann's ass raised up in the air like a cat in heat, and after moistening her fingers with her tongue, Taylor's hand traveled between Ann's ass cheeks before finding and parting her pussy lips. Taylor was only slightly cognizant of her dominant demeanor as her free hand tugged at Ann's hair, raising her head up so that Taylor could nibble on the side of her neck. A series of moans escaped Ann's mouth as Taylor's fingers gently pinched and fondled and probed at her clit and hole. Taylor let go of Ann's hair and she shoved her hand underneath Ann's chest pressed against the bed, as she squeezed and pulled at Ann's tits and nipples. This all felt deliciously familiar, even if in a diffused way, as Taylor then thrust her fingers deep into Ann's pussy and finger fucked her while leaning in to drink in the sweet aroma of her lover's skin and arousal. Ann's moans became louder and Taylor pulled out her fingers just long enough to flip Ann's body around and up onto the bed. With Ann now lying on the bed on her back, Taylor straddled on top of her and shoved her fingers back into Ann's pussy. She leaned down and their mouths and tongues met in a heated, passionate exchange, while Ann's hands filled themselves with Taylor's tits. Ann's pussy began to tighten around Taylor's fingers and she thrust faster and faster until Ann's body contracted and shook against the bed in ecstasy.

Taylor lay in Ann's arms as they watched the dying embers of the fire glow dimmer and dimmer. As they enjoyed a couple of mugs of mulled wine Ann reluctantly informed, or rather, reminded Taylor that her travel through the mirror must only be done during the hours of darkness. For reasons she was unsure of, if one is to make passage through time through the mirror during the daylight hours, they would most likely be stuck in the time of one side, or the other. This gave Taylor cause for concern, and so she decided that it was time to return to her room at the bed and breakfast. She really didn't want to leave, but she needed time to process all the extraordinary events of the past couple of days, not to mention the artifact of being stuck in one time dimension, or another. With a promise to return tomorrow, she gave Ann a passionate farewell kiss as she again assisted Taylor's passage through the mirror back into the year of 2014.

Luckily, Taylor went back through the mirror when she did, because when she returned to her room at the bed and breakfast the brief streaks of color in the sky indicated that sunrise was quickly approaching. Taylor wondered if she would have stayed any longer, would she have been trapped in Old Salem? Instead of getting dressed and heading downstairs for breakfast with the other guests, she instead got undressed and snuggled underneath the covers of her bed where she quickly fell asleep. When she woke around noon, she again wondered if what had happened was a dream.

Taylor kept eluding Sylvia, who was trying to corner her to inquire about her activities, and every night after for the next seven nights, Taylor traveled through the mirror back to Old Salem to be with Ann. The passion they shared for each other was pure and the chemistry they had for each other was intense. While Taylor still couldn't recall any of her past memories with Ann, she was certainly enjoying all of the current memories they were making. With only a few days left of her stay in Salem, Taylor became consumed with the thought that she might never see Ann again once she returned to Los Angeles. This was not something she was happy about, and Taylor kept thinking that there had to be a way that she could continue to see her, to be with her. She had just fallen deeply in love for the first time in years, and with a woman who just so happens to live in the late 1600's. The very thought of it seemed crazy. But, what else was crazy was that she was seriously contemplating just returning to Old Salem to stay.... forever... with Ann. She could easily leave her job and Los Angeles behind, and she in truth had nothing to keep her tied to her present day. So, with a new hope in her heart, Taylor was eager to see her lover later that evening to share with Ann her news of wanting to stay with her.

Later that evening after sundown Taylor traveled through the mirror to visit Ann, but her small home was cold and vacant, and she was nowhere to be found. Taylor's heart sunk as she read a note that Ann had left for her on the table explaining that she was in peril. Her tears stained the parchment as she read:

My dearest maiden,

I have been accused by some of the locals for the crime of being a witch. If your eyes should befall onto this scribe tis because I am in hail awaiting execution. I urge you my love not to come seek me for it is too risky. I hold in my heart now and in the afterlife our love.

My heart,

Ann

With steadfast determination, Taylor knew that she had to find Ann and try to help her. She would risk her life for Ann and for the love they shared, and so she set foot to the streets of Old Salem in search of where Ann might be being held. Taylor knew all too well the history about the Old Salem Witch Trials, and she wasn't sure what she could possible do to stop Ann's execution, but she would just try and figure it out while she went out looking for her. She simply could not allow Ann to suffer a beheading or hanging, or worse…. a burning at the stake.

Old Salem was even smaller than present day Salem and in short time Taylor was able to locate the small courthouse that housed their prisoners in the downstairs jail cells. When she arrived at the building, she noticed that a small barred window to each cell was visible to the outside street. Taylor went to each of the barred cell windows until she located the one that Ann was being held in. She sat in the rain by Ann's cell window and wept for her safety. There had to be a way to stop this. Sobbing, she talked to Ann through the bars of her small mostly underground cell, and Taylor told her that she was sorry for everything that happened. "I can't lose you Ann. It will truly shatter my heart. Tell me what I can do." Taylor pleaded.

Holding her hand through the bars, Ann tried to comfort Taylor while her own heart too was breaking. "Tis naught you can do my love. You shant be here. If you love me, than I beg of you to leave. If they see you, then they will send you to your hanging too."

"I can't just sit by and watch them take your life!" Taylor exclaimed in a hoarse whisper.

"My maiden, I take our love with me to the afterlife. Please do not choose death by staying here," Ann replied as she reached up on her toes to kiss the tips of Taylor's fingers.

A few minutes later, guards came and dragged Ann to the raised platform which was situated out in front of the courthouse with noose and hooded hangmen awaiting, and Taylor's stomach lurched when she heard the crowd cheering in anticipation of her lover's execution. Ann's crime was witchcraft, but no one had ever explained what she really did. Witchcraft was a catch-all fabricated crime used to punish people to death for going against the church. Often, neighbors who didn't like someone would accuse someone of "witchcraft", along with the homeless and prostitutes, and without proper judicial process, the church expeditiously sentenced those accused to death. Taylor knew that she could not bear to witness this atrocity, and so she rushed back to Ann's house and she made a "memory be'gone" potion. At first she wasn't exactly sure how to make the potion because she had never made one, but it seemed like her old self was able to navigate a spell book really well. Knowing her heart could not bear the memory of Ann's death, Taylor drank the potion as she screamed out her lovers name in pain and anguish. She stumbled over to the mirror to travel back to present time before going unconscious, and when she awoke the next morning she was in her bed at the bed and breakfast in present day

Salem, with Sylvia anxiously hovering her.

"Sylvia, what's wrong?"

"I should be asking you that question," replied Sylvia, with a concerned look on her face.

"Why are you in my room?"

"My dear, I heard you screaming and I came rushing up here to check on you. You were thrashing around your bed, but when I checked your head you did not have a fever. I was concerned, so I've been here for the past couple of hours keeping watch over you."

"Screaming? I was screaming? I don't know Sylvia, I really don't."

"Well, perhaps you were just having a nightmare. In any case, I'm glad you're alright. Also, I know you are leaving soon, and I have something I wanted to show you. Something that I think you might find interesting."

Sylvia brought out an old worn log with all the names of the people involved in the Salem Witch trials. Taylor's finger traced over the list of names of people involved in the Witch Trials, and for some reason her finger came to rest on one of the names listed in the section of women believed to be witches, on the name Ann Pudeater. Her accusers said that they believed she was a witch because of the mysterious lotions and potions she supplied to people that inexplicably would heal and mend them. Ann was a masterful natural healer, but many people of the town feared what they did not understand and they turned Ann in for witchcraft. Sylvia watched Taylor's expressions as she browsed through the old log. She knew that Taylor was portal jumping, but she didn't say anything because she knew something, or someone, was making Taylor very happy on the other side. When Sylvia first met Taylor, she seemed to be lost and searching for something. And, even though Taylor never had time to share her time travel experiences with Sylvia, Sylvia couldn't help but take notice to the glow in Taylor's face and the spring in her step. Sylvia believed that whatever Taylor was looking for, it found her.... on the other side of the mirror.

Taylor couldn't quite explain her reasons why, but she decided that she wanted to stay in Salem...permanently. She called her surprised boss, letting him know that she was quitting, as well as her landlord to cancel the lease on her apartment. She would make the trip out to Los Angeles in a few weeks to pack up her belongings. For some magical reason, Salem was calling out to her and Taylor decided that from now on she was going to follow the guidance of her instincts, of her inner knowing. Sylvia told her that she could stay in Room 13 at the bed and breakfast until she could find a place of her own to stay, and somehow that comforted Taylor, despite the fact that she wasn't even sure why.

Taylor decided to use her talents to open up an exhibit strictly dedicated to the Salem Witch Trials. She wanted to educate the public about the horrific wrongdoings that occurred and the many innocent lives that were lost as a result. She even thought about writing a couple screenplays for a few new movies, which would of course be about Salem and witchcraft. One evening while Taylor was shopping at the town grocery store, she spotted a uniquely beautiful woman close to her age going into one of the check-out lanes. She was tall, had long black hair, and there was this mysterious aura about her that drew Taylor to her. Excited at the prospect of possibly making the acquaintance of an available woman in Salem to date, Taylor followed her into the checkout lane and "accidently" bumped her shopping cart into the woman. Taylor of course apologized for her clumsiness, and the two made small talk. The woman was new in town, an herbalist who was about to open her own shop of holistic lotions and potions. Before they could both could finish checking out and paying for their purchases, the beautiful woman invited Taylor out for a dinner date the following evening. Taylor accepted, and the following evening she was set to have a romantic dinner with her new acquaintance.... Annalee, or just Ann for short.

Story #14

Juice Joint Jane

D ark, dreary and disappointing, that is how Grace would have described tonight's outing with her paranormal investigation group. Any light from the moon and stars had been blocked out by the thick rain clouds and fog that hung in the air, and the rain and fog created an ambiance that lent itself to a sure success for tonight's investigation. And, as they trudged through the three floors of the old abandoned building, all of the group's participants were in great anticipation that every creak or gust of wind would lead them to something supernatural. Unfortunately, tonight's outing was a bust, which many of them are. In the end, there hadn't been a single supernatural artifact or experience, and the group decided to leave and have a late night drink at their usual hangout. Their venue of choice was a late-night restaurant in a remodeled gangster hideout that was used by many of the Chicago mobsters in the 1920's. It was a great place to eat, drink and socialize, especially for those who were into things like that, and the place still had many of its hidden passageways, trap doors and secret hiding places all still intact. Grace was definitely a big fan of the place. She loved the old gangster history of Chicago, as well as gangster movies. She loved sitting in this particular restaurant, absorbing the atmosphere and conversing with the staff, even when sometimes she was the only customer in there. She had often wished that the group could conduct a paranormal investigation at the gangster restaurant, but the current owner resisted.

After the group had enjoyed a couple rounds of drinks, her friends started to trickle off, calling it a night. Grace, however, found herself reluctant to go home. It was already nearly 2 in the morning, and even though Grace should just also call it a night and go home, she had an overwhelming urge to stay a little longer.

"You coming, Grace?" the last one in the group called out as she paid her drink bill and paused in the doorway. The lighting was even dimmer near the exit door, so when Grace looked up from her empty coffee cup, she saw that her friend's face was steeped in shadows, shadows with secrets from the hideout's rich gangster history. Secrets that she would love to discover. Somehow her just being in the old hideout restaurant, had filled her with the hope that that was ever a possibility. Grace shook her head at her friend's inquiry. "Ok, just don't forget you have work in the morning."

"I know." She gave the woman one last smile before turning to one of only two staff members who was still there, the pretty bartender standing behind the bar. The door closed with a soft click, blocking out the whistling wind. It still wrapped itself around the old building, though, pushing through cracks and making the entire place sound haunted. If only.

"If it's not too much trouble, could I get one more cup of java?" Grace called across to the bartender, holding her coffee mug up and shaking it a little.

"Sure thing, I just need to put on a fresh pot." The bartender pointed her thumb behind her to the empty coffee pot with an apologetic smile. "If you don't mind waiting a few minutes, it'll be up in just a few."

"No, I don't mind waiting," Grace replied. "I appreciate it." Grace liked the bartender. She was there most nights whenever Grace came in, and she always seemed to have this melancholy look about her. She was pretty, and Grace suspected that both men and women probably regularly tried to make their moves on her, but somehow she doubted that any of them would get the bartender's attention, which always seemed to be off in the distance somewhere. Maybe she had her heart broken, once, or perhaps one too many times.

Grace watched her wiping things down and putting away glasses for a bit before standing to stretch out her legs. She felt restless, and before she knew it, she was headed for a corridor that had caught her eye. She had never been down this particular one before, but when she reached the end of it, she saw a bathroom sign, so at least she knew it wasn't off-limits. There was an antique phone booth beyond the bathroom that didn't even look out of place here. Intrigued, Grace gave a slight smile as she stepped closer to inspect it, wondering if it was just for decoration.

"Hmm…" The door wasn't locked, in fact, it opened effortlessly. She stepped inside the booth, marveling at how the entire thing looked to be in clean, good working order, as if the restaurant made it a point to keep it in good shape. "One 'call' can't hurt, right?" Grace said out loud to herself. She'd just pretend she was calling someone from the heyday of this place, maybe calling her girlfriend who worked for the mob, so she could hear about her dangerous exploits of the day. She reached for the phone and carefully lifted it off its receiver while twisting the silver phone cord in her other hand. After a couple of seconds, though, she heard something click, and the back panel of the old phone booth slid aside cleanly, taking the phone with it. "What the…" Grace started to say, as she dropped the phone piece. "Hello?" she called out into the opening, where the back phone booth wall had just been.

Startled, Grace turned to look back down the corridor, glancing into the restaurant and bar area. The bartender wasn't even looking her way, for she was too concerned with her cleanup work to even take notice to what was going on down the hall. Looking back at the dark, open space, Grace noticed that the open panel had revealed yet another passageway that led beyond the corridor that took her to the phone booth. She wasn't really surprised as this entire building had many secret passageways to hide, and even exit the building undetected, and she had often told herself that she'd like to try and discover them someday. Perhaps that someday, was today. The passageways and hiding spaces hidden within the building were just various tricks that the mobsters would use to elude police as well as rival mobsters that would follow them into the place, which was a speakeasy back in the 1920's and

1930's. In addition to being a cover for mobster activity, the speakeasy was a place where you could acquire liquor, which was illegal then due to it being the time of the prohibition, and speakeasies were often slangy referred to as "juice joints".

Surely the bartender wouldn't mind if she took a quick look around. She would just see if there was anything in the passageway, or at least see where it led to, and then come back and get her cup of coffee. Grace stepped into the dark opening and the phone booth panel slid closed behind her after just a few steps. Grace jumped in surprised, her eyes blinking rapidly as she turned to look back at it, and without the light from the restaurant she was now plunged into total darkness. The entire phone booth was now closed off, and she really had no choice now but to proceed deeper into the secret passageway. With no light to guide her, Grace reached her arms out to the front and sides of her, feeling her way along the dark, damp tunnel. She suddenly felt nervous and apprehensive and could both feel and hear her heart beating wildly in her chest. What if this particular passageway didn't actually lead anywhere? And if it didn't, would she be able to turn back around and get the panel in the phone booth to open back up for her? Grace swallowed hard as she resisted the urge to scream out for help, and she probably would have had she not suddenly felt very disorientated, like when you wake up startled from a lucid dream and you're not sure where you are or what you're supposed to be doing. Her feet kept moving her body forward, yet Grace's mind and awareness felt like they were elsewhere.

After what seemed like forever, Grace could hear voices murmuring at what had to be the end, or at least an opening, of the passageway. It seemed strange, considering she and her paranormal investigations group had been there for a few hours and hadn't seen anyone else coming into the place. Maybe these were people who worked here, and at the very least, maybe they could tell her how to get out of the passageway and back to the restaurant. Grace saw a crack of light escape from the bottom of a closed door. She listened for a moment, before she slowly opened the door and paused in her footsteps. The room was dimly lit and the air was thick with smoke. A few well kept, but intimidating looking men sat across the table from a beautiful woman, who was wearing a sexy evening dress, expensive jewelry and had her hair professionally done. There were a couple open ledgers in front of her, which she immediately slammed closed upon Grace's entrance into the room. Old looking guns were resting on the table in front of the men, whom were each dressed in expensive suits and had slicked-back hair. One of the men, the one in the dark gray suit, looked up, and he pulled the cigar he'd been smoking out of his mouth. "There she is. How you doin' Gracie?"

"We're done here, Tony," the beautiful woman said, while keeping her eyes on Grace. "Tell your client his shipment will be here next week. I don't need to tell you both to be careful when leaving here, but I am anyway. The feds have been casing the joint for weeks now, just waiting for their chance to hook me with something. Now, go, it's time for me to spend some time with my lady."

The moment Grace heard the woman speak, her voice brought a flood of recognition and awareness to her, and Grace suddenly knew where she was and who she was with….her lover Jane LaPietra, sister to mob gangster Angelo LaPietra. Jane was not only beautiful she was also very intelligent and powerful, and kept a handle on the family's illegal liquor business. She ran that underground part of the family operations from a secret room deep within the building, a building that fronted as a high end restaurant and where the gangsters met on a daily basis to discuss and manage their affairs. Grace met Jane when she came in one day looking for a job. Jane took a liking to her, and they've been lovers for over two years now. While they had to keep their relationship hidden from most of the world, whenever Grace came to the club they didn't have to hide their love for one another. It was a dangerous thing to be involved with someone in the mob, but then again, the world was a dangerous place in itself.

"Jane, ya know I don't like hangin' around you guys when you smoke. I don't like the way it makes my hair and clothes smell. I like to smell pretty for you." Grace stepped into the center of the room as the two men each picked up their guns, buttoned their suit jackets and grabbed their hats which were hanging on a hooked coat rack near the door entrance. Both men obliged Grace with a nod and a smile as they exited the room. Jane butted out her own cigarette before getting up from her place on the other side of the table, walked over to Grace and slipped her lace glove adorned hands around her waist.

"Where are they going?" Grace asked.

"They're going outside to keep watch over the place, sweetheart. I don't want my pretty doll gettin' hurt." Jane gave her a grin at that, and pulled Grace down to sit next to her on a small two seat couch that was positioned next to the table and chairs. Grace pouted, and Jane reached up and ran a hand up along the curve of Grace's slender neck and up to her pouting lips. "You know it comes with the territory doll. I deal with some dangerous men, and I always gotta keep my eyes out for anyone who wants to do any harm to the family business, to me, or the ones I care about."

This just got a bigger pout out of Grace. She'd been Jane's girl for more than two years, and even though she was usually compliant of Grace's coming and goings, Jane was also always genuinely concerned about her safety and well-being. Jane loved Grace, she truly did. Jane had told Grace how she loved being able to openly be who she really was around her, not trying to pretend or put on any facades for anyone. She treated Grace with the utmost respect, bought her pretty babbles, and when it came to their love making...Jane made her dizzy with pleasure every time she touched her. Grace truly loved her too, of course. And, truth be told, she was very attracted to the fact that Jane was a dangerous woman. She was the ultimate of "bad girls", and that element of danger was what really drew Grace to her. Maybe she didn't fully understand everything that Jane did as Jane kept the details of her work private from Grace, but she had plenty of ideas. Yes, Grace was in love with a "bad girl", and she loved every minute of it.

Grace continued to pout as she sat snuggled up against Jane on the couch, looking towards the door. She felt like there was something strange about the fact that she was here, but she couldn't quite put her finger on it. She had come here to see Jane, as she did a lot, no matter how much Jane told her that it was dangerous and she shouldn't do so. This was one of the main rooms within the building that was used for the most secret of mob meetings, Grace knew that, and there was never any telling just what kind of not-so-friendly transactions might be happening deep within the hidden bowels of the hideout. The police knew that too, but they had never managed to catch anyone here because there were too many traps and tricks built into the building, so the subject of their stake-outs always seemed to disappear. Still, there was something nagging at the back of Grace's mind that something wasn't right. When she turned to Jane, she caught Grace's lips in a sensual kiss and Grace completely forgot what she was going to ask her.

Jane slowly brushed a hand along Grace's torso, her fingers skimming up her side in a way she knew drove Grace crazy. Jane may have been a tough broad, and depending on where they were, she couldn't always show affection towards Grace publicly. But, whenever they were alone, Jane didn't hesitate to let Grace know just how much she desired and loved her. Jane always knew exactly where to touch Grace and what to do to make her moan.

Jane didn't get much farther than putting her hand on Grace's shoulder, though, before she pulled away, her eyes still closed. "Hungry, baby?"

Grace paused at that. She knew it was late, very late actually, and that had something to do with Grace's gnawing feeling that something was wrong. In truth, she was kind of hungry, but she didn't want to trouble the cook at this hour of the night. "Isn't it too late for dinner?" she asked, and Jane started laughing. Grace frowned. "What's so funny Jane?"

"You know who I am and where we are, right? Doll, they'll make something for us, don't you worry." Jane said it as if it was unreasonable to think it would go any other way, and it sent a shiver of reality down Grace's spine. Had she really forgotten that Jane's family "owned" this place? No, her family didn't have the deed to it, nor did they run any of the front operations of the restaurant, but if Jane or anyone else in her family wanted or needed something, they'd get it, one way or another.

Grace slowly stood up from the couch and waited for Jane to stand. Jane never let her leave the room in front of her if she could help it. Jane always seemed to be afraid of the possibility of Grace being shot. Grace thought it was sweet, in a way, but to tell the truth, she'd probably hate it more if Jane was ever shot vs. herself getting shot. She wasn't that important, after all, and Grace was sure that Jane could find some other woman to replace her if she ever ended up being killed, which was, of course, a high possibility considering Jane's family's line of work. It just wasn't something Grace liked thinking about too much.

The hallway was dark and quiet, the only sounds coming from Grace and Jane's high heels as they clacked along the cement floor. The entire place was cold and damp, and Grace got a sense of foreboding as they walked along, even though it had only been a few minutes since she went through here herself. Flashes of memory flickered in her mind as Grace remembered slipping into the back and walking for what seemed forever, but now that she wasn't distracted, she still wondered just what it was that was feeling "off" to her. They reached the end of the passageway where Jane fiddled with one of the stones in the wall, which triggered the hidden wall in the phone booth to slide open. It was then that Grace fully remembered how she had gotten there, and her mind tried to wrestle with the reality of it all as they walked back into the main restaurant and bar area. The bartender was still there, although it wasn't the usual female bartender. It was an older man, and he was wiping down the bar and humming to himself as he worked. Grace wrinkled her brow in confusion as she glanced up at the clock on the wall, only to see it was now three a.m.. Jane led them to a slightly secluded corner table, which Grace knew was one of her regular spots to sit if she came out to the front area of the restaurant.

"Evening Miss Jane, Miss Gracie, what can I get for you two?" the bartender asked, looking up from the bar and giving them both a bright smile. Of course he was willing to do anything for them. His "boss" was the LaPietra family. And, if the LaPietra family was your "boss", you obliged anyone in their family, no questions asked.

"We're a bit hungry Jimmy. Would you kindly whip us up a couple of plates of your famous manicotti," Jane replied as she helped Grace settle into the back of a large corner booth. "I'll get our drinks. You just start tending to our food." The bartender nodded and went into the kitchen to start their late-night meal without any further dialog.

"Now then, baby, let me get us a couple of cocktails." Jane went behind the bar and made them a couple double martinis, one with extra olives for Grace. She walked the drinks back over to the table and set them down before she slid into the booth next to Grace. "Here's to you, blue eyes," Jane said, holding up her glass for a toast.

"Ahh…, you're so sweet to me," responded Grace.

They clinked glasses and sipped at their strong libations, as Jane tugged off her lace gloves and pulled Grace even closer to her. Grace's body immediately melted against Jane, and she let Jane kiss and caress her body as if they were alone. Well, they were almost alone, with the exception of Jimmy, who was presently preoccupied in the kitchen preparing their meal, and Jane's two henchmen, who were outside keeping watch over the joint. So, yes, they were pretty much alone.

The booth they'd sat in was spacious, and before Grace really knew it, Jane had her on her back. Her clothes were still intact, but Jane was once again running her hands up and down Grace's sides as she did earlier, while grinning seductively at her. Jane's long pearl necklace kept falling against Grace's face, so she reached one hand up to tug it up and over her head before tossing it aside. Jane pressed her lips to Grace's, and Grace could taste the remnants of cigarette tobacco and vodka on her tongue and lips as she deepened the kiss. "You look so good tonight, baby," Jane murmured against her lips before moving her attention down to Grace's neck. Her neck has always been one of her erogenous zones and Grace let out a high-pitched moan as Jane gently bit down on just the right spot, no doubt leaving a mark. Grace had one hand on Jane's ass, and she raised the other up to her neck, feeling the teeth marks and saliva left behind once Jane moved on to other parts of her body.

The top of Grace's dress was button-down, and Jane's fingers easily unfastened them. She pushed the fabric aside, exposing Grace's silky slip and bra, a slip and bra she vividly remembered picking out for her when she treated Grace to a day of shopping. After partially sliding both the slip and bra from her breasts Jane leaned down to lick and suck at Grace's erect nipples, while she reached one of her hands underneath the hem of Grace's dress and hiked it up towards her waist. The silky feel of Grace's stockings drove Jane wild, and as she reached up to tug Grace's panties off over her garter belts, she took her time sliding them down and off her legs, leaving her black high heeled shoes on. Jane loved pretty legs, and Grace's legs were a slice of sensual heaven. She looked great naked, but Jane actually preferred seeing Grace, and even making love to her, when she wore her heels, stockings and garters. In fact, Grace always blushed when Jane would tell her that she was sexy enough to belong on a pinup calendar.

Jane's fingers slowly caressed their way up Grace's thighs until they reached her mound. She ever so gently parted Grace's pussy lips with her fingers, and teasingly toyed with her clit and folds as she passionately kissed Grace's red-stained lips. Grace moaned with pleasure, as her hands reached down the front of Jane's dress to squeeze her tits. She had long since forgotten her surroundings, and that they were romping around in the booth of a mob joint being staked out by the feds and who knows who else. Jane opened her legs farther for her mob lover, and Jane eagerly slid a single finger slowly into Grace's wet pussy. Jane then slid her body off of the bench seat of the booth and kneeled down on the floor, her head positioned perfectly in between Grace's parted thighs, and gently began lapping at Grace's clit with her tongue. Grace gasped and leaned her head back, enjoying the delicious efforts of her lover. Jane stopped as suddenly as she began, and demanded that Grace stand up and take off her dress, slip and bra, but to leave her shoes, stockings and garters on. Too worked up at this point to care if anyone walked in on them, all Grace could do was nod and comply.

As Grace stood naked in front of Jane while she sat in the booth, Grace had to admit that the danger of someone walking in on them only heightened her arousal. Jane stared longingly at Grace's nudeness as her hands reached under her own dress to peel off her panties and toss them to the floor. She hiked up her dress so that she could spread apart her thighs, and seeing Jane's naked pussy before her caused a surge of heat to stir in Grace's belly. Jane casually took a sip from her martini glass before motioning for Grace to come stand in front of her. Grace obliged, and she straddled Jane's legs as she remained seated on the booth bench, moaning as Jane's hands caressed her ass….her fingers then feathering their way in between her thighs, before teasing and pinching and parting her pussy lips open and tickling at her hole. Grace held onto Jane's shoulders as her knees weakened, and when she felt a couple of Jane's fingers seep deep inside of her cunt, she sat down on Jane's lap as Jane finger fucked her. Their mouths met hungrily with passionate, feverish kisses, as Grace reached a hand between both of their parted legs to play with Jane's pussy, which was already wet and swollen. Grace's eyes fluttered shut as Jane's fingers worked their magic. With a couple fingers thrusting in and out of her pussy and a thumb simultaneously rubbing at her clit, Grace literally had to bite her tongue to keep from baying out loud with pleasure.

"Its ok baby, let it out," Jane whispered, leaning into Grace's neck and pressing a kiss to the mark she'd left there earlier. This pushed Grace into the blissful state of losing control, and she allowed the moans to escape her mouth as she rode Jane's fingers, faster and faster. Grace clutched at Jane's back, bucking and moving her hips so that Jane's fingers would reach that sensitive spot, and in just a few minutes, Grace vocally appreciated the orgasm that rippled throughout her body. Grace was sweaty and gasping as her eyes fluttered shut in bliss. She leaned against Jane, her fingers playing with the back of her hair, and Jane held her tightly for a moment before pulling Grace up off of her lap so that she could openly admired her nudeness.

When Jane heard the clinking of dishes in the kitchen, she grunted and reluctantly moved away from Grace, reaching onto the table for some napkins to clean them both off. Grace had more work to do to make herself presentable, so she gathered up her clothes and quickly slipped off to the bathroom to dress and clean up instead of doing it at the table. She glanced over at the phone booth at the end of the hall before closing the bathroom door. She did have a mark on her neck, she observed in the mirror after she finished getting dressed. It could be easily hidden though by a dab of makeup and the collar of her dress, and in truth, she loved the physical reminder of her spontaneous love making with Jane. Jane may not have been the picture of a law-abiding citizen, but she never showed anything less than complete respect towards Grace, not to mention a level of love and passion that she had never in her life thought she'd experience. Add to that, a level of danger and the excitement of sneaking around, and it was nothing more than the perfect relationship in Grace's eyes.

The food was on the table by the time she got back, and Jane was patiently waiting for Grace to return before digging into her plate of steaming hot food. The plates of manicotti did look exceptionally good, Grace had to admit; she'd caught the scent of the freshly prepared Italian fare even when she was still standing there in the bathroom with the door closed between her and the rest of the world. There was light conversation between her and Jane as they ate, and sometimes Grace would look up and see that Jane was looking at her with an intense expression on her face. Was she worried about something? Grace wasn't sure what Jane might be thinking, but something told her to just leave it alone and not ask her. Grace sighed in a contented way as she leaned back from the table, finally done with her food and thinking what a wonderful evening she was enjoying with her girl.

One gunshot… two….. Jane jumped up from her seat before Grace could even ask her what was going on, pulling out a handgun that was secretly strapped to the underside of their table and jumping in front of her seat to shield Grace. There was the sound of scrambling outside, most likely Jane's two henchmen whom she had sent to keep watch of the perimeter. Something was happening. The thuds and clamoring sounds got closer, and Grace dove under the table, catching one of her shoe heels on the leg of the chair and twisting an ankle as her body fell to the floor. Louder sounds of shuffling and struggle could now be heard coming from outside, followed by another few rounds of gunfire. A few moments of tense silence…..and then…. the door burst open!

Grace hesitantly glanced out from under the table. Jane looked relieved and started to lower her gun, when the sound of more gunshots boomed just outside the open door. Grace yelped and hid back under the table, pulling the table cloth back down from where it had caught on the table so she wasn't visible to the people who'd come in. She heard

Jane talking to one of her men, but the sound of gunshots and yelling was deafening and she couldn't really make out what it was they were saying. She thought she heard them say something about them being under attack by a rival mob cartel. Why else would anyone but the police be trying to come after them like this? Jane's family was way too powerful for anyone else to think they even stood a chance. Grace couldn't help but wonder, if the rival mobsters had made it this far, she certainly wasn't feeling too optimistic about getting out of the situation unscathed.

Grace's breath caught in her throat just thinking about it, and she huddled into herself a little tighter. This was just the kind of thing that could happen when you dated someone tied to the mob, like her lover Jane LaPietra was. This was what she wanted though, wasn't it? The excitement of having a bad girl for a lover? The gunfire then erupted like a Fourth of July celebration and the smell of gunpowder permeated the air. Grace's ears were ringing and she felt dizzy and confused. Jane warned her of the dangers of her lifestyle. Grace understood, yet she admittedly didn't think it would ever happen; finding herself in the crossfire....literally. She could hear bullet shells bouncing off tables and walls all around her; the faint sounds of yelling; the odor of burnt gun powder.... and then....the gunfire suddenly stopped. Grace held her breath, afraid to make a sound, and that's when she heard someone scrambling and the front door opening and closing as whoever it was quickly made their getaway. Was it over? Waiting a few more minutes to make sure that there wasn't going to be another round of gunfire, Grace slowly crawled out from her spot under the table, huffing and puffing and swinging all around as she tried to take in her surroundings. The place was a mess. Tables were turned over or splintered, the plates from their late-night dinner shattered on the floor at her feet, and the air was thick with smoke from the heavy exchange of gunfire. It was hard to see anything in great detail.... but then....her eyes adjusted.

Grace let out a blood curdling scream. She'd finally had the courage to step away from the table, but her shoes met with Jane's body, lying lifeless with blood slowly draining out of multiple gunshot wounds and pooling around her head. Tears stung Grace's eyes as she tried to hold back another scream, clapping her hands over her mouth and scrunching her eyes shut. She couldn't look at those blank eyes for even another second. Just as she backed away towards the bar, the bartender emerged from the kitchen. "Go call the police, Gracie! Now!" It was the only thing he said, as he nodded down the hall, towards where Grace knew there was a phone booth.

"I....I... okay." Grace stammered and left, tears running down her cheeks as she had to step over the wreckage. The men who'd come after Jane's juice joint hadn't hesitated to destroy the place along with her life. Grace found herself choking, and she paused and reached up, rubbing away the tears from her cheeks before she was able to continue. She just had to call the police and they'd be able to do something about this. After all, they wouldn't dare try to blame Jane or her family for any of this. She was dead! No. She wasn't going to use that word. If she didn't say it, then maybe it wasn't real.

As Grace stepped into the phone booth, she had the vague feeling that something had happened in this very same phone booth earlier. No, that couldn't be, she was probably just in a state of shock from what had just happened. She shook her head and tried to see through the flow of tears as she picked up the phone. Before Grace could tell the switchboard to connect her to the police, there was a sudden flash of light that literally filled the phone booth. Grace couldn't see anything in front of her, and for a few seconds, she wasn't even sure where she was. Silence and darkness were all that she observed, and then.....it was over.

Grace blinked a few more times as she just stood there, holding the phone. Her head was spinning still, and she honestly had no idea what she was doing, standing there in the phone booth. Hadn't she been waiting for the bartender to make a fresh pot of coffee so she could have one more cup before she went home? She shook her head as she pushed the door open to the phone booth and walked back down the hall, trying to make sense of the flood of segmented flashbacks that were coming to her. About a secret passageway and back room, her beautiful mob affiliated lover, the gun fight, her lover's dead body, and Grace crying as she went to the phone booth. But… it wasn't real, was it?

"Hey, where ya been?" the pretty bartender called out to Grace as she emerged back into the restaurant area. She only half glanced at Grace before turning and picking up the fresh pot of coffee, pouring a fresh cup for Grace and one for herself. There weren't any other people left in the restaurant, and so the bartender came around to the front of the bar and sat down on one of the stools as Grace took the one beside her, cradling the mug of hot coffee in her hands and blankly staring down into its murky depths.

"I'm not exactly sure…" Grace finally answered. She closed her eyes at that, not lifting the cup yet. Grace didn't know why, but the steady gaze the bartender gave her made her think that she might actually believe Grace if she told her what had happened, or at least what she thought had happened. And so, Grace proceeded to tell the bartender everything that she could remember, although she may have skimped on some of the details, not really wanting to go into something as personal as making love with her beautiful mob affiliated lover. The bartender didn't once interrupt her, even though Grace herself thought that she sounded pretty insane. After all, how possible was it to time travel, let alone that she'd end up in the one phone booth in Chicago that was capable of it? Grace knew her paranormal group would eat all this up, but as she finished her story and leaned back on her bar stool, finally taking a drink from her mug of now tepid coffee, she had a feeling she wasn't going to tell them what happened. If that booth really was capable of time travel, surely other people would have discovered it already. Maybe she really was having a moment of insanity. Maybe she is so wrapped up in all things paranormal, that she just imagined the whole experience.

"I'm sorry." Grace said. "You probably didn't want to hear all that. I know I must sound like I'm off my rocker." She took her wallet out and was about to put down a couple of bills on the bar, but the bartender stopped her. "But, I haven't paid..."

"Don't worry about it." A warm, gentle smile graced the bartender's lips as she stood from her own stool and took both of their mugs away to be washed. Before she entered the kitchen though, she looked back to Grace. "Be careful driving home. The storm's getting pretty bad out there and I wouldn't want a pretty doll like you getting hurt." And then she was gone. Grace paused as she was putting her wallet back in her purse, gazing at the kitchen door that swung once or twice before settling back into the frame. Grace had a sudden flash of thought... that she recognized her....her choice of words, and....No, that wasn't possible. Jane? She needed to get home. She obviously needed some rest and time to clear her mind which was reeling with a very active imagination right now.

The bartender had been right when she said that the storm was getting worse. The entire building usually sounded haunted when the wind blew through it, but now Grace could really hear the storm's intensity as she headed for the door. She glanced back down the hall where she'd discovered the old phone booth, but there was nothing particularly ominous about it that she could see. Before opening the door, Grace put a hand up to her neck where Jane had marked her. She couldn't feel anything, and she frowned, dropping her hand. Why was she even thinking about it?

Grace didn't have an umbrella with her, so she made a run for her car. She never heard the heavy bar door fall shut behind her, but given how much more noise the storm made out here right in the middle of it, she figured it was just because she couldn't hear it. Once Grace was in her car, she quickly turned it on and just sat there, letting the heater kick in so she wouldn't be cold while she drove home.

The bartender stood there at the door as the whipping winds and chilling rain assaulted her body, watching Grace, frowning a little as she leaned against the door frame and folding her arms around her body. She was tempted to chase after Grace, to tell her everything. That she believed her story about the phone booth; about the passageway; and about the shooting, because... she too had been there. Her spirited had hovered over her body and watched as Grace had cried over her as Jane bled to death on the floor. But, it was one thing for Grace to tell her a story about something that had happened to her, it was another thing altogether to believe someone else's story. Janie smiled, remembering the way Grace had talked about it. It certainly seemed that she loved her dangerous woman, and that she had enjoyed her experience... until the gun fight, and her death. Janie was unsure that she wanted to bother Grace about it. She'd been thinking about approaching Grace ever since she and her paranormal group had started coming into the restaurant.... their restaurant... the juice joint that Jane, now Janie once ran for the family. Janie was looking for an opportunity that would make sense to Grace. After what happened this evening, it could definitely be the opportunity she was looking for because Janie knew with almost certainty that Grace would be open to what she had to say... or would she? This was something Janie was going to have to ponder, and if she felt it in her heart that it was the right thing to do, she'd do it. But, for now, she'd just watch and enjoy her beautiful doll from a distance.

Grace looked up as the heater finally kicked in and she activated the windshield wipers. The rain was falling even harder, and just as the wipers cleared off the windshield, they'd become covered in a film of water that obscured her vision and frustrated her. There wasn't much she could do about it though, and she'd just have to drive extra careful. The rain was coming down just as hard on the back window, but she thought she saw something out of the corner of her eye. She glanced into the side mirror and raised her eyebrows as she saw the bartender standing there just inside the doorway into the building. She looked like she wanted to step outside, but something was preventing her. Grace couldn't see the look on the bartender's face considering how far away she was, plus the rain was definitely obscuring her view, but there was something inherently melancholy about her, and she paused before shifting her car into gear. Grace was tempted to get back out of the car and see what was wrong, but then she shook her head. She barely knew her. Counting that night, they'd talked maybe once or twice beyond Grace telling the bartender her order whenever she came into the restaurant with her paranormal group. If the bartender was having problems, Grace was sure that she had plenty of people to talk to who knew her far better than she did.

With a long sigh, Grace switched the windshield wipers to go a little bit faster and started off. She glanced in her rearview mirror. There wasn't a single sign of the bartender standing there in the doorway, and Grace had to blink a couple times to make sure she was seeing correctly. It hadn't even been but a few seconds since she'd spotted her. With a puzzled look, Grace switched on her headlights, and slowly inched her way home... confused... confused because she had the strangest of feelings... the feeling that this restaurant was somehow her home.

Story #15

Carnival Crush

C **Y**ou look a lot happier here," Carrie's sister had told her yesterday when they were sitting in a small café together, drinking tea and just taking time with each other. And it was true, she did feel happier here. As Carrie drove along the dusty road towards the carnival she had promised to bring her young nieces to, Carrie couldn't help but take stock in the fact that she was not only a lot happier here in Austin, Texas than she had ever been in New York City, but that she also felt grounded, more at peace, and she began harboring a sense of hope about her future. In contrast, every day in the city had been a blur to her, and certainly not in a good way.

Carrie glanced in the rearview mirror at her nieces in the backseat, watching their bodies wiggle with excitement as they couldn't wait to get in to the carnival. The line of cars was surprisingly long, but it was the weekend, so she should have expected it to be busy. She had agreed to bring her two nieces out today while her sister went to visit a coworker in the hospital, but she was more than happy to do so for it gave her a reason to let her hair down and have some fun. It had been so long since she could just be herself, she admittedly felt like a kid herself today. Carrie reflected on her recent split from her ex and how her partner always managed to stifle her joy, constantly reminding her to act prim and proper no matter where they went. Every day they were together, Carrie felt the life and spirit being slowly drained from her, until she reached that turning point when she couldn't bring herself to walk through the door of their posh New York apartment even one more time. The day she left her partner and rented a small studio apartment in a much less exclusive neighborhood, was the emancipation of Carrie, and she vowed to rekindle the zest for life that she once enjoyed.

"Aunt Carrie, I want a corn dog!" That was the younger of them, at eight years old. Carrie's sister Teresa had given her money to make up for the fact that she wasn't going with them even though Carrie had said she didn't need it. She was more than willing to pay for her nieces to eat whatever they wanted, and of course play a few games. Teresa had insisted, though, and Carrie hadn't been willing to fight about it, finding it silly to argue about who had more disposable income. The sound of carnival patrons and music from the rides was already clearly audible as the three of them sat there in the car, waiting to be directed into a parking spot. Her nieces were literally bouncing in their seats by now, and Carrie quietly locked the doors, just to make sure they didn't just bound out and make a run for it before she could park the car.

Once they finally parked and made their way into the front entrance to purchase their tickets and ride bracelets, it seemed to be no-holds barred. Her two nieces were running far ahead of her, and Carrie had to quicken her pace just to make sure they remained in her sight. The older one was only eleven, after all, and she'd feel pretty bad if she let them disappear and they ended up getting hurt. Carrie sighed happily as the trio snaked their way through the carnival, taking in all the sights while at the same time ensuring that she always had her nieces in her sight. Taking notice to all the laughing, happy couples all around her, Carrie again mused about her future. Austin really was the kind of place she wished she could stay in. Everyone here was friendly and happy, and they even smiled at her as she passed them, despite not knowing her. There was nothing wrong with being friendly, right? If she walked down the streets of New York City like this, she likely wouldn't get a single bit of acknowledgement, and she might even get a glare if she tried to smile or talk to someone she didn't know. Yes, she really was going to put some serious thought into the possibility of moving to Austin. Plus, she already had family here.

"Aunt Carrie!" the younger one called out. She had stopped in front of one of the games, and Carrie had a feeling she knew what was coming next. Her niece obviously wanted to play, and even though carnival games were notorious for being a bit of a long-shot to win, they were always a part of the whole carnival experience. Of course carnivals needed to make money, and they couldn't make money if the games were easy or they gave out prizes for a small victory. There was nothing wrong with that, she supposed, as she brought out her purse and took out a few bills so that they could all play. The carnie was giving her nieces the shtick that she had expected, about how they could win a bunch of really cool prizes if they just hit the target five times. It was an air rifle game, and it made Carrie a little uncomfortable when she thought about it, but she supposed that guns were a lot more common here, and the kids certainly had no problem with it.

"Alright, alright!" Carrie replied to her niece's eager pleas, smiling after she had paid and the three of them were handed their air rifles. Their scores couldn't be combined apparently, but she was determined to win something for at least one of them. They each had ten shots for the amount she had paid, so she was sure she could get the target in that amount and at least get a small stuffed animal. Her nieces were already pulling at their triggers, shooting at the targets and hitting them with extreme ease. One shot, two, three. Carrie never hit the bullseye, but she did manage to at least hit the targets six of the ten shots she was allowed, and when the booth attendant went to look at it, he grinned and swept his arm over to a display of small stuffed animals. They certainly weren't as impressive as the ones that were hanging at the front of the booth, obviously there to entice people and fool them into thinking that's what they'd get if they won at the booth. Well that was another trick, but Carrie decided not to tell that to her nieces, both of whom had each gotten all ten of their shots, and so each of the girls was able to pick from the selection of medium-sized animals.

"I think I'll take that bear," Carrie said, pointing to her selection at the back of the stuffed animal pile. She was picking it out for herself since her nieces didn't need her to save them from the pain of defeat, and she somehow was drawn to the small, unassuming teddy bear. It wasn't that spectacular, and it didn't have anything special about it other than the cute sundress it had been put in, but as the booth attendant handed it to her and went about serving the next people, Carrie smiled as she grabbed the bear from the attendant's hands. As she held onto the small stuffed bear a brief feeling of déjà vu swept through her, but passed as quickly as it came. Carrie thought that was a little odd, but dismissed the feeling as she and her nieces continued along the fairway. There were other games that her nieces wanted to try, but Carrie didn't participate in them. Instead, she decided to hang back and simply hand out the money they needed and watched as they won or lost and got more prizes. It was only after several more games that she remembered her younger niece's request for a corn dog. It wasn't like she completely forgot she needed to feed them, but she'd been so caught up in the attractions and watching after her nieces that it simply just slipped her mind. They'd also gone on a few of the rides in-between the game stops, and so she figured it was okay to sit down and get something in their stomachs. She handed her oldest niece a twenty dollar bill, and took the youngest one to search for a place to sit where they could then eat their food.

"Aunt Carrie!" the older niece called out as she walked over to Carrie, her arms loaded with typical carnival junk food; funnel cakes, licorice whips and an enormous bag of kettle popcorn. Carrie laughed out loud, knowing her nieces stomachs would be protesting later after their consumption of all that sugar. Carrie wasn't sure how they were going to eat all of her niece's choice of lunch items, but she guided them over to a sticky table and bench seats to sit down while she then went back to get them some lemonade.

"So what do you two want to do after this?" Carrie asked, managing to not talk with her mouth full. She was sure that would be a bad example for them. On the other hand, she couldn't help but want to eat more and more, enjoying each mouthful of guilty pleasure carnival fare. Another consequence of living with her extremist ex partner was that

Carrie had been subjected to a purist health food regimen. In fact, her ex had insisted on it, saying that she would feel better if she didn't eat anything that was breaded, fried, that contained any fat, contained any sugar, blah, blah, blah. While the words may have sounded genuine Carrie had never felt that her ex partner's true intentions behind her extreme oversight over what Carrie consumed was ever purely based on wishing her good health. Sure, she may have been slimly concerned about her health, but Carrie had always felt in her gut that her ex partner's extreme vigilance in what she ate had much more to do with her not wanting Carrie to get fat, which her ex would have deemed both unacceptable and embarrassing.

"I wanna go on the roller coaster !" Carrie's younger niece hollered as she pointed across the fairway to a roller coaster that currently had carts full of screaming passengers, descending down the highest loop and twisting around, shaking and rattling in a way that made Carrie slightly nervous. Surely it was safe, Carrie thought to herself, otherwise they wouldn't have been able to set it up. Yes, surely it was safe, yet Carrie always had this strange sense of "danger" whenever she was in or near a carnival or amusement park of any kind. She wasn't sure why, but there was always this definite nagging in the back of her mind. Sure, she'd let her nieces go on the roller coaster, but she wasn't about to let them go on a big twisting, jolting ride right after eating all of that junk food.

They talked some more over their food, somehow managing to eat every last bite, and as Carrie sat there enjoying the company of her nieces, she couldn't help but feel happy over her decision to take this trip. It proved to be very cleansing to her spirit and was just what she needed after her split from her ex. And, she was sure that if she just stayed here in Austin long enough that she would somehow discover a new direction in life, and possibly even a new romance. Carrie was still uncertain about where her life might be headed after her recent split, but the one thing she was clear about, was that she wanted to be far, far away from New York City. She hated her job, she hated the constant hustle and bustle of city living, and she always felt like she was stuck there with no other options. Now, without her domineering ex tying her down, Carrie was viewing her future as a clean slate and an opportunity to explore and rekindle the joy and passion for life that she once had. She hadn't yet told Teresa that she was contemplating moving back to Austin, but she guessed that her sister had assumed that she might. In fact, her sister had already said that she was going to set her up with "a nice, Southern girl." Carrie wasn't sure exactly what that entailed, so she didn't know if she should be grateful towards her sister and for her efforts, or not. Carrie's ex had been a city girl through and through, and she was the reason that Carrie had ended up in New York City in the first place. They lived right in the heart of one of the busiest parts of the city, and she always had a hard time enjoying herself even when she wasn't working. Carrie was much more the country girl, and she just couldn't fathom how anyone would want to live in a place with so many people, so much pollution, and so much noise. And, while Austin, Texas wasn't exactly small-town, it was definitely more her pace. She had enjoyed herself ever since she had gotten off the plane and every time Carrie went out with her sister, or explored the town on her own, she found herself unconsciously looking out for places that were either for rent or sale. She knew she probably shouldn't be thinking about relocating right now. She had barely moved out of the expensive apartment that she had shared with her ex for so many years, and she was sure that she had plenty to still do in New York. Not to mention, she'd have to find a job out here before she could move, because it wasn't like she could just leach off her sister the entire time. But still, it was something fun to think about.

Carrie had been so deep in thought, that she didn't even notice that the food was all gone until both of her nieces stood and started impatiently tugging on her sleeve, telling her that they wanted to go on some more of the rides. Carrie sighed but smiled. She gathered up their food wrappers and cups and deposited them in a nearby trash can before letting her nieces lead her towards the rattling, creaking roller coaster. "Are you sure you want to go on the roller coaster right after you've eaten all that food?" Carrie asked, genuinely more concerned about the safety of the ride more so than the jumbling of their stomach contents. Her eyes went up to it, and she shook her head, turning around and tugging her protesting nieces with her. "I think we should go on something a bit calmer first, and let the food settle in our stomachs."

Her nieces were still protesting as she led them towards the area with the tamer rides, tugging them by the sleeves with one hand and still holding the small teddy bear in the other. She hadn't let go of the thing since she won it back at the game booth, and she wasn't sure why. She should have just put all of their prizes in the car and come back, just because that would be easier, but something made her keep it with her. Carrie stopped when they were in front of the Tunnel of Love ride, and it was the typical cheesy cliché carnival attraction, with flashing lights on the outside and the entire thing decorated in pinks and reds. The carnival attendant was just preparing for a new set of riders, so Carrie tugged her nieces along. "Come on, this one looks good. A gentle, slow-moving ride should be enough time for our food to settle, right?"

Her older niece groaned in protest. "Aunt Carrie, this thing is really corny. And it's for couples. See?" She moved her hand towards one of the train cars. It was clear there was room for only two people in each of the cars, and that was it. Thankfully, without her even having to give them instructions, her two nieces headed for an empty car, and she headed for the one directly behind them. Somehow, it was a little depressing to Carrie to be sitting on a carnival attraction meant for sweethearts and not have someone to ride with. And when she thought about it, she couldn't recall a single occasion that her ex had ever done something cheesy and spontaneous just for the fun of it. In fact, Carrie's ex would have considered just being at a carnival way beneath her. Her complacent attitude was glaringly evident to Carrie after the first year or two of their relationship, when she hadn't thought it was all that important to spend quality time with Carrie, like have date nights or take fun day trips or vacations together. Hell, even sex seemed like a chore to Carrie's ex after a while, and Carrie eventually just stopped trying. She would constantly tell Carrie how lucky she was; living in a posh New York apartment, having influential acquaintances, dining in all the talked about eateries and having just about any material need that she wanted, as if all those things were the keys to happiness. And, while all of that seemed fun for a brief while, it didn't really make Carrie happy. In fact, all Carrie ever felt was lonely, unloved and trapped. Sometimes it's the unpleasant things that act as a much needed catalyst, and looking back, leaving her ex was one of the most loving and liberating things she could have done for herself.

Once everyone had been loaded into the train cars, the Tunnel of Love ride slowly jerked to a start. They were immediately brought into a dark tunnel with flashing lights and plastic red and pink decorations everywhere, as well as animated standee figures that were probably supposed to be moving in time with the music, but were just a little off. The music itself was old fashioned and sounded like it was being played on a record player that had seen better days. It occasionally skipped and the sound quality seemed to vary, but maybe it was supposed to sound that way to enhance the vintage character of the ride. Carrie had no idea how much longer they had on the ride, but when it started to slow down and they hadn't even left the tunnel, she had a feeling something was wrong. That's when they heard a voice coming over a loud speaker system saying something that sounded garbled which Carrie couldn't seem to make out, and she suddenly felt incredibly dizzy and disorientated. Then, with a violent jerk, the ride resumed its forward motion and the train cars started going back to their normal speed. Carrie couldn't help but feel like she was going to throw up. It was then that an arm slipped around her shoulders, and as she looked up, clutching her sundress wearing teddy bear in her arms, she had to blink twice before she recognized who it was.

"You okay, Carrie?" the young woman asked, and Carrie gave her a shy smile and a nod as she looked down at her bear. She had no idea what had come over her, but she was safe, enjoying her favorite carnival ride with her sweetheart Rachel. Carrie always felt safe with her. No matter what was happening, Rachel had a calm steady presence that always made her feel loved and protected. The country was in the throws of the Great Depression and ever since Carrie, just 20 years old, had taken a job with the traveling carnival to make whatever money she could to help her family and their farm, she had found both friendship and love in her relationship with Rachel. Rachel was just one year older than Carrie, and she always looked after her and treated her so well. As the ride's rickety cars continued to move along through the Tunnel of Love, Carrie could feel her heartbeat slow down, and she smiled and settled into Rachel's arms. She gazed down at the small teddy bear she was holding in her arms. It was one of the few times she'd ever let Rachel get her anything from the carnival. Considering they both worked there, they both knew how rigged the games tended to be. But Rachel had worked so hard just to get this small token of her love for Carrie, and she hoped Carrie would treasure it. At first, Carrie had thought that she was maybe a little old to treasure a teddy bear, but nonetheless, it meant the world to her.

It was late at night, both Carrie and Rachel were done working their chores at the carnival, and they had managed to get on the last ride of the Tunnel of Love. There weren't a whole lot of fair goers left, and when they stepped out of the ride and looked around, Rachel squeezed Carrie's hand. "Looks like we've got the place to ourselves," she said, giving Carrie an affectionate smile and a kiss on the cheek. Carrie cherished these tender times alone with Rachel, and she didn't care if they just spent the entire evening just sitting in each other's arms, staring up at the stars. The carnival lights were slowly being put out, and as Carrie looked up and past the huge Ferris wheel and then even further up into the sky, her breath caught in her throat. There she saw a beautiful full moon and slow moving clouds that imparted a hauntingly romantic atmosphere that almost brought tears to her eyes. She reached up and wiped them away before Rachel could see them, not wanting Rachel to think that she'd upset her somehow. Even though life and work at the carnival could be hard and often involved a lot of manual labor, Carrie had somehow come to enjoy it. She enjoyed her time with Rachel foremost, but also with all the others who worked with them at the carnival, and they truly had all become like a second family to Carrie. Carrie spent most of her time away from her family, sending them any money she could spare from her allowance since the carnival gave her room, board and meals. Life during the Great Depression was trying and hard, and you found happiness wherever you could. And, if you were fortunate, you might even find love. Carrie and Rachel were lucky enough to have found both friendship and love with one another, making Carrie feel joy and happiness in a circumstance where many would not.

Rachel grabbed hold of Carrie's hand as she guided them towards the back of the dusty lot, where they were hidden by a cluster of the larger carnival tents. Carrie smiled when she spotted a blanket lying there, with a dark colored jug she suspected was filled with moonshine. Clearly Rachel must have set this up recently otherwise one of the carnival patrons would have surely stumbled upon the blankets and booze, and would have most likely at least taken the booze. Carrie decided not to comment on that though, and instead let Rachel direct her gently onto the old blanket, where Rachel then sat down next to her. She immediately started kissing Carrie, and against her lips, she whispered, "I love you so much, Carrie."

Hot tears stung at the corners of Carrie's eyes again, and this time she just closed them, not even bothering to wipe them away this time. They were happy tears, after all, and when Rachel gently laid her down onto the blanket and touched her face and body just as gently, Carrie wrapped her arms around Rachel's shoulders and sighed happily. They took their time as they lay there, knowing they wouldn't be disturbed. This wasn't the first time they had laid on a blanket in back of the tents and just enjoyed each other, and the other carnival workers didn't seem to mind as long as it was after hours. Carrie was on her back as Rachel kissed her gently, and when Carrie opened her eyes, she couldn't help but again take notice to the full moon and sparkling, star-filled sky above them.

"Is it okay?" Rachel's question broke through Carrie's thoughts, and Carrie realized that she had been paying so much attention to the sky that she wasn't even cognizant that Rachel was trying to do something else with her. They didn't always have sex out here in the open, but it did happen, especially when they hadn't gotten to spend a lot of time together. Sometimes they went days without really even getting to talk, just because they were so busy making sure the carnival went exactly as it was supposed to. They both were very attracted to one another, yet Rachel was always respectful and never once had she tried to force herself upon Carrie. Carrie smiled and wrapped her arms around Rachel again, burying her face in Rachel's neck. "Yes, it's okay baby. I want you to make love to me," she whispered, feeling tears running down her cheeks again. Carrie had no idea why, but she knew that they were happy tears. She had been Rachel's sweetheart for almost a year now, so she thought the overwhelming excitement of simply being around her would fade after a while. Apparently it hadn't. Carrie did have an unusual gift of sixth sense, however, and she often sensed things before they happened. But, that certainly couldn't be the case now. Everything around them was peaceful. She was enjoying a romantic evening with her sweetheart, and there was nothing amiss that would hint to anything tragic. Even the skies were presently dust free and beautiful this evening.

Rachel leaned down and kissed Carrie's mouth with slow, tender kisses as her fingers unbuttoned the front of Carrie's faded and slightly frayed sundress. Carrie removed the large hair comb that was holding her long hair in a loose bun, and her long dirty blonde locks fanned around her head against the blanket. "You look like an angel," Rachel said, looking deep into Carrie's eyes. After Rachel unfastened the last of the buttons, she slowly opened the front of Carrie's sundress, exposing her pert, beautiful breasts. Her skin was milky white and her light pink nipples soon stood erect against the brushes and pinches of Rachel's fingers. Rachel's mouth wrapped around one of Carrie's nipples, and as she gently sucked and tugged at it, her hands gently worked at pulling off Carries panties. Rachel stopped and stood back up so she could quickly remove her own worn sundress and panties before returning back down to the blanket and positioning herself next to Carrie's beautiful, naked body.

Rachel's mouth again found Carrie's, and as she kissed Carrie now with a bit more urgency, her hands trailed across her stomach, hips and thighs. Rachel spread Carrie's thighs open, and her fingers gently traced their way up to the crease that merged with her pussy mound. She tenderly parted Carrie's soft folds and slowly circled Carrie's clit with her fingers. Rachel will always remember from her clumsy early attempts to make love to Carrie, that she much preferred Rachel's touches to be soft in her delicate areas, vs. the over-eager rough probing that her hands initially assaulted her with. Rachel was never offended by Carrie's direction, however, and their mutual intimate explorations of one another's bodies had taught them both to be patient, attentive lovers. Rachel loved Carrie with all her heart and she only wanted to make Carrie happy in all ways that she possibly could. Rachel never viewed their intimate times together as just having sex; to her it was truly love making. Something she came to realize could only happen when there was an intimate union of two bodies, coupled with the intimate union of two hearts.

Rachel could feel Carrie moisten from her finger play, and as she deepened their kisses with a passion and sensual hunger she could hardly contain, Rachel slid a finger into Carrie's warm, wet pussy. Carrie's hand clutched at Rachel's ass, pulling her body up tight against her. As Rachel's fingers continued to rhythmically slide in and out of her pussy, Carrie reached a hand between Rachel's thighs and slowly stroked a finger along the outer folds of her pussy. Rachel's free hand found its way to Carrie's tits squeezing and caressing, before she repositioned herself on her stomach at the edge of the blanket, in between Carrie's parted legs. Kissing her way up Carrie's inner thighs, Rachel's tongue lapped slowly at Carrie's pussy lips, spreading them open wide with her fingers so that she could access that special little bud that made Carrie squirm. Back and forth Rachel flicked her tongue against Carrie's clit, as soft muffled moans vibrated at the back of Carrie's throat. Carrie's thighs squeezed against Rachel's ears as her hips began to buck up off of the blanket. Rachel knew her sweetheart was getting close to cumming, and she slid a single finger back into her pussy as she continued her steady tongue stroking across Carrie's clit. Carrie's hands grabbed at Rachel's hair as her hips started twitching, and Rachel could feel Carrie's pussy start to contract and pulse around her finger. Faster and faster Rachel simultaneously moved her tongue and finger, sending Carrie's body over the edge and climatic waves of ecstasy rippled visibly throughout her body. Rachel loved the sweet, musky scent of her sweetheart's arousal and she continued to gently lick at Carrie's pussy as her trembles slowly subsided.

Rachel crawled back up beside Carrie's body and kissed her tenderly on the mouth. Carrie surprised her by returning her kisses with a renewed sense of urgency. "Rachel, I want to taste you." And with that, Rachel rolled over onto her back and this time it was Carrie who was on top. But, instead of sliding herself down between Rachel's legs, she straddled her legs on either side of Rachel's head and lowered herself into a "69" position. It was a position she discovered in one of the male carnival worker's dirty magazines, and it worked just as well for two women as it did for a man and a women. Carrie slowly lowered herself until she felt Rachel's mouth against her pussy, and then she lowered her head between Rachel's parted thighs to explore and enjoy Rachel's spread pussy. Rachel was already moist, allowing Carrie to easily slide a couple fingers into her hole as she sucked gently at Rachel's bud. Rachel started to moan and she tried to stifle it by shoving her face tighter against Carrie's mound. Carrie was a bit more expert at finding just the right spots to make Rachel cum, and Rachel was always surprised by how quickly she felt her body lose control when Carrie's mouth and hands were pleasuring her. Rachel's tongue was now only intermittently licking at Carrie's pussy, as she was too distracted by the intense sensations her own pussy was experiencing. She never really knew what Carrie did to make her feel that way, but surges of heat and what felt like electric currents spasmed deep within Rachel's belly as her eyes rolled back behind her eyelids. Rachel could vaguely hear Carrie slurping at her pussy as she felt her body tense and tighten and get hot. And then....bam! Over that delicious edge her body went. Rachel's hips involuntarily pushed up against Carrie's mouth as she shook and quivered and moaned out her pleasure.

As her waves of sexual climax subsided, Rachel's body fell softly back against the blanket and Carrie got up to turn herself around and cuddle up against Rachel. Rachel tenderly kissed Carrie's lips, cheeks and forehead while murmuring words of endearment to her. Rachel then reached for another blanket she had tucked underneath the one they were laying on, and covered Carrie's nakedness. She then reached for the small jug of moonshine and poured them each a small pour into two dented tin mugs.

"To my pretty sweetheart," Rachel said, as she held her mug up to toast Carrie. "I promise to always love you and be there for you, no matter what." As they both sipped the harsh tasting moonshine from their mugs, Carrie could not have felt more happy or lucky. There was so much tragedy and hardship happening in the world, yet she felt rich...rich with love. Staring deep into her lover's eyes, Carrie's heart skipped. It was because Rachel was smiling at her in just the right way, and whenever she did that, Carrie fell in love with her over and over again. Rachel leaned her body against Carrie, putting her arm around Carrie's waist as she tilted her mug up to take a long drink. "Well, just one more day here, and then we're moving on again."

"Suppose so." Carrie replied, looking back up at the stars. "No matter where we go, though, we always seem to be followed by those crazy dust storms." The carnival typically stayed in each town anywhere from 1-4 weeks, depending on how business and the weather went. Not only was it the Great Depression, but it was also the time of the great Dust Bowl, and no matter where they went, they just couldn't seem to escape the wrath of the dust storms. There was dirt lazily drifting around them even now, and Carrie found herself starting to shiver against the growing wind.

Rachel gave Carrie another kiss and a smile before reaching for their clothes. Rachel let go of Carrie long enough so that they could both get dressed, but as soon as they did, Rachel pulled her right back down onto the blanket and nuzzled her neck. "I'll always love you. Even when the stars fall out of the sky and we've got nothing left but all this dust."

Carrie giggled at that as she laid her head against Rachel's shoulder. "You're so sweet, Rachel. I'll always love you, too."

It was well after midnight when Carrie was awoken in her small trailer by the sound of shouting. She had no idea what was going on, but once she had gotten out of her half-asleep state, she managed to sit up in her cot and look around as her trailer was violently being tossed back and forth. The sound of wind whipping through the structures was obvious, now that she listened, and her heart skipped a beat. Another dust storm was wrecking havoc. Her first instinct was to go outside, but she knew that the rest of the carnival workers wouldn't like that. She wasn't as strong as the men and even some of the other women who'd been working with them longer than she had, including Rachel, and so she'd probably just get in the way. Still, she couldn't help but worry. Carrie always worried and felt anxious during these storms, longing for the moment when the winds and tidal wave sized walls of dirt fell calm. She sat in bed for close to two hours before she felt like it was safe to go outside. She couldn't hear the wind quite as well anymore, and when she tried to open her door, there wasn't a single bit of resistance. When she looked out though, a puff of dust came at her, and she had to cover her mouth with her sleeve to keep it from choking her.

"Carrie, you really should go back inside." That was the first thing one of the carnival men said nervously to her when they saw her emerge from her trailer, but she didn't listen to him. "Carrie, please. You shouldn't be out here now. It's best if you just stay inside."

Everyone was shuffling around, looking somber and like they had no idea what to do. Carrie's eyes scanned the area, and everything was covered in a thick layer of dust, but other than that, it seemed that the carnival grounds were intact. Everything appeared to have been safely tied down except Carrie noticed that a lone, thick cable wire was hanging from one of the rides. Her eyes followed the swaying cable wire down to the ground, which was covered in mounds of dirt from the dust storm, and her eyes fell on what looked like a body. Yes, it was a body, covered in dust and what seemed to be dried blood. Everyone was avoiding it, but everyone was also talking about it, trying to figure out what they were supposed to do. She kept hearing a name being quietly spoken amongst the men anxiously walking around her body. Rachel..... Rachel..... Rachel.

Rachel was dead. Her body had literally been sliced through with the thick cable that had been broken off from the ride when the men and a few of the women had gone out during the dust storm to secure the rides and tents and trailers. She apparently bled out in a matter of minutes. Carrie stood frozen in a state of shock. She literally felt her heart sink to the pit of her stomach, and she opened her mouth to scream, but no sound came out, as her conscience scolded her. She had just been sitting there on her cot, considering if it was worth it to go outside during the storm and try to help the others. She'd done nothing, telling herself that she'd only get in their way. And now, Rachel's life, as well as her own was over. Carrie could feel her head spiraling as she staggered towards Rachel's lifeless body and wept.

Carrie felt a sudden jolt as the Tunnel of Love ride started up again, and she shook her head, glancing all around. What the….. What just happened? What had she just experienced? She couldn't say for sure, but she knew that it had been important. Her two nieces were in the car in front of her again, and when she looked down, her hands were desperately clutching onto the teddy bear. And then she blinked, and that's when she realized that she had tears running down her face.

"We apologize folks for the ride's technical difficulties. Thank you for your patience. The ride will now resume," said a voice over the intercom, and Carrie looked up at the ceiling where it came from, trying to reorient herself so she wouldn't look quite so bad when she had to get off the ride. Everything was flaring back to life as they rode through the rest of the Tunnel of Love ride, music playing and lights blinking. By the time it was done and the ride attendants helped the passengers out of the train cars, Carrie was as composed as she was likely to get. She knew that her nieces would ask her why she was crying if she let them see it, so she turned away from them for a few seconds even as they walked together through the carnival again, picking out more rides and games to play.

They arrived back at her sister Teresa's house a few hours later, tired and stuffed full of fair food, but all had a good time. Carrie's older niece disappeared into the bathroom, saying something about taking a shower to wash all the dust and grime off herself. As she watched her niece close the bathroom door, Carrie mused over what she had experienced at the carnival. Could it have just been a dream?

"Carrie!" Teresa came bounding through the front door with a sly grin. By this time, Carrie was sitting at the kitchen table, drinking a cup of tea as her mind went in a million different directions, so she hadn't even heard her sister's car pull up in the driveway.

Carrie smiled and looked up from the table, still holding the hot cup of tea between her hands. "Hey, sis. You have a good time visiting your friend?"

Teresa grabbed a bottle of water from the fridge, whistling as she headed towards the living room, and curious, Carrie grabbed her cup of tea and followed after her sister. The teddy bear she'd won for herself was sitting beside her, and she petted its head before she headed out into the living room.

"I did have a good time. My friend's doing fine and..." Teresa paused, staring at Carrie as if she was trying to decide exactly what to say. "Well, don't be mad, but I told my friend that you'd go out for coffee with her cousin while you're here. She's recently single too, and I think you'll really like her."

The smile didn't slip from Carrie's face, but she did roll her eyes in a good-natured way. Of course her sister would still make it a priority to play match maker and hook her up with someone while she was here. "Can I at least know her name?"

"Of course. Her name is Rochelle, I think.... no, no, that's not it. Rachel, yes, that's her name, Rachel." Carrie's face lit up at that, and she wasn't quite sure why. There was just something pleasing about the name, Rachel. Who knows, maybe Rachel might even prove to be her new direction in life.....

Story #16

Lesbian Love Magic:

Sappho Love Potion #9

Amelia carefully stirred the contents of her enameled spell pot. Love potions were always so tricky to mix, and she had just spent the entire morning adding just the right amount of ingredients to the one she was currently working on. She really ought to have been done an hour ago, but since this was one of her most coveted of potions, Amelia was always careful to double check every ingredient and never rush any of the steps, as each and every one was integral to the final outcome. This particular love potion is so potent in fact, that one need not even drink it to reap its benefits. The mere absorption of this potent potion through one's skin would be enough to infuse its intended magic.

Amelia only had three items left to add to her potent love brew. "Red rose petals, gold shavings from a worn wedding band, and dried pansies." Amelia muttered repeatedly the three remaining ingredients to herself as she rummaged through the back room shelves lined with botanicals, oils, feathers, sticks, stones and shavings and chips of various metals, barks and other materials. She grabbed the bottles containing the first two items, and was about to grab the third, when a voice from the adjoining room of the potion shop interrupted her concentration.

"Mel, I'm gonna go on break! Can you watch the front of the store for a bit? You're done making that love potion by now, aren't you?" Amelia's younger sister Stacy popped her head in the door to the incanting room, and it was clear from Stacy's facial expression, that she was a bit perturbed over the delay of her being able to take her midday lunch.

Guiltily Amelia blushed. "Go on ahead Stacy. All the delicate cooking steps are finished. I just have a few final ingredients to stir in and then the potion will be complete"

Amelia quickly grabbed the last bottle of ingredients that she needed, which contained the dried pansies, and strode back over to counter where her mixing pot rested, awaiting Amelia's final touches. The jingle of the front door bell told her that Stacy had already headed out of the shop for her lunch break. Amelia quickly went to work carefully stirring in the last three ingredients to her brew pot, and in just the right order. Amelia frowned a bit at the light color of the dried pansies, and hoped to herself that it would not diminish the strength of the love potion. The dried pansies should be a deep violet purple, but instead they were more of a mauve color. "I need to check our supplier." Amelia muttered out loud to herself. "These pansies are off color."

As Amelia delicately dropped in the last of the dried pansies and carefully stirred the potion in a clockwise rotation, a poof of fragrant pink smoke rose from the brew pot. Amelia removed the long-handled wooden spoon and watched as the potion immediately condensed into a fuschia-colored liquid in the bottom of the pot, indicating that the potion was now complete and ready to be bottled.

As Amelia grabbed just the right bottle to contain the finished love potion, she heard the shop's front door jingle, telling her a customer had arrived. "Hello there," Amelia called towards the shop front. "I will be with you in just a moment!"

Amelia carefully poured the swirling fuschia liquid through a funnel, into a thick purple glass bottle. She then sealed the bottle with a cork plug and walked into the shop area with the love potion firmly in hand where she could create a special label for it.

Standing at the front counter was the form of a well dressed woman whom Amelia did not recognize ever being in there before. And, judging by the nervous expression on her delicate features as she kept looking down at the shop's front counter, and the fidgeting of her body, it appeared to Amelia that she might not be all that comfortable with being in a shop that specialized in the creation and selling of potions and brews for a vast array of needs and desires. Amelia was all to eager however to help put her new customer at ease, and moving up to the other side of the counter, Amelia set the love potion down and smiled warmly to her attractive customer.

"Hello. Welcome to Worrick Sister's Potions and Perfumes. How may I assist you?" Amelia asked the woman.

The nervous woman looked up and Amelia's breath caught quickly in her throat. She was instantly captivated by a pair of the most amazing deep green eyes that were now looking back at her, and a brief moment of stirring purred inside Amelia's chest.

"Umm… a friend of mine said…uh, actually that is…I have this little problem." The woman's voice trailed off, and her ivory skin flushed a bright red, as she turned nervously away from Amelia's gaze.

Amelia sighed softly. Clearly the beautiful woman must either be having some sort of trouble in the bedroom, either with regard to sexual performance or fertility. These were the two most common reasons women came into her shop, and almost all of them wore the same uncomfortable, embarrassed expression as the woman before her now did. Amelia had the ability however to quickly put her nervous customers at ease, and once she gained their confidence and trust, she discreetly assisted their specific needs by supplying them with just the right potion or brew, and they left happy and satisfied.

Amelia never quite understood why women were embarrassed or shy about discussing affairs of a sexual nature, but nonetheless, her aptitude for the subject manner and her craft, along with her carefree and compassionate nature always did put the women at ease. And, she knew they would return to her shop for all their future alchemy needs. For some reason however, the thought that this enchanting woman might be having bedroom issues made Amelia feel disappointed, yet she wasn't quite sure why.

Shaking the feeling off, Amelia smiled reassuringly. "Don't worry my dear. I think I know what your concern is, and I assure you, I get a lot of women who come in who are in need of that sort of assistance."

The beautiful woman looked taken aback. "Uh, you do?" she replied shyly with surprise.

"Of course." Amelia smiled reassuringly, and stepping away from the counter, she directed the woman towards the love and reproduction section of the store.

"It's far more common then you may realize. Follow me this way please, and I'm sure we can find something to address your specific problem."

Dazed by what was happening, the still nervous woman followed Amelia to where the various fertility elixirs where shelved, carefully arranged according to the specific issue needing to be addressed.

Turning to face the woman standing next to her, Amelia stated "Now I realize this may be a bit embarrassing, but in order to make sure I get you the exact potion you require, I need you to be as specific as possible about your problem." Turning from her customer to face the shelf lined with potions, Amelia began the familiar line of questioning. "Now, would you characterize your problem as being related to attraction, performance, fertility or something else?"

"What?" The woman stared wide-eyed at Amelia, blinking, and clearly confused.

"Well..." Amelia started again, trying to clarify. "Are you having trouble being affectionate with your husband, or are you having trouble trying to conceive?"

Startled by what Amelia was implying, the woman shook her head vigorously. "What? No!"

"Ok," Amelia continued gently. "So, is your problem related to your body not responding?" Amelia gave the woman a discreet glance, and from what she could tell, it certainly shouldn't be an issue of body image that was giving her trouble in bed. The woman standing next to her was strikingly attractive, and again Amelia felt a stirring rise up in her chest.

"Well, if you're unsure, I have a wonderful potion that divines the erogenous zones in women" Amelia continued, still trying to get to the root issue. She began to reach for the potion on the top shelf, but was suddenly stopped when she heard the woman gasp loudly.

"What?! You thought I was having trouble with my... with sex life? No, no!" The woman was clearly horrified by the look on her face. "I don't even have a lover right now, but I assure you, I have never had any problems or complaints." She put a frustrated hand over her eyes, and sighed. "Clearly this wasn't the best idea. Maybe I should leave."

Amelia was now horrified with herself, and her assumption of what type of assistance the woman had come into her shop for. "Wait please!" Amelia put a hand on the woman's arm to stop her from exiting the shop, as she turned to leave. "This is completely my fault. I should know better than to assume the needs and request of my customers like that. Please, let me help you, Miss. What did you say your name was?" Amelia smiled gently and affectionately at the woman, hoping she would give her a chance to rectify her mistake.

"It's Gabby Fenton. And, you can just call me Gabby, you don't need to call me Miss Fenton."

Amelia smiled, relieved at the second chance, and stuck out her hand in greeting "Amelia Worrick, It's a pleasure to meet you Gabby. Now, please let me start over. What may I help you with?"

Sliding her soft skinned hand into Amelia's to return the greeting,

Gabby finally explained, still a little nervously, what was really troubling her. "I have to give a speech to a large group of people at work on Monday, and as I think you just found out, I can have a hard time expressing myself. I get especially bad when I'm nervous." Feeling herself blush again, yet relieved she was finally able to articulate what her situation was, Gabby smiled shyly at Amelia, as she anxiously awaited her response.

Feeling suddenly relieved, Amelia asserted "I have just the thing for that. It's a potion for clear thought and eloquent tongue, and it will magically impart upon you the gift of speech".

Gabby's nervousness subsided, and the two women engaged in small talk as Amelia grabbed the appropriate potion off the shelf. Amelia took the bottle into the back incanting room to grab a copy of the usage instructions, when she was interrupted by Gabby's voice calling out to her from the front of the shop.

"Do you really have a potion that divines erogenous zones for women?"

Amelia was instantly distracted by the seemingly flirtatious question, and as she returned out to the front of the shop, Gabby's deep green eyes looking back at her caused Amelia's hand to loosen its grip on the potion bottle, The bottle slipped out of her hand, but thankfully, came to a rest at the edge of the front counter.

Grateful that the potion bottle didn't fall and break, Amelia gathered herself and answered "Yes, I do, and it is quite popular with the ladies." It was Amelia's turn to blush, as Gabby gifted her with a sexy smile.

"I guess I will have to remember that." Gabby replied with a slight gleam in her eyes.

Amelia grabbed the potion bottle along with the usage instructions, and put them in small bag. When Amelia handed the bag across the counter to Gabby, Gabby's soft hand closed over hers for a long silent moment, before she pulled away. "Thank you for everything, Amelia. I'm sorry for the initial misunderstanding, and I will be sure to let you know how my presentation goes." Giving Amelia a little wave and wink over he shoulder, Gabby walked out of the store, with a noticeable spring in her step.

Amelia sat down on the wooden stool behind the front counter, and with a dreamy sigh, she closed her eyes and indulged briefly in a little fantasy involving Gabby and the erogenous zone potion. Amelia envisioned Gabby drinking a double dose of the potent elixir, and once the effects of the potion took hold, Gabby couldn't deny her attraction to Amelia and proceeded to sexually entice her in the candlelit room they shared. Gabby's feminine hands pulled her skirt high over her silky smooth thighs, teasing Amelia with just a peek of her purple lace panties. Gabby's hands then traveled slowly up and over the curves of her hips, over her stomach and continuing on until her hands reached the mounds of her breasts pressing against the thin fabric of her chemice blouse. Lost in thought, eventually Amelia's hand came down to rest on the counter, and the cold feel of the countertop startled her back to reality, as the sensual daydream quickly evaporated from her mind.

Looking down, Amelia picked up the little green glass bottle sitting next to her hand, and frowned as she read the words on the front of the bottle. "Clear Thoughts and Eloquent Tongue" the little label read, in Stacy's elegant, swooping hand writing. A horrible tightening feeling suddenly manifested in Amelia's stomach. If this was the speech potion that she had specifically chosen for Gabby off the shelf, then what exactly did she wrap up for her beautiful new shop customer to take with her? Looking around the entire shop counter space, as well as the wall shelf in which she retrieved the speech potion from, Amelia's heart jumped in her throat when she realized her newly made bottle of love potion was missing. "Oh, no!" Amelia gasped in horror, and she ran out of the shop door in hopes of catching up with Gabby so she could exchange the love potion bottle she had accidentally given to her, with the speech potion elixir that Gabby thought she had purchased.

Frantically looking all around as she ran down the street, Amelia spied Gabby at a park just around the corner from the shop. Gabby was sitting at one of the park's picnic tables, and it appeared she had already unwrapped her package. Amelia could see just a glint of light reflect off the uncorked purple glass bottle in Gabby's hand, as it appeared she was getting ready to uncork it and take a drink. Seeing the purple elixir bottle confirmed Amelia's suspicions, and she now knew for certain that she had accidentally given Gabby the wrong potion!

"Gabby stop! Gabby, don't drink that!" Amelia called out, running like a wild woman across the street towards her. Amelia's heart beat like a drum in her chest, as she watched seemingly in slow motion as Gabby brought the shimmering bottle to her lips to take a sip of the pink potion.

"No!" Amelia shouted, as she reached Gabby, slamming into her a little too hard. The potion bottle was knocked free of Gabby's grip and fell onto the hard picnic table top, spraying both broken glass and liquid up into the air. An odd mixed sensation of dripping liquid and pain shot through Amelia's hand, and looking down, she realized that she had cut herself on the glass from the broken elixir bottle, and the love potion was absorbing into her skin.

"Amelia? My goodness, what on earth is the matter?" asked Gabby in utter shock over the shop owner's frantic display. "By the way, that potion sure tastes delicious. It is just slightly sweet, and do I detect some hint of flowers in there?"

With a groan, Amelia realized that her efforts to stop Gabby before she could consume any of the love potion had been too late, and that Gabby had already drunk some of the powerful elixir. Staring at the beautiful woman who was looking at her like she had just lost her mind,

Amelia tried to explain her wild behavior.

"I accidentally sent you away with the wrong potion, and I was trying to catch you before you could drink any of it. I had just brewed a potent love potion earlier this morning, and I realized after you had left, that I had put the love potion in your bag by mistake, instead of this one." Amelia explained, her breath slightly winded from running, as she then handed Gabby the correct potion bottle, which miraculously remained unbroken even after her crashing into Gabby at the table.

Gabby stared at her dumfounded, allowing Amelia's words to sink into consciousness, while Amelia absently brought her hand to her mouth and sucked on the cuts to the back of her fingers. The subtle taste of vanilla and flowers blossomed on Amelia's tongue, overwhelming the slight metallic taste of her blood, which trickled out due to the cuts she sustained from the broken glass pieces. Amelia closed her eyes and gave a second groan, realizing what she had just done, a second too late.

"That was a love potion? I just drank half a bottle of a love potion?!" Gabby sputtered at Amelia, her voice halfway between amazement and horror. "How exactly does this love potion work?"

Amelia sighed, exasperated at how all of this was playing out, and explained. "It's actually pretty straight forward, but also, very powerful. Once you drink some of the potion, within the next hour, if the object of your affection also drinks some of the potion, there are only two possibilities that can occur. If the two people who consumed the love potion are compatible, the potion quickly goes into effect, and the magical properties of the elixir allows their potential love and passion for each other to come forth. Should there be no compatibility between the hearts and souls of the two people who consumed the love potion, then nothing will happen at all."

"Ok," Gabby replied, still sounding a bit confused. "But, I didn't mix that potion with anything, and you spilled the rest when you knocked into me, so it should be ok, right?"

Amelia shook her head no. "You drank some of the potion straight from the bottle, and when the bottle broke on the picnic table, cutting my hand, some of the potion spilled on my cut fingers." Amelia showed Gabby her cut fingers, which glowed pinkly. "Even worse, I licked at my cuts, which I remembered too late, had some of the spilled potion on it. That love potion is very strong, and it isn't meant to be taken directly in such a high concentration. And, it's really not meant to be applied directly into the bloodstream, or mixed with blood and drank, whether deliberately or accidentally. This particular elixir is much too potent for that."

Amelia avoided looking at Gabby, afraid of what her beautiful customer might be thinking of her in this awkward moment, and instead, she examined the remains of the broken potion bottle. Just as she had feared, the shattered glass and pavement were completely dry.

"My skin must have absorbed the rest of the potion through my wound." Amelia cursed under her breath, and getting up, took Gabby's hand with her uninjured one. "I know you are confused by what has just happened, but, we really need to leave the park immediately and remove ourselves from the viewing eyes of any passerbys."

Gabby hesitantly started to follow Amelia, as she turned to leave the park. "Why do we need to leave the park? I don't feel any different. Is something supposed to........." Gabby's voice suddenly dropped off. "Oh, my goodness Amelia, you're right. We need to leave!

Pulling Gabby into her arms, Amelia could tell that the love potion was obviously starting to affect the both of them, which Amelia knew could only happen if the two of them were compatible with one another. Amelia quickly guided the two of them out of the park, and down the street, quickly covering the distance to her potion store in swift, long strides. Amelia tried to calm herself as she opened the door to the shop and guided Gabby inside. Amelia too could feel the potion's magic coursing through her veins, and already she could feel her heart beating with longing for the beautiful woman she had her arms wrapped around.

Amelia quickly locked the door to her shop and flipped over the 'open' sign on the front window to say 'closed'. Taking a moment to calm her breathing, Amelia turned back around to look at Gabby, whose appearance was a combination of surprise and lust, and in Amelia's mind, she was staring at the most beautiful creature she had ever laid eyes on. Thoughts raced silently through Amelia's mind, as she stood for a moment staring at Gabby with a mixture of feelings churning inside her chest that she was quite unprepared for. Was her sudden desire to make that love potion earlier this morning a result of divine intervention? Were there magical forces already directing and preparing her for the run in she'd have with Gabby later in the day when she entered her shop? Was there a deliberate overlap of circumstance that prompted Amelia to hasten her final steps with the elixir, thus causing a state of unfocused attention that resulted in her giving Gabby the wrong potion? Amelia had never accidentally given a wrong potion to a customer. Why today? Why Gabby?

"Amelia, what's happening?" Gabby asked, in an almost breathless voice. "I'm sorry if this sounds too aggressive, but I really want to wrap my arms around you, and kiss you, and taste you, and make passionate love to you. I'm so overcome with desire for you right now, that if you say 'no', I think I shall faint!"

Reaching behind the front counter, Amelia wrote a quick note for her sister. "Magical mishap. All is ok(ish) for now. The love potion I made this morning is much more potent than I could ever have realized!!!! Will explain more later. Amelia"

Leaving the note next to the cash register where Stacy was certain to see it, Amelia turned back towards Gabby, who was watching her intently. "My apartment is just upstairs. We are definitely going to need some privacy right now." Amelia practically bolted up the flight of stairs located in the back of the store that led up to her apartment, with Gabby following her only a few steps behind. While she fumbled with the key to unlock her front door, Amelia nervously tried to chat with Gabby, but her small talk was cut short when Gabby leaned in and gave her a deep, hungry kiss that made her knees melt like warm butter.

"I couldn't wait to do that" Gabby said, pulling back from her sensual kiss with Amelia. "All I'm feeling right now is this intense need to meld my body and soul with you. Is that crazy? After all, we just met, yet I feel my heart yearning to know you."

Amelia's body too was screaming to meld with Gabby's, and clearly, after Gabby's words of sentiment and initiation of physical intimacy, Amelia could only affirm that the love potion she mysteriously felt so inclined to create that morning, was indeed working its intended magic. Amelia finally managed to successfully maneuver the key into the lock, and opened the door to her apartment. She quickly closed the door, and led Gabby by the hand through her living room, past the kitchen and down the short hallway, not stopping until they reached the foot of her bed.

The next several hours passed in a blur for the two, as they made love repeatedly, exploring and honoring each other's body with a passion that could just not be contained. Amelia had never before experienced such a deep soul connection when making love to a woman before. It was so much more than raw lust between them. It was literally as if she and Gabby had been custom made to fit together. Every curve of Gabby's beautiful body fit just right against Amelia's, and there was this unspoken connection that was literally palpable between them. The rhythm of their love making was flawlessly in sync, and their hearts beat together in matching rhythm. Every time one of them reached their climax, the orgasmic electricity literally travelled through to the other.

When they were both finally too exhausted to continue, Amelia held Gabby's nakedness against her, and they drifted off to sleep.

"That sure is one hell of a potion you brewed." Gabby murmured in Amelia's ear, as her eyes fluttered closed. Amelia smiled in blissful agreement, closing her own eyes and joining Gabby in some much needed sleep.

A loud, aggressive knocking on Amelia's apartment door woke the two. Pulling on her robe, Amelia whispered to Gabby to remain comfortable and to stay where she was. Amelia hurried to answer the door, wondering who would be bothering her at this hour with such a frantic pounding on her door. Amelia was surprised to see her sister, Stacy, standing there holding out an ingredient bottle in her hand. Amelia suddenly remembered that she had left that note for Stacy near the cash register before her and Gabby came upstairs. Stacy was just probably making sure that she was alright.

"Amelia, is everything ok up here?" Stacy asked, looking a bit hesitant.

Blushing at the inquiry, Amelia smiled and shook her head. "Yes, I'm fine. In fact, I feel utterly alive and amazing!"

"Me too. I can honestly say that I have never felt more wonderful!" Gabby's voice sounded behind Amelia from the bedroom door. With widening eyes, Stacy looked around her sister, trying to see where the reply came from, and saw the very alluring stranger walking towards them wearing Amelia's bed sheet around her as a cover. It was quite obvious to Stacy, that this tousled hair beauty had clearly spent the night with her sister.

"We had a little accident with the love potion I made yesterday." Amelia admitted, blushing.

"Yeah, about that love potion. There's something you should know." Stacy opened up the bottle she had been holding in her hand, and shook out a few of the mauve colored petals onto her hand. "Did you put these in the potion you brewed yesterday? I found the bottle next to the spell kettle."

Amelia nodded her head. "Yes, I did, and we really need to talk to the herb supplier about quality control. Those pansies are really off color." Amelia's mouth transformed into a love-struck smile as Gabby came up to stand next to her, and wrapped an arm around her waist. "Let me officially introduce you two ladies." Amelia continued. "Stacy, this is Gabby. Gabby, this is my sister Stacy."

"Very nice to meet you Gabby" replied Stacy, offering her hand in greeting. Stacy then turned her attention back to her sister, and handed the ingredient bottle over to Amelia. "Read the label sis." Stacy directed.

Amelia read the label out loud, "May Day Peonies. "Peonies? I put peonies picked on May Day into that love potion instead of pansies?!" Amelia stood staring at her sister, flabbergasted, and her mind reeling with the implications of what that little potion mix-up really meant.

Worried by what she just heard, and witnessing Amelia's reaction to the revelation, Gabby chimed in her concern. "I don't understand. Does putting in a different flower make some sort of difference in the potion?" Gabby asked.

"Oh, yes, it makes quite an important difference." Stacy confirmed for Gabby. "If you substitute May Day peonies in place of the pansies during the brewing process, instead of getting a love potion, you end up with a seeking potion instead."

Bewildered herself by the turn of events, Amelia finished the next sentence for Gabby, "You get a seeking potion, that takes you directly to your true love."

Stacy giggled out loud. "No wonder you put that note next to the cash register, Mel. That potion is infamous for some pretty intense fireworks between a heart-aligned couple when they finally meet. If your true love was right in front of you when you drank that potion, I'm not surprised the two of you were....well, let's just say, busy all night!"

Stacy turned to Gabby, and gave her a hug. "Well, welcome to the family Gabby!" Turning back to her sister, "I will take care of the shop today, Mel, so don't worry about needing to come down and check on anything. When things calm down a bit up here, maybe you can take the time to brew me up some of that potion too, huh?" Laughing, Stacy went back downstairs to tend to the shop, leaving the bemused couple standing together in the doorway.

"So, that was a true love seeking potion, huh?" Gabby asked Amelia.

"Yes, it is remarkably hard to brew correctly, but it never fails." Amelia answered, a wide smile spreading across her lovely face. "It certainly wasn't the potion I had intended to brew, but I think there was definitely some magical interference going on when I made it."

Gabby laughed gently, as she pulled Amelia around to directly face her. "Well, it looks like you were right after all Amelia."

"What do you mean?" Amelia asked inquisitively.

Chuckling, Gabby replied "Well, it would appear that I really was looking for a love potion after all!"

Available Books by
Spirited Sapphire Publishing

Lavender Love Diaries Vol. 1: Lesbian Sex Fantasies

Lavender Love Diaries Vol. 2: Lesbian Taboo

Lesbian Cop: Unlawful Strip Search

Lipstick Lesbian Lust: Carnal Candied Kisses

Lesbian Domination: Submitting to my Lesbian Mistress

Lesbian Romance: College Girls First Lesbian Experience

Lesbian Love: Best Friends Turned Lesbian Lovers

Lesbian Sex Stories Vol. 1: Lavender Love Erotic Shorts Volumes 1-5

Lesbian Domination: Water Bondage Discipline

Lesbian Sex: Cowgirl Seduction at the Wild West Ranch

Lesbian Adventure in the Sky: Sappho Seduction into the Mile High Club

Lesbian Sex Stories: Lesbian Love and Seduction Collection

Lesbian Love Magic: Sappho Love Potion #9

Lesbian Sex Story Short: Dial 'M' for Mistress

Lesbian Sex Story Short: Intern by Day – Dominatrix by Night: My Journey into the World of Bondage and Domination

Lesbian Sex Stories: Bondage and Domination Collection